The Glastonbury Triangle

Stephen Ford

LEAF BY LEAF

Published by Leaf by Leaf
an imprint of Cinnamon Press,
www.cinnamonpress.com

The right of Stephen Ford to be identified as author of this work
has been asserted by him in accordance with the Copyright,
Designs and Patent Act, 1988. © 2024, Stephen Ford.
Print Edition ISBN 978-1-78864-891-2

British Library Cataloguing in Publication Data. A CIP record for
this book can be obtained from the British Library.

Designed and typeset in Adobe Caslon Pro by Cinnamon Press.
Cover design by Adam Craig © Adam Craig.
Cinnamon Press is represented by Inpress.

About the Author

Stephen Ford is Walks Secretary for the Surrey branch of the Long Distance Walkers Association (LDWA), whose membership relishes longer distance treks at a brisk pace over challenging terrain.

The son of a geologist, he had a varied and nomadic childhood in Africa and the Middle East. From childhood, Stephen has been inspired by wild places, mountains, rivers and forests, places where nature reigns, not people.

Now, inspired to write, Stephen explores these themes: What is nature? Is nature alive? What is life? What distinguishes a human from an animal? Do people have spirits? If people have spirits, then perhaps animals do too? Can spirits exist also in inanimate entities, rivers, trees, mountains, valleys?

The Glastonbury Triangle is Stephen's third novel, following *Destiny of a Free Spirit* and *Walking out of this World.*

The Glastonbury Triangle

Knights of Camelot

An ancient mustiness hung in the room, the lingering essence of centuries of dust, clinging to nostrils like air breathed through an old blanket.

On the library bookshelves were old tomes covering natural history, meticulously illustrated studies of botany, the complete works of Shakespeare and publications of nineteenth-century authors I'd never heard of, beautifully bound in fine leather.

My eye was drawn to a volume on a side table. I sidled over to take a closer look, taking the liberty of opening it; the title promised mythical creatures of Greek legend. It flopped apart, revealing a finely drawn illustration of a satyr, with the upper body of a man and the horns and hind legs of a ram, prancing and priapic, improbably well endowed.

My attention was diverted by a discreet cough and shuffled feet. I glanced behind towards the Marquess's butler, a tall, immaculately groomed gentleman of indeterminate mature age, an edifice of starched formality, impassive and imperturbable, with a well-honed ability to subtly convey disquiet by slightly clearing his throat. He raised his eyebrows, lowered his chin. He had a basilisk stare of disapproval on the open book.

Resisting the temptation to turn the page I backed away, letting my eyes wander around the portraits of the Marquess's illustrious ancestors, admirals, British generals who enjoyed victories around the globe, exquisitely costumed countesses and, incongruously, a couple of racehorses poised to gallop across Epsom downs.

A door at the end of the room opened. The Marquess, a lofty and solidly built man in his mid-fifties, emerged accompanied by a wide eyed excited looking man in his forties. The man wore a crumpled and ill-fitting off-the-peg greyish suit from a mass market department store, a creased shirt with a check pattern, a thin blue tie twisted to one side and scuffed unpolished brown shoes.

'These new coding sequences are particularly exciting,' claimed the Marquess's guest as they wandered past me. 'We are seeing outstanding progress in the accelerated breeding programme.'

The Marquess and his butler halted as they reached the end of the library, their gaze cast expectantly in the direction of the door leading into the vestibule, but the man continued with his animated explanations. 'With our xeno-tolerance developments we have really opened the doors for hybrid organisms in a groundbreaking way.'

As his guest paused for breath the Marquess seized his opportunity. 'Dr Shorbody, thank you so much. It was illuminating to have heard such a thorough and detailed report of the excellent progress you are making in your research. It will be delightful to hear more in due course.'

His butler, sensitive to his lordship's wishes, held open the door, positioned to make it clear at this point the man was expected to depart.

His excitable guest having withdrawn, the Marquess glanced in my direction, nodding to the butler as he made his way back to the door opposite. The Marquess was expensively but understatedly dressed in country style tweeds, expertly tailored, probably by the same Saville Row firm outfitting the Mendip family over generations. He moved decisively but was unhurried, exuding confidence.

'His lordship will see you now,' the butler announced to me.

As he came up alongside in the middle of the room, the Marquess stopped and beamed at me. 'You're the gentleman from *The Daily Trumpet*, I take it. Welcome to Mendip House.'

'Yes, your lordship. Simon Chewton. How do you do, sir.'

The quarter of a century age difference between us was insignificant next to our difference in styles. The Marquess, still in the world of the 1920s, was a full century behind my contemporary dress, with my lithe six foot frame clad in a pair of chino trousers, a light blue open neck shirt and a tailored denim jacket.

The Marquess beckoned for me to precede him, with the butler taking the lead. For a moment I felt like a prisoner escorted by guards, front and rear. The butler held open the double doors and stood aside for us to pass into what was evidently the Marquess's study, withdrawing back into the library, closing the doors behind him.

The study on the corner of the frontage of Mendip House was generously proportioned. Around the edges of the room were side tables laid with models of what I assumed were the Marquess's latest project. Also scattered were drawings and sculptures featuring another of his evident interests, mythical beasts: centaurs, griffins, dragons, sea monsters and mermaids. Some illustrations were in a strangely detailed style, as if of dissections in a medical textbook.

In the corner of the room, away from windows, the Marquess's expansive Georgian mahogany desk faced out, overlooking his estate's extensive landscaped grounds. The Marquess led me to the opposite corner where antique easy chairs and a sofa were set out within the area well-lit by the hazy April sunshine beaming in from the large windows on two sides of the room.

As we approached, a striking blonde woman in her mid-thirties stood in acknowledgement. Without having spoken, her presence, the gaze of her flashing eyes, her commanding stance, dominated the room. She was in the style of Queen Guinevere and must have been playing some central role in the Marquess's enterprise, the Knights of Camelot theme park. Her outfit was sumptuous, made of the finest of fabrics, adorned with subtle but intricate patterns, set off by fine jewellery and exquisitely tailored to accentuate the lithe curves of her figure. It was altogether far more elaborate than the kind of cheap outfit a theme park might normally provide.

'May I introduce Philomena, my spiritual and cultural advisor. Philomena, this is Simon Chewton from *The Daily Trumpet*,' announced the Marquess.

I sensed his deferential manner was more than mere good manners.

Her eyes were on me, unsettlingly, like a cat looking at its prey. I couldn't discern her motivation, but sensed something carnal. She held out her hand, which I grasped in a firm handshake. She gripped mine softly, but as I let her go, she let hers linger as if claiming possession. Her eyes fastened me with an examining gaze, her face almost expressionless yet asserting authority.

'Pleased to meet you, Mr Chewton,' said Philomena in a neutral, formal tone. I had work to do building rapport while reclaiming my autonomy.

'Likewise, Philomena, delighted to make your acquaintance. I must congratulate you on your outfit. It ties in with the Arthurian theme of your new park wonderfully, and tastefully too, if I may say so?'

Just the barest hint of a smile flickered on her dead pan face. 'Nice of you to say so.'

'Please, do sit,' said the Marquess. 'May I offer you coffee?'

'Lovely, thank you.'

'What do you think of the Somerset countryside, Mr Chewton?'

'The epitome of traditional England,' I enthused. 'Charming, bucolic and fruitful.'

'It has more than surface charm. There are deep cultural roots too, stretching eons into the rich legacy of legend woven into what makes us English, heritage which is the driving inspiration for the Knights of Camelot.'

'It is good to see our heritage celebrated.'

The butler padded in quietly with a tray, setting out the coffee and accoutrements.

'Our park is entirely different from those established elsewhere, in Florida or California.' The Marquess's face wrinkled. 'For the Knights of Camelot authenticity is key. We offer a vision of real history situated in the very landscape where the legendary events occurred.'

Content everyone had been served, the butler drifted silently from the room.

'Are there particular legendary events that you focus on?'

'The Round Table experience is one of our highlights. Visitors are invited to take their place at the table among the knights of King Arthur's court, served mead and authentic comestibles.'

'Sounds fun.'

'Jousting between Sir Lancelot and the Black Knight is a great favourite.'

'Could be dangerous, couldn't it?'

'We take precautions. It is well choreographed. Then there are the magic powers of the wizard Merlin.'

'I guess the magic is choreographed too.'

'Yes, and we have tremendous special effects people too. We bring in the young prince Arthur proving his entitlement to the throne by drawing the sword from the stone and the sword Excalibur appearing from the lake in the hand of Lady of the Lake.'

'I have always been confused by those sword legends. How is it Excalibur could both come from the stone yet also be provided by the Lady of the Lake?'

Philomena intervened. 'The sword in the stone was Arthur's first weapon,' she explained. 'It was broken in combat with King Pellinore. It is after Arthur is rescued by a spell of enchantment cast by Merlin when he is equipped with his indestructible replacement Excalibur by the Lady of the Lake.'

As she spoke I was drawn to her beauty, how her eyes lit, oozing charisma and femininity. I reflected she made an excellent Guinevere. Sir Lancelot would have been putty in her hands.

I would have welcomed more time to drool over Philomena's allure, but this was curtailed by the opening of the double doors. The butler led two purposeful men in semi-formal cheap suits, chain store shirts and ties. 'I am sorry to interrupt, my lord, but these gentlemen were most insistent.'

The older man stepped forward. 'I am Detective Inspector Bellard from Glastonbury CID and this is Detective Sergeant Lunnton. We have a warrant to search these premises in pursuit of enquiries into missing persons whose last known whereabouts were in the vicinity.'

If the Marquess was shocked, his face showed no sign; there was only a slight quizzical tightening of his eyes followed by a subtle sardonic twist of his mouth. He rose. Far from betraying annoyance the Marquess approached them as honoured guests.

'Well, gentlemen, I'm sorry to hear of these missing persons. It is most important they are found. It must be terrible for their loved ones. We will assist in any way we can.'

The two police officers were taken aback, presumably more accustomed to hostility.

The Marquess's sangfroid was impressive; his aristocratic upbringing had instilled effortless superiority combined with a suave diplomacy. Far from putting him at any disadvantage, his perfect manners accentuated his command, crushing the police inspector's authority. He turned to me.

'Mr Chewton, we will have to curtail this interview. Please accept my sincere apologies.'

'Of course, I quite understand. I would be happy to wait here while you take care of matters,' I replied, cheekily hoping to listen in on details about the missing persons for what promised to be a juicy story for *The Daily Trumpet*.

Inspector Bellard's face contorted; he stood poised to regain the initiative and have me thrown out, if necessary by force. Sergeant Lunnton, heftily built, spread his legs and jutted his elbows.

The Marquess smiled. Before DI Bellard could intervene he said, 'You will be wanting to see the park, I am sure. If you accompany Barstairs he will happily arrange a guided tour.'

Barstairs, the butler, said nothing but, standing hard against the easy chair I was sitting in and eyeing me expectantly, his intention was clear.

Despite the pressure, I tested the situation by remaining seated a few more seconds, feigning indifference to the various stares. It was only when the two police officers advanced in my direction my defiance cracked.

I stood, playing for time with conversation. 'Well, my lord, I am most grateful for your time. It has been wonderful hearing about your marvellous Knights of Camelot attraction.'

'The pleasure was mine. Barstairs will provide you with anything more you may need.'

I turned to the Marquess's charming spiritual and cultural advisor.

'And, of course, Philomena. It has been delightful to make your acquaintance. I do hope we can continue our most interesting conversation in due course.'

'Goodbye, Mr Chewton. Enjoy the tour,' she replied coldly.

I looked around, hoping for further means of prolonging my presence.

As I reached the doorway I paused, hoping to linger in the background eavesdropping. Barstairs closed in like a sheepdog encouraging a reluctant ewe into a pen.

Night out in Glastonbury

It was mid-afternoon when I extricated myself from the throng of excited children and teenagers among whom I had shared the thrills of St George slaying a scary fire-breathing animatronic dragon, Queen Guinevere's rescue from the clutches of the evil Maleagant, unfortunately not on this occasion played by the delightful Philomena, mortal combat between Sir Lancelot and the Black Knight, noble Sir Galahad rescuing a damsel in distress and a boat trip through the magic grotto into the sparkling court of King Arthur accompanied by a musical arrangement of lutes and lyres.

Still surrounded by noisy families I took the Knights of Camelot shuttle bus service into Glastonbury, depositing me near a large supermarket. The earlier sunshine had given way to wet blustery clouds. I huddled to withstand the drizzle and chilling breeze for the brisk five minute walk to the Ananda Guest House, a dwelling decorated in eastern style with statues of Buddha and scented with incense.

'The yurt is still available, if you prefer,' offered Adelena, the landlady.

'Well, I don't know.'

'Wonderful for connecting with the natural world outdoors, with ensuite open air shower.'

'Not sure how I feel about being outdoors.'

'It's wonderfully peaceful now overflying has been banned.'

The noise from low flying aircraft was not my primary concern. I was more deterred by the bracing chill when I took a shower. 'I think I'll stay indoors, if it's alright.'

'Have you plans this evening?'

'Yes, I'm meeting someone.'

'Anything beforehand?'

'No, I've got a few hours to kill.'

'We offer alternative therapies. I can do reiki, crystals and chakra massage in the meditation room through here.' She beckoned to a conservatory extension laid with cushions, candles, smouldering incense sticks and a statue of Ganesh, a Hindu deity with an elephant's head on a human body with extra arms.

I shook my head. 'I think I'll just go for a walk in town.'

Having established my territory in my room with toiletries and spare clothing extracted from my rucksack I made my way out. I glanced at a copy of the *Glastonbury Gazette* laying on the hall table. The headline complained that north Somerset had the worst mobile phone reception in the UK with dead zones especially prevalent in the Mendips.

Opposite the guest house I was enticed over the threshold of the Mendip Grenadier by their promise of a wide range of local ciders and real ales. The pub was a workaday place geared for the needs of the working population without a hint of hippy or new age aesthetics. It was old and would have still felt familiar to someone returning after an interval of 30 or 40 years. The bare bricks and rough wood fittings were largely unchanged for a hundred years. Some chairs and tables would have been replaced in the interim, but their replacements were in the same simple style as their predecessors. The same could be said for the pub's patrons, different individuals hewn out of the same gene pool and West Country tradition. I propped myself on a barstool and ordered a foaming pint of Meadow Dew ale.

'You're not from round here, are you?' said the tough young man sat on the neighbouring stool in his broad West Country accent. Dressed in working clothes, blue jeans, check shirt and a denim jacket, he had a mop of longish unkempt curly blonde hair framing a confrontational expression on his broad face. His sturdy frame indicated a physically active profession and his assertive stance suggested he would not hesitate to deploy his muscular physique.

'No, I'm from London.' I felt a slight bristle of hostility, as if I represented a class of oppressive overlords.

'What brings you here then?'

I pondered. 'Girlfriend problems.'

'Ha! You're not the only one. What sort of problems?'

'She's run away, from London.'

'What did she run away from?'

'I wish I knew. Jacked in her job, too. Doesn't make sense.'

My companion eased closer on his stool, his air of suspicion ebbing. 'I've got problems with mine and all. She's got mixed up in hippy witchcraft stuff.'

I swung to face him. 'Really? Mine too. She's really into it, Wicca and all that.'

'Yeah, Wicca, that's what mine calls it too. Can't get my head around it.'

We were almost bosom buddies now. We introduced ourselves. He was Harry Mallet, working as a storeman at Mendip Constructions, a civil engineering contractor in Glastonbury.

'My girl, Ivy, these days she cares more about Wicca hocus-pocus than me. She's into chakras, ashrams and that.'

'Whatever they are. From what I've seen, there's a lot of that sort around here.'

'Too right. Too much of it altogether. She's got daft ideas too. Told me she should take charge of sex and that. Had to give her a good slapping to put her right.'

I paused. 'They get those ideas, I know.'

'What about your bird?'

'Mine is called Jenny. I had only just got to know her and then she's off, back here for some weird reason, spiritual empowerment or something. Got my boss to send me here for work, so I could catch up with her.'

'What work's that?"

'Investigation, finding things out, reporting things.'

'What, you mean, like a detective?"

'Sort of. I'm a journalist.'

'Look, empty glasses,' Harry observed. 'Fancy another?'

'No thanks, better be going,' I replied, draining my glass. It could easily have become a long session of mutual commiseration, but I was due to be seeing Jenny later.

Ambling into town it felt like passing a portal gradually transitioning from the normal world of earning, raising kids, pastimes like ten pin bowling, football and bingo, into an alternative lifestyle of legend, hippies and the supernatural. Interspersed among the artefacts of everyday life were cards in shop windows advertising talks by gurus, tarot readings and spiritual healing.

I passed a Georgian building, now a holistic health and educational temple dedicated to the supreme Goddess

Gaia. According to a notice, a Mother Earth Temple where the incumbents lived and worshiped following the ideals of love, care and support for each other, Mother Earth and Her spirit the Goddess Gaia. What would that involve? Reiki, crystals and chakras I shouldn't wonder.

I was diverted by a commotion opposite, close to the entrance to Glastonbury Abbey, a loud confrontation between a fervent group of conventional well-groomed individuals and an assortment with unkempt hair clad in shabby chic outfits, mostly ragged, a mixture of brightly coloured patchwork and black adorned with pagan emblems, pentangles and phases of the moon. Smelling not only the hippies but a potential story for *The Daily Trumpet*, I moved in.

The shaggier group had placards proclaiming themselves Pagan Pride. A woman dominated their opponents, loudly decrying their desecration of a sacred place with the works of Satan. I had seen her before, Lady Ophelia Jardinair, leader of the Moral Multitude, a crusading organisation asserting Christian moral standards and what they referred to as common decency. She was accompanied by a tall, heavily built, serious clergyman, who, when he could get a word in, spoke in pontifical terms like a modern Jerimiah, warning of the calamitous dangers of the occult and invoking heathen deities.

Considering the conservative leanings of *The Daily Trumpet*'s readership I focussed initially on the Moral Multitude's viewpoint. I caught the eye of a concerned middle-aged woman on the fringes. 'What is all the fuss about?"

'It's these pagan people, they've got hold of my girl,'

she replied in a broad West Country accent reminding me of cream teas in the countryside. 'Corrupted her, they did.'

'Oh dear,' I commiserated. 'What do you mean, corrupted?'

'Devil worship. Strange goings on. And I always brought her up to be a good Catholic.'

'I'm Simon, by the way.'

'Elsie Langport, pleased to meet you.'

'And your daughter, what's she called?'

'Ivy. Don't know what got into her, getting mixed up with this lot.'

'So, what just happened, to bring all this about?'

'That lot, they've been doing filthy things, jumping around with nothing on, over there in the Abbey. That's sacred ground, that is. Disgusting.'

'I can see it would be upsetting.'

'Well, I wasn't going to stand for it, I wasn't. So, I calls them Moral Multitude to put a stop to it.'

A policewoman pushed between the jostling groups.

'How dare you interfere with our worship,' proclaimed a corpulent woman clad in an expansive robe featuring a prominent pentangle emblem.

'The Abbey's management are within their rights to eject those they consider undesirable,' said the policewoman.

'Religious persecution, that's what it is,' shouted the large woman. 'They have Christian services all the time. But they don't allow Wicca. It's discrimination.'

'This is a Christian site,' boomed Lady Ophelia Jardinair. 'We can't have this sacred place desecrated by Devil worship.'

'Leave it to me, madam, please,' said the policewoman.

She turned back to the Wicca woman. 'You are free to conduct your religious ceremonies as you see fit, but you must do it elsewhere, somewhere it is allowed.'

'This has been a sacred site for thousands of years, long before there were Christians,' asserted the large woman.

'I dare say, madam, but you still can't do your devotions here. You will not be permitted back on Abbey premises. Now, if you don't all disperse I will have no option but to make arrests for a breach of the peace.'

Elsie Langport exclaimed excitedly, 'There she is, our Ivy.'

Elsie made her way towards the motley band of pagans and I followed. It was then I saw Harry Mallet, the threatening fellow from the pub, striding in front of us, reaching Ivy first.

Ivy was a fresh faced girl in her late teens among the other women dressed like her in what they must have considered witch's outfits, typically a loose fitting smock dress tie-dyed or otherwise patterned in assertion of their rebellious pagan identity, together with some form of cloak, decorated by an assortment of pendants and brooches.

Harry seized Ivy roughly by the wrist, making to haul her forcibly from the throng.

The next moment I was taken aback to see my Jenny thrust herself forward between them, grabbing Harry's arm to make him to let go. Her rescue attempt was futile, Harry used his superior strength to shake her off, dragging Ivy across the road before the approaching policewoman could intervene, followed closely by her mother, Elsie.

The upheaval having subsided, Jenny and I were left

facing each other. She had gone to some lengths to emphasise her counterculture pagan identity: her naturally blonde hair streaked with red and black and plaited into spiky dreadlocks, goth style makeup, black lipstick, whitened face, dark smudges around her eyes and ragged garb. With Ivy departed, despite what some would see as her unsightly outfit, Jenny stood out as the youngest and prettiest of the group, her bright blue eyes and a loose-fitting dress doing little to disguise her lithe but curved figure.

I put on a smile, but Jenny glared back in disgust.

'What were you doing over there with those bigots?'

'It's alright, I'm not with them. I've been here to see the Marquess of Mendip about his new Knights of Camelot theme park. I was just passing when I saw the commotion.'

'But you were over there with them, talking to them and helping them abduct Ivy.'

'I was only trying to find out what was going on.'

'But you won't get anything useful from them, just hate and bigotry.'

'I was only trying to find out the basic facts. Besides we need to understand their point of view.'

'Their point of view is hatred and prejudice. There must be no platform for their intolerance.'

'But wouldn't it be intolerant not to listen to them?'

'But some points of view, like theirs, are unacceptable,' Jenny insisted.

'How do I know until I hear them out?'

Our heated conversation was interrupted by the policewoman. 'Come along, you two, move along now. You can't go on like that in the street. Any more and I'll have to arrest you both under Section 5 of the Public Order Act.'

I looked at Jenny in what I hoped was a winsome fashion. 'Come now, we don't want to fight, do we? Let's go over there and make up.' I suggested, indicating a bench on the other side of the road.

Jenny looked back defiantly.

'Please.' I was trying to look charming.

She pursed her lips, weakening slightly.

'Come on, peace and love.'

'Oh alright.'

I took a seat towards the middle of the bench. Jenny sat at one end to leave as much space as possible between us.

'Look, honestly, I was just passing and all I did was ask the first person I came up against what was going on. I don't agree with their busybody interference and intolerant religious attitudes at all. Nor with them dragging Ivy away. Not in the least. Believe me.'

'Well, alright. But I don't know if I can trust you, given who you write for, that hate rag, *The Daily Trumpet*.'

'Journalism is difficult to get into. When you are starting like me, you can't be choosy.'

'So, you just sell out, is that it? I'd prefer you had principles.'

'Well, the fact I have a job means I can afford to take you out to dinner tonight, if you still want me to, that is.'

Jenny weighed me up. I did my best to look friendly and playful. 'Well, alright, but I'll be keeping an eye on your attitude.'

'Righto. No time like the present. Where shall we go?'

'What, you don't mean now, surely? I'm not ready.'

'How do you mean, not ready. We are only going out

to eat something. It doesn't require preparation.'

'Of course going out needs preparation.'

'What would you be preparing for? We're only going for something to eat and a chat.'

'Yes, but I don't want to go out like this,' she said, looking down at herself.

'But you look great, as far as I am concerned.'

'What do you know? You're a man.'

'But you're going out with me. If I think you look nice as you are, surely that's what matters. Who else are you trying to impress, apart from me?'

She was stumped. 'But I want to go home and freshen up, get changed.'

I leaned across and sniffed her neck. 'You smell great. No freshening up needed as far as I am concerned. And your witch's outfit is fetching too. You're my perfect partner for the evening already, just as you are.'

For once Jenny was at a loss for words.

'Right, well, there's a nice pub over there on the corner. Shall we go?' I concluded.

In its style the Oak and Holly was simultaneously in tune with the latest trends while purporting to of a bygone era, a simpler medieval time of mystery replete with folk memories from ancient legend. The decorative motifs were of goblins, dragons, gallant knights, wood nymphs and pre-Christian deities. At the bar I ordered Jenny a half of Natural Dry cider and a pint of Meadow Dew ale for myself. As the pretty barmaid served us, Jenny was sullen. Realising I was better letting her mood subside, I turned my attention to the barmaid, catching her eye and smiling, which did not escape Jenny's notice.

'Did you notice the commotion outside just now?' I

enquired.

'I heard something but I was stuck in here so I didn't see anything. Do you know what it was about?'

'Some morality campaigners objecting to pagans doing stuff at the Abbey. It got shouty and confrontational and the police had to calm it down.'

'Yes, it's happened before. That morality lot have really got it in for the pagan folk. Live and let live is what I say,' replied the barmaid.

Jenny curled her lip. Saying nothing, her face set in annoyance, she took her drink and sat in a quiet corner of the bar while I paid.

'Wasn't quite right, what you told her, was it?' accused Jenny, a steely look in her eyes.

'How do you mean? I only told her what happened.'

'Some bigots aggressively obstructed our freedom to worship, that's what happened.'

'I didn't know what her attitude to these things was. I had to keep it neutral.'

'No you didn't. You are with me. You could stick up for me, and what's right.'

'It's better not to get into fights with people, if possible.'

'Some things are worth fighting for.'

I considered for a moment. 'I notice you didn't say anything. You could have done.'

'It was you talking to her, not me. Anyway, how come you were talking to her instead of me?'

'You weren't very talkative. I was being friendly.'

'Are you usually that friendly with other women when you are taking someone out?'

'Oh come on, it was just normal conversation. I wasn't

chatting her up or anything.'

Jenny glared, saying nothing.

'Well, why didn't you say anything yourself about what happened?' I reiterated.

'You were doing the talking.'

'But you didn't like what I said. You could have put your own point of view, if you'd wanted.'

'I didn't want to contradict you.'

'You mean you left it to me as the man to do the talking and take the flak for it.'

'If you were a proper man you would be glad to stand up for me.'

'I did. I handled things diplomatically to avoid causing you embarrassment.'

'But that's not what I wanted.'

'Jenny, when we met you told me how much you were in favour of women's equality. Actually, there was more. You told me women were superior. So how come you are now saying you expect men to fight your battles?'

Jenny grimaced. Something in her face told me she wasn't feeling quite as antagonistic as she pretended.

'I am right though, if you weren't so obsessed with being diplomatic you should have said hate-filled bigots were forcibly obstructing our freedom to worship, shouldn't you?'

I turned and beamed a smile at her, taking both her hands in mine. She didn't resist.

'Yes, of course that is what I would have said, if I had been speaking my mind,' I assured soothingly.

'Well, that's alright then.' She sipped her cider. 'Why is it you think those Moral Multitude people hate us so much?'

'From what they said, they think you were defiling the Abbey's grounds, land they consider sacred.'

'Well, yes, it is sacred, which is why we need to hold our ceremonies there.'

'The problem is, each religion considers itself to be the only true one, so in their opinion they deserve exclusive use of what they consider sacred.'

'You are annoying. You always see everybody else's point of view.'

I sensed she wasn't really annoyed, enjoying the parry and thrust. As was I, entranced by her feistiness. Relieved to have got over our difficulty, I acted quickly to turn things around. 'Jenny, love, you have only told me a little about Wicca. I'm interested.'

'What would you like to know?'

'From reading up about it, Wicca comes in various guises. What variety does your coven follow?'

'We follow the True Natural Path. We come out of the Dianic Wicca tradition, so we believe in the supremacy of the feminine, but unlike the original Dianic Wicca we have reincorporated the male, but put him in his appropriate role.'

How convenient, I thought; men do stuff for you and protect you, but you put them back in their place under your thumb when it suits you. I questioned why I was still there, but then I looked at her and knew. She was gorgeous.

'What is the reason behind the feminine being supreme?'

'The Earth is our Mother, the embodiment of the feminine, nurturing us, and Gaia is her spirit, the Goddess. We owe our whole existence to Her.'

I nodded, wide-eyed at Jenny's beauty, if not her words, encouraging her to expand.

'Gaia, the Earth Mother is both the supreme spirit and physical embodiment of every other entity on Earth, both spiritual and physical. There are millions of spirits and physical sentient beings on Earth, those of rivers, mountains, trees, flowers, insects, birds, animals and people, all of which are nurtured and suckled by Gaia. Harmony on Earth requires every spirit be aligned with and incorporated into the body of the Earth Mother, literally at one with and built into Her Being.'

'Surely there must be some role for the masculine too.'

'Yes, the Horned God, Green Man, Holly King and Oak King stimulate fertility and mark the seasons, forming part of Gaia's realm to fulfil Gaia's purpose.'

'The Horned God is supposed to be sort of on a par with the Goddess, isn't he? I've seen them depicted side by side as if they were equal and opposite, like Yin and Yang.'

'We in the True Natural Path don't believe that. The Goddess Gaia is supreme and must be for the sake of peace and harmony. The evils prevalent in the world stem from the inherent supremacy of the feminine being usurped by an out of control patriarchy. The patriarchy is the paramount form of oppression from which all other forms stem.'

'Really? How is that?' I raised my eyebrows.

'Take warfare, wars are motivated by male aggression and planned and fought by men. Male greed leads to male-dominated corporations looting the world's resources, subverting governments through bribery and extortion and suppressing technologies threatening their commercial domination. The male priesthood of established patriarchal religions drives societies with dogma to justify and perpetuate the status quo of male domination. Men form secret societies to advance the dominant male clique. Wherever you look it is toxic masculinity wrecking things.'

'How is it just a masculinity thing? Might it not be human beings in general?'

'No,' Jenny said firmly. 'The very nature of men and their testosterone inspired tendencies made them unsuitable for leadership roles; their domineering nature has driven them to seize. The evidence is clear. Criminals, especially violent criminals, are mostly men. All men are potential rapists if left unchecked and permitted to indulge testosterone-driven urges. Male dominated society makes it routine and normal to reduce women to the status of sex objects.'

'So, what is the answer to those problems?'

'The only way is to overthrow the existing patriarchal order and replace it with the natural order, a reconstituted society based on feminine leadership, under the guidance of the spirit of our Mother Earth, the Goddess Gaia.'

'That could take a while,' I mused.

'We can't afford for it to take a while. This is urgent because advanced technology makes warfare too dangerous to be tolerated and only female supremacy can realistically shape society to make warfare obsolete and unthinkable. Female supremacy will place Woman, the civiliser, in charge of Man, the warrior. Women being fundamentally more moral than men will, with feminine leaders, raise the moral standards of society, including the moral standards of men. Feminine power with its different set of values and energies, softness, wisdom and intuition rather than abstract intellectualism, combined with mutual nourishment and emotional expression as a creative form, will raise civilisation to a higher level.'

'So how might this improved state of affairs be brought about?'

'We must revive the ancient religious order that held dear the Earth Mother, Gaia, before being usurped by the false patriarchal beliefs of the Judeo-Christian era. This new spirituality will unleash a reservoir of healing, comfort, tenderness, sensitivity, feminine dignity and purity, to the benefit of all, including men. Men will be guided to curb their coarse and aggressive instincts and instead channel their strength and energies as directed by women who get their inspiration from the Earth Mother, Gaia.'

'Well, fascinating,' I said, truthfully more fascinated by her feminine curves than a female led society. 'Why don't we continue over something to eat? Is there anywhere you can suggest?'

'Nature's Bounty Café, that's good.'

Jenny ordered falafels with a green salad, olives, hummus, pitta bread, chilli sauce and mint yogurt, while I went for mushroom and cashew nut flan, garlic potatoes and tarka dahl. We washed it down with a bottle of potent, locally made organic elderflower wine.

I encouraged her to expand on the benefits of the new order she envisaged under the blessed guidance of the Supreme Mother, Gaia, while I hung on her every word, conveying my appreciation of the wisdom of everything she was saying. She was not to know this was a standard journalistic technique, showing myself to be credulous, a convinced convert, enthusiastically eager to learn, tempting her into indiscretions.

Jenny was enjoying herself now, and, I sensed, increasingly warming to me.

As we finished our meal I placed my hand on her thigh, leaned in with a cheeky grin on my face. 'What should we do now, do you think?'

She looked back at me frowning. 'What do you have in mind?'

'Well, I was thinking it was probably time we got to know each other better.' I stroked her thigh gently with my fingers.

She clasped my wandering hand, firmly pushing it away. 'You can't have heard a word I said.'

'Oh, sorry, about what?'

'About toxic masculinity, treating women as sex objects, that's what.'

'Oh, right. Is it not allowed? You know, sex and that sort of thing. I didn't realise.'

'Love flows down from Gaia, channelled through women. Men have to let it come to them, not make demands. Male energy needing to be harnessed and channelled under feminine control.'

'I take it Gaia's love isn't going to be flowing today.'

She looked at me with narrowed eyes. 'No, not today.'

'Does that mean not ever?'

She smiled slightly. 'Not necessarily. Let's see how it goes.'

I put a sad hangdog look on my face.

'It is an important and significant step, making love with someone. First we would need to make sure the energy flow is right. You can't just do these things on a whim. Spiritual energies have to be correctly aligned.'

I nodded, reflecting this might involve reiki, chakras and crystals. She sweetened the pill by cuddling to me, softly stroking my cheek and giving me a gentle kiss.

'When are we going to see each other again?'

'When I'm back in London.'

'You're going back?'

'Yes, next week. I've still got my flat share. I'm looking for another job.'

'But you already had a job at Drembold Industries. What happened?'

'It was only temporary, filling in.'

Oldest Profession

The brown glazed tiles facing the old District Railway entrance of Earls Court underground station were reminiscent of an Edwardian public lavatory.

Having stoked up on a Cornish pasty I grabbed in passing at Paddington, I ignored the fish and chips on offer every day from the pub opposite the station.

At 7pm it was still peak business hours for the small shops lining the street, catering to folk like me, transient Londoners living in the tiny rented flats slotted into every crevice of the surrounding sprawl of residential buildings, an assortment of sandwich shops, fast food restaurants, pharmacies, foreign currency exchange kiosks and convenience stores.

On my side of Pembleton Gardens most late Victorian era terraced town houses were now small down-market hotels with imposing names, the rest generally converted into warrens of tiny studio apartments. One such miniscule rabbit hutch was my abode, one of four crammed into the third floor of one of shabbier buildings at the street's end.

A man surreptitiously emerged from the building's basement flat, glancing around warily, as had many previous men entering and leaving the basement premises of the lady calling herself Miss KattyKins—her online profile offered intimate consultations for generous gentlemen. Weeks before I had met the lady and adjourned to the pub for a chat.

I dumped my bag in the flat before popping out for a drink at the local hostelry, the Brunswick Star. As I was ordering my pint of London Best ale, Miss KattyKins made an entrance, dressed in a leopard skin effect skirt, beneath which suspenders held up her black fishnet stockings, visible along with her uplift bra pushing out her cleavage from her tight bright green tee shirt with ruffled sleeves. Her heavily made-up face failed to disguise a haggard, careworn expression.

'Hello Kitty,' I greeted. 'Would you like a drink?'

'Thank you, dear. Vodka and coke, if you don't mind.' I nodded to the barman. 'After what happened today, I need it, I don't mind telling you.'

'Make that a double,' I said to the barman.

'Hard day, then?'

'Yes, definitely. One of those days.'

'Don't know about you, but I need to take the weight off my feet. Why don't we take a seat over there?'

'Too right, I need a sit down.'

We took our drinks to a quiet alcove.

'So, Kitty, what happened?'

'How do you mean?'

'You said, after whatever it was you needed that drink.'

'Oh, right, yes, I did, didn't I?'

'So, tell your Uncle Simon all about it.'

'What, with you working for *The Trumpet*? Not on your nelly!'

'Kitty, I'm off duty and nothing will get in *The Trumpet* about it, at least not from me.'

'I don't believe you. You reporter types are never off duty.'

I put my hand on her arm and looked into her eyes. 'Whatever we say stays between us, I promise you.'

'Yeah, right. I wasn't born yesterday. I've heard

promises from men before.' She looked back at me defiantly.

A man looked over at us and blatantly stared at Miss KattyKins. He leaned over in my direction. 'I wouldn't get too close to her, if I were you. You might catch something.'

Kitty leapt to her feet. 'Keep your dirty comments to yourself,' she screeched, causing several people nearby to swivel in our direction.

'That was uncalled for,' I said to the man, hotly. 'Mind your own damned business.'

'They shouldn't let the likes of you in here,' said a prim woman to Kitty.

'I've got as much a right to be here as you, stuck up cow,' retorted Kitty.

'Not if you're in here propositioning the men!'

'What's it to you?'

I stepped between them. 'Leave it, Kitty. It's not worth it.'

The landlord came out from behind the bar. 'Enough of that. I won't have shouting in here. Any more of that, you're barred.'

'This man was grossly insulting to this lady,' I explained.

'Right, you, out,' said the landlord to the man. 'I've told you about this before.'

'Wouldn't want to be here anyway, if you let in low life like her.'

There was more shuffling and confrontation between the landlord and man in the process of him being ejected.

'And you,' said the landlord in our direction. 'Just watch it, that's all.'

We settled again. Even through her thick makeup I saw Kitty's face was flushed red.

'Bastards,' I said. 'Sorry you had to put up with that.'

Kitty sighed. 'Don't worry, I'm used to it.'

'It was already a bad day, from what you said, even before that unpleasantness.'

'Yes, it was.'

'So, what was the trouble?'

Kitty looked at me with narrowed eyes. 'Nothing you need know about.'

I shrugged. 'You're right. None of my business.'

'Yes, it's my business who I have come visit. Nobody else's'

'Of course. You can invite who you like. It's a free country.'

'Wouldn't think so, the way some people go on.'

Kitty slurped back the remains of her drink.

'Here,' I said, reaching for her glass. 'Let me get you another.'

'Oh, would you? You're a dear.'

I went to the bar and came back with our drinks replenished.

'Ta, dear. You're a diamond.'

'Whatever it was that happened today, my commiserations.' I rested my hand on her forearm.

'It's what some of them make me do, that's all.'

I paused, wondering how best to draw her out. 'By them, you mean the gentlemen who call in from time to time.'

'Yes, them.'

'Saw one coming up from your place a few minutes ago. Was it him that upset you?'

'Yes. Well, not only him, but he's the worst.'

'Bad then, what he did?'

Kitty shuddered, curling her lips. 'I don't mind, usually. I'm used to it these days. But some things, they're not right.'

'Yeah, some things must be too much.'

'Not really, if they're paying they think they can do anything they want and I have to pretend to like it.'

'Not anything at all, surely.'

'They think so. Entitled to whatever they want.'

'So, what did this guy think he was entitled to?'

She frowned, pursing her lips. 'If he just wanted it one way, it wouldn't be so bad,' she said after seconds of hesitation.

I weighed this in my mind, failing to make sense of it. 'I don't quite follow.'

'Well, you know, front or back or blowjob, one or other is okay, but more than that is just greedy.'

'So, what did he want?'

'All three, one after the other.'

'You mean …' I said, indicating in turn with my finger downwards, down behind my back and towards my mouth.

'Yes, that. But worst of all, he wanted the blowjob last, which is disgusting.'

'Yuerk,' I said, screwing up my face. 'He had better be paying well.'

'Oh, he paid. He wants it three ways, that's three tricks.'

'So, like three times normal.'

'Yes, but then afterwards he slapped me around and called me a slut and a whore and other things in Russian.'

'Russian?'

'Yes, someone from their embassy, I think. One time I saw him picked up in a car with diplomatic plates.'

'So, he wasn't just a one off punter.'

'No, he comes regular.'

'With what he does, I'm surprised you let him.'

'It's horrible, but he pays good money. Can't afford to be choosy in my game.'

'They're not all as horrible as him though, are they?'

'No, not nice, but not as bad as that.'

'You have to go through a lot.'

Kitty reached her hand out under the table and stroked my thigh. 'I wish they were like you.'

'Come off it, Kitty.'

'I mean it. It would be a pleasure if they were.'

'Sorry to disappoint you, I'm spoken for.'

'Pity. Lucky girl.'

'Some of your gentlemen must be alright, surely?'

'Well, yes, some are quite nice.'

'What are the nice ones like?'

'The posh ones, public school types, they're usually nice. Polite and respectful too.'

'What sort of things do they like?'

'Usually like me to be their nanny, schoolmarm, and such, telling them off and spanking them.'

'Ever thought of doing something else? A different line of business.'

'I used to escort, strip; I did lap dancing and that sort, but I'm too old for it now.'

'I meant something else completely, not on the game at all.'

'Can't think what. I don't know anything else.'

'Well, chin up. Tomorrow might be better.'

'Could do with a day away from it, but I can't afford to. Got bills to pay.'

News Desk

My piece on the Knights of Camelot theme park was tucked within the leisure and holidays section, but I was gratified to see my second opportunistic story about protests by morality crusaders against lewd pagan rituals in the grounds of Glastonbury Abbey appeared much more prominently, although not on the front page.

I was with my friend, Tim Bennston, who was manning *The Daily Trumpet*'s news desk as I caught up with things on my return to the factory like bunker of a London office situated on land reclaimed from the old London docks, a location seen ablaze behind the City in old wartime photographs from 1940. The formerly derelict land had been cheap in the 1980s when *The Trumpet* moved out from the traditional Fleet Street district. Now, right between the traditional City financial district and the newer financial quarter in Canary Wharf, *The Daily Trumpet* was sitting on a gold mine.

Tim was companionable, in his thirties, short, well-rounded, a ruddy complexion with thinning hair, cheerful, humorous, level-headed and helpful even under pressure.

'You did well with the piece on the devil worshipers,' Tim observed.

'Just a chance happening while I was there.'

'Yes, but you spotted it and you were in there. That's what makes a good reporter.'

'Nice of you to say so.'

'I don't matter. Rebekah was impressed. That's what counts.'

'Really?'

'Sure, you did well.'

'So, what else have we got today?'

I looked over Tim's shoulder and skimmed the main stories.

One catching my eye concerned a British scientist, Dr Marcus Shorbody, winner of the prestigious Cheong Ping prize for Biological sciences for his work on genetics. From the accompanying photograph I recognised the man I saw talking to the Marquess about coding sequences and a breeding programme as he left through the library at Mendip House.

Another story concerned Russian agents feeding one of the Kremlin's enemies with poisoned tea in the bar of a hotel in Kensington. I always recognise a face and I could swear the Russian ambassador shown in the photo refuting the allegations, was the man emerging from Miss KattyKin's basement flat.

Scanning on, holidaymakers were complaining about flight delays, blamed by airlines on new airspace restrictions over north Somerset, especially affecting Bristol Airport. I recalled Adelena from the Ananda Guest House mentioning planes weren't flying over there anymore.

An editorial proclaimed wokeism as going mad over a law suit about radio suppression technology in prisons, supposedly infringing prisoners' human rights by denying them the use of radios and mobile phones.

Activists from BUFUIG, the British UFO Investigation Group, had been dispersed by military police using a controversial heat ray system to prevent them invading the Wookey Vale Military Facility, claimed by police to cause only temporary discomfort and no lasting harm. BUFUIG countered that the flight restrictions over north Somerset were a cover up for alien creatures harboured in the facility.

'Come on now, no time for you two to be idling,' intervened the editor, Rebekah Nemmberg, sweeping past. She was an expensively groomed woman in her mid-forties who did everything in her power to appear younger, including cosmetic procedures, a strenuous exercise regime, and fashion conscious outfits designed to display her carefully sculpted figure to its best advantage. The result was not elegant, more brassy, showy and in-your-face, nevertheless in keeping with the content of *The Daily Trumpet*, not a publication known for subtlety.

'What did you think about my story about the devil worshipers at Glastonbury Abbey?'

'A bit weak,' Rebekah replied. 'Where was the picture of the lewd ceremony? Without the naked flesh what do we have for our readers?'

'The lewd ceremony was over once I arrived.'

'You'll need to be quicker then, won't you? And as for the piece on the Knights of Camelot, pathetic. Where was the sensation?'

'What sort of sensation did you have in mind?'

'Do me a favour. Call yourself a journalist? A feud in the Mendip family, one of the rides breaking loose, the Marquess shagging Guinevere, use your imagination.'

'Funny you should say that. I have an idea he might be shagging Guinevere.'

'Why wasn't it in your story then?'

'Another thing, I saw the scientist guy, Dr Marcus Shorbody. He was talking to the Marquess.'

'What about it?'

'I don't know yet.'

'Well, find out.'

'The police came into Mendip House looking for missing persons.'

'It could be a story, but it isn't one yet. *The Daily Trumpet* doesn't pay you to stand around chatting. Get out there and find out who those missing persons are and why the police are interested. What are you waiting for?'

Chastened, I was quickly on the phone to the Glastonbury police. Neither DI Bellard, DS Lunnton nor any other officer were available for comment.

Lacking any other leads I browsed online for further avenues. I glimpsed Rebekah glaring at me from the other side of the office, presumably irate I was idly browsing the internet when I should have been hustling for stories.

As I idly explored the question of devil worship, witchcraft and the deep concerns of Christian folk about the forces of darkness, Rebekah appeared at my desk.

'What is all this nonsense about devils?' she demanded. 'You were supposed to be tracking missing persons.'

'There was this clergyman among the Moral Multitude protesters in Glastonbury. I was wondering if he might be a lead to future devil worshiping, so we could get a picture.'

'Never mind that,' said Rebekah. 'We're invited to a briefing from Dr Marcus Shorbody, the man you saw at Mendip House. Go along and dig about what he and the Marquess are cooking up.'

I felt an imposter among the throng of journalists gathered for the briefing in a lecture theatre at Dr Shorbody's alma mater, Britannica College in

Kensington.

Normally in a press conference I would have known most of my fellow journalists representing other publications, but here there was nobody. In contrast, the others present were a close circle chatting animatedly as we awaited Dr Shorbody's presentation.

This wasn't subject matter *The Daily Trumpet* would normally cover. Those attending included science correspondents from specialist periodicals, magazines covering economics and technology and so-called 'quality' newspapers aimed at the educated metropolitan elite. Some were themselves alumni of Britannica College and practically all had science degrees from prestigious colleges. My own diploma in Communication Studies from the East London College of Media Arts was not in their league.

Having nothing to talk about with my colleagues I took the opportunity to secure a seat in the front row slightly to one side, not directly in the limelight, but close enough to step in with a pertinent question.

A professor from Britannica College introduced Dr Shorbody, emphasising his groundbreaking research carried out during a long association with the college, laying the foundations for his recent award of the prestigious Cheong Ping Prize for biological sciences.

Dr Shorbody was relaxed, comfortable, looking around nodding to several journalists as he took his place on the podium. I caught his eye for a moment but he showed no recognition. Not surprising, I reflected; when I saw him in Mendip House his entire attention had been on the Marquess. That was good, he would be off his guard.

Dr Shorbody posed the rhetorical question: how long

would it take to engineer a completely new morphology into a species of organism? Or to put it another way, to engineer it into an entirely new species.

Well, it would depend upon the type of organism. If we were dealing with microbes that could reproduce a new generation in minutes, it could be achieved fast. But for larger more complex organisms, if one were to rely on conventional cycles of reproduction, it could take a prohibitively long time.

Fortunately there were other mechanisms that could be brought into play. Viruses, cancers and epigenetics adjusted genetic sequences and expression during the lifetime of a single individual. Dr Shorbody had been working for some time on harnessing these processes to make adjustments to the morphology of individual animals during their lifetime. He had demonstrated the transfer of substantial DNA coding sequences from one organism to another and, so doing, introduced new physical and bio-chemical characteristics. These characteristics could be controlled so as only to be expressed in particular parts of the organism, producing what was in effect a chimera.

At this point Dr Shorbody brought up a series of display slides illustrating the action of Cas9 enzymes, plasmids, CAS crRNA complexes, phosphodiester bonds and a bunch of other technicalities. There was rapt interest among the scientifically literate about the astounding accomplishments Dr Shorbody was describing. For my part I understood Dr Shorbody had figured out how to make genetic changes to a creature while it was still alive rather than waiting until it bred the next generation—beyond that I was lost.

Unlike those around me, I failed to be spellbound by Dr Shorbody's virtuosity, so I filled in the time to discreetly make searches about him on my phone. I discovered there was a Dr Marcus Shorbody on the electoral role for Mendip District Council and his recorded residence was a house on the Marquess's estate. I found no direct evidence of what Dr Shorbody and the Marquess were up to, but, recalling the illustrations of exotic mythical beasts I saw lying around in Mendip House, I had a hunch.

During the question and answer at the end of the talk Dr Shorbody dealt confidently and at length with matters relating to the bio-chemical mechanisms and potential malfunctions. As the technical questions were petering out I intervened with one of my own: 'Is it true you are working with the Marquess of Mendip to recreate mythical beasts to appear in the Marquess's theme park for the amusement of visitors?'

Dr Shorbody's cheeks first blushed a deep crimson and then quickly blanched to a deathly white. He remained silent for seconds. 'I have nothing to say about collaboration with the Mendip Estate,' he stammered eventually, turning to the professor beside him, mouthing 'Who is he?'

'*Daily Trumpet*,' replied the professor, *sotto voce*.

'Talk of mythical beasts is sensationalist nonsense,' blustered Dr Shorbody, 'unfortunately all too typical of *The Daily Trumpet*.'

After the briefing we were invited by the professor hosting the event to join Dr Shorbody and senior members of the faculty in the Senior Common Room for refreshments, but, realising I was unlikely to be welcome, I called my old friend Jim Mendolsen, a senior fellow at Britannica College working on cutting edge electronics.

To reach him I had no need to leave the premises; the campus was melded into an integrated hive of scientific endeavour by a rabbit warren of corridors and walkways. Guided through the labyrinth by a coding system and signposts intelligible only to those of higher intellect, and a hike familiar to passengers disembarking at a major airport, I eventually found Jim in his lab. He was an awkward looking young man, medium height and rather thin, wearing heavy spectacles beneath an unruly mop of blonde hair.

Jim's workspace was a jumble of paraphernalia, books and papers relating to overlapping projects, left lying across the floor and on every surface. 'Hello Simon, great to see you.' He hurriedly shifted a heap of papers off a chair. 'Take a seat a moment. Bear with me for just a couple of minutes while I wrap up a few things.'

He returned his attention to the three computer screens running simultaneously. It must have been a good half an hour before he surfaced from his projects. 'Sorry to keep you waiting Simon, shall we get a drink?'

'Yes, that would be great.'

'Let's go over to the Senior Common Room.'

'Er, perhaps not. Marcus Shorbody is entertaining the press there at the moment, and I'm trying to avoid him.'

'Oh, why?'

'He didn't like the question I put to him after his talk.'

'We could go to the Union Bar.'

'Could be a bit rowdy.'

'Pub then.'

The Shetland Pony on Bute Street was a traditional pub situated on a street corner, with ornate mouldings picked out in gold and black paint, etched glass windows, lit with repurposed industrial light fittings, blackboards listing the various special food and drink offerings of the day. We settled in a quiet corner with our pints of Meadow Dew ale.

'Well, Jim, what are you currently working on?'

'I'm using automated radio frequency signal cancellation by out of phase signal reflection,' Jim elucidated excitedly, gesticulating.

'Oh, I see, what does that mean in layman's terms.'

'It is similar in principle to noise cancellation headphones, but they do it with sound. We're applying it to radio signals.'

'How would it be used?'

'It allows an area to be screened from outside radio signals so within the protected area only white noise, essentially just hiss and crackle, can be picked up.'

'So, jamming radio signals then. That isn't anything new, is it?'

'The beauty is it applies across the entire radio spectrum, rather than just jamming particular frequencies. It also only transmits as necessary to achieve signal suppression rather than generating its own unwanted noise.'

'Has this been put in use anywhere?'

'Indeed. I've been working with Drembold Industries to develop it into a system for use in prisons, already deployed in a couple of high security establishments and proving effective, not only in blocking mobile phone, radio and television signals, but suppressing the use of drones to deliver contraband, drugs and so forth, into the jails.'

'How does it suppress drones?'

'Two ways. Radio signals are suppressed so they can't be remotely controlled, and at close range the signals within the built-in electronics can be cancelled by the suppressing system.'

'You mean, even if the drone has built in artificial intelligence to work on its own, it still gets shut down.'

'Exactly,' Jim acknowledged. He seemed about to expand, but apparently thought better. 'Anyway, enough about me. What is hot in the news at the moment?'

'Funnily enough, we ran a story about that prison system of yours.'

'Oh, what about it?'

'Prisoners' human rights being infringed, supposedly, by being cut off from radio and mobile phones.'

'Yes, there were demonstrations about it at Drembold's.'

'Talking of demonstrations, we have a story about BUFUIG, you know, the UFO people. They are claiming the MOD are secretly keeping aliens at Wookey Vale.'

I expected Jim to be amused or interested but he remained dead pan and looked away.

'There was something else about poor mobile phone coverage in the Mendips area.'

Jim frowned slightly. He took a swig of ale from his glass, but without signs of enjoyment, more as something to distract attention.

'I don't suppose the flight restrictions over the area are connected,' I went on, now suspecting I was on to something.

'You need to be careful, if you are talking about the military,' said Jim, clearly uneasy.

'I was at Drembold Industries myself recently, as it happens.'

'What about?'

'We were running a story about criminals using a Drembold device to hijack mobile phones. But that wasn't all. I am now seeing the young lady administrator I met there.'

'What, you mean, you just met her and picked her up, just like that?'

'Yes, I mean she is gorgeous, but at the time I hoped, if I got to know her, she might spill the beans about Drembold's fancy technology.'

'You've certainly got a cheek,' said Jim. 'I couldn't imagine doing that.'

'I didn't really expect anything, but in my trade you have to take every opportunity.'

'I wish I had your touch,' Jim lamented.

For want of anything else to pursue, I returned to my online exploration of devil worship and the occult. Among the random obsessive and often insane ramblings I encountered a blog by Dr Theophilus Pottinger, unremarkable except I identified him from his picture, having seen him during the fracas outside Glastonbury Abbey, as the clergyman with Ophelia Jardinair, leader of the Moral Multitude.

I saw Dr Pottinger was a chaplain and Religious Education fellow in Royal Pentonville College, with an intense obsession about the threat of dark forces, devils and demons, equating pagan cults such as Wicca and druids to devil worship. He saw spiritualism as a grave danger, at risk of summoning demonic forces from Satan's realm.

Sensing themes *Daily Trumpet* readers might relish, ah, I put in a call to Dr Pottinger and arranged to see him at his chaplain's residence in Royal Pentonville College.

The main college building was a large Victorian gothic edifice constructed mostly of dark red brick, adorned with spooky turrets on the corners and gargoyles, arranged around two quadrangles surrounded by cloisters, with a magnificent central clock tower.

Dr Pottinger was a big man, built like a bear, yet on a first impression, polite, mild and reasonable. He met me at the main college entrance, bringing me through to his cramped but cosy quarters built into the clock tower. He made a mug of tea for each of us and emptied some biscuits onto a plate, before we both settled onto the ancient sagging scuffed leather easy chairs he had in his tiny living room.

'Welcome, what would you like to talk about?'

'It concerns the dangers of dark forces, something I understand you are an expert in.'

'Well, I wouldn't go that far, but it is a speciality of mine.'

'We have been hearing of tragic cases and we would like to inform our readers of the dangers involved with dabbling in the occult.'

'The dangers are many,' said Dr Pottinger gravely. 'By delving into these things you open the door to Satan and his servants.' He took a book from a shelf and opened it. This featured a case of a possessed woman who murdered her children.

Without pausing the anecdotes and supporting documents flowed. Dr Pottinger's explanation superficially unhurried and sensible, but unrelenting, permitting me only to nod acknowledgement. Despite his patient delivery on the working of Lucifer, there was an earnest seriousness in his manner suggesting a quiet and determined fanaticism bordering on derangement. He reminded me of Professor Van Helsing in *Dracula*, impressing on people the grave dangers presented by vampires.

Dr Pottinger was especially worried by what he encountered with Ophelia Jardinair in Glastonbury: a Satanic cult purporting to be a bona fide religion. He was deeply concerned about how dark spiritual forces were allowed to invade the hearts of the credulous by masquerading as a beneficent faith. Cults worshiping perilous deities from the ancient world and pagan folklore, practising witchcraft and diabolical rituals, promoting themselves as equivalent, valid alternatives to established Christian faith. So-called spirit guides conjured in séances and invited to enter the minds of unsuspecting participants. Under the influence of the Dark Powers, spreading like a cancer through our society, all manner of hitherto unspeakable activities accepted and normalised.

Also alarming were diabolical practices within a Christian context. Satan, whose business is to pervert truth, could easily lead us astray, not only by undermining Christian worship by infiltrating pagan practices into our devotions, but by mimicking the Divine Sacraments within pagan rituals. Dr Pottinger warned dark forces could be unleashed and immortal souls of ordinary people be placed in peril by these hideous practices. There was an urgent need to restore faith in our Lord Jesus Christ.

There was no end to Dr Pottinger's misgivings about the machinations of Satan and the cunning of his agents. I struggled to tear myself from the endless flow of revelations. Even when I finally managed to convince Dr Pottinger it was time for me to leave, I was first obliged to join him in a lengthy, heartfelt and earnest session of prayer.

Going Away

I was accustomed to Jenny's emotional volatility, but unprepared for the state she was in when I arrived for our date at the Natural Food Café, an alternative lifestyle restaurant in Islington. I found her outside, leaning against the wall alone, staring at the pavement. Oblivious of her surroundings, shut in her own world of gloom from the scrunching of footsteps from passers-by and clatter of traffic. She did not notice my approach.

'Hello Jenny,' I greeted, with a cheery note in my voice but not entirely hiding my concern.

'Hello,' she replied, expressionless. Her dark goth-style makeup, crudely applied, was streaked and smudged with her tears.

'What's wrong?'

'Nothing.' She neither elaborated nor moved from her spot against the wall.

'Look,' I said matter-of-factly 'we can't stay out here moping. Let's go in and you can tell your Uncle Simon all about it.'

I took her by the arm, but she remained in her leaning posture, a dead weight. Taking hold more firmly I heaved her onto her feet, propelled her firmly through the door and into the brightly coloured restaurant, dodging foliage spreading out from the large chipped lichen stained planters, salvaged from the grounds of a country estate. There was a deliberately rustic air, rough-hewn furniture as if crafted by peasants in an unidentifiable Mediterranean nation, expensively selected by a fashionable interior designer. Enticing aromas of blended herbs, spices and fresh baked bread tempted the palettes of the throng of diners whose voices, chomping and clattering cutlery echoed.

Sensing we had private issues to discuss, the waiter guided us to a table in a quiet alcove. I ordered us the best cheer-you-up remedy, a large glass of prosecco.

'Now then,' I said once we were seated, 'tell me what's the matter.'

Jenny just shook her head and looked glum.

'Come on, spit it out.'

'There's nothing which concerns you.'

'Of course it does.' I felt rage build inside. 'In case you hadn't noticed I have become very fond of you, so if you're unhappy it concerns me. How dare you say it doesn't?'

Jenny looked up, shocked. 'I'm sorry, I didn't mean it like that. I meant it's just my problem, something you can't fix for me.'

'How do you know I can't help until you share it with me? Perhaps I can.'

Jenny shook her head. 'No, you can't do anything.'

'Is it something I have done?'

'Oh no, not you. You haven't done anything wrong.'

'Well, what is it then?'

'It's my parents. They're impossible.'

'What have they done?'

'They have tried to subvert my faith.' She looked at me wide-eyed with indignation.

'How have they done that?'

'They want to stop me worshiping and separate me from my fellow believers.'

'But you're grown up. You can do what you like. You don't need their permission.'

'They'll call the police. Get us arrested. That's what they said.'

'But what has religious worship got to do with the police? It's none of their business. Why should they care?'

'We were in the Jardinairs' garden. They say we were trespassing.'

'The Jardinairs' garden, you said. Would that be the same Jardinairs as I am thinking about? Ophelia Jardinair, the Moral Multitude woman, the one leading the protest about you being in Glastonbury Abbey?'

'Yes, her.'

'But why her garden, of all people? Why anybody's garden, come to that?'

'It's the energy flows. Where the ley lines coincide. We can't just worship anywhere. It has to be a sacred spot.'

'But how come these energy flows always seem to lead to somewhere that's going to antagonise people?'

'What do you mean?'

'Well, Glastonbury Abbey and now Ophelia Jardinair's garden. It'll be Buckingham Palace next.'

'We go where the energies lead us, which takes us to religious sites like Glastonbury Abbey, because those who built them were guided by spiritual energy flows just like us.'

'That explains Glastonbury Abbey, but it doesn't explain the Jardinairs' garden. That isn't a religious building.'

'Actually it is. Their house was originally a monastic farm building that came into the Jardinair family after Henry VIII dissolved the monasteries.'

'Okay, I can see how you would have enraged the Jardinairs. But it's your parents you are upset about. What has this got to do with your parents?'

'My dad interfered. It was after that when it got unpleasant at the Jardinairs.'

'But how come your dad was there?' Not for the first time I felt I was losing the plot in this bizarre saga. 'You didn't tell him you were going in there, did you?'

'No, I didn't tell him. But he heard the noise and saw what was happening.'

'But if you didn't tell him, how come he was there? Was he following you or something?'

'No, not exactly. I suppose he sort of followed us. But he was only next door.'

'But what was he doing next door?'

'He lives there. It's our home.'

I shook my head, clasping my fore finger and thumb into my eyes as if trying to gouge them out. 'You don't mean your parents, and you, I suppose, when you're at home in Glastonbury, live right next door to the Jardinairs' place. Have I got it right?'

'Yes, that's right.'

'But I still don't understand why your dad had to rescue you.'

'He didn't. All was fine until he blundered in and made a fuss.'

'What made him blunder in?'

'He was spying on us from his side of the fence and didn't like what he saw.'

'He must have been spying on you for a reason.'

'The other members of the coven came to my place, well my parents' place, and we had all gone out into the back garden. I think he must have been suspicious.'

'So, what did you do in the back garden?'

'Nothing, we climbed over the fence into the Jardinairs' garden.'

'So, he saw you going over the fence and went to see what you were up to.'

'Yes.'

'What then?'

'We were just getting into our celebration of the spirits of nature, when my dad charged in shouting and telling us to get dressed and back over the fence.'

I cradled my fingers and thumb against my forehead. 'Wait a minute. Did you say, get dressed? Did I hear right?'

'Yes.'

'Don't tell me you had nothing on?'

'Skyclad. That's right. We are always skyclad when we commune with nature.'

'So, what happened then?'

'My dad's noise and commotion, shouting his head off, alerted the Jardinairs.'

Later, when I learned more of Jenny's family, I would picture the scene. Sir Nicholas Jardinair and Lady Ophelia Jardinair witnessing their neighbour, Colonel Henry Potterswell (retired), surrounded by a coven of naked witches in their own back garden. In other circumstances it would have made a great story for *The Daily Trumpet*. It might even have earned me grudging approval from Rebekah. But, with Jenny involved... 'So what was the Jardinairs' reaction?'

'Lady Ophelia was just about to call the police, but her husband held her back.'

I could understand that. Sir Nicholas Jardinair was the Member of Parliament for South Mendips and Minister of State for Defence Establishments. The publicity of having naked witches in his back garden would not have done his political career any good. 'So what then?'

'The Jardinairs agreed not to call the police if my dad promised it wouldn't happen again. My dad grovelled horribly and hustled us back to our side of the fence.'

I scratched my chin. 'But so far I can't see what your dad did that was so terrible.'

'He shouted at all the other members of the coven and told them to get out and never come back.'

'I can see why he would have been annoyed.'

'Afterwards he set on me, told me I had to stop seeing them. They weren't allowed in the house or anywhere near. And he told me if I ever did anything like that again, he wouldn't wait for the Jardinairs to call the police. He would call them himself.'

'And what then?'

'My mum shouted at me too. She told me I was a selfish little child and it was about time I grew up.'

'Then what?'

'I left home. I'm never going back. I hate them.'

'I see. So, you're going to be in London then?'

'No. I'm going to be living a new life dedicated to Gaia.'

'What has this got to do with being in London? Can't you dedicate yourself to Gaia here in London?'

'No, I'm going into a commune, out in the countryside, where things are natural.'

'Where?'

'It's in a secret location.'

'But you can tell me, surely.'

'Actually I don't even know exactly where it is myself

yet.'

'Well, whereabouts?'

'Somewhere not far from Glastonbury, I think. At least that's where I'm going to be meeting with the Ethereal Guide to be taken over.'

'So, when are you going?'

'Tomorrow.'

My eyes widened. 'Literally tomorrow? You are going to just disappear tomorrow.'

'Yes. I only waited this long because I wanted to tell you first.'

'But we can keep in touch, meet up now and again, can't we?'

'No, we wouldn't be able to. The True Natural Path eschews unnatural modern technology, so no phones or internet.'

'But what about us? I'm fond of you, you know? You can't just walk away from me, surely.'

'That's why I wanted to see you. I want you to come with me.'

I stared at her incuriously. 'You mean, drop everything and disappear into a commune with you, literally tomorrow.'

'Yes, why not? You'll do it if you love me.'

I paused a long time, then shook my head. 'No, Jenny love, I can't do it. I'm sorry. Not in a rush like this.'

Jenny pouted. 'How dare you refer to me as love. You don't love me at all.'

'Look, I do. But it's too much of a hurry. I don't know enough about Wicca yet. I don't know what we'd be getting into.'

Jenny creased her face, but relented, reaching out her

hand and putting it over mine.

'Simon, I'm sorry. I realise it's asking too much and you aren't prepared yet. I'd love it though, if you followed me later, when the time is right for you. You will think about it, won't you?'

'Okay, Jenny, I'll definitely think about it. I'm torn apart by the thought of you going. I wish you would stay here in London, with me.'

'Sorry, Simon, I must go.'

My shoulders slumped. 'What brought this about? I mean, leaving all of a sudden.'

'It was this.'

She reached into her bag and brought out a crudely fashioned pentangle charm formed of a white metal alloy, configured as a necklace or brooch. It had a chunky handmade look, consisting of a flattened circular ring three inches in diameter and about half an inch wide over a plain pentangle, its points folded under and over had been mounted. This circular ring was embossed with symbols. A different coloured cut glass jewel was mounted on the ring between each of the pentangle's points and over the filled in centre. It conjured images of painstaking craftwork in a mini-smithy operated by a bearded man dressed in beads and sandals next door to his micro-brewery in a lean-to shed, itself producing thick treacly ale, mead and elderberry wine.

'It's a sort of pendanty Wiccary charmy thingy. What's it got to do with rushing off to live in a commune somewhere?'

Jenny set the charm out on the table. 'You'll see. Take out your phone and put it next to the pendant.'

I did. My phone's screen lit. Initially only the usual

wallpaper and icons were visible, but then the image faded and flickered. Another image emerged translucently over the top: a woman against a background of floating mist and water flowing over rocks. The woman was clad in vines and other foliage set off with flowers, morning glory and cherry blossom as far as I could make out.

We could hear the babbling stream in the background. The woman's stomach bulged as if pregnant, but in the place of her baby was a cavity containing a globe, a perfect image of planet Earth replete with oceans, clouds, weather systems and continents.

The woman spoke. The sound from the phone was faint and indistinct and I found it hard to follow above the background clatter and chatter. It had something to do with living a life in harmony with our sacred home, Earth. She was urging the listener to follow her way, the True Natural Path, concluding with a cryptic instruction about how the listener would be guided to this utopian existence, something about Yuletide blossoms and healing waters.

The image faded and the phone returned to its normal appearance.

'Well,' said Jenny, 'she's calling you.'

'Who?'

'Gaia, of course.'

'You mean that was Gaia?'

'Yes, of course it was. We are called to serve Her and save our wondrous planet Earth.'

'Right.' I was sceptical. There was an electronic trickery built into the pendant taking, I postulated, the sort of thing Drembold Industries produced, but I hid my scepticism.

'Well, will you come with me, now you've seen for yourself?'

I sighed. 'Where did the pendant come from?'

'Camden Market. There's a stall.' Jenny picked up the pendant and dropped it back in her bag. 'Well, are you going to come'

'Well, I can't just walk out on everything all of a sudden.'

'Why not? What could be more important than the fate of our planet.'

She looked beautiful at that moment. The prospect of eloping to live in the bosom of Gaia was appealing, but not practical. 'Sorry, Jenny, I can't just like that.'

'But you could follow me later, couldn't you?'

'Well, yes, I suppose so.'

In my heart I didn't believe I would. It was a silly dream of hers. I'd have to bide my time until the silliness blew over and she returned from her commune to normal life.

When it arrived we found we didn't have much appetite for the Wabi-Sabi salad of kimchi, almonds, oyster mushrooms, avocado and butternut squash with sunflower seed and sour plant-based cream dressing. We prodded the excellent vegan fare without appetite, nibbling here and there and spreading the rest around the plates.

Outside we lingered, holding hands and kissing languidly. Reluctantly we parted, our fingertips clinging together for a moment.

On the Trail

Had I been a cold-hearted accountant only motivated by hard economics and practicality, I might have drawn a line under my budding relationship with Jenny.

I had only known her a short time, she was volatile, immature, had strange beliefs and was likely only to cause me problems. Furthermore she had just chosen to walk away. It was questionable whether she even wanted me, although I sensed she did. There must have been other women with whom I could have enjoyed a less troublesome existence.

The love instinct does not function in those terms. Her fate was of paramount importance for me. I resolved to be patient, clinging to the hope she would tire of the commune nonsense and return to me, but waiting helplessly left an ache in my gut.

I only half believed I wouldn't be able to contact her. These days people simply didn't disappear so easily. I tried calling, left messages, texts, emails but with no response. Was she ghosting? Should I just accept she wasn't interested? It didn't make sense; she had implored me to come with her. With two weeks gone by, I needed to act.

She had called me once from her parent's place and I had the number on my phone. Calling there felt like stalking, but needs must.

It sounded like Jenny's voice on the other end.

'Jenny, is that you?' I stammered.

'No, I'm sorry, Jenny isn't here just now,' said the voice, still sounding like Jenny.

'Oh. Do you know where I could get in touch with

her?'

'No, I'm afraid not. I'm her mother. I'd be happy to take a message, in case she calls.'

'I'm Simon Chewton, a friend from London. I haven't heard from her for a while, so I was hoping really just to check she was alright.'

'We haven't heard from her either.' I sensed the urgency and worry in her mother's voice. 'We've been getting concerned too. When did you last hear from her?'

'It would have been a couple of weeks ago. We met up in London. She said she was on her way back to Glastonbury.'

'But she didn't reach us. She didn't say anything else about where she might have been going, did she?'

'Only she intended to join some commune.'

'Did she say anything about this commune?'

'It was to do with paganism, witchcraft, that sort of thing.'

'Yes, I thought it might,' said Jenny's mother, sighing. 'We've been frantic with worry.'

'I'm worried myself. She told me she couldn't keep in touch, but to disappear completely doesn't feel right.'

'We put it down to us having a row and her not wanting to talk to us.'

'She and I parted on good terms, so it can't just be that.'

'I hope to God she hasn't done anything stupid after what happened.'

'She was definitely planning on going to this commune, so I don't think she will have harmed herself.'

'I hope you're right.'

'I'll keep looking and of course I'll give you a call if I find anything.'

'Yes, please do.'

Galvanised by my conversation with her mother, I resolved to track Jenny down.

Pursuing her, urging me to join her, was now my only remaining avenue.

But how? There had been the pentangle pendant that displayed a message on my phone, concluding with a cryptic instruction, unfortunately garbled by the background noise—something to do with Yuletide and sacred waters, but that wasn't much help.

It was from Camden Market, she said. I remembered it having a chunky white circle of metal overlaid with a pentangle set with multi-coloured cut glass jewels. If I could find another such pendant, perhaps the message would come again for me to de-cypher.

Later, as I wandered among the market stalls in Camden, those situated within the labyrinth of brick arches near Camden Lock seemed the most promising.

There was a cornucopia of sights, sounds and colour. Stalls, kiosks and small shops selling a dazzling array of trinkets, cheap jewellery, brightly coloured glass light fittings, shabby chic clothing, exotic oriental herbs and spices, symbols of exotic religions and beliefs, unusual fruits and vegetables. There was an air of counterculture, an alternative lifestyle separate from most people's everyday existence, a slight grubbiness, a waft of narcotic substances penetrating the scents of incense, aromas of foods originating from a multiplicity of cultures, Thai, Turkish, Chinese, Indian, spices, vegetables, an oily watery stench from the nearby canal and the body odour of the jostling crowd.

A tattoo parlour declared itself as belonging to the renowned Suzy Fontanzana. A woman, perhaps Suzy herself, sat outside her little tattoo parlour, made-up goth-style, her hair dyed black, black smudges around her eyes, dressed in baggy black trousers hung low on her hips and adorned with buckles and chains to no apparent purpose, with a dark purple and gold tee shirt. Among the pictures illustrating her work a photo depicted a tattoo of an octopus spreading its tentacles across a female client's belly and thighs, her private parts forming the cephalopod's mouth as if about to chew up and devour any male member having the temerity to intrude. Observing me circling aimlessly, bemused by the spectacle and variety of the market, she caught my eye.

'Looking for something?'

'Erm, I'm not quite sure. Sort of jewellery, I suppose.'

'Ever thought about a tattoo? I'm good you know. They all say that.'

'Hmm, not just now, not today. Perhaps some other time.'

Within the myriad shops in tiny enclaves was a cornucopia of choice, items of a spiritual and mystical nature, an eclectic mix of Buddhism, Paganism subdivided into Druidic traditions, Wicca and witchcraft, Feng Shui and Nordic Runes, magical crystals, necklaces and amulets adorned with occult symbols of varying origin, tracts on auras and energy flows, ley lines and solstice rituals, incense sticks, scented candles and lace net bags filled with sandalwood and herbs. Fighting my fascination, I struggled to keep my focus on items with affinity with Wicca or jewellery.

In shop after shop there was every exotic item one

could imagine, goth clothing and accessories, fiendish leather book covers, fancy flickery lights, brooches and necklaces of every shape, size and style, but nothing resembling Jenny's pendant.

I had searched nearly every nook and was on the verge of giving up, when there they were. Pendants in the style as Jenny had shown me. Unmistakable, the same folded silvery metal strips forming the pentangle, overlaying the chunky engraved metal ring and set with brightly coloured glassy jewels, each unique, individually handmade, and clearly by the same hand.

My pulse racing and hand shaking, I brought out my phone, holding it next to one. The display faded, overlaid by the figure of the Goddess Gaia.

'Yes,' I cried, startling the stallholder.

'Found what you want?'

'Yes, I think so. How much for this pendant.'

'Ten pounds.'

'Where do you get them from?'

'I couldn't say,' he replied, looking at me suspiciously.

I didn't believe him, but, lacking leverage, I left it there.

As I arrived home in Earls Court I saw Miss KattyKins laboriously clambering up from the steep steps of her basement flat. She looked away to avoid catching my eye.

'Hello Kitty. How's things?'

'Okay, I suppose.'

I could see her face now, swollen and caked with thick makeup in a futile attempt to disguise a black eye. She was limping slightly and holding her body awkwardly.

'Kitty, you don't look okay to me. What happened?'

'Nothing.'

'It wasn't nothing, was it?'

'It was that Russian bloke.'

'What did he do?'

'Beat me up, punched me and that.'

'Why?'

'I didn't want to do what he wanted, so he shouted at me and said I had to and hit me until I did.'

'What a bastard! I'm sorry.'

'Not your fault.'

'Anything I can do to help?'

'No, best you keep out of it.'

'Are you sure?'

'Yes, I'll be alright.'

Back up in the flat, I concentrated closely on what was playing on my phone, trying to pick up every clue and nuance from the Goddess's message.

From the preamble I perceived nothing beyond reverence for and exhortation to the service of the Earth Mother and her spirit Gaia, but the final call to action yielded more.

'Come and join with me,' said Gaia. 'Be in harmony with your home, your planet Earth. Follow me in the True Natural Path. Where the Yuletide thorn blooms beside the healing waters, as Sulis fades following Esbat, you will find the Ethereal Guide.'

From a quick search I discovered Sulis to be a Celtic God of the Sun, so perhaps Sulis fading might be sunset. Esbat was the Wicca celebration of the full moon, so perhaps the time was sunset on the day following the full moon.

Yuletide blooms and healing waters remained a

mystery, but I guessed it was probably in or around Glastonbury. I would need to get back there.

However, beforehand, there was another avenue to investigate. Not so long ago I had been at Drembold Industries enquiring about criminals using technology for hijacking mobile phones, and here was a pendant doing exactly the same thing, perhaps too much of a coincidence. I made a call to Alex Drembold, the founder, principal shareholder and chief executive of the company

'Mr Drembold, Simon Chewton from *The Daily Trumpet*. Just calling about a story we are running involving your company.'

'What story is that?'

'It involves a religious sect making use of Drembold Industries technology to groom children for sexual exploitation.'

The line remained quiet.

'Mr Drembold, are you still there?'

'Yes, I'm here. How is this sect supposed to be using our technology in this way?'

'You have technology for taking control of mobile phones, don't you?'

The line went quiet again.

'Mr Drembold, you do provide this technology, don't you?'

'We have investigated means by which the security of mobile phones may be compromised. We do not publish our results, which are made available only to reputable clients in the industry or government agencies.'

'But these results must have leaked, mustn't they, if criminals and religious fanatics have managed to get them.'

'Look, I don't see why I should make any comment, given presumably *The Daily Trumpet* are going to run the story anyway, whatever I might say.'

'Don't you want to put your side of the story.'

'Not particularly.'

'If we run the story with what we have so far we'll simply say Drembold technology has been used for this purpose, which won't reflect well on your brand.'

'And your point is?'

'Although we have identified the nature of the sect, we haven't been able yet to flush out the guilty individuals. If you could help us do so we could make them the villains of the piece and possibly keep Drembold out of it.'

'Why would you do that?'

'Each story needs a villain, but we only really need one. If there are multiple villains it confuses the readers.'

'I see.' He paused. 'How can I trust you?'

'No guarantees, but, as I said, we only need one villain for the story.'

'Alright, you had better come over and we can talk about it.'

Drembold Industries was one of several companies occupying a modern campus style office complex in Chiswick, a West London suburb. Multiple low rise office buildings were set out in landscaped grounds including a lake with waterfall and a fountain attracting ducks and other water fowl, lawns, park-style benches and flowering cherries. Besides offices, the site offered coffee shops, a children's nursery and a health club.

As I approached the office building my way was obstructed by a small group of demonstrators being hustled away by security guards. A placard identified them as BUFUIG, the British UFO Investigation Group, protesting against Drembold Industries. *'DREMBOLD, WHAT HAVE YOU GOT TO HIDE?'* read one placard.

'What are Drembold hiding?' I enquired of the placard's holder, an agitated scrawny little man with straggly hair clad in a stained misshapen anorak.

'Aliens.'

'Where?'

'At the Wookey Vale Military Facility.'

'Wouldn't that be the army?'

'Ah, but Drembold are in league with them, using their Area Denial System to keep us away.'

'What does it do, this system of theirs?'

'It's a ray gun. You can feel the heat from it.'

The security guards hustled the man away before I could get any more out of him.

Drembold Industries' reception area featured posters illustrating young studious scientists smiling happily in futuristic laboratory and factory settings, impressive communications satellites and blow-ups pictures of tiny intricate electronic circuitry.

A company product brochure on display described the Area Denial System: a non-lethal directed energy technology. It deployed millimetre waves to encourage 'avoidance behaviour due to harmless thermal discomfort arising from radio induced excitation of fluid molecules in the bodies of intruders, whether persons, livestock or wild animals.'

A new young office administrator, Jenny's replacement, met me in reception to show me up. On this occasion I resisted the temptation to flirt with her.

Alex Drembold was a chunky man in his mid-forties, average height, clean-shaven with tidy short dark hair, brown eyes set in a round lived-in face.

'So, what's this story of yours about?' he demanded.

I pulled out the pendant I had obtained from Camden Market. 'It's this.' I said, setting it next to my mobile phone. We watched and listened as the woman portraying the Goddess Gaia said her piece.

'Well, Mr Drembold, can you confirm this technology originated from Drembold Industries?'

'I couldn't say.'

'Come now, I have seen a demonstration myself of a Drembold Industries device controlling a mobile phone remotely. It must at least be a possibility.'

Mr Drembold considered, then nodded. 'It's possible, but it could have been from a different company.'

'No, Mr Drembold. I have had the pendant analysed and traced back to your company.' I was bluffing.

'Seems you have done your homework.'

'Well, are you able to tell me who you provided this to?'

'And supposing I don't?'

'As I said earlier, Drembold Industries are currently the villain of our story, unless you can point us elsewhere.'

'So, to be clear, if I can provide an alternative scapegoat, you'll leave us out of it?'

'Yes.'

'And you won't reveal the source of your information.'

'No, fundamental principle of journalism, that.'

'Alright, lend me the trinket a moment. I'll be right back.'

After ten minutes Alex Drembold was back. He tossed

the pendant back onto the desk.

'The electronics were provided to a Philomena Abballon, acting on behalf of the Marquess of Mendip.'

'Thank you, I appreciate your help.'

'Blackmail, I'd call it.' Funnily Alex Drembold demeanour wasn't hostile, more like good humoured admiration.

'Well, Mr Drembold, blackmail is strong. I'd call it more a business agreement.'

'Call me Alex.'

'Well, Alex, on an entirely different story,' I went on.

'How many damned stories have you got on us, for goodness's sake!'

'We are doing a piece on the supposed infringement of prisoners' human rights by Drembold Industries's radio suppression system being deployed in prisons.'

Alex laughed. 'It is nonsense of course. Ludicrous to consider it a human right for prisoners to have the use of mobile phones.'

'Glad you think that. It's the view we are taking at *The Daily Trumpet*. For the story, there are a couple of things I would like to clarify about what the system does.'

'The technical details are confidential.'

'Just in general terms, not the technicalities. I take it the system blocks all radio signals, so not just mobile phones, but radios, televisions and radio controlled drones flying in contraband.'

'Yes, that's right.'

'If the system interferes with drones, could it pose a problem? For example could it also potentially interfere with legitimate aircraft such as helicopters?'

'The system guidelines advises against the deployment

of helicopters in the space above the premises up to a height of 3000 feet,' Alex explained.

'Presumably the system is scalable, up or down depending on the size of the premises,' I postulated. 'I have in mind the mega-prisons in the USA, Los Angeles County Jail or Rikers Island for example.'

'Oh yes,' Alex confirmed. 'The system would scale to whatever size is required. I couldn't imagine the size of the prison being a limitation. As a matter of fact Drembold Industries are already in discussion with American penal institutions.'

'If it was scaled in terms of ground area, would it also increase the height up to which drones would be disabled?'

'Well, yes, a larger installation would reach higher as well as wider.'

'So, the 3000 feet limitation in the guidelines, does that allow for the larger installations?'

Alex thought. 'We set the 3000 feet limitation to allow for the largest installation we envisaged. But for the very large premises such as the examples you mentioned in the USA, it might need to be higher.'

'So, if hypothetically, if there was a system implemented to cover somewhere like, well, for example, the Wookey Vale Military Facility, then height restriction would need to be much higher, perhaps making any kind of over-flying unsafe.'

Alex froze. His face flushed, then quivered. 'This interview is at an end.'

As his office administrator escorted me away, Alex caught my eye, nodding ever so slightly.

When in the front line of the popular news sector you must get used to being unpopular and thrown out of places. From a news gathering perspective hostile reactions substantiate what was only speculation.

Further confirmation came when I returned to the open plan hanger-like expanse news floor within *The Daily Trumpet*'s brutally functional offices in the former docklands. Rebekah Nemmberg observed me coming onto the news floor. She beckoned.

'What on Earth have you been asking Alex Drembold?'

'Why?'

'Because we've had a D notice slapped on us, that's why.'

'Interesting, what does it say?'

She thrust the paper into my hand. It was an issue of advice from Her Majesty's Government stating it would not be in the national interest for information relating to national security to be published. Clever, I thought, Alex Drembold had it drafted so broadly it closed both the story I had threatened about remote control of mobile phones and the one we might have published about the use of the radio suppression technology at Wookey Vale, and indeed almost anything concerning Drembold Industries.

'You'll have to leave Drembold alone, Simon,' Rebekah announced. 'I would rather not have the security services crawling all over us, if you don't mind.'

'Even with Drembold off limits, I'd like to get back to Glastonbury.'

'What for?'

'There are potentially juicy stories there,' I assured. 'For example, the police are giving nothing away about their missing persons enquiry, with its connection to the Marquess.'

'Good, what else?'

'There is a strong link between the Marquess and Dr Marcus Shorbody. I'm not sure what yet, but I think he may be breeding strange mutant creatures.'

'Mutants running loose, great. Anything more?'

'Well, there are those bizarre witch's sabbath rituals involving naked cavorting. I'd like first-hand accounts and pictures.'

'You'd have had those already, if you'd been sharper.'

'I've also got a hunch there might be a connection between the witches, the missing persons and Dr Shorbody's activities with the Marquess.'

'How come?'

'The electronics in the witch's pendant thing was delivered by Drembold to Philomena, the Marquess's advisor.'

'You're being very persuasive. Too persuasive. Have you some kind of personal reason for being in Glastonbury? Some girl, perhaps.'

'Oh no, nothing like that,' I lied.

'I don't believe you. You wouldn't have gone to so much trouble arguing your case otherwise.'

'But should I go?'

'Yes, I think you should. But, you have a maximum of two weeks and I won't be signing off any lavish expenses. Find yourself a cheap bed and breakfast and live frugally. Got it?'

'Yes, Rebekah.'

'And you had better deliver those stories. That's all.'

Missing Person

'Lady Jardinair, it's Simon Chewton,' I announced as she answered the phone. 'I saw you outside Glastonbury Abbey and I just wanted to say how much I appreciate the stand the Moral Multitude are taking to protect places of Christian worship from desecration.'

She paused, probably trying to remember who I might be. 'Thank you for your support,' she eventually acknowledged.

'I have been in touch with Dr Theophilus Pottinger. He was emphatic about the need for Christians to rally our forces against the grave danger presented by the gathering Satanic threat.'

'We all greatly value Dr Pottinger's stalwart efforts on behalf of the Moral Multitude.'

'I represent *The Daily Trumpet* and the reason I am calling is because we are running a piece on the lamentable decay of Christian morality in British society. We would greatly appreciate your input and especially to feature the excellent work of the Moral Multitude to uphold traditional family values.'

Lady Jardinair went quiet for some seconds, perhaps apprehensive talking to a journalist.

'Are you still there, Lady Jardinair?'

'Yes, I'd be glad to talk to you,' she replied.

'Should I pop round to see you at home?'

'Yes, please do.'

The Jardinairs' house was an unruly conglomeration of construction accumulated over centuries by successive

Jardinair generations, adapting to the needs and fashions of the times. An architectural historian would have identified the embedded remnants of the original fifteenth-century monastic building. The most prominent style was a veneer of Victorian gothic overlaying a predominantly Georgian framework, fragmentary Tudor elements and twentieth-century adaptations. Overall it was a substantial pile with an intriguing rabbit warren of rooms and passages with strange alignments and differing levels accommodated by unexpected steps and sloping floors.

Lady Ophelia Jardinair was a bulldozer of a woman in her early fifties, in a sensible outfit and clunky shoes without the slightest concern for fashion, ballasted by her substantial physical presence and unshakeable self-belief, faith in her Christian religious doctrine and mission to uphold moral rectitude across the nation in conformity with Christian values.

She conveyed me in for tea in the drawing room. As we moved, out of the hall, around corners, from one passage to another, I sensed how with every turn the atmosphere changed, as if each location was haunted by its own ghost, a change in temperature, draughts blowing in a different direction, eddies above, below or the side, varying musty smells of ancient dry rot, decades old furniture polish and rising damp.

With us both seated on the chintz furniture I opened our discussion. 'Lady Jardinair, I realise there was some pagan ritual carried out in the grounds of Glastonbury Abbey, but I'm not completely clear about what took place.'

'Call me Ophelia, please.' She shuddered. 'I wouldn't

want to repeat the hideous activities. Indescribably ghastly.'

'The pagans claim they were carrying out a religious rite.'

'Since when has it been religious to prance about without clothes waving antlers in disgustingly suggestive poses among a symbol of the Devil?'

'A symbol of the Devil? Was some sort of shape laid out on the ground?'

'They marked it out in sand.'

'Just poured out on top of the grass? What was the shape?'

'Yes, it was a sign of the Devil, a pentangle, marked out within a big circle.'

'Where exactly did they do it?'

'Right in the midst of the ruins of the old church, in the nave.'

'I thought it was outside.'

'The nave has fallen in, so, open to the sky now. But in a church. Sacrilege.'

'What were they doing around this circle?'

'It was just too repulsive to contemplate.'

'Oh dear. Repulsive in what way?'

'Doing lewd things with nothing on.'

'Very disturbing. Who was doing the lewd things?'

'It was the large portly woman, the one leading the whole thing. She was in the middle with a man wearing antlers on his head and not much else.'

'You mean, sexual things?'

Ophelia shuddered. 'Yes, brazenly, right out there in the open, in the middle of that sign of the Devil.'

'You mean they were having actual sex?'

'They could have. I couldn't say if it was real or they were just simulating, but it looked real enough.'

'What were the others doing?'

'Holding hands in a circle around the two of them doing… well… you know.'

'What, with nothing on as well?'

'Yes, quite naked. Disgusting.'

At this moment Sir Nicholas Jardinair, a suave gentleman in his mid-fifties, the Member of Parliament for South Mendips and a Minister of State in the Ministry of Defence, came into the drawing room. Even at home he was elegantly and expensively turned out in a Saville Row outfit, expensive silk shirt and tie set off with tasteful cufflinks and an understated but exclusive Swiss watch.

'Who was naked?' Sir Nicholas enquired.

'Those Satanists carrying on at Glastonbury Abbey,' Ophelia explained.

Sir Nicholas turned to me. 'I don't think we've met.'

'Simon Chewton, *Daily Trumpet*.'

He didn't shake my hand. 'I see. Not sure it is wise to be discussing these tawdry details.'

'*The Daily Trumpet* is behind us in our battle with this dangerous cult,' said Ophelia.

'Rest assured we are,' I reiterated.

'Well, Mr Chewton, I expect you have the details you need now,' said Sir Nicholas in a tone strongly suggesting the interview was over.

'Well, there was one other thing. I understand there was a similar incident that took place here, in your garden.'

Sir Nicholas and Ophelia both swallowed hard and

looked at each other in alarm. Sir Nicholas was the first to recover his senses. 'We have no knowledge of any other incident and we would have nothing to say about it if we did. Now, Mr Chewton, time is getting on and we should conclude this discussion. I will show you out.'

Undeterred by the resistance I had provoked in the Jardinair household I seized the opportunity to call in on their neighbours, Jenny's parents, the Potterswells.

Their home was an Edwardian villa, a mass of meticulously laid deep red brick embellished with decorative detail, fancy scalloped bargeboards, bay windows with a fancy arrangement of panes and elaborate frames, fronted by a substantial porch with a floor of black and white ceramic tiles and a front door topped with stained glass panels. I pressed the old ornate ceramic bell push button resulting in a resonant two tone bell chime I could hear echoing inside the house.

It was Jenny's mother, Mrs Delia Potterswell, who answered. Not having met each other in person, she showed no recognition as I stood in the porch.

'Mrs Potterswell, I presume. I'm Simon Chewton. We spoke on the phone.'

Her eyes lit up. 'Yes, of course, do come in.'

She was a woman of around fifty, dressed elegantly but not in the height of current fashion, with a slim build, without appearing sporty or athletic. Her face was nicely shaped by virtue of her fundamentally good bone structure, but now bearing the signs of care and worry, a stiffness in the way she moved revealing fatigue.

On either side of the hall were framed group photographs of British Army training teams, in Kenya and Belize. We went through into the sitting room where a man in his mid-fifties stood smartly to greet me. I introduced myself and the man reciprocated, announcing himself as Colonel Henry Potterswell, Jenny's father. He had a firmly set jaw and close cut greying hair. He was a fraction above average height and not heavily built, yet by his bearing he conveyed unyielding strength. His voice was crisp, authoritative.

I recognised his face as one of those in each of the pictures I had seen in the hallway, the central one, the officer in command. Around the room were more items of military memorabilia, a large calibre brass shell case serving as a wastepaper basket, a cavalry sword mounted on the wall, some silver shooting trophies on the mantelpiece.

Anxious and impatient, Henry kept his preliminary greetings to the least required for the sake of minimal politeness. The moment we were seated on the comfortable, well-worn easy chairs he got to business.

'Well, have you discovered anything about Jenny?'

Delia looked at her husband disapprovingly. 'Now Henry, where are your manners? Simon could probably do with some refreshment.'

Henry looked apologetic. 'So sorry. Quite right, dear. Simon, can I offer you a drink?'

'No thanks, Colonel. Perhaps a little later.'

Delia reached over and put her hand on my arm. 'Simon, you'll have to forgive us if we're not as hospitable as we would normally be. It has been a very trying time.'

'That's quite alright, Mrs Potterswell. I entirely understand how you must be feeling. I'm anxious about her myself. Anyway, about Jenny. She told me she was joining a commune, near Glastonbury, so presumably not far away, which is why I'm here.'

'Any idea what sort of a commune?' asked Henry.

'To do with Wicca, female supremacy, Mother Earth, and so forth.'

'Might have known it would be those weirdos. I can't understand how Jenny could have got involved with all that hocus-pocus.'

'You really shouldn't be rude about it, Henry,' said Delia reprovingly. 'Jenny is a grown woman and she is entitled to have her own beliefs. If it wasn't for your intolerant attitude she might still be with us. You drive people away, the way you talk sometimes.'

'Oh, alright. Of course she is entitled to her own opinions. And I have been a bit hard on her at times. I share the blame for this, I admit. But beating myself up and wearing a hair-shirt won't get her back.'

'You owe Simon an apology as well, Henry. He wouldn't want Jenny's and perhaps his own beliefs being dismissed as hocus-pocus.'

'Oh, I see. Simon, I'm so sorry, last thing I'd want to do is offend you. I wasn't thinking. Put mouth into gear before brain. So sorry.'

'That's alright, Colonel, no offence taken.'

Chastened, Henry kept quiet.

'Simon, do you have any idea how she got drawn into this commune thing?' enquired Delia.

'As it happens I do.'

I pulled out the pentangle pendant and placed it on the coffee table alongside my smartphone. The aggressively pagan object clashed with the conservatively Anglican Christian conformity of the Potterswell home. Delia edged away from its uncivilised influence. Henry's face snarled like a guard dog. Suppressing their distaste, they watched in fascination as the woman purporting to be Gaia conveyed her message via my phone.

'How can we track down this rendezvous it mentions? So we can get her out of there,' demanded Henry, released from the penitentiary time-out imposed by his wife.

'I'm working on it,' I replied. 'However, now I've told you what I've discovered, is there anything you can tell me, to help us find her?'

Henry and Delia looked at each other.

'Did she say anything when you last saw her?'

'We weren't on good terms. She just said she was going away and not coming back,' said Delia, tears welling.

'She was hysterical and we weren't happy either. Feelings on all sides running high,' Henry summarised.

'Not helped by your loud and intolerant remarks,' said Delia sharply.

Henry looked sheepish.

'That would have been after the incident next door in the Jardinairs' garden, I suppose?'

'So you know about that,' observed Henry.

'Yes, Jenny told me.'

Henry and Delia looked at each other again.

'We agreed with the Jardinairs we wouldn't say anything about it,' said Henry.

'I've just come over from the Jardinairs, so they already know the cat is out of the bag.'

'I see.'

'Is there anything you can tell me about the incident to throw some light on where she might have got to?'

'I suppose there would be those friends of hers, the

ones she had with her at the time,' said Henry.

'I don't suppose you have any idea of who they are and how we might get in touch?'

'Sorry, I don't. At the time we were more intent of getting them off the premises and out of Jenny's life than exchanging contact details.'

Delia said nothing but she had the face of a disapproving nanny. I smiled slightly, a picture forming in my mind of Henry forcefully ejecting a coven of witches.

'There must be some leads. Is there anything among Jenny's stuff that might throw light on it?'

Delia looked uncomfortable. 'We didn't want to pry.'

'No time to be squeamish about her privacy. She's disappeared and we need to track her down.'

'Quite right. Let's get on with it,' Henry boomed. Without further hesitation, he was on his feet and ushering me and his wife upstairs and into Jenny's bedroom.

There were posters and symbols on the wall depicting aspects of Wicca, the calendar of Wicca festivals, triple aspects of the Goddess, the casting of spells, treatises on pagan philosophy and history.

'Sorry, but is it okay if I have a rummage?' I hesitated. 'It's intrusive, but needs doing.'

Delia looked nervous, but Henry rode roughshod over any misgivings she might have had. 'Yes, go ahead. Let's get to the bottom of this.'

I began the painstaking process of looking in each drawer, scanning every shelf, under and beside the furniture for any clue.

Dropped on the floor of the wardrobe was a scuffed leaflet promoting Glastonbury Pagan Pride. It featured an assortment of pagan entities, among them a group photograph of the Mendip Moon Coven, among whom Jenny could be seen.

'Do you recognise any of these people from when Jenny went into the Jardinairs' garden?'

'Couldn't say for sure, but some of them look slightly familiar,' said Delia.

On the leaflet was a contact number and name next to the picture.

'Leave this one to me. I'll follow it up,' I promised.

Having exhausted Jenny's belongings in the search for leads we adjourned downstairs.

'I think we could all do with tea,' said Delia as she disappeared into the kitchen.

'So, Simon, what is it you do?' enquired Henry.

'I'm a journalist at *The Daily Trumpet*.'

'Ever considered a military career?'

'Well, not really. But I can't help noticing your own military career has been an interesting one.'

'It's had its moments.'

'What were its highlights?'

'When I was in the special forces, I suppose. But I can't talk about it. Hush hush.'

'You did other things though.'

'Ended up in a desk job, commanding officer for some training establishments.'

Delia came in with the tea trolley.

'I don't suppose Jenny has been reported to the police as a missing person yet, has she?' I enquired, as Delia served out tea and cake.

Delia and Henry looked at each other anxiously. 'We haven't. Do you think we should have done?' asked Delia.

'Well, all you knew was Jenny stormed out in a huff, but you didn't exactly know she had disappeared completely. You can't blame yourself.'

'But we know more now, don't we?' Henry intervened, picking up on my cue.

'Yes, we do. I think the time has come for us to report her as missing.'

'Quite right. We should do it right away,' said Henry, beaming approvingly.

On the way to the police station, as Henry drove us past the Mother Earth Temple, he had to slam on his brakes as a young woman rushed across the road. I recognised her as Ivy Langport, the teenage daughter of Elsie from the Moral Multitude demonstrators at the Glastonbury Abbey incident. Moments later Harry Mallet, the bruiser I had met in the Mendip Grenadier, ran across in hot pursuit. He got to her just as she was reaching the temple entrance, roughly grabbing hold of her and trying to haul her away.

'What does that swine think he's doing?' exclaimed Henry.

'Whatever it is, he needs to leave her alone,' I said as I jumped out of the stationary car. Henry followed me.

'Cool it, Harry,' I said.

'Nothing to do with you,' said Harry. 'Keep out of it.'

'Get your hands off her, you brute,' said Henry.

As Harry continued to drag Ivy away, Henry punched him hard on the chin. With Harry momentarily dazed, Ivy broke free and dashed towards the front door of the temple. Coming to his senses Harry made to run after her, but I stepped into his path. He collided with me forcefully.

'Leave it, Harry. Let Ivy do what she wants.'

For a second Harry looked as if he would go down fighting, but faced with the two of us, shrugged and gave up.

'What did you have to interfere for? What's it got to do with you.'

'I have never allowed any man to assault a woman,' declared Henry, 'and I'm not about to start.'

'Come on Colonel, we've done our good deed for the day,' I said, steering him back towards the car.

As arranged on the phone, Detective Sergeant Keith Lunnton met me and Henry at the kiosk-style reception desk at Glastonbury Police Station, a forbidding utilitarian brick and concrete construction with only a few small opaque windows. He let us through an electronically operated door separating the internal police domain from the general public, along a plain corridor into a minimally furnished interview room.

DS Lunnton was a large heavily built man in his late thirties. He had a full head of slightly curly brown hair, a wide friendly face, his eyes conveying warmth as did the placid unhurried tones of his strong West Country accent.

Waiting for us to be introduced and comfortably seated, DS Lunnton methodically went through each item on a missing person form, carefully writing the relevant information, pausing before moving on to the next topic. At times, instead of proceeding to the next section on the form, DS Lunnton mused in deep contemplation before asking supplementary questions. At points new information prompted him to glance backwards and reopen a discussion we assumed concluded. I noticed him becoming particularly pedantic about detail when we referred to Jenny's interests in radical feminist politics, paganism or witchcraft.

From the moment Henry arrived he was already straining at the leash to muster a police squad to comb the surrounding countryside searching every shed and barn, bringing in suspicious characters for questioning, especially pagans and hippies. As the interview progressed he was getting increasingly impatient and irritable in the face of DS Lunnton's languid, reflective style.

'We don't need all this damned red tape,' Henry exclaimed, thumping his fist on the table. 'We need to get out there and find her.'

To Henry's great annoyance DS Lunnton did not respond right away, carefully continuing with what he was writing until he reached the end of his sentence. Henry puffed and growled like an angry guard dog.

'Now then, sir. We need to get all the details down right so we know what we are doing. Otherwise we would be chasing our tails, wouldn't we?'

'Don't talk to me like that,' yelled Henry. 'I want to talk to your superior officer.'

I reached across and placed a hand on Henry's arm. 'Colonel, please, let him do his job. The sergeant's right. We need to go over all the details. We shouldn't try to rush it.'

DS Lunnton was not a man to allow himself to become flustered by other people's irritability. He continued the information gathering process calmly and systematically. Henry fidgeted and harrumphed. I reined him back enough to prevent him exploding.

As DS Lunnton reached the end of the interview, I felt ready to intervene. 'How does Jenny's situation compare with your other missing persons cases?' I kept my voice calm.

'I assure you, sir, we treat each missing person case very seriously,' replied DS Lunnton. 'They all get looked into thoroughly.'

'It wasn't that. I'm sure you'll do a proper job. What I meant was, are there parallels, things in common, with your other cases?'

'I'm sure you will understand we have to respect confidentiality. We can't discuss other cases. You wouldn't want us to go talking about Jenny to other people willy-nilly, would you?'

'I don't care who you talk to, nor what you say to them, so long as you get her back,' said Henry, hotly.

'Let's stop messing about, shall we?' I demanded. 'I know perfectly well you have ongoing enquiries into other missing persons and Jenny's case is relevant to those enquiries.'

'Our missing persons enquiries are entirely routine, I can assure you,' replied DS Lunnton in a reassuring tone that did not mollify me.

'So it's routine to carry out a raid on Mendip House, is it, the country home of the no doubt very influential Marquess of Mendip?'

DS Lunnton had a moment of realisation. He looked at me closely as if remembering where he had seen me before. 'I'm sorry, I can't discuss ongoing police operations.'

'Look, let's cut to the chase. Is Jenny's disappearance connected with those other missing persons cases?'

'We always look for possible patterns, that's standard police work.'

'You haven't answered the question/'

Henry looked at me approvingly.

'It's too early to say,' said DS Lunnton.

'No, it's not. It is perfectly clear to me there is a strong connection.'

'What exactly makes you think there is a connection?' Police officers were the ones who were supposed to put pressure on people with their questioning, not those they were interviewing. He sought to restore our respective roles.

'You wouldn't have spent so much time taking down minute details about Jenny, her associates and interests, if you didn't think so. This case is clearly not just routine.'

'Why are you so interested in other cases?'

'Because, forgive me if this sounds insulting, I don't intend to leave it to flat foot PC Plod to find Jenny. I will be pursuing my own enquiries as well.'

'Oh, I wouldn't advise it, sir. Best leave it to the police.'

'I appreciate your advice, but I'm still going to be investigating this myself.'

'In which case just make sure you keep it within the law.'

'Right, I think we can take it now that there are other missing person cases similar to Jenny's. You still haven't told me what connects them.'

'I'm not in a position to comment,' he said defensively.

'Let me suggest what they might be then. You took down details about Jenny's interest in Wicca, witchcraft and so forth. There has to be a reason. What is it?'

DS Lunnton was clearly uncomfortable. He stood.

'Well, I think I have all the details we need. Thank you for your patience.'

Henry stood too. 'Oh no you don't,' he spat in the crisp tone of a colonel reprimanding a transgressing junior officer. 'Sit back down and do your job. We haven't finished. What do you know about this witchcraft stuff?'

Subdued by the combined onslaught, DS Lunnton sat back down. 'I can't reveal details of police enquiries, you must respect that.'

'It may interest you to know I have a lead to Jenny's associates I will be following up.'

DS Lunnton's interest perked up.

'Would you like me to keep you informed about what I find?'

'Yes, actually I would.'

'In which case you'll need to open up a bit to me.'

'I'm not sure I can.'

'Well, to begin with, if I do pursue this lead, from what you already know, would I be putting myself in danger?'

DS Lunnton sat still, struggling with how should respond. Eventually he relented. 'Well, alright, you have already worked out for yourself there are similarities with other missing person cases, so I won't deny it. Jenny is not the first person who has told people she was joining this cult, commune, whatever you want to call it, and then subsequently vanished. Since we don't yet know what happened to Jenny or the others, yes, you could be putting yourself in danger.'

'Well, you want to get to the bottom of this, as we do. Can we collaborate?'

DS Lunnton nodded slightly. 'I'll have to talk to my inspector. Leave it with me. I'll call you.'

As Henry and I drove back sedately to the Potterswell home in Henry's classic Jaguar, Henry was full of praise.

'You did a cracking job bringing that policeman to heel.'

'Thanks. Handling people is part of my job.'

'You had the blighter on the run. Excellent work.'

'Well, thanks.'

'Are you sure you weren't in the military?'

'No, I went straight into journalism.'

'Pity. You'd go far in the military. Officer material if ever I saw it.'

'I'll bear it in mind.'

'This business about joining up with this cult, are you sure? It could be dangerous.'

'Yes, I'm up for it. If there's anything we can do to get Jenny out of there, we have to try.'

'You don't have to go on your own. I'll be there with you.'

I sighed and shook my head. 'No, sorry Colonel, but it just wouldn't work.'

'Why not? I'm not afraid and I'm still tough as old boots.'

'Colonel, you could never convince anybody you're a new age, hippy, Wicca type of person. Besides they already know you from when you threw them off the premises after the affair in the Jardinairs' garden.'

Henry considered. 'I suppose you're right. Damned good show, you're going in after her. I've got every confidence in you. You're a fine chap.'

My mobile phone rang. It was a call from DS Lunnton, informing me his boss, Detective Inspector Bellard would like to see me at my earliest convenience.

Henry turned the car around and dropped me back at the police station. 'Do you think I should come in myself?'

'No, I don't think it's necessary.'

'More than happy to.'

'Easiest if I do it alone, I think.' I did not relish having Henry blustering and exploding in the background as I had delicate conversations with the police.

'Yes, you can do it. Every confidence in you,' Henry conceded.

'Thank you.'

'Should I wait?'

'No need. I don't know how long I'll be. I will report back to you later.'

DI Bellard was an energetic man in his mid-forties with thinning gingery hair, blue eyes set in a freckly face and a purposeful expression. His compact body and wiry frame gave his movements an elegant cat-like precision. His manner was brisk and decisive.

'I understand you are Jenny's partner and you intend to try to follow her wherever she has disappeared,' said DI Bellard, for clarification.

'I'm not exactly her partner, well, not yet, but we are close and I do want to track her down.'

'It could be dangerous, what you are suggesting? We simply don't know what you might be getting into. It's not something we could advise you to do, as police officers.'

'I understand the risks and I'm prepared to take my chances.'

'In which case, would you be prepared to take a tracking device?'

'Perhaps. But before we get into that, I saw you both at

Mendip House, didn't I? Looking for missing persons. Did you find anything?'

The two police officers looked at each other and winced.

'I take it from your reaction it didn't go well.'

'That is police business. We can't talk about it,' said DI Bellard.

'I should at least know; are the missing persons you were looking for the ones who disappeared in the same way Jenny did?'

'We can't talk about it,' reiterated DI Bellard.

'In which case you can stuff your tracking device where the sun don't shine.' I declared. Calming down I added, 'You can't expect my help unless you are prepared to provide information. I'm only being reasonable.'

'Alright, you've got a point. Yes, those cases are related to Jenny's disappearance,' said DI Bellard.

'Another thing. I don't understand the need for a tracking device. Nearly everyone these days carries a mobile phone. Couldn't you just track their phones?'

DI Bellard remained silent a few seconds, as if weighing what and how much he should say. 'Trouble is, when the people vanished their phones vanished too.'

'You must know where the phones were last located before they dropped off the radar.'

'Yes, we do know that.'

'So, don't keep me in suspense. Where was it? Different locations for each, or always the same location.'

DI Bellard went quiet again a moment, before relenting. 'It was the same location in every case, in the vicinity of Mendip House.'

'Ah, so now I get it, why you were there. What did you

find?'

DI Bellard shook his head. 'Nothing of interest, unfortunately.'

'Can't you just go back and tear the place apart until you do find something?'

'No, unfortunately. The Marquess has friends in high places. After our last visit we have been warned off.'

'Okay, I understand now. Thanks for levelling with me. What is this tracking device you want me to have?'

'You wear a belt, don't you?'

'Yes.'

'We'd like you to wear this belt. The buckle contains the tracker.'

Mendip Moon Coven

The grand Georgian style of the Mother Earth Temple building was at odds with the New Age alternative society ethos of its current occupants, built as the residence of a pillar of the establishment, a wealthy merchant or minor aristocrat. The bright naïve designs of the posters displayed near the front entrance and the multi-coloured ribbons tied around the pillars of the front porch were reminiscent of a radical student society occupying a grand historic college building within a centuries-old university.

While externally it had been the building's ancient grandeur overshadowing the colourful interventions of the worshipers of Mother Earth, I sensed a change in the balance of power as I passed through the front door. Inside it was primitive, pagan, with eastern and mystical dominating motifs; the conservative Anglican touches only showed through subtly with the sweep of the Georgian staircase, ornate plasterwork on the ceilings, architraves around the doorways and the dado rails. All around was a garish mix of bright, clashing colours in interlocking shapes. Handwoven mats depicted abstract patterns and pagan symbols were scattered on the floors. Against the walls nestled a variety of old tables, their originally brown polished wood now decorated with a full palette of bright lacquer paints and adorned with statues of goddesses, alongside murals of further goddesses among idyllic natural settings.

There was nobody in the hallway to ask, so I looked around for a clue for where I should be heading. A large board in the hallway mounted within a rough frame of recycled driftwood had a mass of notices describing a variety of activities pinned to it, their times and locations.

In the Mother Earth Temple Chamber there were regular chanting and meditation sessions led by the High Priestess. Goddess Gaia Embodiment evenings would allow Her healing presence to nourish the soul. Tantric Fulfilment sessions would ensure climactic alignment of cosmic energies. Spiritual Midwifery classes took place on Tuesday mornings. At last, there it was, the Mendip Moon Coven, Freya Room on this particular evening.

A sign on the wall indicated the Freya Room was upstairs. I made my way to the first floor landing, where I spotted a hand-painted sign above a door announcing Freya. On the door itself was a naively crafted painting of a goddess on a chariot drawn by what looked like a pair of domestic cats, the sort one would expect to see purring on a sofa.

I stepped into the room. The walls were painted in a bright pink and adorned with paintings and symbols representing Norse Valkyries and runic messages. The floor was spread with hand woven rugs and cushions. Various accoutrements were spread around, a cauldron, a brass gong, a witch's broom and burning incense sticks. A broad circle encompassing a pentangle shape was drawn on the floor with coloured strips of cloth held in place by sticky tape.

An assortment of about eight women of varying ages and in all shapes and sizes were already present with just two men. One of the women was Ivy Langport, who Henry and I had recently rescued from the clutches of bruiser Harry Mallet. There was an unmistakable atmosphere of sexual apartheid, a dominant sisterhood with the men as ancillaries.

One of the men, around 40 years old with longish brown hair hung loose and a short straggly beard, was evidently the partner of one of the women, hovering in a supporting role rather than as a primary participant. The other, still a teenager by my estimation, a little less than six feet tall but gangly, thin as a rake, was separate from the group looking unsure of himself.

Conversation stopped and heads turned as I arrived. I announced myself. 'Hello, I'm Simon, I called earlier. Hope I'm in the right place.'

'I'm Hetty. You spoke to me,' said a bulky woman in her mid-forties wearing a dress decorated with glittery spangles in an extra-large size draped over her like a tent.

'Nice to meet you,' I acknowledged, holding out my hand.

'Merry meet,' she said in a cold, formal tone, ignoring my offered handshake, before turning her attention back towards the other women with whom she had been conversing before I had rudely interrupted.

As no introductions from her were forthcoming, I resolved to introduce myself. Taking one woman at a time, seizing an opportunity when a particular individual was not actively engaged in conversation, I made myself known. Each woman thus accosted looked at me with suspicious distaste as if she had just been indecently propositioned by an inebriated sex pest in a bar. I hoped I might gain a foothold with the delectable Ivy.

'You're Ivy, aren't you?'

'Yes,' she acknowledged, turning away towards the other women.

'Last time I saw you, Harry was trying to stop you

getting in here.'

'Yes, thanks for getting him off me.'

'That's alright. He was dragging you away outside Glastonbury Abbey as well, wasn't he?'

'Why, do you know Harry or something?'

'Yes, I had a chat with him in the Mendip Grenadier.'

'You're no friend of mine then, if you take his side.'

'My girlfriend Jenny was fending him off, when he was dragging you away.'

'Do you drag her around forcibly as well?'

'No, but I am concerned about her. She's disappeared and I can't trace her.'

'Perhaps she wants to keep away from you, doesn't want you to find her.'

'She wanted me to join her, where she was going.'

'Why didn't you?'

'At the time I couldn't just drop everything.'

'But now you've got second thoughts.'

'I'm worried what might have happened to her, that's all.'

'Angry she's escaped from you more like.'

'No, not at all. Worried for her safety.'

'Safer away from you, I'd say.'

Having exhausted the conversational possibilities, I turned my attention to the two men.

The gangly teenager hung back meekly, tongue-tied and avoiding eye contact.

The unkempt older man beamed a welcoming smile when I caught his eye. 'Hello, I'm Nathan.'

'Simon.' We shook hands.

'Are you new to Wicca?'

I nodded.

'Thought so. Don't worry, I'll guide you through it.'

Hetty invited the group to gather with harmonious friendship and love in the presence of our spiritual Earth Mother, the Goddess Gaia.

Nathan being the only one so far who had offered any sort of welcome, I sat beside him on the cushion-strewn floor.

Hetty declared the circle once cast must not be broken. Looking particularly intently in my direction, she demanded to know whether anyone present would break the circle.

'You've got to stay in the circle, mustn't break out of it, or you destroy the spell,' whispered Nathan in my ear.

The group stood around facing inwards and held hands to form the circle. Hetty declared the banishment of all evil forces, patriarchal oppression, unnatural chemicals, degradation of our beloved Mother Earth, all to be cast out of the circle. The group walked around one circuit turning towards the left.

'Widdershins, anti-clockwise, for casting out,' explained Nathan softly.

'May we be cleansed and fertile,' declared Hetty.

Three of the women broke away.

One took up the witch's broom and circled around sweeping outwards from within the circle.

'Using the besom, the broom, to sweep the circle clean,' whispered Nathan.

The woman then took the besom and dipped it into the cauldron, which was half full of water. She made a circuit of the circle of people sprinkling us with water from the bristles of the broom.

'Asperging, blessing us with water,' explained Nathan

under his breath.

The second woman followed behind scattering crushed fragments of white crystal over people's heads.

'Salt, for fertility,' said Nathan.

The third woman made a circuit with an incense stick, wafting the smoke around.

'Smudging, blessing us with smoke,' Nathan said.

Hetty declared welcome to all who come in peace and love. The group walked around another circuit but this time turning to the right.

'Doesil, clockwise, to invoke the circle.'

Hetty took up a fearsome dagger and thrust it down towards the floor, then upwards towards the ceiling.

'The sword thing, it's the athame, it invokes the Goddess into the circle.'

Four of the participants faced outwards, uttering incantations for each of the air, fire, water and earth.

'The four quarters, east, south, west and north, and their elements and spirits,' informed Nathan.

The spirits of the Goddess Gaia and Her consort Cernunnos, the horned God were invited to join within the circle. Hetty took the athame and thrust its tip into an ornate chalice held by one of her women assistants. More incantations were spoken.

'Symbolic representation of sexual union between the Gods to fertilise the Earth,' Nathan explained.

The ritual began to run down from this point of climax. Thanks were given to the Goddess for Her goodness, to the four quarters and their spirits. We circled around anti-clockwise, or widdershins in pagan terminology.

'Opening the circle,' Nathan explained.

Another incantation about the circle being open and never broken, and how we had met merry and would merry meet again.

Hetty announced we would meet again the following evening, on the sacred hill to celebrate Esbat.

My heart raced as I realised the significance. The instructions given by the pendant mentioned what I took to be sunset on the day following Esbat, so only two days' time, if I was to meet up with the Ethereal Guide, whoever that was.

There now followed a ceremonial sharing of cake and wine, following which the group remained to informally socialise. As before, we men were marginalised.

I approached the quiet young man. 'Hello, I'm Simon.'

'Oh, hello.'

'I didn't catch your name.'

'Frankie.'

Evidently Frankie's role was to serve as an invisible slave. He slipped away from me, employing himself tidying the various artefacts.

'Great to have you with us,' said Nathan.

'Glad to be here.'

'It's nice to have another man to talk to.'

'I know what you mean. The women don't seem to like talking to us.'

Unwilling to accept the gender apartheid I tried my luck with a woman who I had seen looking and nodding in Nathan's direction.

'Do you mind if I ask you something?' I enquired.

'Depends what it is.'

'It's about my girlfriend, Jenny. I haven't been able to reach her.'

'Perhaps she doesn't want you to reach her.'

'I know it's not that.'

'How do you know?'

'She asked me to join her.'

Seeing us talking Hetty intervened. 'What's the matter with you?' she demanded. 'You're mancroaching again, as you have been doing incessantly. Show respect.'

'I'm just introducing myself.'

'Pestering everybody is not the way to do it.'

'I'm sorry. Didn't mean to intrude.'

'We have had quite enough of your manterrupting. Behave yourself.'

Nathan, seeing me chastened from my fruitless and evidently unwanted attempts at conversation with my betters, guided me to one side, in shadows where menfolk evidently belonged.

'This Jenny of yours, you really want to find her?'

'Yes, of course.'

'She's not far from here.'

'What do you mean?' I asked, an urgent note in my voice.

Nathan looked uncomfortable, as if he realised he had said too much. 'Can't say any more now. We, me and Megan,' he glanced over to the woman I had just been talking to, 'run a shop in Glastonbury High Street, Megan's Magick Shoppe. Pop in tomorrow and we can talk about it.'

The group were now dispersing. Only Hetty acknowledged me. 'Will you be coming to the Esbat ceremony tomorrow evening?'

'Yes, I'll be there.'

I tried to catch the eyes of some of the other women,

but all ignored me.

I made my way along Glastonbury High Street relishing the sights, sounds and scents of this gateway from humdrum daily reality into an alternative world of fantasy, make-believe and the supernatural where fairies, goblins, spirits and the wisdom of past ages run free.

There was a better class of graffiti adorning the walls of the alleyway leading into the top end of the street, a splendid stag in a leafy woodland grove set between a giant squirrel wielding an axe and a huge cyclops of an eye peering from under an arch, all beautifully painted.

For those with the disposable income to opt out into their chosen alternative world, the High Street catered to their every need. I took my time gazing at the window displays and wandering in and out of establishments as my fancy took me.

An ecological food store offered every type of lentil, nuts, organic vegetable, fair trade coffee, ethically sourced dark chocolate and locally baked wholemeal bread. A variety of hippy style décor was available for the home, sculpture, carved wooden items, wall plaques depicting the Green Man, animals and mythical figures. There was a plethora of shabby chic clothing for the discerning pagan's wardrobe. Inexpensive jewellery was plentiful together with boxes to store it in. An array of gleaming crystals was offered with books explaining the meaning and power of each colour and form of the dazzling minerals. My head spun with the scents hitting me as I came into a specialist botanicals shop. Aroma therapy specialists were available to explain the power of each exotic fragrance. To feed the mind specialist bookshops featured Norse, Celtic, Greek and Asian pantheons of gods and goddesses, spirituality, shamanism and transcendental use of mind-altering substances.

Seeking to fit in with the mood of the place and my new associates in the Mendip Moon Coven, I invested in Goth style ragged black trousers, a dark tee shirt emblazoned with an elaborate gold pentangle motif and a green hooded cloak.

Eventually I stumbled across my destination, Megan's Magick Shoppe. Nathan, the shop's co-owner, seeing me come in, nodded and smiled. Nathan had a laid-back hippy air. His bony body hung loose, his long lank hair draped across his face and onto his shoulders. The hair on his unshaven face was trimmed short making it wispy.

'Hello Nathan.'

I gazed at yet another cornucopia of new age goods. Here there was everything remotely associated with Wicca, witchcraft, spells and some others things beside. There were small glass jars of magical powders and oils, herbal spell mixes in brown paper packets, pentagram tealight holders, crystal globes for divination, amulets with runic symbols and aerosol sprays of magical miasmic mists.

Megan, Nathan's wife, a gone-to-seed hippy of around forty but still clinging to the alternative lifestyle of her rebellious youth, was busy in a quiet corner doing a tarot reading for a client.

'Impressive range you have on offer,' I said to Nathan.

'Anything particular caught your eye?'

My attention fell on a display of brightly coloured little bundles described as spell bags, each consisting of a strip of torn fabric wrapped as a package around supposedly magic ingredients, organic herbs and the like, secured with a length of frayed string. 'What can you tell me about these?'

'The colours denote the nature of the spell, so here we have spiritual healing, this one breaks a curse, over here we have the bringing of love.'

'Not sure if I need to cast any spells just now, but I'll think about it.'

'No worries, just look around.'

'About what we mentioned last night, my girl Jenny, you said you thought she wasn't far from here. Any idea where she might be, specifically?'

Nathan shrugged. 'To be honest, I don't know exactly. It's sort of a secret, I think.'

'But you must have a clue.'

Nathan contorted his face slightly. 'Not really. I wish I could be of more help.'

Torn between wanting to progress but not alienating Nathan, I changed the subject. 'That *Familiar Witchcraft* book attracts attention as you come in.'

'Yes, it's is very popular at the moment. The black cat on the cover attracts attention.'

'I can see it would appeal to cat lovers. But what has it got to do with witchcraft?'

'Cats are often witches' familiars. It has heart-warming stories about the loyalty and exploits of Wicca folks' feline friends.'

I was hunting for some other avenue for spinning out our conversation when another visitor came through the door, one I recognised: Philomena, the stunning blonde woman I met at Mendip House with the Marquess. I had remembered her as striking, but I hadn't appreciated how tall and athletic she was, almost as tall as me. Dressed informally in figure hugging leggings and fleece top, I could see she was built like an Amazon warrior. She held a package, which she handed to Nathan. I nodded in recognition, which she acknowledged.

'Nice to see you again,' I said.

Philomena looked me up and down in a predatory fashion. 'The pleasure is mine.'

After she departed, I watched Nathan unwrapping the package to reveal a shipment of pendants, but not just any pendants: the same design as I had found on sale in Camden Market. He laid them out on display. I took out my own pendant for comparison and there was no doubt they came from the same source.

I took one of the new pendants and placed it on the shop counter with my smart phone alongside. The figure representing the Goddess Gaia appeared and made her speech. Nathan stopped what was doing and watched.

'I didn't know they did that,' he said, when the Goddess had finished her spiel.

'Where do they come from?'

'I don't know. Philomena brings them in. That's all I know.'

'The last bit, where the Yuletide thorn blooms beside the healing waters, what's that about?'

'It'll be at the Well of Avalon. They have one of those Glastonbury Thorn bushes there, a special magical breed of hawthorn that blooms at Christmas time.'

I punched the air. 'Oh, thanks. That's really helpful.'

'Why? Do I take it you're intending to go there yourself?'

'Yes. I believe it's how Jenny made contact, so I need to

follow her myself, if I'm to find her.'

'Oh, I see. You know you could get stuck there, don't you?'

'Yes, I understand the risk involved.'

'You're not the first who's done this,' said Nathan sadly.

'I know. For a start there is Jenny and the other missing persons the police are interested in.'

'I meant not the first I've got to know personally.'

'Who else?'

'Bloke called Cadfael. Like you, he came over and joined the Mendip Moon Coven. It was good having another bloke there to talk to.'

'What happened to him?'

'He just disappeared, like your Jenny. Then I suddenly got a message from him, over from where he is now, in a place called Abballon.'

'Abballon, you say. Do you know anything about this place, where it is, for example?'

'No sorry, just that it's called Abballon.'

'How did you get the message?'

'It was as a note in one of the shipments Philomena brings in.'

'Great. So, he's okay. Did you manage to reply?'

'Well, not right away. I can't send him a message directly, but there was another person, one of the witches in the coven, who I found out wanted to go over to them. I sent a message over with her.'

'Did he get it?'

'Yes, he sent me a note in another shipment later saying he had heard from me.'

'What happens now?'

'He sends more notes now and again.'

'Right.'

Nathan thought. He looked over towards his wife to make sure she wasn't listening. Lowering his voice, he continued. 'Actually, if you are going, there is something you could take for Cadfael. If you don't mind?'

'Alright. What is it?'

'You'd need to be careful. What you would be taking isn't allowed over there. Just give it to Cadfael and don't let anyone else see. Alright?'

'Okay. What is it makes it so secret? Drugs or something.'

'Well, yes. Something like that. Not illegal as such, but not something the True Natural Path folk would approve of.'

There was obviously some risk involved, but then Nathan had identified the rendezvous place. I owed him a favour.

'Okay, I'll do it.'

Checking again to make sure his wife wasn't looking, Nathan rummaged in a drawer, pulled out a locket with a pentagram emblem on a silver chain and handed it over.

'Is that it? Why wouldn't the True Natural Path approve of it?'

'It's not the locket, it's what's inside.'

Later, back in my room in the bed and breakfast, the one with the Buddhas, reiki and a yurt in the garden, I fumbled with the locket until I figured out how it opened. Tightly wrapped in tissue paper and crammed into the space were diamond shaped sky-blue tablets. Viagra, if I wasn't mistaken.

Wearing my newly acquired Wicca-themed outfit, I

joined the members of the Mendip Moon Coven outside the Mother Earth Temple as they gathered for the Esbat celebration. Nathan was wearing a headdress with antlers and a shaggy green coat adorned with leafy twigs hanging loosely on his gangly frame.

'Great outfit,' I observed.

'I'm representing the Horned God Cernunnos,' he explained.

In due course we made our way to a hill a short distance from town, not the famous Tor but a smaller mound in the opposite direction looking over the more work-a-day part of Glastonbury, an industrial and commercial quarter including the offices and warehouse of a construction company, a superstore, chain hotel and builders supply merchant.

We laid out a circle and pentangle on a flat grassy area atop the hill near a grove of trees. The moon was full but only showed through intermittently from the cloudy sky.

Hetty, the priestess, declared the ritual would be more meaningful and spiritually fulfilling if carried out skyclad. Of the ten people attending only Hetty, Nathan's wife Megan and young Frankie chose to be naked, others being deterred by the wet ground and damp chilly night air as much as for the sake of modesty. Nathan was excused because he was obliged to wear his Horned God outfit. Being my first time, I excused myself, intent on seeing how it went first.

Hetty's floppy breasts and large belly drooped over her wide spreading hips giving her the appearance depicted in Stone Age Venus figurines. Next to Hetty, Megan's sturdy figure was sylph-like in comparison. The two women formed a startling contrast to Frankie's naked form of spindly bone and sinew. The remaining women for the most part wore cloaks of various descriptions, typically green or black and decorated with pagan symbols.

Hetty and the entourage formed a circle and chanted homage to the full moon, drawing down the Goddess of the moon, Queen of the night, keeper of women's mysteries. Hetty urged those present to raise their arms to welcome the Goddess, feeling Her surge of energy as she came into their hearts.

As arms were raised in unison a middle-aged couple crashed into the circle and dashed towards youthful Ivy to remonstrate with her. One I recognised as Elsie, Ivy's mother, and I guessed the other to be her father.

Ivy's mother scolded her as if she were still a child while her father shooed her as if one of his cows were recalcitrant about going through a gate. Ivy shouted back at them to not spoil things for her like this. Other members of the coven united to confront the intruders. Eventually, with Ivy resolutely refusing to budge, Elsie and Eddie withdrew, venting their frustration in their agricultural West Country vernacular.

By this time the penetrating chill from the drizzly rain was numbing us to our bones, draining our will to linger in the cold outdoors. But, our expectations of a peaceful return into the warmth offered by the Mother Earth Temple were dashed when Harry Mallet emerged near the entrance. He roughly seized slightly built Ivy and almost carried her away in his muscly arms.

Harry had an intimidating look, which was reflected in the reaction of the members of the coven as they surreptitiously followed what was happening out of the corners of their eyes while sheepishly appearing to look elsewhere. A few looked around hesitantly as if wanting to intervene but hoping for some moral support before daring.

I caught Harry's eye. 'Hello Harry,' I said, looking and sounding as friendly as I could.

'What are you doing here?' growled Harry.

'Learning about Wicca.'

'What do you want to learn about that rubbish for?'

'To improve my mind.' It was neither the time nor place to explain my search for Jenny.

'Ain't going to improve nothing, this crap.'

'Won't know until I find out, will I?'

'I really thought you had more sense.'

'You should leave Ivy alone.'

'You going to stop me?'

'If necessary.'

'What's it got to do with you?'

'Ivy has the right to make up her own mind.'

'How do you know what Ivy wants?'

I looked directly at Ivy. 'You alright Ivy?' I asked, giving her the opportunity to ask for help.

Ivy nodded. 'Yes, alright,' she confirmed.

I shrugged. If Ivy was content to be forcibly dragged away there really didn't seem much point in further intervention to a domestic situation. Harry walked off purposefully with Ivy firmly in tow.

With Harry and Ivy departed I became aware all eyes were focussed on me, the faces showing a blend of fear and awe.

'I wouldn't have done that,' Nathan confided.

'Done what?'

'Stood up to Harry Mallet like you did.'

'Why not?'

'He's a hard nut. Not someone you want to tangle with.'

The women were looking at me with admiration replacing their previous disdain.

We adjourned gratefully out of the chill damp air into the warmth of the Mother Earth Temple, where Frankie, under Hetty's instruction, served cake and wine.

Nathan's wife Megan was the first to make conversation. 'You did well, standing up to that thug.'

'Only did what needed doing,' I replied.

'Simon wants to go over to Abballon,' said Nathan.

'Really,' said Megan. 'It's a big step.'

'My Jenny went over and she wanted me to follow.'

Megan shared the news with the others, who were soon all around me, praising my boldness and courage.

Into the Unknown

The first light of dawn brought no joy, only foreboding, that this might be my last day on Earth, or at least on the Earth as I knew it. I would be following Jenny and the other missing persons, vanishing without trace.

Nobody was forcing me to do this. But, were I to back out, how might Jenny and the others be rescued? I must take inspiration from the gallant knights of King Arthur's Round Table.

In previous centuries, before the world became a global village with ubiquitous instant electronic communication, people would have felt like I did before a long uncertain voyage. They would have been advised to get their affairs in order, lest they not return.

I had no dependents, but I did have my collaborators, on whom I might later depend to rescue me.

I casually mentioned to Adelena, my landlady over breakfast that I had some business possibly coming off in the next day or so, which might take me away.

When I called to see Jenny's parents, Delia and Henry Potterswell, to minimise their anxiety and avoid spurring Henry into some impetuousness, I was deliberately vague.

'I have a lead, which might take me away a while; please don't worry if I'm not in touch.'

'What sort of a lead?' Henry demanded.

'It's tenuous and sensitive, so I can't say much.'

'At least give us a general idea.'

I shook my head. 'I'm sorry, but it isn't safe for me to say anything more.'

'More!' scoffed Henry. 'You haven't said anything yet.'

'Calm down, dear,' Delia intervened. 'Simon has his reasons.'

Glastonbury police station was my next port of call, where I informed Sergeant Lunnton of my developments. 'This is on the strict understanding, if there is to be any police surveillance, it must be discreet.'

'Don't worry, we won't blow your cover,' Sergeant Lunnton assured.

Finally there was my editor, Rebekah. I drafted an outline of a story about the Mendip Moon Coven and its connection with Megan's Magick Shoppe, with some of the photos I had discreetly taken over the previous days. I also worked in quotations from my encounter with Dr Theophilus Pottinger about the spiritual dangers of Satanic practices and witchcraft. I sent a brief email with the full story and other background information separately posted in the form of a mailed package, to ensure she would not receive it until after I had departed lest she take action to prevent it.

As I stepped towards the sacred spring, the Well of Avalon, the sun slipped towards the horizon, already a deep yellow deepening into an orangey red.

A gentle trickle emerged from the foliage-covered rocks forming a miniature waterfall into a channel carved from the rock, the flow restrained by a build-up of slippery green slime to ooze out among the nooks and crannies of the surrounding gardens.

Facing the source of sacred healing water from a quiet enclave where visitors could meditate, were three women draped in multi-coloured capes softly chanting a magical incantation in unison. Like the three witches encountered by Macbeth, situated beside the healing waters at the specified time, perhaps they had a message for me.

I hovered in the three devotees' line of sight to make my presence felt. The women, enwrapped in their ritual, took no notice. If one of them were the Ethereal Guide, they were in no hurry to make contact.

There was one thing that didn't fit the instructions, there was no thorn I could imagine blooming during Yuletide. I scanned the vicinity for anyone else who could possibly be the promised Ethereal Guide. Looking up there was a grassy bank on which stood a scrubby tree, quite plausibly the miraculous Christmas flowering hawthorn, alongside which was a standing woman silhouetted against the fading light.

As I walked up the slope in her direction, I recognised Philomena, the Marquess's Guinevere. On this occasion she was dressed in the style of a warrior woman of ancient legend, with a heavy dark green cloak bearing an ornate pentangle emblem marked in gold and held in place with a chunky bronze clasp. Under her cloak she was clad in a figure-hugging leather tunic. Hanging loose around her waist she wore a thick metal studded belt suitable to take a sword and scabbard. As I came close she challenged me. 'Who do you seek?'

'I seek the Ethereal Guide,' I responded, remembering the words of the summons from the Gaia figure projected onto my phone.

'You have found her. I am the Ethereal Guide,' Philomena announced, with a look of a raptor poised to seize its prey. 'Are you ready to follow the True Natural

Path?' she asked in a commanding tone.

I considered a moment. 'I am ready.'

Philomena's eyes drew me in. 'Come closer.'

I came up to within a more intimate distance.

'Do you understand what is entailed in following the True Natural Path?' Philomena enquired, speaking more softly, now soothing and seductive.

'Well, not exactly,' I confessed.

'You will forsake all contrivances of modern technology and live the natural life Mother Earth intended. Do you accept this?'

I hesitated. I would have to accept the conditions, whatever they were. It was the only way for me to reach Jenny. 'Yes, I accept.'

Philomena accepted my acquiescence with satisfaction. With each utterance I was falling ever tighter into her clutches.

'No electronic or mechanised contrivances. Everything made will be by the strength, dexterity and skill of Gaia's children. Are you prepared for this?'

'Yes, I am prepared.'

'No artificial chemicals will be allowed to sully and corrupt our Mother Earth. Do you forswear filthy chemicals?'

'Yes, I forswear them.'

Philomena's hold on me passed beyond seduction to raw domination.

'Do you renounce and reject toxic masculinity and patriarchy embracing the feminine love flowing from our Earth Mother, our Goddess Gaia channelled through Her Ethereal Guide and the sisterhood of women?'

I pondered what this meant. What she was saying

sounded like female supremacy under Philomena with herself as dictator and, by the way she was looking at me, probably carnal predator as well. To my shame, I found myself turned on by the prospect of being dominated and ravished by her. Not that it mattered, pleasurable or not, I would be doing whatever she decreed.

'I do,' I conceded.

Philomena's lips twisted in annoyance at this less than fully explicit response.

'You do what? You must renounce and reject toxic masculinity and embrace feminine love.'

Philomena was like a big cat gliding in seductively for the kill. I knew what was happening, but I did not resist, nor even wish to resist.

'I renounce and reject toxic masculinity and embrace feminine love,' I pronounced obediently.

Philomena was poised for the coup de grace. 'Do you embrace the True Natural Path never to return to the corruption and evil of the Patriarchy?'

'I embrace the True Natural Path,' I responded.

Philomena glared at me expectantly. 'And what else?'

'...never to return to the corruption and evil of the Patriarchy,' I continued.

She looked pleased, satisfied she had achieved the total ownership she required. Relaxing she switched to a more conversational tone. 'Well, Simon, I hadn't expected you to be taking this step. You didn't strike me as someone who would so readily accept the new order of feminine leadership. I am very pleased you have, though.'

I paused, trying to compose a suitable response. I couldn't very well confess my motivation was to rescue Jenny and the others from the grip of this cult. I knew I must say something to reassure her of my allegiance.

'I have come to see the only way for humanity to survive and thrive is for us to revert to the true natural order under the loving nurturing way of Mother Earth.'

Philomena smiled in satisfaction. This was what she wanted to hear. However, she had one other concern. 'You do of course understand the True Natural Path requires physical acts of love must always to be initiated by a woman and flow from her. Men must be patient, never demanding, awaiting love's call and be grateful for what is granted them. Are you content and capable of constraining yourself in this way?'

I had already suspected this condition, but it wasn't an issue uppermost in my mind. My first priority was rescuing Jenny. Assuming she still subscribed to this philosophy, I could handle her taking the lead in our relationship.

'Yes, I understand and accept this rule.'

Philomena looked me up and down. Her tongue protruded from her mouth and she quite literally licked her lips.

'I don't think you need to be overly concerned in your case,' Philomena cooed. 'You will be called upon, I promise you.'

From her manner I had a good sense of what she had in mind. I was ashamed to admit, despite my feelings for Jenny, I was rather looking forward to the prospect of Philomena calling upon me, as she put it. If I was acquiescing Philomena's demands, it wouldn't exactly be cheating on Jenny, would it?

'Now, the only further matter is to bring you across to your new life in the land of Abballon. Are you ready to come over tomorrow?'

'Yes, I'll be ready.'

'Excellent. You must meet me at 11am tomorrow at the Grotto in the Knights of Camelot Park in the grounds of Mendip House. Do you know where it is?'

'Yes.'

Philomena handed me a ticket.

'Use this ticket. It gives you special entry into the park so you can reach me behind the scenes. You must go through the Staff Only barrier at the back end of the Grotto.'

I joined the throng of families, with excited younger children enraptured with the fairy tale magic of Merlin and Arthurian Knights, their older teenage siblings affecting disinterest in everything except the scariest dare-devil rides.

Making my way to the Grotto I glanced only briefly at visitor amusements, a damsel chained to rocks, menaced by goblins, rescued in the nick of time and hoisted onto his steed by a gallant knight, galloping into the forest, a loud arrogant knight in black contemptuously challenging the romantic Sir Lancelot to a duel.

The Grotto was an immense spooky cave set into a hillside, lit by a myriad of multi-coloured fairy lights making the long stalactites glitter and sparkle, within which were further exciting happenings, an elegant medieval Royal Barge conveying chattering families along the subterranean river terrorised by fearsome dragons surging from the depths rocking the boat, somehow arriving unscathed at the underground Royal Court of Avalon where King Arthur still reigns.

Emerging from the barge visitors surged to the subterranean banqueting hall to partake of victuals and mead from the King's table. I dropped back, located the Staff Only gateway Philomena mentioned, which clicked open as I offered up my ticket to the sensor.

I was in a works and storage area, equipment laid out in racks alongside humming machinery. Wandering through for a short distance I emerged into a control room where Philomena sat in a swivel chair surveying a bank of display screens showing videos of the people at control points within the Knights of Camelot Park overlaid with status information and numbers.

Standing to greet me, she was dressed in the green uniform of the Knights of Camelot Park staff, a stylised supposedly medieval green tunic with tight leggings, a hood over her head and boots decorated with plaited leather straps, in the style of the Merrie Men in a Hollywood Robin Hood movie. Her uniform carried gold braided military markings of rank, indicating her position of authority within the park.

She did not waste time. 'Good, you're here. Are you ready to make the transition?' From her manner and tone it was not a question leaving room for discussion.

'Yes, I'm ready.'

Philomena discreetly operated a control I could not see directly. What had previously appeared a solid face of the bedrock slowly folded back revealing an entrance way leading even deeper into the hillside.

'This way,' Philomena announced, as she stepped through.

I was apprehensive, claustrophobic, deep underground in a secret control room, already enclosed, now invited to entomb myself even deeper. Despite my nerves, her air of authority compelled me to obey.

We were in a rocky chamber, within which stood a small pod similar to the cockpit of a fighter plane, just large enough to accommodate one seated person. The heavy rock doors ground shut with a whirring of motors, ending with a solid rocky crunch.

'This machine will convey you to Abballon.'

I nodded.

'You will sleep as you go. When you awake you will be in Abballon.'

I wondered whether Abballon might be a hoax, cover for the gullible missing people used in some fiendish experiment by the sinister Dr Marcus Shorbody. Then I remembered Nathan in Megan's Magick Shoppe had received messages from his friend Cadfael. Was Nathan in on it? No, too paranoid. I couldn't imagine Nathan plotting.

I had no time for lengthy foreboding. Philomena continued with her instructions. 'Seat yourself inside, please.'

I hesitated.

'Come along now, nothing to be frightened of.'

Her command overrode my fears. I squeezed myself into the seat. Philomena reached across to strap me in securely.

'See you in Abballon.'

Does that mean she'll be there too? I wondered. This thought made me feel better. I was now quite taken by Philomena.

She closed the front of the pod. I heard the clunk of clamps being secured. I was encapsulated, deep underground in a fiendish machine. Nothing to be frightened of at all!

I heard the whirring and grinding of the rocky doors of the hidden rocky chamber re-open and then re-close. Presumably Philomena had gone, leaving me alone in there.

The pod shook and vibrated as if in preparation for something.

There was a faint hiss like an escaping gas. I was light headed. The surroundings rotated about me. The vibration intensified. I felt a sensation of movement as everything went blank.

Abballon

Cool air caressed my skin, permeating my nostrils with outdoor scents, wet leaves and other earthy notes. Bright light penetrated my closed eyelids. The chill from a cold hard surface permeated the soft damp material I lay on. Soft voices talked in hushed tones.

For some moments I had sensory awareness but lacked memory or context. My mental faculties tortuously grappled to restore themselves.

'Where am I?' was my first thought, then 'I need to see where I am.' My mind struggled to regain control of my body. With a surge of effort I compelled my eyes to open. The blurred scene briefly revealed the shadowy shapes of people silhouetted against a bright sky with rough splodges of green shrubs and trees in the background, before the glaring brightness forced my eyes shut again.

I screwed up my face and blinked. Flashes of active thought flickered in my sluggish brain, fighting the fog of unconsciousness, struggling to gain traction like wheels spinning in a muddy mire. I forced my eyes open and strained to bring the scene into focus.

People were stood around, dirty and unkempt, tunics and leggings roughly tailored from coarse hand-woven cloth decorated with zigzig patterns in earthy colours from vegetable dyes.

I felt a rough scratchiness against my skin and saw I was clad in the same fashion as the others, laying on a heap of damp moss spread out over a slab of rock.

'What about my stuff?' I thought with alarm. My original clothing was gone, together with whatever had been in my pockets. Smart phone, wristwatch, wallet were all missing, as was the belt DI Bellard had given me with the tracking device in the buckle. So much for the police tracking my movements. I checked around my neck to find I still had the crudely decorated pentangle pendant that could hijack a smartphone and the locket Nathan gave me to pass on to his friend, Cadfael.

'He's waking up,' someone said. Glancing towards the sound I observed a studious looking man in his mid-thirties, slightly built, thinning blonde hair and a narrow face, tapered chin and a thin pointy nose.

'Hello. I'm Simon. Where am I?'

'You're in Abballon,' he replied. 'Merry meet, Brother Simon. I'm Brother Tarquin.'

Raising myself on my elbows I perceived to my rear a steep rocky cliff-face, attached to which was a wooden building, ornate, decorated with carved timber depicting Wicca symbols.

We were on the outskirts of a small hamlet one might describe as hobbit houses, set in an untidy mosaic of small holdings and clearings within a setting of mixed woodland. Chickens, sheep, goats, cats and a couple of cows wandered freely between dwellings, as did a few grubby looking children. Located to one end of the settlement was a large timber and thatch Anglo-Saxon great hall.

'Let's get you up,' said Tarquin, helping me to my feet. 'Come along to the hall and meet everybody.'

It was by now late in the afternoon, with the sun just dipping towards the horizon. It had been only eleven o'clock in the morning when I departed the Grotto in the Knights of Camelot theme park, leaving hours unaccounted for.

The small scattered rustic dwellings constructed exclusively from local materials could have been in the Iron Age, with wood smoke emerging from rough mud brick chimneys protruding through their turf and thatch roofs, mingling with the cool dampness of the chill evening air making a not unpleasant waft resembling an autumn bonfire.

The central hall stood apart in the grander style of a Dark Ages nobleman. Leading the way, Tarquin swung open the heavy door made from sturdy roughly hewn oak planks. We emerged into a large hall, dimly lit by small unglazed windows and half a dozen lanterns. It was redolent with a mixture of wood smoke, sweaty bodies, soggy rarely washed woollen clothing, well-trodden woven reed mats strewn over flagstone floors and aromas from cooking pots simmering over a log fire in a stone hearth at the hall's far end.

Some members of the community tended the cooking or relaxed on rough-hewn wooden chairs, stools and benches alongside a long table I took to be large enough to seat the entire community.

At the head of the communal table laid in the middle of the floor space was Philomena, dressed as I had seen her at the Well of Avalon, in the female warrior outfit of the Ethereal Guide, radiating authority. Her gaze sought and held me like a searchlight.

'Merry meet, Brother Simon. Welcome to Abballon,' she declared.

All eyes turned to acquaint themselves with the newcomer to their community.

I scanned the scene, hunting for Jenny, but she was not

there.

'Who are you seeking, Brother Simon?' asked Tarquin quietly.

'Sorry, Brother Tarquin, I must have appeared rude. I was hoping to see a good friend of mine, a young lady by the name of Jenny. She wouldn't be here by any chance?'

'I'm sorry, Brother Simon. Jenny isn't with us anymore.'

The news fell like a sledgehammer blow. I had made this trip to follow her into the unknown, only to find I had left it too late. I went pale and my knees felt like jelly.

Seeing me falter, Tarquin took me by the arm. 'Brother Simon, are you alright? You seem unwell.'

With my six feet of lithe muscle and confident demeanour I was not usually a man who crumpled under stress, but with Jenny already gone I felt as if my legs had been chopped at the knees. I would have to dig deep to find fresh resources. With gritted teeth I resolved to steady myself and continue my quest. I must secure my place in the community. 'Just faint for a moment, Brother Tarquin. I'm alright now.'

Tarquin stood by me anxiously a few seconds while the colour returned to my cheeks. Reassured I had recovered, he led me over to a sturdy man in his late forties, muscular from hard physical work, with shaggy matted shoulder length hair and a thick reddish beard.

'Brother Simon, this is Brother Cadfael, our community Moderator. He takes care of us, adjudicates and settles any points of contention within the community, as directed by the spiritual influence of our Ethereal Guide,' Tarquin explained.

'Merry meet, Brother Simon,' acknowledged Cadfael.

'Very glad to meet you,' I replied, hesitating a moment,

having realised I wasn't following the community's conventions. 'Brother Cadfael,' I added after a second or two.

'A lot will be new to you,' replied Cadfael. 'You will need to conform to our ways. There will be things you don't understand at first, but stay with it and learn. In time it will become clear. Are you ready to take the True Natural Path?'

'Yes, Brother Cadfael, I am ready.'

There was a talkative woman and two rather more taciturn men huddled as if plotting. All three were lean, muscular and tough, including, perhaps especially, the woman; definitely not folks you would want to get in a quarrel with. They looked up.

The woman called out. 'Come over here, Brother Simon, let's take a look at you.'

I went over, with Tarquin hovering in the background.

'I'm Sister Brenda, but you can call me Bradders,' the woman announced. Bradders had the hearty manner of a swashbuckling pirate, no settling into a feminine gender stereotype for her, she was one of the chaps.

'Brother Hugo, call me Huggs,' said one of the men. He was in his late 20s, tall, slim yet broad, strong and muscular with brown curly hair, big brown eyes in a cheerful welcoming face, his posture open and relaxed.

'Woody,' said the other man without elaborating. He was about forty, medium height with a compact frame, yet wiry and robust, his thinning fair hair brushed back. The lines on his weathered face set into an expression of perpetual scepticism, suggesting a general suspicion.

'What brought you here?' asked Huggs.

Should I confess honestly that I was there to find

Jenny, or spout worthy platitudes? The latter felt prudent. 'To get away from a world dominated by capitalist exploitation and environmental destruction to something natural, free and in tune with our Mother Earth.'

'Wouldn't you know it! A bloody idealist,' muttered Woody, his Yorkshire accent emphasising his cynicism. 'There's work to be done here, some of it bloody hard work. You're up for it, are you?'

'I'm not afraid of hard work.'

Bradders looked at me sceptically, observing my soft smooth hands. 'Well, you look as if you could shape up. You're pasty and soft from city living. We'll see how you manage over the coming weeks. Come on, I'll introduce you to some of the others.'

Bradders led me, with Tarquin following, across the hall to an assortment of large pots simmering on an antique wood burning kitchen range; a cauldron containing stew bubbled directly over the fire in the stone-built hearth. I briefly overheard the two women attending the cooking, '… no, he's yours, don't worry about me, I've got my eye elsewhere …' before the conversation halted abruptly as we approached.

One of the cooks, a well-rounded woman, radiating a spirit of universal motherhood, smiled with an expression suggesting I might be her favourite nephew. She wore a kaftan-like garment of roughly woven but highly decorated fabric adorned with a brightly coloured pattern, the deep V neck of the garment revealing an endless cleavage between her ample unsupported breasts. Across her breasts tenuous tendrils of a creeping plant were portrayed, tattooed into her firm curvaceous flesh, in the unmistakable style of tattooist Suzy Fontanzana in

Camden Market.

'Merry meet, Brother Simon,' she said in a reassuring West Country voice reminiscent of Devon cream teas. 'I'm Sister Hypatia.'

'And this is Sister Elsa,' said Bradders, introducing the other woman, in her thirties, a leathery face from an outdoors lifestyle and straight brown hair tied into a pony tail, her stance and sturdy build suggesting she could happily wrestle any opposition into submission.

'Sister Hypatia does a fantastic job feeding us all and Sister Elsa takes care of our various animals,' Bradders continued. She lifted the lid on one of the pans. 'They are doing a particularly good job today, by the look of things.'

'Merry meet, Brother Simon,' said Elsa, looking me up and down, assessing my potential with a critical eye as if inspecting one of her livestock.

A clatter distracted attention as a ladle bounced off one pot and toppled to the floor. Tarquin was occupied adjusting racks holding food stocks and kitchen utensils.

A bell clanged, drawing my focus to Philomena standing, placing the bell back on the communal table. The men stepped back passively as the women considered where to sit and which if any of the men to select to join them. There appeared to be a pecking order.

Philomena was the first to choose. I felt a shiver of excitement and apprehension when she momentarily fastened her gaze on me, before looking towards Huggs. With her arm raised in invitation, Huggs compliantly came forward.

The matriarchal Hypatia was next in the dominance hierarchy. Cadfael looked expectantly in her direction, but her eyes swung towards Woody, who at first didn't react, nonplussed, as if thinking, Who? Me? Are you sure? until with the focus of the entire room on him, he was compelled to take notice. Cadfael looked anxious and crestfallen, shock and loss evident in his eyes, as Woody stepped over uncertainly to join Hypatia.

Elsa was next. She did not hesitate, her penetrating eyes went straight in Cadfael's direction, full of triumphal possession and lust. Cadfael's expression switched from loss to fear. He hesitated. When Elsa gestured impatiently with her hand, Cadfael complied in resigned acceptance.

When all the selections had been made, Bradders, Tarquin and myself were among those unpaired for the evening. After everyone else had settled into their places, the three of us settled together at the far end of the long table.

At the head Philomena said the blessing.

'Blessed be the Earth for giving birth to this food, Blessed be the Sun for nourishing it, Blessed be the Wind for carrying the seed, Blessed be the Rain for quenching its thirst, Blessed be.'

Those around the table responded in unison, 'So mote it be.'

'Is this what happens every evening?' I asked.

'Yes, pretty much,' Bradders confirmed.

'I see the women choose from the men, but not you. You didn't choose anybody.'

'You might have already guessed, if I was choosing, I'd be choosing from the women, but that isn't how it works.'

'Anyway, just us then,' I remarked.

'I wouldn't be much good to them,' said Tarquin. 'I'm gay.'

'I doubt if you'll be at a loose end for long,' said Bradders, 'judging from the way Philomena was looking at you. I reckon Hypatia fancies you too. As for Elsa, she'll have anybody. She'll be after you at some point.'

'Cadfael looked less than entirely happy about having to go with Elsa,' I observed.

'I'm not surprised. From what I've heard she's an animal. Insatiable,' said Bradders, snorting raucously.

I pictured being seized by the rapacious Elsa. Any appetite I might have had for carnal delights ebbed. I sought to change the subject.

'So, what do you two mostly do around here?'

'This and that. Physical stuff. Building, working the fields, kind of thing,' said Bradders.

'I mostly fix things, make things, mechanical stuff, pipework,' said Tarquin.

'You do more than that. You're a bloody technical genius,' said Bradders.

'What are you making at the moment?'

'I've got some work to finish off on the windmill and windows. When that's done it'll be drainage and composting toilets. It's quite interesting actually,' Tarquin said.

The food was hearty, the main course a stew containing potatoes, carrots, turnips, onions and mutton pieces, with hunks of a heavy bread-like food to soak the gravy. To follow was a compote of apple and blackberry. We washed it down with tankards of robust ale which from its taste I imagined could have been brewed from a range of organic ingredients, pigeon droppings, floor sweepings and dead rats for example.

The bread-like chunks weren't any food I recognised.

They were dense and consisted of a blend of processed ingredients I couldn't identify, fragments of fruitiness mingled with starchiness, something like nuts but not a kind I could pinpoint, together with a creaminess somewhere between a soya paste and cream cheese. It was as if someone had formulated a kind of cake to be a complete diet by itself, containing all food types.

'This is good, whatever it is,' I remarked as I chewed.

'It's manna,' said Bradders. 'Food provided by Gaia Herself.'

'How does She provide it?'

'It arrives overnight in the temple,' said Bradders.

'The temple, is that the wooden building set up against the cliff?'

'Yes, that's it.'

'So, this manna, it just arrives there, all by itself?'

'Well, no, it come from Gaia. She puts it there, to sustain us,' Bradders explained.

Over the course of the meal, with Tarquin explaining at greater length than was needed about the construction and operation of the composting toilets, I distractedly cast my eye over my new companions. Philomena caught my glance, smiling suggestively. If her companion Huggs felt concern or jealousy, he showed no sign.

After the meal those paired up dispersed, with the woman taking the lead. An awkward scene ensued as Elsa stood from the table, the first to make a move, but Cadfael remained seated. Elsa tugged on his arm. He said something quietly I couldn't quite hear. The sound of talking around the table subsided as people turned to observe what in this community was evidently a scandalous turn.

Philomena intervened, turning towards Hypatia. 'Is this true?' I heard her ask.

Hypatia shook her head and indicated towards Woody, sitting beside her. Philomena turned back towards Cadfael. There was anger in her eyes as she pronounced loudly and emphatically. 'Gaia's love flows through the Sisterhood who are fashioned in Her image. Men do not choose, but must accept feminine love gratefully whenever it is offered and from whoever it is offered. Go now, as you have been commanded.'

There was shocked silence, all eyes on Cadfael. Dejectedly he stood, defeated, allowing the triumphant Elsa to take his hand and lead him outside.

In a short time all the various couples rose and departed in pairs. Huggs went with Philomena. To me he appeared chilled out, content with his fate, if not particularly excited. On Woody's face as he accompanied Hypatia, I sensed disbelief and elation.

The hall cleared leaving Bradders, Tarquin and me alone. Bradders poured us each another tankard of ale.

'It's usually just Tarquin and me. Glad to have you with us, Brother Simon,' she said.

'Yes, it's wonderful having you with us, Brother Simon,' Tarquin agreed, looking fondly in my direction.

'There was quite a stir, just now, I mean with Cadfael and Elsa,' I observed.

'Yes, he was breaking the rules. He can't pick and choose,' said Bradders.

'He's been with Hypatia a long time. It would have been a shock for him when she suddenly picked Woody,' said Tarquin.

'It is quite a humiliation for him actually,' said

Bradders. 'It's about more than just getting to shag Hypatia. He is the Moderator, making him the senior member and leader of the men in the community. Hypatia casting him aside and selecting Woody in his place, well, let's just say it makes one wonder about his future.'

I wondered where I might end up for the night. Tarquin was quick to answer. 'You're more than welcome to stay over at my place.'

'You sure? I don't want to intrude.'

'Think nothing of it. You won't be intruding at all,' Tarquin assured, putting his arm around my shoulder.

'Well, just for as long it takes to get my own place.'

'Stay as long as you like. I'd love having you around. Really.'

'I'll be on my own as usual,' said Bradders. 'Don't worry about me. I'm used to it.'

With the sleeping arrangements decided, following Tarquin into the night air, we picked through the darkness the hundred yards or so to Tarquin's quaint hobbit house.

Tarquin's home would have been cosy had there been fewer bits and pieces related to his many technical projects. It was simultaneously a home, workshop and scrapyard. I stepped over gear wheels Tarquin had hewn out of timber, squeezing past window frames, on my way to the seat Tarquin indicated for me while he shimmied around making herbal tea.

As we sipped our tea I raised the subject on my mind all evening. 'You know when I asked you about Jenny and you said she isn't with us, where exactly is she, if not here?'

'I really couldn't say,' replied Tarquin with an edge of caution.

'Well, what happened to her? You must have some

idea.'

Tarquin looked away awkwardly. 'She was cast out,' he answered eventually.

'How do you mean cast out?'

'Cast out for breaking Gaia's law.'

'Which law? And who decides if the law has been broken?'

'I'm not sure exactly what she did. It was to do with wanting something put to a democratic vote. Philomena says you can't put Gaia's law to a vote. It would be putting yourself above Gaia. Then Jenny said something about Philomena being a dictator. Anyway, it upset Philomena and it is her who decides.'

'So, calling Philomena a rude name gets you cast out?'

'Yes. Philomena called it defamation of the Ethereal Guide.'

'So where do people go when they are cast out?'

'I don't know. They just disappear and we don't see them anymore.'

I had a horrible feeling in my stomach, as if an angry python was squeezing my guts. People just disappearing for challenging the leader—like Stalin's Russia.

Tarquin showed me to a little alcove where I could bed down on a mattress of straw bales. Racked with dread, though tired, I slept fitfully that night.

A New Day in the Community

Spasmodic sleep was broken by unusual noises, not the familiar London traffic—police sirens, footsteps clattering on pavements, drunk people shouting—but the howling of what I took to be wolves, owls hooting, shuffling and rustling of foliage. There was a wild jungle around Abballon.

An itch on the inside of my elbow, a pinprick, suggested the taking of a blood sample, presumably occurring during those lost hours between leaving the Knights of Camelot grotto and arriving in Abballon.

It was getting light, not quite dawn. Feeling a need to offload some of the ale from the previous evening it felt like a good time to try out the composting toilet Tarquin had explained in such detail the previous evening.

I heard Tarquin moving around. Presently he came into my alcove with a rough hand-thrown mug filled with hot herbal tea. 'Blessed be the morn.'

'Oh, good morning, Brother Tarquin, thanks.'

Tarquin lingered. 'It's a delight for me having you here, Brother Simon,' said Tarquin gazing fondly at me with his pale blue eyes. He reached over and gently placed his hand over mine. Unsure how to react, wishing neither to encourage him nor hurt his feelings. I left my hand under Tarquin's but kept it still.

'It's nice being here. Thanks for putting me up,' I acknowledged politely. The need to drink my tea gave me a reason to move my hand without making Tarquin feel rejected.

'What does one do to get a wash around here?' I

enquired.

'There's the stream. I'll show you.'

Dodging between tools and pieces of timber, Tarquin led the way a short distance along a foot track to the stream running along the edge of the village's main clearing.

From there, as I had a quick wash with a good view of the cliff forming one of the boundaries of the community's land, a massive edifice of almost vertical sheer rock. I couldn't imagine anybody except a mountaineer scaling it. Near the top of the cliff was a layer appearing smoother, flatter and more reflective. Its colour and the shapes of the rocky features the same as elsewhere on the cliff, so it wasn't different at first glance. An optical illusion, perhaps.

As I gazed, in the distance I noticed Hypatia and Elsa emerge from the temple, the ornate wooden building set against the cliff. They held large trays of something. I couldn't make out exactly what, but it could have been the mysterious manna.

Having washed, we shared breakfast of mixed grain porridge Tarquin had prepared, washed down with more herbal tea.

A bell tolled, a single chime repeatedly.

'What's that?'

'The bell summoning people for work duties.'

'Do we have to go?'

'Normally you would, but you can skip it today and work with me, if you like?'

'Don't you go?'

'No, not usually. I've plenty of my own projects and Cadfael lets me get on with it.'

I spent the morning with Tarquin assisting in his higgledy-piggledy home-cum-workshop. He took the opportunity to inform me about the community, its beliefs and practices as well as the technical intricacies of his innovations.

I enjoyed an explanation about the uses for oil in the True Natural Path religion rituals; Tarquin paused in the middle of explaining its role in initiation into the community, branching off into the growing of echium to provide the oil.

I enquired what echium was, barely establishing it was a flowering plant with seeds from which oil could be squeezed, whereupon Tarquin launched into a detailed explanation of the intricacies of the oil press he had devised, leading to him pulling out some of the parts of the device for me to ponder.

Before I could take in any idea of how the parts functioned, Tarquin veered into a discussion about the cultivation of the plant and its need for a reliable water supply, in turn moving to the irrigation system he had devised for the community's crops by diverting the flow of the stream I had washed in earlier, making it necessary to inspect the flow valve components he had contrived to regulate the irrigation water.

Tarquin had heavy timber machinery laid on the floor, a system of interlocking gears; replacement parts for worn components in the community's windmill, he explained.

As time went on I became so befuddled I understood less about the Abballon community than I had first thing in the morning, quite an achievement when my knowledge had started from practically zero. Tarquin's confusion of information had conveyed the mathematically impossible, negative knowledge.

My head spun as Tarquin launched into an explanation of the construction of window frames, consisting of small panels each of which held a small uneven pane of greenish tinged glass with wobbly circular ripples, like those used decoratively in Olde Worlde shops in quaint touristy villages in the Cotswolds. As he launched into the finer points of the process he had invented for making the glass, the bell tolled again.

'Time for lunch break in the hall.'

Under the wooden beams spanning the smoky, dimly lit great hall, members of the community helped themselves to hunks of manna from the trays laid out on the long table.

To one side of the hall on another table I glimpsed familiar looking pentangle pendants. Investigating I could see they were unmistakably of the same distinctly hand-made manufacture as the one I had bought in Camden Market and seen again delivered by Philomena to Megan's Magick Shoppe.

Cadfael, the community's Moderator, a weather beaten hunk of muscle, was nearby.

'Do you like them?' he asked.

'Yes. I've already got one,' I replied. I pulled mine out from under my jerkin. 'Here, look.'

'You got it from Nathan, I expect.'

'Actually no, although I saw Nathan selling them. I bought mine in Camden Market.'

'I do the metalwork.'

'Very nice.'

'How they look is as much down the Sister Hypatia as me. She does the decoration, carving, setting the stones and so on.'

'What happens to them?'

'Philomena takes them away with her into the temple as an offering to Gaia.'

'But you've already figured they go on from there.'

'Yes. I worked it out when I saw a new member wearing one, like you have.'

Moving to the table to pick up a piece of manna I was greeted enthusiastically by a cheery Bradders. 'Brother Simon, merry meet. Slept in, did you?'

'No, up with the lark, me.'

'Didn't see you in here this morning.'

'No, I've been working with Brother Tarquin.'

'Doing what?'

'Making windows, mostly, and a bit with the irrigation system.'

'What are you up to later?'

'Don't know. What have you been up to?'

'Working in the vegetable plots. Proper work, unlike playing about with Tarquin's gadgets.'

Proper work would be less tiring than trying to absorb a further torrent of disjointed information. 'Mind if I join you?'

'We'd have to ask Woody. He's in charge.'

She led me to where Woody sat. 'Mind if Brother Simon joins us this afternoon.'

Woody looked over at me sceptically. 'You'd have to work. I don't want anybody getting in the way and slowing us down.'

'I'll work, I promise,' I assured him.

He scowled. 'Alright then, as long as you get stuck in.'

The work planting carrots, onions and cabbages was physically hard but a merciful relief from mental overload.

As I stretched my limbs from time to time I took in my surroundings. The tallest building was a windmill, presumably the one for which Tarquin was fabricating wooden machinery. Besides the vegetable plot, were fields of wheat and maize, an orchard with apple and pear trees and some pasture for cows, sheep and goats. Beyond the fields was a strip of ground with bracken and low shrubs, further out from which was dense wild woodland. I could not see anything through the trees, but now and again glimpsed a wild animal, mostly deer but I also made out an unusual gigantic cattle-like animal with enormous horns, a creature from a bygone era, something I had seen illustrated in a book about the Ice Age, I think called an auroch.

'What goes on in those woods?' I asked my companions when we had a break.

'That's the Wild Side,' explained Woody. 'We don't go there.'

'Oh, why not?'

'It's Gaia's realm, reserved for Her creatures. We're not allowed.'

'Some of those creatures are quite big, I fancy. I thought I heard wolves last night. Don't they sometimes come over here?'

'No, they can't. Gaia doesn't allow it.'

'I don't suppose they know about Gaia. What stops them?'

'Don't you go talking like that. Gaia's wisdom is everywhere and in everything, plants, animals, streams, rocks and clouds, all things natural.'

Woody was sharp. Apparently I had made something of a faux pas. Bradders smirked.

'Sorry, you're right. I should have had more respect. But what actually does stop them?'

'Gaia has put a force there blocking the way. If they or we stray into the scrubby area between us and the wood, they get pushed back,' Bradders explained.

'So this force doesn't just stop the wild animals coming here, it stops us going there as well. Is that right?'

'Spot on. It blocks both ways. Keeps us apart. Just as well. There's bears, wolves, sabre cats, mammoths, dangerous beasts of all kinds,' Bradders elaborated.

'So how does it push back, this force? I can't see barriers. It looks as if you could just walk across with no problem.'

'Well, you get to feel a massive heat. So hot you can't stand it. Like getting really close to a raging fire. You really don't want to stay there long.'

'How do you know?' demanded Woody, with a shocked look.

'Sorry. Just curiosity. I know I shouldn't have. Just wanted to see what would happen.'

'You're wicked. You could get into real trouble. People have been cast out for less.'

After our work was done the three of us freshened up with the cool stream water. Woody took himself off, while I lingered with Bradders, hoping to chat with her alone.

'You know you said you'd been over into that kind of no-mans-land between us and the woods, Wild Side, whatever you want to call it, just to see what would happen? Could you really get cast out for doing it?'

Bradders nodded. 'Definitely. It's forbidden. A grievous breach of Gaia's law.'

'Who decides these things? I mean, casting out and so on.'

'Philomena. She is the Ethereal Guide, which makes her the boss.'

'But you like to live dangerously?'

Bradders smiled wickedly. 'I suppose I do.'

'You know Jenny, the one I mentioned. Tarquin told me she got cast out. What was she cast out for?'

'She upset Philomena. Never a good idea.'

'How did she upset her?'

'Philomena thought she was making a play for Huggs. She saw them chatting.'

'She is possessive then, Philomena?'

'Not half. It's an unwritten rule. Never take any man she wants for herself.'

'Tarquin mentioned stuff about her wanting to have a vote on something and her calling Philomena a dictator or some such, and that being the reason.'

'Trumped up charges. Bottom line is, it was about Huggs. Mind, it wasn't smart to defy Philomena or challenge her authority. It gave her the pretext she needed.'

'I see. Any idea where people who are cast out end up?'

'No, afraid not. They just disappear. Not with us anymore.'

In the distance I made out Philomena emerging from the temple at the base of cliff. The shape and movements of her alluring figure radiated sexuality and power. I nodded in her direction.

'Talk of the Devil!'

Bradders elbowed me hard in the ribs. 'You'll get cast out yourself, saying things like that.'

'Sorry. Does she go in there a lot?'

'Yes, she's there most of the time actually. Typically all day, but on occasion she's been gone days at a time.'

'So, what does she do when she's in there?'

'Communes with Gaia, I suppose. I don't know exactly.'

'Does anyone else go in there?'

'No, not usually. Hypatia and Elsa collect the manna of a morning and we have ceremonies sometimes, but mostly it's just her.'

'So, what's in there?'

'There are benches and an altar, but behind the altar is a secret holy place, forbidden to the rest of us, a place only Philomena may venture.'

I made a mental note. This must be the portal allowing Philomena to enjoy her double life as ruler of Abballon while simultaneously spending time outside in Glastonbury.

As we gathered for the communal evening meal the Abballon community hall had its unique aroma arising from the mingled scents of its surroundings, gathered provisions, damp unwashed clothing and the body odour of its inhabitants.

The pairings were the same as they had been the previous evening.

Huggs's position by the imperious Philomena's side put him in an ascendant social position, but from his chilled manner Huggs seemed unconcerned with status. In contrast Woody was relishing his new privileged position as Hypatia's chosen companion. Cadfael looked diminished, meekly accepting his new position at Elsa's side, though not enjoying it.

Remaining on the shelf, Bradders and I found our eyes glazing over as Tarquin explained his repair work on the windmill, oblivious of our lack of attention.

At the end of the meal brief words exchanged between Cadfael, Elsa and Philomena.

As couples dispersed, Elsa stood on her own, leaving Cadfael seated. Looking around the room, her eyes caught mine. I averted my gaze, but glancing back, she was still staring at me as if with carnal intentions. My heart pounded as she took steps in my direction. She half closed the gap between us, hesitated, then turned and departed alone.

Seeing Cadfael still in the hall, I took the opportunity to slip away from Bradders and Tarquin to talk to him alone.

'Hello Brother Cadfael, do you mind if we have a quick chat?'

'Merry meet, Brother Simon. Not at all. Chat away.'

I slipped off the locket I was still wearing.

'Nathan in Glastonbury asked me to give you this.'

'Oh, so he has been getting my messages then?'

'Yes, he has.'

'Wonderful. You don't know what it is then?' Cadfael asked nervously.

'It's none of my business. I'm just the courier.'

Cadfael looked me up and down. 'You do know though, don't you? I bet you had a peek. I would have done.'

'Yes, alright, I know. But I won't say anything. As I said,

it's none of my business.'

Cadfael unclipped the locket and saw the diamond shaped blue tablets. 'Phew. Those are a life saver. Without those my days as Moderator would be over for sure.'

'How come?'

'It's Beltane tomorrow.'

'What happens at Beltane?'

'As Moderator, I'm Cernunnos, the Horned God, and, well, you know, it means I've got to fertilise and so on, if you get my meaning.'

'You mean you have to do, you know, how's your father, for real in the ceremony.'

'Yes, for real.'

'With… who exactly?'

'Philomena, in the ceremony she will be the Goddess.'

'Well, glad I could help,' I said, making to move away.

Cadfael gestured for me to stay. 'Don't go. Let's have a drink.'

He indicated for me to take a seat with him at the long table at the opposite end to where Bradders and Tarquin were still seated. He took a couple of tankards and filled them with ale. 'Fact is, these days I haven't always been able to get it up, as you probably guessed. I expect you know from the others I used to be Hypatia's man. Have been for some time, until yesterday when she chucked me in.'

'Yes, Bradders and Tarquin told me.'

'It wasn't usually too much of a problem with her. I'm used to her, you see. It just sort of feels natural and comfortable, so it mostly works out okay. There have been a couple of times it didn't work out, when I've been tired. It's been alright later, once I've rested.'

'Well, you can't expect, y'know, to manage it every time. You have to be in the mood.'

'Tell that to Hypatia! She has high expectations. She's fickle, mind. Depends upon time of the month, being pregnant, hormones and so forth, so there are times she doesn't want anything at all. But, other times, when she's in the mood, she's insatiable.'

I was squirming. It wasn't even as if I even knew Cadfael yet, although I was certainly getting to know him fast! Perhaps he needed a relative stranger to confess to, who was sympathetic. 'But Hypatia appears to have moved on now,' I observed.

'Yes, I suppose she must have felt I didn't measure up any more.'

'I guess she thinks Woody will live up to his name.'

'Yes, I see, yes, wood, right. I wouldn't mind so much, but it was shocking having Elsa move in right away, before I had got a chance to adjust to losing Hypatia. They must have cooked it up between them.'

I remembered the snippet of conversation I overhead when being introduced to Hypatia and Elsa. 'Yes, I think they did.'

'Last night it was bloody impossible. It wasn't because I didn't try. I didn't really want to go with Elsa, as everybody saw, to my embarrassment, but once I was there I did try, honestly, but nothing happened. Her reeking of her precious sheep and goats didn't help.'

'Yes, it could put anybody off,' I mused.

'Elsa didn't take it kindly. Accused me of doing it deliberately. She was angry and whipped me.'

'Whipped you? Really?'

'Yes. You didn't know about that? Being whipped, I

mean.'

'No, nobody mentioned it.'

'Well, you see, here in Abballon men are required to behave and control their sexual impulses, taking their lead from the woman who chooses them and fulfilling her wishes. A woman is empowered to beat any man who fails to control himself as required. Normally it applies to men who get ahead of themselves and do stuff the woman doesn't want, but in this case Elsa thought I must have been failing to perform deliberately, so I deserved a whipping. She's tough. She gave me quite a thrashing.'

'You're not with her tonight. How did you get out of it?'

'I mentioned to her and Philomena I should really keep my strength up for tomorrow. Philomena agreed.'

'I see.'

'She then went and told Philomena she had had to discipline me last night. She didn't tell her why, at least I don't think she did, not in my earshot anyway.'

'I guess she wouldn't want to explain. Rather have folk believe her to be so ultra-desirable she had to fight you off.'

'But now there is tomorrow. Philomena can be intimidating and in front of all those people. It could have been a problem. You brought those pills just in the nick of time.'

Beltane

My second full day in Abballon was a special occasion for the community, the celebration of Beltane.

I didn't linger among the clutter at Tarquin's place when the morning bell sounded, but made my way to muster for work with the others in the hall.

Most of the women were already present in the cooking area, with Hypatia as mother hen corralling her chicks. There was no sign of Philomena.

I joined the other men and Bradders gathered around our Moderator, Cadfael. We chewed on hunks of manna from the trays laid out on the long table.

'We need to finish planting the vegetables,' said Cadfael.

'What about the building work?' Woody demanded.

'Food supply has to come first,' Cadfael insisted. 'We have to eat.'

'We need a roof over our heads too.'

'Let's allocate the planting first and then see who we have to spare for building work.'

'There's drainage to be dealt with,' Woody insisted. 'The crops won't grow if they're flooded.'

'We can deal with the drainage later,' Cadfael retorted.

It felt like a nature documentary where, the equilibrium disturbed by a change in the affections of the alpha female, Hypatia, silver back alpha male gorilla, Cadfael, was being challenged for dominance by a rival, Woody.

'Who do you need for your building work?' Cadfael conceded.

'I'll have Huggs, Bradders and Simon.'

Huggs outranked both Woody and Cadfael in the female determined pecking order, I reflected, yet he accepted his assignment cheerfully and without quibble.

Woody's building project was a new dwelling, a home in the prevailing hobbit house style, in a consistent form, size and style, yet unique, moulded by the demands of the site and variations in the building materials.

As usual it consisted of a single storey blended into the terrain with a turf roof, a timber framework infilled with straw and cob, windows consisting of the small panels of wonky glass made by Tarquin. Few if any of the timbers, sourced from the modest patch of woodland within the community's land rather than the inaccessible Wild Side, were straight, the random variety of branched and curved forms making each structure appear organic and unique.

'We'll start with these,' said Woody, indicating a couple of relatively straight branches. 'Trim them off here and here,' he said, looking at Huggs and pointing where the smaller side branches were to come off.

'We need to anchor them here,' he said to Bradders showing where they were to be fastened into the wall.

'Brother Simon, I need you on top, securing t'rafters with these pegs.'

I cast my eye from my vantage point. momentarily mesmerised by a primeval sight emerging from the trees over in the Wild Side: a shaggy furred woolly mammoth with immense tusks, followed by its baby, a scampering miniature version of the adult without the tusks and about the size of Shetland pony.

'What's the matter with you?' Woody demanded.

'It's a mammoth and baby. Over there.'

'We're not here sightseeing. We're 'ere to get t'ouse built,' grumbled Woody.

Later, when we took a break, Huggs took Woody to task for being so driven. 'You need to chill out, man, take in the vibe of nature, like Brother Simon with those mammoths.'

'We've got to get stuff done. I suppose you think you can just chillax how you like now you're Philomena's bit of stuff,' retorted Woody.

'Lucky sod. Wish I could be Philomena's bit of stuff,' lamented Bradders, quietly so I could hear, but Woody and Huggs, intent on squaring up to one another, probably didn't.

The atmosphere remained tense when we resumed working, but it wasn't for long because we finished early due to it being the Beltane celebration in the evening.

As usual we freshened up in the stream after work. Woody and Huggs didn't linger long, departing in quick succession, but separately, leaving me and Bradders at the water's edge. I examined my hands, smarting after I rinsed them clean.

'Let's have a look at those poncy soft hands of yours,' Bradders said.

I showed them to her, raw, blistered and blood-stained from cuts.

'Torn to bloody shreds already. Not used to hard work, are you?'

'Well, I admit, not the hard physical kind. I'm not frightened of it, though.'

Consideration of the state of my hands and my fitness

for work were interrupted by the captivating sight of Philomena emerging out of the temple.

'There she is again. Philomena. Just like yesterday,' I observed, glad to change the subject.

'I know. Lovely, isn't she?' replied Bradders wistfully.

'You really fancy her, don't you?'

'Not half. I would do anything, just to have one night with her. You wouldn't believe how jealous I am of that lucky sod Huggs.'

'You say that now, but after you'd had the one night you crave, you'd lament giving her up and particularly hate seeing her going with someone else.'

'Well, perhaps. But I'd accept it. Just having been with her the once. I'd have those memories to fall back on. It would be worth it.'

'Supposing such a thing were to happen, it would be Philomena who would be in charge, holding the reins and having the whip hand, so to speak. You'd be doing what she wants, not what you want. You might not like it.'

Bradders shook her head. 'No, you don't understand. I would happily do whatever she wanted. I don't care what it might be. It could be as humiliating, degrading or painful as it pleased her. Just being with her for a time would be enough.'

'It almost sounds as if you think it would be humiliating, degrading and painful.'

Bradders smiled wryly and inclined her head. 'I don't know, but from what I've heard I think it might be.'

'Oh, I see.'

'You'll be finding out for yourself soon enough, I reckon,' said Bradders.

'What do you mean?'

'I've seen the way she looks at you.'

'But she's got Huggs. She doesn't need me.'

'She'll tire of him. She always does. Besides you've got an air of youthful vigour and virility she couldn't resist.'

I squirmed. 'Come off it. Women resist me all the time only too easily.'

'Well, you're not my type obviously, but I know what straight women go for, and you are a good example, believe me.'

This observation, while flattering, was somehow demeaning too. I sought to change the subject. 'How long will Philomena and Huggs be an item, do you think?'

'Not long. He is at least her third, or is it her fourth, since she chucked Cadfael aside.'

'So Cadfael was with her once?'

'Oh yes. That was when she appointed him Moderator.'

'But he remained Moderator afterwards.'

'Yes. He is good at it. Everyone respects him. Actually, I think he was happy to be released from being her lover. I don't think that he enjoyed it much. Hypatia picked him up straight away. He definitely likes her better.'

'But now he's lost Hypatia.'

'Yes. It was a shock. And Woody is so bloody full of himself now he has taken his place. It makes me sick.'

Wandering back into the village my mind whirled with contradictory feelings about being Philomena's plaything, helplessly obliged to fulfil her desires, a prospect as fascinating as it was frightening, with twinges of guilt about betraying my true love, Jenny, with this lust.

As I came through the rough-hewn timber doorway into the hall, Bradders's prediction felt more real and immediate. Philomena's eyes focused on me, following me like a cat tracks its prey as I approached the table laid out with snacks to sustain us through the forthcoming Beltane ceremony.

I let out my breath as Philomena's attention moved to other people. I saw Tarquin and caught his eye. 'Hello Brother Tarquin, this looks like a good spread. What would you recommend?'

'Sister Hypatia's pasties are good.'

I bit into the excellent Cornish pasty prepared by the matronly Hypatia, a culinary genius in my estimation. Looking around to congratulate her, it was Elsa who caught my gaze. Her eyebrows raised and head tilted in acknowledgement, her coy look sharing some secret between us. Blushing involuntarily, I quickly turned away.

'What have you been up to today?' I asked Tarquin.

'Repairs and improvements to the windmill.'

'What sort of improvements?'

'Expanding the sails to give us more power.'

'What does it entail?'

'The tower has to be raised another storey, the fan blade expanded, a new main shaft fashioned as well and replacement cogs and gears. You see, the extra power means everything needs strengthening accordingly. The choice of timber is critical.'

I began to wish I hadn't asked.

The air was still warm from the day as we stripped, so as to be skyclad in our circle facing the sun as it set over the dense forest on the Wild Side. We were stood on a small mound set aside for sacred purposes just beyond the village buildings.

A life size woven basketwork figure of a man was set up atop a pyre of assorted brushwood and timber offcuts positioned centrally within a pentangle and outer circle marked in white chalk.

Philomena presided, adorned with garlands of spring flowers, alongside Cadfael, clad in a cloak of woven greenery and horned headdress.

At the precise moment the sun dipped out of sight Philomena nodded and Hypatia set the pyre alight. With the flames taking hold, proceedings began.

'Hail Gaia, our beloved Earth Mother, Hail Cernunnos, the bringer of fertility, Hail Guardian Spirits of this place, spirits of wind, fire, water, trees, plants, birds and animals, We come here in peace to celebrate Beltane. We ask you accept our presence and share with us to bring fertility this year.'

All around responded in in unison: 'So mote it be.'

'Blessed be this day of Beltane, Day of Sacred Union of Gaia, our Mother Earth and Cernunnos, Great Horned God of the forest, Her consort, The bringer of Summer, The dark time of Winter behind us.'

'So mote it be,' responded the community.

'The Beltane fire sends its flames to the Sun, The promise of summer warmth to come, Cernunnos, our Horned God, dances through the green, In pursuit of Gaia, our Earth Goddess and Queen, Their Sacred Union empowers the Earth, And we seek their blessings for future birth.'

'So mote it be.'

In her right hand Philomena took up a richly decorated dagger, a ceremonial blade known as an athame, and held it in front of her for all to see.

In her left hand she took up an ornate chalice, a ceremonial drinking vessel, and held it alongside the athame.

'We greet this time of Sacred Union and give honour to our beloved Gaia and Cernunnos, our Earth Mother and Her Consort, for Their fruitfulness, May Their union be fertile and productive.'

'So mote it be.'

Philomena slowly lowered the athame blade into the chalice to symbolise the union of the deities. Then she placed the items on the ground a short distance from the rising flames of the fire.

Philomena and Cadfael faced each other. She reached out and took his male member in her hands, which to Cadfael's relief raised itself as required as she encouraged it with her fingers.

She took his hand and drew it towards her own intimate parts, where guided by her he prepared her symbolic fertile soil of Mother Earth, now swollen and moistened to take the sacred manly plough of Cernunnos, which fortunately for Cadfael remained hard and straight, thanks no doubt to the blue tablets I provided for him earlier.

Philomena's breathing quickened and voice raised in pitch as she spoke the next words of the ritual, her hand still holding Cernunnos's plough embedded within the moistness of Mother Earth.

'Gaia, Queen of the Night, Our Earth Mother, Cernunnos, King of the Forest, bringer of fertility, From Your mating shall spring forth life anew, We celebrate Your union.'

Philomena gestured down and Cadfael sank to his knees. She gestured again and he laid back on the ground. With their figures silhouetted against the firelight all could see Cadfael's manhood remaining aloft as Philomena knelt astride him facing his head, each of her knees on the ground beside his thighs to bring Mother Earth to meet him.

Breathing heavily now she almost shouted the next words.

'As They are one, They become one, As They become one, They are one, And we too are one with Them.'

As she uttered the words she lowered herself onto him taking Cernunnos's plough within her.

'And we too are one with Them,' responded the congregation.

With the union of the spiritual leaders reaching its climax the women of the community selected their partners for their personal enactments of the fertility ritual.

The ritual over, we had put our clothes back on, but for most, I suspected they would shortly be coming off again.

Woody, beaming with triumph, was taken by Hypatia. Philomena, preoccupied with Cadfael, had no requirement for Huggs who was contented to be left free to converse with Bradders, Tarquin and myself.

For a few moments I happily anticipated a relaxing chat among the unattached folk, but Elsa, having been deprived of Cadfael's company, settled her gaze on me.

'Come on, Brother Simon, show me what you've got,' said Elsa in her rough Black Country accent as she took me by the elbow.

Bradders gave me a quick dig in the ribs and a slap on the back as Elsa drew me away. 'Yes, you show her, Brother Simon. Give her one for me,' she said by way of encouragement.

Elsa, pumped up with passion, set a cracking pace towards her place on the village outskirts, but I neither shared her urgency nor wished to break my neck tripping in the dark over ruts, brambles and tree roots.

'Come on, chop-chop,' called Elsa, chivvying me along as if I were a member of her herd of assorted livestock.

I could hear and smell Elsa's hobbit house before I could see it. Animal noises and a rich farmyard aroma wafted from the surrounding animal enclosures, shelters and corrals for the assortment of sheep, goats, pigs and cows under her care.

Reaching her home Elsa flung open her front door, physically propelled me inside as if I were a sheep being thrust into a pen, slamming the door shut behind us. Even inside the room was redolent of animals. The only light was from the faint glow of the embers still smouldering in the fireplace. Elsa lit a lantern to reveal her abode and tossed a couple of logs onto the fire's remnants. Home comforts included rush matting on the floor, roughly hewn table and chairs with the fireplace doubling as a cooker. In the corner was a bed spread with a quilt formed from the woolly hides of former members of her flock.

Wasting no time, Elsa thrust her arms under my clothing. 'Come on, Brother Simon, don't be shy,' she urged, encouraging me to disrobe.

My outer garments shed, Elsa tossed aside her own clothing. She was a round sturdy woman, with powerful thighs, broad hips and full pendulous breasts. 'Come along over here,' she said, drawing me towards the bed.

She lay back onto the bed. Holding each of my hands she pulled me over towards her. 'Before you sow the seed you need to prepare the ground. Do you want to prepare the ground, Brother Simon?' said Elsa softly as she placed my hands on her body, one on her breasts, the other on her thigh. She placed her hand on the back of my head and pushed it down between her legs. 'Eat me, Brother Simon. Make me moist. Make me ready for you.'

Smothered in the earthy aromas of the farmyard and wetness of sexual juices my bodily responses kicked into life automatically driven by the primitive unconscious circuits of the brain inherited from distant evolutionary ancestors shared with fish and frogs. As surely as Elsa's stud ram fulfilled his duties, Cernunnos's plough found its furrow, not once but thrice that night on Elsa's sheepskin rug.

Trapped

Joining the community in the malodorous hall for the morning allocation of work duties, I was overwhelmed by a frantic urge to escape Abballon at the earliest opportunity.

Only a short time before Elsa had prevailed on me to satisfy her lust, twice more in addition to our energetic coupling after the Beltane celebration. In between I slept fitfully while clasped naked in her arms under her fetid sheepskin bedding.

I hated the way my body had responded involuntarily to Elsa's sexuality, automatic reactions, physically exhilarating, enjoyable in a crude carnal way, as out of my control as the beating of my heart and rumblings of my bowels. In my gut were conflicting feelings, nausea and disgust competing with fulfilment and satiety.

Bradders, glancing in Elsa's direction, nudged me in the ribs, winking knowingly. 'She looks in a good mood. Like the cat who got the cream. You must have done a good job rogering her,' she remarked, laughing raucously.

I had been coming to like Bradders, but right now I did not like her at all. She could be rude and crude and I was not in the mood.

Huggs was more sympathetic. 'I'm getting bad vibes, man. Like it wasn't a good scene last night.'

'Yeah, it wasn't the best.'

'Not what you would have chosen, I guess,' said Huggs.

'I wouldn't have chosen it, no.'

'You need to go with the flow, man. Give her what she wants.'

'But it's not what I wanted.'

'Don't overthink it, man. Best just let it happen.'

I was back under Woody's direction, working alongside jaunty Bradders and chilled out Huggs on the construction of Woody's latest hobbit house, my mood not improved by Woody's arrogance and sarcasm, nor by the sexualised banter from Bradders.

In the evening, when partners were being chosen, I was tense. For a moment, when Elsa looked in my direction beaming, I thought I was condemned to accompany her again, but this time she raised her eyebrows and shrugged as if in apology and the ordeal was to be Cadfael's.

During the night, back by the alcove at Tarquin's place, I resolved to make good my escape, or at least make a serious attempt. I tiptoed around the myriad scattered artefacts to not disturb Tarquin and made my way to the empty stillness of the sleeping village.

Standing under a clear sky and bright moonlight at the edge of the strip of bracken and scrub between Abballon and the deeply forested Wild Side, I resolved to make a rush for freedom, brazening it out through the heat barrier I had been warned about.

With an energetic spring I made a frenzied dash into the forbidden space. Almost immediately my body lit up with a searing heat, as if I had been plunged into scalding water. My momentum propelled me on for four or five steps before the fiery heat became too much. I collapsed, but the heat persisted. In agony I staggered back towards my starting point. The heat subsided, but my skin continued to smart as if suffering from a severe sunburn.

A ghostly figure of a woman appeared suspended and glowing over the forbidden ground, the very woman who had lured me here, representing Gaia on the screen of my mobile phone when placed near the eye-catchingly bright pentangle pendant. 'Go back. You are forbidden to encroach onto the Wild Side,' boomed the voice of Gaia.

On the edge of the forest a monstrous cat like figure emerged, head and ears focussed on me like a search light. It was like the largest lion I could imagine and then some, larger than life, akin to the lion statues in Trafalgar Square. Glinting in the moonlight were its monstrous fangs, foot long daggers, a sabre cat like those from the last Ice Age, as if I had travelled into pre-history through a time warp.

The cat, hungry for its prey, surged forward directly towards me. By rights the heat ray barrier should have worked equally well to keep out the cat of Abballon as it had to keep me in, but not being confident enough to put it to the test, I quickly retreated to the nearest of the village hobbit houses. Surrounded by animal pens and a familiar farmyard smell, with a sinking feeling I recognised Elsa's place, but at this moment Elsa was slightly less terrifying than the cat.

As I reached her door I heard a growl and yowling from the direction of the Wild Side. I looked back to make out the cat at the forest edge squirming and licking itself. By good fortune I had been spared both actual death from the gigantic cat's teeth and claws and a fate worse than death with Elsa.

I flopped on a grassy mound to catch my breath and collect my thoughts. Bodily frailties once again defeated my best intentions, and crushed under the weight of disillusionment in myself, my musings were interrupted by a figure approaching from the direction of the main village. My heart rate quickened. I sorely missed the safety and comfort of my bed.

'Is that you, Simon?' It was Tarquin.

'Yes, Tarquin, it's me.'

'What have you been up to?'

'Oh, I don't know. I was just trying to get away.'

Tarquin dropped onto the grass and put his arm around my shoulders. 'You're shivering. You can't stay out here in the cold.' He helped me onto my feet. 'Come on now, let's get you home.'

Back at Tarquin's we sat with hot mugs of herbal tea.

'You shouldn't have done it, trying to get across to the Wild Side. You really shouldn't. I know you did because I saw Gaia ordering you back. People get cast out for such things,' he chided.

'I just needed to get away.'

'What did you need to get away from?'

'Well, I don't know. Just things.'

Tarquin was quiet a moment. He took my hand in his, waiting until I was ready to open up. 'Come on now, tell your uncle Tarquin what it is.'

'It was what happened with Elsa. I just couldn't face it happening again.'

Tarquin's eyes opened wide as if this was something he hadn't anticipated. 'Oh, was it so bad? She was full of herself this morning. I thought it must have gone well.'

I groaned and shook my head.

'So, it didn't go well then?'

'Well, in a sense it did go well, if you mean we had a lot of sex. But I didn't want to.'

'But it must have been okay if you had a lot of sex. You didn't have to have sex.'

'I feel so ashamed of myself. I did it and I kind of enjoyed it. I'm disgusted with myself for it. It's not what I wanted.'

Tarquin considered a while. 'So, you did enjoy it, but at the same time you didn't want it. Right?'

I nodded.

'So your enjoyment, if we can call it that, was just a physical thing. You're disgusted with yourself for reacting in that way. Am I on the right track?'

I nodded again.

'It's as if your physical reaction, including the physical pleasure, was something which just happened and you couldn't control, but you would have preferred not to have it happen.'

'Yes, you've got it exactly. I hate myself for it.'

'And you wanted escape, even to risk your life in the Wild Side, to prevent it happening again.'

'Yes.'

Tarquin was quiet, figuring out what to say next. 'You know, Simon, I am very fond of you.'

I looked at him sideways, unsure how to respond. 'Tarquin, you're a great mate. You've been very good to me and understanding. I appreciate it.'

Tarquin hesitated. 'I meant more than just good mates.'

I had already figured it out, but I still struggled how I might handle the situation. 'I see,' I said noncommittally.

'Well, Simon, how do you feel about it?'

I summoned my brain into gear, honing my diplomatic skills. 'I'm sorry, Tarquin, you are a great bloke. But it just wouldn't work, the way you want it, I mean.'

'Don't be hasty Simon. I know the women fancy you

and you will be obliged to go with them if they want you to. I don't mind. I could accept it. If you come back to me, I'm okay about it.'

I shook my head. 'Tarquin, it's not you. It's me. It's not the way I'm made. As Elsa demonstrated. I'm straight. Entirely straight. So flipping straight you can put me with any woman, even one as rough and course as Elsa, then once we are in an intimate setting, I am like a rutting stag, and there is nothing I can do to stop myself. But blokes don't do it for me, couldn't ever do it for me, even thoroughly nice decent loving blokes like you.'

By the morning I felt calmer. To add to my shame about what I had done with Elsa, I now felt regret for having turned down Tarquin's advances. I gave him a close manly bear hug by way of reassurance.

I still wanted to get away from Abballon, if I could, but the urgency was less now Elsa had Cadfael to divert her again, so, I wouldn't rush to escape in a panic as I had attempted the previous night, taking my time, figuring things out carefully, seizing an opportunity when it arose.

I gave up pestering people about Jenny, partly out of guilt about betraying her, also because it would make them uneasy without providing any further useful detail.

I took the opportunity to absorb the ways, customs and beliefs of the Abballon community, if for no other reason than to aid my escape.

Tarquin was a great friend I felt I could trust completely. Despite his feeling about me in a way I could not reciprocate, he accepted the situation and was glad to be with me.

I had gone off Bradders after her insensitive innuendo,

but I forgave her and found her to be good to talk to; although there were intimate matters I wouldn't share with her.

Cadfael, as Moderator, coached me in my role as a man in the community. He had a steadfastness, an air of solidity, great physical and spiritual strength, but a good strength, protective rather than threatening, strength you could rely on to keep you safe rather than being turned against you.

The principal responsibility of the menfolk was to develop and maintain the physical necessities, the growing of crops, making of tools and construction of buildings. If the community's rules were infringed the men of the community were required to see those responsible brought to justice, to act as a police force. However the men were not judges. That was the role of the Ethereal Guide and the women she chose to assist her, whose orders must always be obeyed.

Hypatia coached me on the spiritual side of the community's culture and beliefs. One day, instead of having me go to work with the menfolk and Bradders, who considered herself one of the men, Hypatia had me remain with her in the hall.

In a blasphemous way I felt a wave of happiness and contentment from being close to Hypatia, as if she was the embodiment of Gaia Herself. Philomena, as Ethereal Guide, was clearly the community ruler, but in this role she was a more remote figure, cold, detached, powerful and vengeful, holding the community in awe through fear, whereas Hypatia, ever present, was everybody's loving beneficent mother figure.

I watched while she worked on the decoration of the

distinctive pentangle pendants. Cadfael brought in the roughly formed items. There was a small flat black object to be fitted inside, made of some modern synthetic. Hypatia explained that Gaia provided them to incorporate her essence. Philomena brought them in from time to time when she returned from conferring with Gaia in the sacred realm at the back of the temple.

Having demonstrated her handiwork on the pendants, Hypatia took me with her into Gaia's temple, nestled against the cliff face. If the community's solid and functional great hall represented its robust heart, the temple was its soul. The timberwork was more delicate, more finely worked, decorative, and symbolic, its focus on style as much as function. Around the room's perimeter were depictions of a variety of Goddesses from a range of cultures, Brigid and Morrigan from Celtic Irish folklore, Kali and Lakshmi from Hindu tradition, Ishtar from Mesopotamia, Freya and Frigg from Norse mythology, Juno and Minerva from ancient Rome, Hera and Aphrodite from ancient Greece. The main body of the room was open with rush matting on the floor and scattered rugs and cushions.

At the front of the room on a table set out as an altar was a carved painted wooden representation of the Greek goddess Artemis set behind three smaller carvings of a young maiden, a mother and an older woman representing the triple Wicca goddess of Maiden, Mother and Crone.

Behind the altar a decorative carved screen aligned with the cliff face against which the temple was built, beyond which I could make out signs of a chamber carved into the limestone rock. As I advanced to the edge of the screen to look behind, Hypatia called me back sharply. 'That is a sacred space. We are forbidden from entering.'

Hypatia had us sit on cushions in the space before the altar. I felt like a young child drawn to Hypatia as if she was my kindly kindergarten teacher on my first day of school as she set out to explain the tenets of the True Natural Path.

'It begins with reverence for Gaia, the Goddess spirit of Mother Earth. She requires the substance of Earth Herself be treated with reverence and respect as it is the flesh of the Earth Mother. The Earth must be loved and nurtured to provide humankind with her bounty. Only natural means must be used for the growing of food and other necessities. Use of chemicals or genetic modified organisms are a desecration of the Earth and sacrilege to Gaia.'

I thought about the blue pills from Nathan I illicitly gave Cadfael. 'Does the use of chemicals apply to people as well as farming?'

'Most definitely. We are part of Mother Nature as much as the earth we stand on, the wind, water, sky and any other creature. We may consume only natural products. To consume chemicals would be a desecration of our Mother Earth. We need to understand the root cause of the desecration of Mother Earth. The root of it is the Patriarchy.'

I nodded, but frowned. 'How has Patriarchy done this?'

'The destruction of nature by humans and the oppression of women by men are both aspects of an oppressive and destructive patriarchy. They have in common political theories and social practices in which both women and natural resources are treated as objects to be owned or controlled by men.'

'How is this resolved?' I asked.

'Just as Gaia, our Earth Mother is supreme in nature, so must women govern society. Our Mother Earth guides us through women, not men. Men must be guided by women who are guided by Gaia. The cherishing of Mother Earth, the avoidance of violence and the spiritual leadership channelled through women will defuse conflict. Feminine guidance will ensure peace and love prevails.'

'But couldn't we just have equality between women and men? Wouldn't that be enough?'

'It is not sufficient for women just to have equality within a society created by men and shaped for the benefit of men. It is necessary for society to be fundamentally reshaped, designed to suit the needs of women with women in the leading role, as we have here in Abballon as a model for the world to follow.'

I let these ideas settle. The prospect of leadership by Hypatia bringing peace and love was comforting. For men, I reflected, such a life would be simpler and more peaceful, no more of the confrontation and hard choices arising from leadership, just the comfort of a loving mother to guide us. If this mother were Hypatia, what was not to like?

Hypatia looked at me with irritation, expectantly for an acknowledgement of her wisdom rather than staring dreamily into space. I took the hint. 'Does it mean men are owned by women here in Abballon, rather than the other way round?'

'No certainly not. Leadership by women is for the

benefit of all. The concept of ownership of other human beings comes from the Patriarchy. Here love is free, so there is to be no ownership or exclusivity of relationship between individuals. Traditional marriage stems from the outdated masculine concept of ownership, setting up the spouses to act like vigilant jealous hounds guarding each other from the attentions of rivals, weighing themselves down with duties and sacrifices. Here love flows freely, as it should.'

'Does that mean anyone may make love with anyone?'

'No. Acts of love flow from Gaia. Gaia channels her love through women. The only legitimate love is what flows from and is initiated by women.'

'Where do men's preferences fit in?'

'Men must be grateful and accept all acts of love from any woman as a flow of love from Gaia. Rejection of a woman would be rejecting Gaia's love.'

I recalled my recent experience with Elsa with horror and remembered Cadfael's reaction in the same circumstances. I wasn't a huge fan of this provision of True Natural Path teaching. 'Are men ever allowed to express a preference?' I persisted.

Hypatia crushed my notion. 'By Natural Path law all intimate activity of any kind must be solely at the initiative of the woman. We do not permit the sexual harassment which happens under the Patriarchy. Men are strictly forbidden from making any kind of suggestion, hint or move of any kind towards sexual activity.'

This arrangement felt one-sided, but not something I could challenge. 'What are the advantages of this?'

'Feminine control is the natural and harmonious order of things under Gaia, preserving the harmony of the community and the happiness of both sexes. Women are happier knowing they are safe from sexual pressure and harassment and can relax confident of being in control over their own bodies and participating only in sexual activity that pleases and satisfies them. Men are happier knowing any sexual activity demanded of them by a woman is desired and pleasing to her, freeing them of guilt and emotional havoc inevitably caused by crass testosterone-driven clumsiness were they to act outside of feminine guidance.'

I was left alone that evening, having brief looks from Elsa and Philomena with hints of carnal intent, but for the time being, they were preoccupied with Cadfael and Huggs respectively, leaving me free to converse with the other singletons, Bradders and Tarquin, but it felt like only a temporary respite.

My recent experiences left me less easy-going and tolerant than I would normally be, so when Bradders made yet another ribald remark about my time with Elsa my patience was exhausted. 'Will you just shut up about me and Elsa! I'm sick of it. Just shut up!'

Bradders was taken aback, having clearly not understood how sensitive this was for me.

'Sorry. I didn't want to upset you. Sorry,' Bradders grovelled.

I calmed down. 'It's alright. It's just it wasn't something I wanted, what happened, I mean. Nor something I want to repeat. I'd rather not be reminded of it. And, for me, it's not a bloody joke.'

'Oh, I see. It didn't go well for you. I'm sorry. I didn't realise. I'll shut up about it.'

'Look, it's okay. I'll get used to it, I suppose. I'm not used to this, if she wants me, I've got to just accept it.'

'You know, when I make jokes and tease and stuff. I'm sorry about doing it. I think it's me being jealous makes me do it, if I'm honest,' Bradders confessed.

'Jealous? I hadn't thought of that.'

'You know, if Elsa wanted me, or Hypatia, Philomena, any of them, I'd be in heaven. But it never happens. Truth is, I'm green with envy for all you guys who get to go with them. I'd change places any day. I wouldn't care what it's like, what they made me do or how they treated me. They could do anything with me.'

'Changing places. Nice idea. But it's not us who decides. It's them.'

'Elsa's got Cadfael back now. She'll probably leave you alone.'

'She might get tired of Cadfael, and his heart certainly isn't in it. When it happens she'll be back for me, I shouldn't wonder,' I lamented.

'You need to catch Philomena's eye. I can tell she fancies you. Once she has you, Elsa wouldn't dare encroach.'

'I see, using Philomena as a shield.'

'Notice Elsa didn't even look at Huggs. She wouldn't dare.'

'But, Philomena! It feels like jumping out of the frying pan and into the fire.'

'Having those choices, feels like a nice problem to have from where I'm sitting.'

Later that night, in my alcove bed at Tarquin's, I mused. Evidently there was some kind of a way out of Abballon behind the temple altar, which Philomena used to come and go. When all was quiet, I ducked and shimmied my way around the half-assembled pre-industrial machinery scattered in Tarquin's living room.

As I picked through the village, slowly and noiselessly, I heard the howls of wolves and hooting of owls from the Wild Side, but in the village all was still.

I edged into the temple, now dark and cold, the feeling inside as crisp and sharp as the rocky cliff face looming above, tiptoed across the floor carefully to avoid tripping over the strewn rugs and cushions, slinking to the edge of the screen behind the altar.

As I encroached on the holy precinct it was as if I opened the door of a furnace. A wave of invisible heat slapped my face. I reeled, toppling over a cushion and landing on my back spread-eagled across the floor. As I did, the now familiar figure representing Gaia rose up. By the eerie light from the apparition I made out a long tunnel hewn of the rock. 'Go back. How dare you enter this sacred place!' the apparition boomed.

As I collected my thoughts the figure faded and once more all was still.

I had hoped my attempted escape had remained between myself and Gaia, but in the morning my ears burned as I overheard a conversation between Hypatia and Elsa. 'Someone tried to get into the sacred space in the temple last night,' Hypatia remarked. Her eyes were on me. It may only have been my guilty conscience, but I felt I was suspected. 'I heard Gaia order somebody back.'

'It might have just been an animal,' said Elsa.

'I don't think so,' said Hypatia. 'Gaia knows the

difference between an animal and a person.'

'People get themselves cast out for that,' said Tarquin, also looking intently in my direction. Oh dear, he knows, I thought.

My life set into a pattern. The work roster, some work of one kind or another with fellow members of the community, instruction and coaching on the beliefs and practices of the True Natural Path, the communal meal in the evening, pleasant conversation with my new friends, usually Bradders and Tarquin and sleeping over at Tarquin's place.

One evening as we were about to settle for the night, sitting at the roughly hewn kitchen table in Tarquin's hobbit house with a mug of herbal tea, peering around the partially assembled foot operated wood turning lathe spread out across the table top, and Tarquin broke the silence. 'You realise it is two weeks today since you arrived with us.'

'Is it really? I'd rather lost track of time.'

'How are you feeling about your life here now?'

In my mind, I debated whether or not to put a favourable gloss on my feelings. On reflection I felt I trusted Tarquin enough to be frank. 'Resigned to my fate,' I lamented.

'Doesn't sound as if you are full of the joys of spring,' he observed with a concerned look on his thin bony face.

'Well, I'm stuck here and there is nothing I can do about it.'

'But you wanted to be here, didn't you? You chose to come, like we all did. You must have believed in what we stand for.'

I hesitated again. 'Look, can I be candid? Will you keep what I say just between us?'

'Yes, of course you can trust me. You mean the world to me, you know. I would never betray you.'

'I came here to find Jenny and bring her back. I was never a great believer in Gaia, female supremacy and all the rest.'

'I guessed that,' said Tarquin, after a pause.

'Now I find Jenny isn't here anymore and I can't get out. So, no, I am not full of the joys of spring.'

Tarquin nodded. 'I see. But you've come to terms with the situation, haven't you?'

'Yes, I suppose. Broken in, you might say. Like a horse comes to terms with being harnessed and ridden. I don't necessarily like it, but I accept it.'

'You've come to understand more about the True Natural Path since you've been here, though. You must see some of the truth and wisdom of it by now.'

'I don't really have a choice, do I? Being here in Abballon I have to accept the tenets of the True Natural Path irrespective of whether I like them or agree with them.'

'There must be good things about being here.'

'Yes, definitely. You're one of them, Tarquin. I really appreciate your friendship.'

Clearly touched, tears welled in Tarquin's eyes. Seeing him so affected I stood to give him a hug. 'I do wish it could be more than just friendship, I really do. I know you'd like it to be. But friendship is what it is. I'm straight you see, and it isn't going to change.'

'I'll settle for friendship.'

'And it's not just you. Bradders, Huggs, Cadfael and

the others, they're all the best of mates. I value them too.'

'So, it's not all bad then.'

'No it's not. The way of life is good too. I'm feeling as energetic and healthy as I have ever been. The hard physical work, good food and lack of stress. It's doing me good.'

'So, it's actually quite good, if you'll only admit it.'

'I'm really not adjusted to being a plaything at the whim of any woman.'

'But other than the one time with Elsa, they've left you alone.'

'Yes, but it's the idea of it.'

'Many men would relish being used like that. They'd jump at the chance.'

'That's them, not me.'

Tarquin looked at me quizzically. 'I don't quite believe you. You've admitted to me yourself you fancy Hypatia, and Philomena for that matter.'

'Well, alright. Hypatia's lovely, I must admit. Woody's a lucky sod. And, yes, the thought of Philomena turns me on.'

'You'll get your wish with Philomena, I reckon.'

'But in the meantime, there is Elsa to contend with.'

'She's well occupied with Cadfael. She won't be troubling you, I shouldn't think.'

'I wish I could be so sure.'

'Does she really not turn you on at all, Elsa I mean?'

I blushed and squirmed in my seat. 'She bloody does, which is what I hate most of all. Since that night I can't get her out of my mind. I get turned on as hell thinking about her and there's nothing I can do about it. I hate myself for it. I wish it didn't happen. If she selected me I

179

know I'd shag her like a machine, over and over, until her ruddy cows came home. I couldn't help it. Yet I don't want it. What's wrong with me? It's doing my head in.'

'Give up women, there's my advice. It's much simpler being gay,' observed Tarquin.

'Doesn't work like that though, my old mate. We are what we are and we can't do anything about it.'

Tarquin shrugged. 'So, are you still feeling dejected about stuff?'

'I'm feeling trapped, I think that's what it is.'

'How so?'

'Being here, it's like being in a Garden of Eden, trapped in a nice comfortable enclosure controlled by a deity.'

'But isn't the whole world, the whole of Mother Earth, like that? The planet is just the minutest fragment of the universe, but all Gaia's creatures are confined there. The confines of Abballon help us understand this truth better.'

Favoured by Philomena

'All good things come from Gaia,' pronounced Philomina. 'Give us the wisdom to follow Her way of the True Natural Path.'

'So mote it be,' acknowledged the Abballon community congregated in the hall.

I joined in the words, not daring to abstain, let alone object, a non-believer among believers, a secret outsider embedded within the Abballon community. Unable to escape, I passively coasted along.

Then one evening I came under Philomena's penetrating gaze. Her attention did not unsettle me because she had looked at me before in that way, lustfully, part rapaciously.

Surely her eyes would pass to Huggs, but they remained on me, looking with intent. She dipped her chin and head jerked to one side, an instruction to approach. Frozen like a deer in headlights, my cheeks glowed, my heart fired like an over-revved motorcycle. She gestured with her hand in reiteration of her summons. I complied, wobbling.

'Brother Simon, we need to talk about your dedication onto the True Natural Path,' Philomena announced as I arrived at her side. 'You may sit with me this evening and we'll discuss it.'

'Yes, Sister Philomena,' I acknowledged, unable to utter anything of substance.

'Sister Hypatia and Brother Cadfael have coached you in our laws and rites, I understand.'

'Yes, they have.'

'So, you are clear now about what we stand for.'

'Yes, I'm clear about it.'

'We must get you dedicated then.'

'Yes, Sister Philomena,' I replied meekly, capitulating my principles to her authority.

'Good. We'll do it tomorrow, when we celebrate Esbat.'

Had it really already been a month since I had participated in the Esbat ceremony with the Mendip Moon Coven on the hill above Glastonbury? It must have been.

I had been fantasising about what carnal delights might be in store, but, partly to my relief and partly disappointment, Philomena had no conjugal requirement of me on this particular evening, leaving me alone with the other singletons.

Huggs was already sitting and chatting with Tarquin and Bradders. Could I face his jealousy, I wondered. Perhaps best to slink off alone back to my billet with Tarquin, but that was no longer an option when Bradders beckoned me.

'Sorry Huggs, I didn't mean to break it up between you and Philomena.'

'Hey, it's cool man. No sweat. If she wants you, you must do what she wants. No need to worry about me,' Huggs assured, pouring me a tankard of ale.

'So, what happened? She didn't take you away with her,' Bradders enquired.

'We just talked about my being dedicated. That's all really.'

'When's it going to happen?'

'Tomorrow, at the Esbat ceremony.'

Later, before we turned in for the night, sitting perched on one of his partially assembled inventions, I sought guidance and solace from Tarquin. 'What exactly does dedication entail?'

'You commit yourself to the True Natural Path, upholding its values and obeying its laws.'

'That's what worries me. Can I be candid? You won't repeat anything I say?'

'Everything you say is just between us. I won't breathe a word of it, ever. I promise. What's on your mind?'

'Right now, if I'm truthful to myself, I wouldn't go through with it because I don't believe it all.'

Tarquin considered. 'But you do believe some of it, don't you?'

'Well, yes, some of it.'

'Well, it's probably okay then. If we are honest with ourselves I don't suppose any of us completely believe in every single detail.'

There is a difference between not believing some small detail and not believing the fundamentals, I thought. 'So, you think it would be okay to be dedicated, but still question one or two things?'

'Yes, but you need to be careful who you voice those questions to. With me it's fine. I'd never condemn or betray you. But with some others, it could get you in trouble. Worst case, it could get you cast out.'

'I'll bear it in mind. But the dedication ceremony, itself, what does it involve?'

'There's an ordeal of purification but you get mushroom juice to help you through it.'

'Purification, what does it mean?'

'Philomena whips you basically. It's supposed to be

183

symbolic, but she gets enthusiastic, so there is pain involved.'

'I see. And the mushroom juice, what's that?'

'You must have heard of magic mushrooms.'

The Esbat ceremony over, it was time for my dedication.

I was skyclad, stood within Nature's circle, laid with sprinkled river washed sand on Abballon's sacred mound.

Philomena's eyes betrayed an appreciation of my naked form as she handed me the ceremonial goblet of magic mushroom essence to open my mind to Nature's spirits.

She blindfolded me, bound my ankles with a cord, my wrists behind my back, securing the cord around my neck.

Hypatia ran the ceremonial bell.

'Before thou art taken onto the Way of the True Natural Path, art thou willing to suffer an ordeal and be purified?' asked Philomena.

'I am and I will.' I responded, as instructed.

'Kneel for thine ordeal.'

My attendants, Woody and Huggs, assisted me while I complied. Philomena took up a plaited leather whip, dense and heavy where she grasped it, tapering to a single thin tail.

'Thou must endure the scourge, thrice, seven and nine,' she announced.

As a ceremonial process there was no need for the purification to be forcefully applied, but Philomena preferred it, laying on with gusto. She swung the whip with a well-practised flick, lightning fast and with brutal force, an angry swish a moment before the sting. Despite being warned by Tarquin, the blazing intensity of pain came as a shock, scorching a line into my flesh as if from a strip of white-hot metal. Involuntarily I yelped and squirmed, willing myself to remain in position. Even in the dim light from the fire those watching would have seen the long red weal slowly darkening, wrapping all around my body, with a small trickle of blood where the tip of whip had cut in.

As Philomena leaned over and spoke quietly into my ear, she oozed sadistic gratification. 'Well done, Brother Simon, you took it well.'

I waited in tense anticipation while she took her time to lay on the next lash. When it came it was equally as painful, but no longer such a shock. When I held my reaction to just a grunt and momentary tensing of my body, Philomena allowed no time for the pain to subside before laying on the third lash to force a squeal out of me.

Hypatia rang the bell three times.

'Well done, Brother Simon. Take a little rest now, before we go on,' said Philomena softly, her face glowing in satisfaction.

'Thrice, now seven,' Philomena announced after a brief interval.

She resumed the whipping with undiminished severity. I gasped and squirmed as I absorbed the pain. With all my willpower I remained in place. At last it was over. The bell rang out seven times.

'Good going, Brother Simon. We'll pause a while. Relax,' Philomena said quietly into my ear.

My chest heaved with panted gasps, my body processing the pain. Philomena stood still grasping the whip watching while my heavy breathing subsided.

'Seven, now nine,' she announced at last.

With gritted teeth and summoning all my willpower,

almost in a trance now from the pain and mushrooms, I absorbed the final nine lashes of my ordeal. In my imagination a sea serpent had risen from the depths and was lashing me with its scaly tail. I twisted and squirmed but somehow I remained kneeling. Then it was over. A nine-fold ringing of the bell.

'Nine. Thou hast bravely passed the test,' Philomena announced.

She leaned over and whispered into my ear: 'Well done. You took it better than most. I'm proud of you.'

She stood again to proceed with the ceremony.

'Art thou ready to swear thou will always be true to the Way of the True Natural Path?'

In a trance, I said nothing.

'Come on Brother Simon, we have been through this. You know what to say.'

'I am and I will.'

'Art thou ready to swear thou will honour all women as the conduits of the love from our divine Gaia, our Earth Mother, and seek no love and no carnal pleasure except what comes freely from a woman flowing through her in the name of Gaia?'

'I am and I will.'

'Art thou ever ready to protect help and defend thy sisters and brothers of the True Natural Path even though it may cost thee thy life?'

'I am and I will.'

My attendants, Woody and Huggs, helped me back to my feet.

Philomena picked up an oil flask and poured a little into her hand. With her oil-soaked hand she marked an inverted triangle on my body, stroking and fondling my skin.

'I consecrate thee with oil.'

Philomena then leant forward and kissed my body at the corners of the triangle.

'I consecrate thee with my lips.'

Woody and Huggs then removed my blindfold and untied my binding cords. They helped me into my initiation robe, a kaftan decorated with a brightly coloured pattern.

'Welcome onto the Way of the True Natural Path, Brother Simon,' Philomena announced.

The congregation cheered and clapped, then all adjourned to the great hall where there was merry-making and the consumption of ale and mead under the protective shield of the building's sturdy timbers.

'I'm glad it's over,' I remarked, as I sat with Tarquin, Bradders and Huggs.

As the others looked at each other knowingly, in my mind for a moment they were jackals waiting in the wings for a lion to make its kill.

'Don't think it's quite over yet,' said Tarquin gently, wistful. I saw him as a wise owl.

I turned to Huggs. 'I expect Philomena will want you later on,' I observed.

'She'll have other plans for tonight,' said Huggs looking meaningfully in my direction. 'She won't be wanting me.' I saw him as a sorrowful bloodhound.

The others looked at me and Huggs in turn before looking away evasively, a pair of chameleons with swivelling eyes.

Philomena approached, a sleek panther. The others backed away discreetly. 'It is time for the next stage of your dedication, Brother Simon,' she purred.

I followed her into the night, a dark abyss, the footpath like stepping stones over water, reaching her hobbit house, appearing as an island in a lake covered in weeds and rushes. Her place was larger and more elegantly appointed than other Abballon homes, with furniture and artefacts of higher quality and free of miscellaneous debris and clutter. She led me to the rear into the bed chamber.

'We must be skyclad, Brother Simon.' She lit a lantern.

Once I had slipped off my robe, she did likewise, indicating I lie down on the bed.

She opened a box to reveal large coloured stones, twinkling in the lamp light like Christmas lights.

'Lay down still on your back while I use the crystals to rebalance your energy vortices.'

She took each stone and laid it on my body to form a line from my head to my crutch.

'Each crystal represents one of the seven chakras. Its energy will replenish and strengthen you for the True Natural Path lying before you.'

The crystals seemed alive, each like a glowing eye watching the scene.

'Now you must kiss the fount of my womanhood, take my juices and absorb their strength.'

She knelt astride my torso and moved herself upward so the lips of her intimate parts came forward onto my mouth.

Before my vision of her was blocked as the curves of her body enveloped my head I had a clear view of the tattoo around her nether regions, a depiction by the famed tattoo artist Suzy Fontanzana of a tropical creeper in flower spreading its bloom laden tendrils from her crutch as if growing out of her pudenda and spreading across her belly and thighs with just a hint of a tendril wrapping itself all the way around to her buttocks. As she rocked her body, grinding her wet pussy into my face, it was as if an aggressive carnivorous plant exploded out from deep within her to consume me.

'Lick me, eat me out, Brother Simon, go for it.'

There was nothing I could say. I could barely even breathe. I did as I was told and licked and licked until her body quivered and she moaned in climax.

'Now, dear Brother Simon, we must have tantric sex. You must remain still and let it happen, slowly so we can be replenished and energised. Just lie still.'

She slid down and lowered herself slowly onto my now very hard male member and held herself there without moving.

In the ensuing hours I was initiated into the panoply of sexual practice the gorgeous Philomena had in her repertoire. In my state of mind I couldn't be sure how much was a weird dream. It was a blur and at some point I lost all recollection.

When I awoke disoriented at dawn's first light, back in my cramped billet at Tarquin's place, I had no memory of getting there, my last recollection a vague impression through a mist of my encounter with the awesome Philomena.

Philomena's intimate juices on my lips and smeared over my face flooded my nostrils, with a carnal scent as rich and fertile as Mother Earth Herself, conjured a spectral presence of her in the room, proud and naked, about to crush my face between her thighs. With the apparition closing in around me, I sensed her wet private parts blocked my nose and mouth, my breathing smothered, the scent of her snuffed out, her phantom existence in retreat so I could breathe again, only for her aroma to draw her back crushing herself against my face.

Cutting the overawing influence of her sexuality were the stinging welts from where Philomena lashed me with her whip, wrapping around my back, torso and stomach like tendrils of poison ivy pulled tight against my body.

I remained held in this terrifying yet sexually stimulating state, unable to rouse myself, able only to grab the gasping breaths Philomena's phantom spirit would occasionally permit.

Tarquin rescued me from my breathless state with a mug of herbal tea, placing his hand on my shoulder. 'My, Brother Simon, you look terrible. Are you okay?'

My voice was croaky and rasping. 'Yes, I think so. My head's still in a spin.'

'It'll be the mushroom essence, making you light headed and prone to seeing things.'

I swigged the tea, clearing my head to some extent, Tarquin's reassuring presence banishing the phantom Philomena so I could breathe again.

Later, by the stream, I hesitated to wash myself despite, or perhaps because, of the disturbing hallucinations arising from Philomena's intimate scent, until another urge pushed through, the desire for freedom, to be a normal person again. Like Samson breaking out of his bonds, I cleaned and rinsed frenetically until all I could taste and smell was fresh air, countryside, damp leaf mould and moss from the woodland.

The evening confirmed me as Philomena's new preference, leaving Huggs to join the singletons Tarquin and Bradders at the far end of the table.

Captured by her, I was racked by guilt at my disloyalty to Jenny, yet helpless as an insect in a spider's web, held by Philomena's savage beauty, her overpowering sexuality and raw authority, a combination of imperial Earthly power and her embodiment of Gaia's divine beneficence.

During the meal Philomena showed me no more than a passing interest, a companion she took for granted while conversing with those surrounding her. I had anticipated her requiring me again after in her quarters, but instead I was casually dismissed with a flick of her fingers.

I should have been relieved, permitted to keep myself for Jenny, yet it was an anticlimax leaving me as forlorn as a child's toy tossed out of a pram on a city pavement.

Bradders, Tarquin and Huggs chatted happily at the end of the table as they quaffed tankards of ale. Dejected, I considered slinking away, but Bradders waved me over.

My toes curled in embarrassment as I, his usurper, took a seat next to Huggs. It was Huggs who poured me out a tankard of ale.

'She didn't want you tonight then,' Bradders observed. 'No.'

'What a shame. I bet you're disappointed, aren't you?' she continued tactlessly.

'No big deal,' said Huggs. 'She doesn't always fancy it. It's cool.'

I was thankful for Huggs's intervention, not only heading off Bradders's uncomfortable thread of conversation but providing an opportunity to clear the air between us. 'Look Huggs mate, I'm sorry about what's happened, I mean with me and Philomena. I didn't want to get between you. I didn't do anything to encourage her. Honest.'

Huggs put his arm around my shoulders. 'Don't beat yourself up about it,' he assured me. 'She does what she wants. She never keeps one guy for long, always ready to move on to the next one. It's the way it is. Nothing you could do about it. I'm cool with it.' He picked up his tankard and bumped it up against mine. 'Here, drink your ale.'

I felt a breath of relief and the welcoming warmth of comradeship.

A new pattern established itself in my life. Each evening Philomena required my presence next to her at the dinner table. During the meal she would acknowledge me there as her consort, yet show no signs of intimacy, conversing with others. At the end of the meal I wondered whether she would require me later, only to be dismissed back into the company of the singletons.

Throughout day and night, body and soul, I yearned for her, mesmerised by her charms. On the fifth evening over dinner I felt compelled to ask: 'Do you have plans for me later on?'

Philomena looked back at me with annoyance. 'If I did, I would let you know.'

'You haven't needed me for these last few days.'

'What of it?'

'I hoped you might sometime.'

Her eyes blazed. 'Don't ever talk to me or any other woman like that. Got it?'

I kept quiet for the remainder of the meal, at which

time, as usual Philomena waved her fingers at me. 'You may go.'

With my frustration at breaking point, instead of obediently making myself scarce, I lunged forward to put my arms around her in an attempt to kiss her. She roughly broke away, drew herself up in a regal stance and addressed me sharply. 'How dare you? Don't ever do it again! I am the Ethereal Guide. You will show me proper respect. You have had the taste of my whip already. You will get it again tenfold if you try it on again. Clear?'

Philomena's outraged tones had attracted the attention of the gathered community, who gazed shocked and fascinated.

'Yes, Sister Philomena. I'm sorry. I won't do it again,' I stammered.

'You had better not.'

I looked at her pleadingly. 'But, Sister Philomena, after our time together, I thought we might, well, you know...'

Philomena looked at me through narrowed eyes, deciding whether to tear me off another strip or take pity on me. She decided on the latter. Leaned over close she spoke softly. 'That was special, for your dedication, to make your union with Gaia, our Earth Mother. It has nothing to do with us.'

'Oh, I see. I'm sorry for the misunderstanding.'

She smiled. 'Don't worry. Gaia may yet have need of you now and again. We'll see how it goes. But it will be when She requires it. You must wait for Her call. Do you understand?'

'Yes, Sister Philomena, I understand.'

Philomena departed from the hall, outwardly oblivious, but I stood nervously, blushing crimson as if heated by the focussed stares of a hundred onlookers. Sheepishly I looked over for support from my singleton buddies. Bradders had a knowing look tinged with enjoyment. Tarquin's face looked pained, embarrassed and concerned for me. From Huggs I sensed a genuine warmth and empathy combined with a laid back reassurance. Gratefully I joined them, out of the glaring spotlight of attention.

'My, you were brave,' Bradders remarked barely stifling her urge to chortle.

'Not brave. Very unwise. People have been cast out for less,' said Tarquin with deep concern.

'Chill man, she's not going to cast you out,' Huggs reassured. 'No rush man. Let her decide when she wants you. Leave it to her. You don't need to do anything.'

'You've really got the hots for her, haven't you?' observed Bradders. 'Couldn't help yourself, could you? Can't say I blame you. She's flipping gorgeous.'

'Just leave him alone,' said Tarquin, putting his arm around my shoulder protectively.

I stared at the table in front of me, sensing wonder, outrage and curiosity in the fleeting glances still coming in my direction from around the room. 'Thanks guys. I really made a fool of myself, didn't I?'

'Well, actually you did,' agreed Tarquin. 'It was really dangerous, what you did then. Better not do it again.'

The following evening I sensed the staring eyes as Philomena selected me to accompany her for the evening meal. There was a feeling of anticlimax as if the folk were expecting, perhaps even hoping for some drama that did not materialise.

'Brother Simon, I hope I can trust you to behave yourself today,' Philomena said softly once we were seated.

'Yes, Sister Philomena,' I responded meekly.

'I am pleased to hear it. I am going to require your presence tonight, Brother Simon.'

My pulse quickened. At last, an end to my frustration. I shivered. 'Yes, Sister Philomena.'

'I must teach you self-control, though, mustn't I? We can't have more outbursts like we had yesterday, can we?'

'No, Sister Philomena.' I swallowed with a soft gulp and my fists clenched slightly.

The myriad eyes were on us again at the end of the meal as Philomena casually indicated for me to follow her. I walked out a few steps behind her, my eyes looking down to avoid the surrounding gaze.

'I'll have you skyclad, Brother Simon,' Philomena announced as we entered her bed chamber.

I obediently slipped out of my clothes and laid them into a neat heap to one side of the room. I stood slightly sideways to disguise my male member, swelling involuntarily.

'Now then, Brother Simon, we have some unfinished business, don't we?'

I stood, still at an awkward angle. My face would have betrayed my confusion and worry. 'Unfinished business, I don't understand.'

'The business of you making a lunge at me yesterday evening.'

'Oh, I see.'

'You attempted to sully Gaia's love with your toxic masculinity.'

I let the words sink in, trying to make sense of them.

Philomena's eyes bore into me.

'Yes, Sister Philomena, I suppose I did.'

'Yes, indeed you did, and for that you must be purified.'

Any uncertainty of what she meant was dispelled when she opened a rustic cupboard, which, from its style, would have been made for her by Tarquin, taking out the same plaited leather whip she had lashed me with for my dedication ceremony.

'You need to be taught self-control and respect. We'll start your learning now with twenty lashes. It's what you need, isn't it?'

I swallowed hard. My body was still decorated with and stinging from the livid stripes from my dedication whipping. I shook, but I had disgraced myself and knew I must take the consequences, apprehensive, yet grateful to her for the purification. 'Yes, Sister Philomena, thank you.'

'On your knees and hands on your head,' Philomena ordered with a harsh edge.

I obeyed. Philomena picked up her whip, flexed it for a few moments and then lashed it hard onto my already well bruised flesh. I winced but held my position. Philomena's whip had quickly erased one source of embarrassment laid bare by my nakedness as my erection collapsed, all arousal eclipsed by the pain.

Nineteen more times was the whip laid on. Each time I gasped or squeaked and my body jerked, but I remained in my place.

Philomena was pleased. 'Well done, Brother Simon. You took it well.'

'Thank you, Sister Philomena.'

'Real progress after yesterday's outrage. You have learned restraint and obedience.'

I was hurting, but my gratitude was genuine. I was enjoying being the centre of the awesome Philomena's undivided attention. The pain was worth it.

'Lay yourself on your back, here on the floor,' she ordered.

I complied without hesitation, now trained to obey without thought.

'You must kiss the fount of my womanhood, take my juices and absorb their strength.'

She stood astride me, lowering herself onto her knees, sliding forward so her already wet vulva met my lips. I wondered if the sadistic pleasure from whipping someone was enough on its own to turn her on, or whether it depended on who she was whipping.

Philomena's overpowering feminine scent filled my nostrils and the slippery wetness from her intimate parts smeared over my mouth and chin as she rocked against me, spreading her juices over my face. 'Lick me, Brother Simon, go on, lick out the Goddess's love juices and take in Her divine strength.'

I licked as ordered. She adjusted to get herself into a better position for my tongue. 'Not there, higher, reach up a bit, that's better, a bit deeper, do it quicker.'

I followed her instructions as best I could, keeping at my task, sucking in breaths of air as best I could, her wet privates squashing against my nostrils, ooze dribbling and smearing my face, pace and urgency building as she made little moans and cries. I felt pumping contractions from her pussy and a more copious flow gushed over my face.

As Philomena's climax subsided she let her crutch slip away from my face and slid off me to one side. Observing my rampant erection, she leaned forward and patted me on the cheek. 'No, Brother Simon, there will be no release for you today. You must first learn self-control.

In the morning I intentionally did not wash my face, wanting to keep those delicious fragrant juices there as long as possible. After working for the day with Woody, Huggs and Bradders, I washed my hands in the stream, splashing water over my arms and chest, still refraining from washing. I noticed Bradders looking at me with a wry smile.

Woody and Huggs went on their way leaving me and Bradders to dry ourselves in the last of the afternoon sunshine.

'You've still got grime on your face,' remarked Bradders.

'Oh, have I?' I said, blushing slightly.

'Not all you've got on your face, is it? Grime, I mean. There's something else too, isn't there?'

'What do you mean?'

'You know what I mean. Philomena had her way with you last night, didn't she?'

'Actually, yes. How did you know?'

'I can smell her on you, you lucky bastard, and you want to hang on to her scent, don't you? That's why you didn't wash your face, isn't it?'

I cringed. 'You really are a tactless cow, Bradders,' I replied irritably.

'Sorry, mate. I know I am. It's only because I am jealous as hell.'

'What? You mean you would have liked to have been in my place last night?'

'Too right I would.'

'I got whipped too, you know. Would you have wanted the whipping too?'

Bradders considered. 'Certainly. I'd gladly take it for her.'

It was my turn to reflect. 'Yes, I was happy to take it too. It didn't half hurt though.'

'Well worth it, I'd say,' said Bradders yearningly.

For a minute or so nothing was said, until Bradders broke the silence.

'Go on, tell me what happened.'

'Bloody cheek. Go to hell. It's private.'

'Don't be like that. Come on, what happened?'

'Well, she was in my face, if you get my meaning.'

'I can imagine,' said Bradders dreamily, as if visualising the scene, complete with a rich heady fug of sexy scent, moans of carnal rapture and squelchy sound effects. She sighed.

'You're getting off on this, aren't you? You pervert,' I accused her, wrinkling my nose.

'She wouldn't even look at me, unfortunately. She isn't that way inclined, more's the pity. All I might get from her is a whipping, if I'm lucky. I'm consumed with jealousy.'

'You were right when you said she had her way with me. It is only on her terms. Nothing for me except getting whipped and getting her off.'

'I'd gladly settle for that. I still think you're a lucky bastard,' said Bradders wistfully.

'But what she did was hugely frustrating, enticing me to get incredibly intimate with her, leading me on, and then just leaving me hanging there in limbo.'

'It fits her character. It's a power trip. Keeping you helpless under her spell, yearning for her, unfulfilled, suffering at her behest. She likes seeing people suffer, hence her thing about whipping. The whipping is supposed to be symbolic, but not with her, she does it to satisfy her sadistic desire.'

'But not everybody can take the frustration. Sooner or later someone will lose control and try to force themselves on her after she has led them on the way she does.'

Ivy

'We have a new arrival, a sister.'

It was Tarquin calling across the field where I was busy hoeing the rows of cabbages alongside Bradders and Huggs. Being towards the end of the afternoon we were happy to finish a little earlier than usual.

She was asleep, laid out over the same moss-covered flat rock in front of Gaia's temple set into the steep rocky cliff where I had arrived myself a few weeks before.

I recognised the community's new member right away as Ivy Langport from the Mendip Moon Coven, a succulent peach of a young woman, the one with the intimidating boyfriend, Harry Mallet. She was now clad in the community's style of coarse peasant attire with its naïve decoration, not something she would have been wearing when she left from Glastonbury.

'Did anybody see her arrive?' I enquired.

People shook their heads.

'Does anyone get to see when new people arrive?' I asked Tarquin.

'No, I don't think so,' replied Tarquin. 'They kind of just appear. Never heard of anyone seeing it happen.'

'Always like this?'

'Yes, always the same, really.'

'What, you mean, laid out asleep on this stone as if from nowhere?'

'Yes, just like this.'

Ivy stirred. She tipped over slightly on her side. Her eyes blinked. People noticed, touching their neighbours to alert them. The hubbub subsided.

Bradders, her eyes gleaming, had positioned herself close to Ivy, but it was Hypatia coming to the fore to welcome the new arrival.

Hypatia and Elsa took Ivy under their wing and escorted her back to the community's hub, the great hall. Bradders hovered a few steps away, her face glowing with lust, but not daring to challenge Hypatia's lead by getting closer. Ivy nodded an acknowledgement as I briefly caught her eye from the outskirts of the throng.

For the evening meal Ivy was seated among the women and their selected consorts towards the head of the long table. Seated beside Philomena I was nearby, as an escorted man I was only permitted to speak when spoken to, so unable to open any dialogue with Ivy, limiting myself to smiling in her direction a couple of times.

'I won't be needing you tonight,' Hypatia told Woody.

He slipped back to the outskirts of the throng, looked around sidelong before surreptitiously slipping out of the hall. I could understand him wishing to avoid the inevitable indignity of remarks made by Bradders and others had he remained among the singletons.

It was Ivy who Hypatia took out to stay over at her place.

Huggs and Ivy chatted as I arrived for the morning muster parade, relaxed and enjoying each other's company. Bradders came in soon after, cutting across their conversation.

'Hello Sister Ivy, welcome to Abballon,' she said loudly, cutting Huggs off mid-sentence.

'Hello,' acknowledged Ivy.

'I'm Sister Brenda, but they call be Bradders.'

'Hello, Bradders.'

'What made you come over to Abballon?'

'Dunno, really. Lots of things.'

'What sort of things?'

'Men pushing me around, for one.'

'You don't have to worry about that here.'

Huggs had been hovering, but at this point he shrugged and wandered off.

'That was rude of her,' I observed. 'Bradders, I mean.'

'It's cool,' said Huggs. 'I can talk to Ivy another time.'

'But you were having a nice conversation with her, before Bradders butted in.'

'They're enjoying talking to each other now. It's cool.'

I did not get to overhear exactly what passed between Bradders and Ivy, but Bradders's move had clearly met with success because Ivy selected her to accompany her for the evening meal, during which they continued to talk animatedly.

At the end of the meal Ivy and Bradders lingered chatting for a short while, but Hypatia was nearby looking impatient. I sensed some hesitation on Ivy's part before she broke away to accompany Hypatia back to her place.

Woody had now been spurned by Hypatia two nights in a row. He looked on glowering with his jaw set in an angry frown. His face darkened all the more as he observed his rival Cadfael escorted out by Elsa. He hesitated between retreating to avoid embarrassment and remaining to brazen out any loss of face with the singletons. He remained. I joined them too; on this occasion Philomena did not require my presence.

Presumably on the principle attack is best defence, Woody was aggressive from the outset. He rounded on me. 'Philomena not want you tonight then? Not surprising after your behaviour with her. You should've been cast out after what you did.'

'Yes, well. She dealt with it in her own way. It's behind us now.'

'Leave him alone. It's all dealt with. And it's none of your business anyway,' said Tarquin, his thin face set in defiance.

'Cool it, man. It's no big deal. Philomena has to be in the mood. I should know,' said Huggs in support.

'As for you, I saw you this morning chatting up the new girl, Ivy. Bloody cradle-snatcher. Disgusting,' said Woody turning on Huggs.

'What's the problem? She's new. We should be getting to know her, welcoming her.' said Huggs. Unusually for him he was showing his irritation.

'Hypatia not need you tonight then?' said Bradders, looking straight at Woody.

'No. She had to look after Ivy.'

'Prefers Ivy, then, I guess,' said Bradders.

'I know who prefers Ivy. Jealous of Hypatia, aren't you?' replied Woody.

Tarquin tugged my elbow. 'Come on, Brother Simon. Let's go home. We don't need this.'

'Bloody dykes and queers, the lot of you,' jeered Woody, as his companions melted away.

'Building work is behind schedule,' said Woody as we gathered for the morning work. 'I'll need fourteen guys.'

'But you want practically everybody we have,' Cadfael said.

'What of it?'

Over the preceding weeks Woody was increasingly challenging and confrontational about allocating work tasks. Until this point, for the sake of a quiet life, Cadfael had smoothed things over by largely acquiescing to Woody's demands, but this time Woody was pushing things to a confrontation.

'Dealing with the crops is more important, otherwise we don't eat,' replied Cadfael.

'I need to get the work done.' Woody raised his voice, which caused others to stare.

'I can spare you four people. You'll have to make do with them.'

'Who says you get to decide?'

'I'm the Moderator, that's why.'

'Not for much longer, I'd say, now Hypatia prefers me.'

The commotion drew the attention of all around, including Elsa and Hypatia. I sensed a lust in the way Elsa looked at Woody, as if she perceived his aggression and power from the new alpha male destined to usurp Cadfael.

Hypatia's perception was different. 'Don't you get above yourself, you nasty little man,' she shouted at Woody. 'You'll do as Brother Cadfael tells you.'

Hypatia further demonstrated her displeasure when she cut Woody dead at the evening meal, leaving him to find his place among the singletons who he had rudely alienated.

Wary of her since our earlier carnal encounter, I tended to keep Elsa under observation. Until now she had been wearing Cadfael like a badge, using his seniority among the men to enhance her status, but this was changing. In the evening, although she had Cadfael beside her, her focus was on Woody, the enticing rogue male. At the end of the meal she did not require Cadfael's presence, leaving him free to join the singletons, among whom there was a split, with the majority clustering around Cadfael and a sizeable minority paying court to Woody.

The following evening there was a further change in allegiances as Elsa selected Woody as her consort, leaving Cadfael at a loose end with the singletons.

Bashful Ivy and forthright Bradders were now clearly established as partners, with Ivy adjourning to spend the night at Bradders's place.

After the meal I struck up conversation with Cadfael. 'How do you feel? About Elsa, I mean.'

Cadfael looked uncomfortable.

'Don't worry, forget I spoke. None of my business,' I assured him.

'No, it's alright. I'm bloody relieved actually.'

'I had a night with her. I expect you remember.'

'Yes, I recall. I think you got off lightly, speaking as the guy who was stuck with her for weeks.'

'You didn't like it then?' I enquired.

'Well, it's an odd thing. I've never had more sex. And it wasn't just any sex. It was the most energetic mind-blowing sex you could imagine. Yet all the time I couldn't help feeling, I don't want this. It was just too crude and animalistic. There was something disgusting about it. Do you know what I mean? Am I talking sense?'

'Yes, perfect sense. I felt exactly the same. The sex took me over, but not in a nice way.'

Cadfael smiled. 'Woody's welcome to her.'

'I reckon she'll suit him, actually. He has a crude aggressive way that fits her style.'

'Reckon you're right,' Cadfael paused, gulping ale from his tankard. 'You must have noticed things haven't been good between us recently. Woody and me, I mean.'

'Yes, I think everyone has noticed by now.'

'Well, until now Woody was my sort of deputy, backing me up and so on, but I don't think it can go on.'

'Oh, I see. No, I don't suppose it'll work anymore.'

'What do you think about you stepping up and helping me out, organising things?'

I looked at Cadfael with surprise. 'What, you mean me?'

'Yes.'

Over the coming days a new pattern established itself.

Ivy and Bradders were very much in love, spending every available moment together.

Hypatia and Cadfael were back together, which made Cadfael happy.

I remained Philomena's chosen consort. Sometimes she required my presence overnight, sometimes not. Anything taking place between us was strictly on her terms and for her gratification, but I didn't mind. It was a rare privilege to be chosen to serve a demi-goddess and I was happy to have her on any terms. Pushed to the deepest recesses of my mind was any guilt about not saving myself for Jenny.

One evening, a week after Ivy's arrival, instead of turning in for the night right away Bradders and Ivy chose to remain in the hall with the singletons for a drink and chat. I was present, Philomena having not required me.

'What made you take the plunge and move to Abballon?' I asked Ivy.

'It was your fearless example for one thing. I might not have had the nerve otherwise.'

I felt a surge of guilt.

'You were in *The Daily Trumpet* too.'

'Really? What did it say?'

'How you disappeared while investigating strange happenings in Glastonbury. How terrible the police were in their investigation of missing persons.'

I was heartened to hear my ruthless boss, Rebekah Nemmberg, had not abandoned me.

'It can't just have been my courageous example bringing you here. There must have been something else,' I insisted, to minimise my culpability as the author of Ivy's fate.

'I wanted a fresh start and to live a better life.'

'Ever been worried about those you left behind?' I was thinking of Harry Mallet.

'They'll get over it,' she said, through gritted teeth.

'I was the newbie around here until you arrived. Feels strange becoming an old hand.'

'What brought you here?' Ivy enquired.

I pondered, aware of the dangers of being too frank. 'Well, like you, fresh start and better life. But I was also hoping to find someone I was close to. I expect you remember Jenny. She's not here though, at least not anymore.'

Ivy looked me up and down as if assessing my character. 'Sorry you didn't find her.'

'Yes, it has been a disappointment.' I looked back at her, wondering if I should probe more. 'You had a bloke you were close with, if I recall. Harry, wasn't it?'

Ivy frowned in disgust. Bradders intervened. 'Sensitive subject. Better not go there.'

'Sorry, didn't want to open any old wounds or anything. I'll shut up.'

The following day Bradders and I lingered by the stream freshening ourselves after work. I picked up on the previous evening's conversation with Ivy. 'I obviously touched a nerve with Ivy yesterday evening.'

'You did. Her ex, Harry is not her favourite person just now.'

'Oh, I see. What did he do to upset her?'

'Tried to force himself on her for one thing.'

'Ah. Sorry to hear that.'

'Silly beggar. She doted on him. He could have done anything he liked with her. All he had to do was be nice and gentle about it. He spoiled his chances and upset Ivy being a coarse, ugly brute.'

'I don't know him well but from the little I saw of him I can't imagine him being much good at the lovey-dovey coochycoo routine.'

'As a result of what he did she is now here and has gone off men entirely. Prefers to make out with women, which has worked out well for me.'

'That's great, Bradders. I hope you both will be really happy.'

Bradders nodded and smiled. 'How are things with you and Philomena?'

'Well, okay, I suppose.'

'You don't sound ecstatic about it.'

'I am basically just her slave and plaything, to be toyed

with at her whim.'

'You want more than that?'

'Not necessarily. Strange thing is, I feel honoured to be her plaything. If it's all she wants from me, then as far as I am concerned, it's enough. I'll settle for that.'

'Until a week ago I would have been jealous. I'd have settled for what you've got from her or even less. I'd have been content to just have her whip me now and again.'

'But you're not jealous anymore.'

'No, not since Ivy.'

I splashed my feet in the flowing water. 'There is one thing nagging at me about being with Philomena.'

'What's that?'

'When I'm with her, enjoying her awesomeness, I still feel a twinge of guilt about Jenny.'

'I can understand how you yearn after Jenny.'

'How come?'

'It's my turn to make you jealous now.'

'Go on.'

'When she was here, before she went, I fancied the hell out of her.'

I looked at Bradders hard, my imagination spinning. 'Did anything come of it?'

'Not really. Not for lack of trying on my part. It might have, if she'd been here longer.'

While I saw no signs of quarrelling or animosity between Ivy and Bradders, I sensed the relationship was running its course.

Rather than withdrawing from the evening meal at the first opportunity they were lingering in the hall in the company of the singletons.

There was a preponderance of conversation between Ivy and Huggs, nothing deep, just chat for its own sake, smiles, exchanged glances, demonstrating closeness. From the third occasion Ivy made a point of sitting next to Huggs. I could see Bradders was unhappy about this attachment, but she was either powerless or chose not to fight it.

During the working days Bradders became increasingly subdued and a tension developed between her and Huggs, although neither expressed overt animosity.

One evening Bradders withdrew into the shadows, out of character for someone who was habitually loud and brash. I could see she had been crying, not something I had seen before. I considered asking her about it, but sensing she had no wish to engage with people, left her be.

Later Bradders resumed her familiar place among the singletons when Ivy selected Huggs to join her for the meal, but she was not the brash cocky Bradders we knew. Along with others of her friends, I offered my sympathy for her estrangement with Ivy.

Bradders remained subdued and silent during the following working day, carrying out her tasks mechanically without enthusiasm, like a zombie. As we finished for the day, refreshing themselves by the stream, I took matters in hand.

'Bradders, you need to talk to someone about what happened with Ivy. You can't keep it to yourself,' I advised gently.

Bradders shook her head. 'There isn't anything to say.'

'Yes, there is. And you're going to say it to me. No

arguments.'

'What is there to say?'

'Well, let me guess, you had really hoped you had something good going with Ivy and now you're devastated it hasn't worked out. Am I right so far?'

'Yes, about right.'

'It obviously felt right for you, both of you, to begin with, I mean,' I prompted.

'Yes, I think she's lovely. I fell for her right away.'

'I noticed!'

'Was it so obvious?'

'Yes. But what about Ivy? What did she like about it?'

'That boyfriend of hers. Harry. He was a brute. She swore after what he did she would never go with any man again. And then, well, she could see I really fancied her and she liked me, so it went from there.'

'What happened to change things?'

'She said Huggs is different and she found out she isn't really a lesbian. She likes me as a friend but she needs a man to, you know, turn her on and stuff.'

'Oh, I see. I thought it must be something of the sort.'

'She said she wanted to love me. She said when she held me she would shut her eyes and think of me being a man and it would be okay but then when she opened her eyes and saw it was me it wouldn't be the same.'

'Hmm. Yes, I can see why it might not have felt right for her.'

'But might it just be it's men she's used to. She could come to love me, couldn't she?'

'I couldn't say. Only Ivy herself could tell you.'

'She did say to me she'd never let a man touch her ever again. She wouldn't go back on it, would she? She told me now she had a lovely strong woman like me, she'd never need a man. She could come round then, don't you think?'

I feared Bradders's hopes could not be fulfilled. Not wanting to depress her further, I changed the subject. 'She's right about Huggs being different. Not at all like Harry.'

'You knew Harry then?'

'Not well, but we had a couple of drinks together.'

'So, what do you think of him?'

'Well, he has an intimidating manner. There is aggression there, certainly. And from what I saw, I'd say he was controlling, wanting things his way.'

'So, a bad bloke then?'

'I wouldn't go that far. He probably means well. If I was in a scrap I wouldn't mind having him by my side. There are some women who probably like blokes like him.'

'So, is Huggs right for Ivy, do you think?'

'I couldn't say for sure, but there is a good chance he is, I'd say.'

'Why do you think that?'

'Well, he is the opposite of Harry. He's so calm and chilled out. He'd never pressurise Ivy into anything. She could feel relaxed with him, yet he's no wimp. He's strong and tough. I think she'd feel protected by him, which seems to be what women want from a guy, but, hey, what do I know?'

Bradders looked deflated. 'So, no hope for me then, as far as Ivy is concerned?'

'I would say, probably not. Sorry to be the bearer of bad news.'

Tears welled in Bradders's eyes. I reached over and put my arms around her. 'I'm sorry it worked out this way.'

'Story of my life.'

'How do you mean?'

'Women come here, disillusioned with men. For a while they feel safer with another woman, not threatened, feeling they have more in common. Then after a few weeks they rediscover they're straight and it's all over.'

Frankie

Summer bloomed in its fullest glory, leaves shiny and glowing green in the hot bright sunlight under a dazzling blue sky and puffy white clouds, when Frankie arrived in Abballon.

'It's Frankie,' I said to Tarquin as we came across him laying across the mossy rock platform reserved for new arrivals.

'You know him then,' said Tarquin.

'Yes, but I don't know him well. Met him shortly before I came over myself.'

'What do you think?'

'I think he'll need our support.'

Frankie stirred slightly and blinked.

'Hello,' said Tarquin. 'How are you feeling?'

'Don't really know,' said Frankie, trying to focus his eyes on us. 'Alright, I suppose.'

'I'm Brother Tarquin.'

'Hello Frankie, you know me, I'm Simon.'

Initially groggy, Frankie was properly awake within a minute, whereupon Tarquin and I helped him to his feet and walked him to the hall. Frankie was diffident and unforthcoming as we did the rounds of introductions. I sensed a familiar predatory look in Philomena's eyes as we presented him to her.

Later, while I was beside her at the head of the table for the evening meal, I had déjà vu, with myself as Huggs had been, fickle Philomena weighing Frankie, for the time being among the singletons at the far end. I was no more jealous than Huggs was of me, but concerned for the innocently virginal Frankie, soon to be subject to Gaia only knew what sexual trauma from the predatory Philomena.

I was concerned for myself too. Philomena had me in her thrall. More than Gaia's priestess, a goddess in her own right, being parted from her would be a wrenching loss, like having a limb torn off. Even were I to content myself worshipping her from afar, being under her protection kept others at bay, in particular Elsa.

Dismissed by Philomena as usual at the end of the meal I convened with the singletons where Frankie sat shyly hugging himself as Tarquin held forth about the construction of drainage ditches.

'Where is Frankie going to stay?' I asked, breaking into Tarquin's detailed explanation about the effectiveness of reed beds for breaking down bodily wastes.

'He can stay over with us,' said Tarquin.

'Yes, of course. It'll be a squeeze, but we'll manage.'

Frankie flipped his gaze between us, slightly panicking. He nodded his head.

'Well, it's settled then,' I said. 'You're coming back with us.'

It was indeed a squeeze, with Frankie and I sharing the same cramped alcove I had to myself since my arrival in Abballon. The congestion at Tarquin's place was not helped by the assorted paraphernalia strewn about, technical contrivances at various stages of development, pieces of wood and metal piled up in case they came in handy.

Tarquin was particularly attentive to Frankie's needs, if not exactly flirting, at the least seizing every opportunity to be as close and personal as he could. It had already been tight when there was two of us, but now it became a challenge. Tarquin shoved bits and pieces aside on his bench to make space for Frankie to squeeze in tightly next to him.

'Any news from outside?' I enquired.

'Don't know,' said Frankie. 'What sort of news?'

'About me and Ivy, for example. Anybody saying anything about us?'

'Yes, you've both been in the paper.'

'Which paper?'

'*The Daily Trumpet*. Mr and Mrs Langport were in there as well, talking about their Ivy going missing.'

'What did they say?'

'Not so much them, more about the police.'

'What about the police?'

'Indolent and incompetent was what they said.'

I smiled, imaging my boss Rebekah laying it on thick in her editorial. 'Anything else?'

'The police did a raid on the theme park, Knights of Camelot. Searched around in the grotto they've got there.'

'What did they find?'

'Nothing. Marquess wasn't happy though.'

'Oh, what did he do?'

'Got an injunction against them.'

'Injunction against what?'

'Marquess's brief said it was a vexatious raid. They can't go into anywhere on the Mendip estate.'

Frankie suffered the next day when he was assigned to work alongside me and Bradders on Woody's construction work, quickly tiring with strained muscles and joints.

'What's the matter with you?' Woody grumbled.

'Sorry, I'm tired.'

'If everyone else can do it, so can you.'

Before the day was out Frankie's hands were bloody and his exposed skin crimson with sunburn. Bradders and I fell behind with our work as we took the load off him.

Woody's disgruntled expression was darker than ever. 'What's the matter with you lot. The work today has been shocking. Is it some sort of go slow or working to rule, or what?'

The time had come for me to get a place of my own, so I tackled Cadfael about it.

'As you know I have been staying with Brother Tarquin for some time. Now our new Brother Frankie has moved in with us, which is making it a little cramped.'

'I'm sure we could find another billet for Frankie. I'll ask around.'

It wasn't quite the answer I was after. Apart from my own preference to get away, it wouldn't have suited Tarquin either because he liked having Frankie around.

'Actually I was rather hoping I might be able to move out into a place of my own.'

It was Cadfael's turn to look uncomfortable. 'You would have to talk to Woody about it. He takes care of allocating accommodation.'

Cadfael is the Moderator, so Woody should do what he's told, I thought, but, understanding the tension between them, I resisted the temptation to voice this opinion.

I took my leave from Cadfael and looked for Woody, spotting him at the other end of the hall in an altercation with Elsa. I didn't catch what was being said, but I gathered in her view he was a miserable git and she didn't want anything more to do with him.

Woody was in a foul mood, but this was nothing unusual. It would have taken a month of Esbats before catching Woody in a good mood, so after allowing a moment for the unpleasantness to subside I girded my loins to raise the matter with him.

'Brother Woody, I was wondering if I could talk to you about accommodation.'

'What about it?'

'Well, it's for me actually. It's a bit cramped at Brother Tarquin's with Brother Frankie there now as well.'

'If you want to billet with someone else you'll have to talk to Brother Cadfael.'

'It wasn't exactly what I meant. I'm wondering if there was a chance of getting a place of my own, one of the new houses we're putting up now perhaps.'

'Nothing doing. There're all allocated.'

'Well, perhaps I could put my name down for one of the next ones to be built.'

'What next ones? Cadfael doesn't even allocate the people I need to finish the current lot, let alone build any more.'

'Perhaps he will once the growing and harvesting season is over.'

'Even if we did build more, what makes you think you deserve one? You didn't exactly bust a gut today on the building work, you, Bradders and that useless wimp Frankie.'

Realising I was going to get no joy from Woody, I wandered to join Tarquin and Frankie.

'I raised the subject of accommodation with Cadfael and Woody.'

'Oh, what's happening?' asked Tarquin, looking concerned.

I had anticipated the subject might be sensitive.

'I was vaguely enquiring if I might get one of the new homes we're building.'

'Aren't you happy with me?' asked Tarquin, looking hurt.

'Yes, of course I am, but it's more than a bit cramped with Frankie as well. It's okay for now, but we need to be thinking ahead.'

'Look, if I'm in the way, there must be somewhere else I could stay,' offered Frankie.

'No,' said Tarquin and I in unison.

'You're more than welcome with us,' I said, trying to repair the damage.

'So, was anything decided?' Tarquin asked anxiously.

'I didn't get anywhere. Cadfael referred me to Woody and he turned me down flat.'

'But you'll still be looking to move out though?'

'No, unless you want to throw me out.'

'I'd never throw you out.'

I put my arms around both Frankie's and Tarquin's shoulders. 'Good, so we'll all stick together then. Team. Right?'

'Yes, team,' said Tarquin with relief.

It was at this point Elsa interrupted the conversation. She eyed Frankie. 'So, you've been keeping this new young man away from me, have you?'

'Oh, hello Sister Elsa,' said Tarquin through gritted teeth.

For the moment I was too stunned by the intrusion to say anything. Elsa sidled close to Frankie, eyeing and circling around him as if he was one of her goats.

'Bit skinny aren't you,' she observed. 'Bit of fresh air, exercise and good food. We'll soon get some flesh on those bones.'

She reached down and slapped her hand on Frankie's thigh. 'Wonder what else you're packing down there,' she said, running her hand up into Frankie's crutch.

Frankie leapt back in shock. Both Tarquin and I looked on in horror. Frankie was little more than a child and the idea of him being ravaged by this rapacious monster was repugnant.

I stepped in quickly between Elsa and Frankie. 'Please, Sister Elsa, I'm much more meaty than poor little Brother Frankie here. Why don't you have me?'

Elsa curled her lip. 'Show some bloody respect. You have just broken True Natural Path law. How dare you? You know perfectly well it is forbidden for any man to proposition a woman.'

'Yes, Sister Elsa. I'm sorry. I got carried away.'

Elsa switched her attention from Frankie's scrawny frame and onto my more substantial muscly figure. 'Jealous of poor little Brother Frankie, were you?' Elsa raised her eyebrows.

'Yes, Sister Elsa.'

'Couldn't bear the thought of someone else having it off with me, then?'

'No, Sister Elsa.'

'Wanted me so much you couldn't contain yourself?'

'Yes, Sister Elsa.'

'I should whip you for that.'

'Yes, Sister Elsa.'

She inspected me lustfully. 'You're right though. You have got more meat on you. But you're spoken for by Philomena. I wouldn't want to step on her toes.'

I felt relief. I had been prepared to sacrifice myself for Frankie's sake, but I hadn't been relishing the prospect.

'I should refer you to her, after what you've just done. You know that, don't you? She'd whip you for sure. Actually it's the very least she might do. People have been cast out for less.'

'Yes, Sister Elsa.'

Elsa leaned up close to me. 'I won't though. When Philomena's finished with you, you'll be mine. You'll like that, won't you?'

'Yes, Sister Elsa.'

'Mind you, when the time comes, I'll have to whip you first. After what you've just done.'

'Yes, Sister Elsa.'

Elsa turned back towards Frankie. 'I think I'll leave you for now, young Brother Frankie. Your time will come, once you've filled out a bit.'

Later, at the evening meal, while I accompanied Philomena, Elsa, now alone having dropped Woody, kept casting me suggestive looking glances, something Philomena didn't appear to notice, her eyes now being cast in Frankie's direction.

Appalled as I was by the idea of intimacy with Elsa, somewhere deep inside me a horny beast was relishing the prospect, stirring my loins.

The evening before the Litha celebrations found me once more among the singletons for the community's evening meal, Frankie having superseded me at Philomena's side.

'You didn't last long with her, did you?' goaded Bradders.

Once I might have been offended, but by now I had become used to her manner and took it as intended, as teasing banter.

'I don't suppose anybody lasts long with her. She has a wandering eye,' I observed philosophically.

'On the lookout for fresh meat,' said Bradders.

I reached under the table and pinched Bradders's thigh. 'You're only jealous because she hasn't picked your meat.'

'Actually, seriously. How are you feeling about the situation? You okay?' asked Bradders, evidently having decided to inject a little sympathy into the situation.

'Yeah, I'll be okay.'

'It might turn out good for you. Look at what it did for Huggs, the lucky sod,' observed Bradders, wistfully looking up the table towards lovebirds Huggs and Ivy.

'I have a feeling my immediate prospects are not as favourable,' I remarked.

It was Elsa I would be saddled with, I reflected, triggering an involuntary yet shamefully disgusting stirring and swelling in my groin.

The air had a crisp chill and the grass was laden with dew as the community stripped naked, our bodies goose pimpled in the twilight before dawn on the day of Litha, so as to be skyclad to face the first rays of the rising sun.

'Let our celebrations commence,' Hypatia pronounced as the bright tip of the sun's disk appeared on the horizon.

'So mote it be,' responded the congregation.

A puff of what looked like smoke burst from the sacred circle, an eruption of fine ash released from a spring loaded cylinder triggered by Tarquin operating a lever of his contrivance. Behind the smoke a wooden panel covering the top-most point of the pentacle within the circle slid aside, revealing a second wooden panel freed to tip upright. As the smoke cleared Philomena was revealed standing with her back against the panel, dressed representing the Earth Mother, radiating divine power as only she could.

Adorned with green vines, plaited and twisted which could be imagined as being the tentacles of a sea creature, Philomena stepped forward into the centre of the pentangle, from where she took over officiating of the ritual.

'Blessed Litha! Sacred Fire! Magical sunrise stirs desire, We see your first blessed ray, On this sacred solstice day, Forever warm our Mother Earth, sacred Sun.'

'Forever warm our Mother Earth, sacred Sun,' responded the congregation.

Philomena went on.

'Oak King and Holly King, Light and Darkness bring, Oak King and Holly King, Season's cycles bring.'

'Oak King and Holly King,

Season's cycles bring,' responded the congregation.

Philomena continued.

'Oak King and Holly King, On this Litha day so bright. Now is time for your great fight.'

Tarquin, from a laying position in a hollow dug into the mound, operated two more levers, releasing smoke puffs. With a creaking noise panel covering the two bottom points of the pentacle slid aside and two more panels tipped upright. Stood against the left panel was Huggs, adorned in oak twigs and leaves. Stood against the right panel was Woody adorned in holly twigs and leaves, arranged as far as possible, but not totally successfully, to avoid pricking his naked flesh.

Philomena stepped aside to permit Huggs and Woody, adorned in their foliage costumes, each armed with a stout stave, to advance to the centre of the pentacle, where they faced each other brandishing their gnarled weapons. They circled each other, taking swipes at their adversary who would parry the blow with his stick, at times lunging with their rod like it was a spear, growling and grunting, their stick clattering, Woody wincing in pain now and again from scratches form his costume's spiky holly leaves.

After some minutes of sparring, to Woody's relief as he was by now in some discomfort, Philomena intervened.

'Oak King you must step aside, Leave us now until Yuletide.'

Obediently Huggs fell back and Woody pressed the end of his stave into his chest in victory.

'Holly King you rule us now, Harvest riches for us you endow,' Philomena pronounced.

Woody raised his stick in the air in triumph.

Frankie's dedication took place on the same sacred mound as had been used shortly before for the Litha festival.

Skyclad, blindfolded, bound with cord around hand, foot and neck, dosed with magic mushroom potion, Huggs and I as his attendants, Frankie undertook the ritual and endured his purification whipping. I winced at the guileless innocent youth, Frankie, struggling to absorb the pain Philomena applied with unnecessarily excessive force. I looked across at Tarquin, suffering the impact of every lash as intensely as Frankie himself. A few times it was too much for Frankie. Philomena coaxed him into composing himself, whereupon she continued with undiminished intensity.

At last, Huggs and I removed Frankie's blindfold and untied the cords binding him, helping him into his initiation robe, a kaftan decorated with a brightly coloured pattern.

'Welcome onto the Way of the True Natural Path, Brother Frank,' Philomena pronounced.

The gathered congregation were downbeat, awed by, yet, I sensed, uncomfortable with the spectacle of suffering we had witnessed in as they would have been with an act of cruelty inflicted on a child or animal.

There was a slight cheer and a small ripple of clapping that quickly died. Several people gathered around Frankie, hugged and comforted him, congratulated him on taking his ordeal and welcomed him as a full member of the community. There was a subdued atmosphere as we sipped ale and mead in his honour.

After a little while Philomena looked over in Frankie's direction and caught his eye. With a slight toss of her head she indicated for him. He looked around nervously and then complied. As he came near I overheard her as she whispered to him quietly.

'Now you must taste the secret juices of your Goddess Gaia, Brother Frankie. Come with me.'

Tarquin, Huggs, Bradders and I exchanged glances, sharing our discomfort, doubting Frankie was yet ready for what Philomena had in store.

Tarquin and I were ruminating over mugs of herb tea in Tarquin's living and working space when we heard faint sounds from outside. I looked over while Tarquin opened the door to investigate, to see Frankie sat crumpled on the ground with his back to the mud walls of Tarquin's hobbit house, shivering from the cold, or it may have been shock, or a little of each. Tarquin rushed over and crouched beside him.

'Frankie, what are you doing there? Come on in to the warm,' said Tarquin.

'I didn't want to disturb you, wake you, or anything,' Frankie explained.

Tarquin hustled Frankie indoors and set him up with a mug of herbal tea.

'What happened?'

'She sent me away.'

'You mean Philomena?' I asked, for confirmation.

'Yes.'

'Why did she do that?' I enquired.

Frankie blushed a deep crimson and looked away.

'Come on, now, you can tell us. You're among friends here,' coaxed Tarquin gently.

'I… you know… couldn't help it. It just happened.'

'Let me guess. She told you, you had to control yourself and you couldn't. Am I right?' I ventured.

Frankie nodded. Tarquin looked alarmed.

'So she sent you away because she thought you had disgraced yourself?'

Frankie nodded again.

'What was this disgraceful thing you did?' I asked gently.

Frankie visibly cringed and curled into a ball.

'He's embarrassed, poor dear. Come, Frankie, you can tell us. We'll understand,' said Tarquin.

Frankie squirmed. He opened and closed his mouth a few times. Tarquin and I looked on encouragingly, nodding to coax out some words.

'She was, well, kind of playing with me, touching me... there, you know... but she told me I had to hold back, control myself. But then, it well, you know, just squirted out, I couldn't help it.'

I nodded. 'Yes, I know that one. It's the sort of thing she does. What then?'

'It went over her, squirted onto her. Made a mess. She was really angry. She swore at me and then told me I was filthy and must go.'

Tarquin put his arms around Frankie.

'You poor dear. It's not your fault. You couldn't help it.'

The following evening Frankie was not entirely out of favour with Philomena because she had him join her at dinner, but having no requirement for his services after the meal he was allowed to join the singletons later and return home with Tarquin afterwards.

I did not join them because, as I had feared, Elsa had me sit with her at the meal and, unlike Philomena, she very definitely required my services back at her place afterwards.

As we left the hall I noticed a salacious glint in Elsa's eye as if she had something special in mind. I did not have to wait long to find out what. She let me go in front of her into the living room of her little hobbit home, followed me in and slammed the front door ominously behind her.

'Brother Simon, we have a little matter to deal with

now, don't we?'

'Oh, do we?'

'Yes, Brother Simon, a disciplinary matter.'

Elsa was a strapping energetic woman who clearly had both the temperament and strength to apply whatever discipline may be required. She strode to a cupboard and took out a vicious looking leather whip, which she cracked in the air.

'We'll have you skyclad for this, Brother Simon.'

I was bewildered a moment, wondering whether to argue or resist, but by now I knew enough of the customs of the Abballon community to appreciate resistance was futile. Dutifully I stripped off my clothes and left them in a heap on one side of the room.

'You know why I must discipline you, don't you, Brother Simon?'

I shook my head.

'Let me remind you. You made a suggestive remark to me, a flagrant breach of True Natural Path law. You were unable to contain your lust, letting rip to your toxic masculinity. You surely remember?'

'Yes, Sister Elsa.'

She wandered to stand right next to me letting her body brush against mine. She spoke softly into my ear.

'You are very lucky I have decided to deal with the matter myself. It might have been much worse for you... had I referred it to Sister Philomena.'

'Yes, thank you, Sister Elsa.'

Elsa, evidently inspired by the recent example of Philomena's dedication of Frankie, lashed the whip forcefully so its tip wrapped right around my body, biting into my flesh with a fiery intensity. For some minutes she lashed me over and over, without finesse, just raw strength and power, all the while smiling as she relished the spectacle of me squirming, writhing, grunting and squealing under the lash.

Then, flushed with her exertion, her sadism satisfied, she cast the whip across the room. She grabbed me by the arm and hauled me towards the bed. She reached greedily into my crutch and fondled my private parts, which responded almost immediately. At this point matters were beyond the control of my mind and soul, the sexual beast within me took over and eagerly did what the horny Elsa required.

For nights the pattern persisted. I spent evenings and nights in the company of the insatiable Elsa, sucking my sexual energy dry in her rustic farmyard love nest. It was animalistic and devoid of grace and subtlety. My finer feelings were appalled by the coarseness and filth, while the sexual brute within revelled. Meanwhile, Frankie was Philomena's escort for the evening meal, released to Tarquin's tender care each night.

Then one night, I noticed Philomena had a look of stern decision.

'Now then, Brother Frank, we have some unfinished business, don't we?'

Frankie looked like a startled rabbit.

'Yes, Sister Philomena, I suppose so,' Frankie stammered.

'Yes, we do. You have to learn self-control and I am going to teach you.' Philomena stood. 'Well, come then. We'll start your lessons now.' She hustled Frankie away.

Hoping I might slow Elsa down a little, I persuaded

her to linger in the hall for a drink before we retired. We enjoyed one drink but she decided this was enough, so we made our way out of the hall setting in the direction of her place.

Having barely stepped out of the door we heard a shrill scream and a frantic ringing bell. The voice sounded as if it might be Philomena's. We stopped, twisting our heads to figure out where the sound was coming from.

Moments later Cadfael and Woody rushed out of the hall. Seeing me, Cadfael called. 'Brother Simon, Sister Philomena's in trouble. Come on, we need your help.'

Elsa and I hurried after them towards the clanging bell, to Philomena's home, the largest and most elaborate hobbit house within the settlement.

The posse rushed through into Philomena's bed chamber where she stood swinging her hand-bell vigorously. Frankie, pathetic and feeble, was on the floor cowering under the wrath of her imperious gaze.

As we came in Philomena tossed the bell onto the bed where it landed with a muffled clunk. 'Arrest this toxic abuser who has violated my person.'

Woody wasted no time. He rushed forward and kicked the already broken Frankie hard in the body as he lay on the ground.

'You filthy pervert. You disgust me,' said Woody as he put the boot in. Cowardly kicking a man when he was down, I thought; it wasn't even a man he kicked, merely a callow youth.

Cadfael pushed forward to intervene. 'Enough. We'll do this properly, with due process.'

He thrust himself in Woody's way. As the two jostled the leather strand around Cadfael's neck snapped releasing the locket so it fell away, releasing the catch to spill out small blue objects on the floor.

Cadfael dropped to gather them, but it was too late, all present saw the offending articles.

'Let me see what you have there,' commanded Philomena.

Reluctantly Cadfael opened his hands to reveal the diamond shaped blue tablets.

'Brother Cadfael, those are toxic chemicals from the unnatural world, are they not?'

Cadfael nodded.

'Chemicals whose purpose is to boost a man's toxic masculinity,' she continued.

Cadfael stared at the floor.

'You are dismissed from your role of Moderator, forthwith.'

'Brother Woody, you are appointed Moderator. You will place the perpetrators of these outrages, Brothers Cadfael and Frankie, under arrest. We will deal with them in the morning. Brother Simon will assist you.'

'Yes, Sister Philomena,' said Woody, a glint of satisfaction in his eyes.

'Come on, you two,' said Woody as he shoved the culprits towards the door. I followed behind as we made our way into the night, back towards the great hall. As we left Philomena turned to Elsa. The two of them sat on the bed, Elsa comforting her community sister after the violation she suffered at the hands of her toxic male abuser.

Woody shoved and pushed the accused through the length of the community hall in the manner of a secret police officer in a totalitarian regime. At the far end was a small room big enough to not-so comfortably confine one person. Woody roughly attached metal shackles on the wrists and ankles and both men and locked them tight. He shoved them into the confined space, slammed the sturdy door and bolted it from the outside.

'You can wait in there for now, you two. We'll deal with you in the morning.' He turned to me. 'You're on guard for now, Brother Simon. I'll relieve you later on.'

Woody walked out briskly, only turning briefly to check I was standing on guard as instructed.

Woody having departed, I dragged up a seat, settling myself next to the holding cell. After a couple of minutes I unbolted the heavy door and swung it open.

'I'll leave the door open and we can have a talk. But first you have to promise you won't try anything on. Do you both promise?'

The culprits both nodded.

'I'll have to close it up again before Woody returns, but it won't be for a while.'

'Thanks, I appreciate it. It's claustrophobic in here with the door shut,' said Cadfael.

'So, Frankie, what exactly happened? What kicked off all this fuss?' I enquired.

'I'd like to know too,' reiterated Cadfael.

'I'm sorry. It's all my fault,' said Frankie, fighting back tears.

'Never mind being sorry, just tell us what happened,' I reiterated.

Frankie crunched himself forward holding his hands across his chest and stared at the floor. I reached over and rested my hand on his shoulder.

'Come on, mate. We're your friends. We'll understand,'

I said gently.

'I'm too ashamed. I did wrong. I know that,' said Frankie, voice shaking.

'What did you do wrong, Frankie?'

'I tried to force myself on Philomena.'

'Oh dear,' said Cadfael.

'But you didn't do it all of a sudden, did you? Something must have built up to it?' I asked.

'Well, she said I had to learn to control myself. Then she sat on top of me with her pussy in my face. She made me lick her down there, but I wasn't allowed to do anything else.'

'I thought it would have been something of the sort. So, what happened then?'

'I had to keep, you know, licking her. First she got all wet. She made me keep licking, making me do it quicker. Then she started moaning and squeezing herself against me.'

'Okay, so, don't tell me. She told you, you just had to stay there and control yourself.'

'Yes.'

'But you didn't?'

'No.'

'What did you do?'

Frankie bent over and stared at the floor, shaking his head.

'Come on, Frankie, spit it out,' I coaxed.

'I rolled over on top of her. I was going to, you know, have sex with her.'

'But it didn't quite happen?'

'No. I was going to. I would have done. But she pushed me off and jumped up. She screamed at me. Then she grabbed the bell and started ringing it. After that you came in.'

'Oh dear,' said Cadfael. 'I fear the worst, for both of us.'

'Look, Brother Cadfael, it was me who brought in the pills. I should own up to it. It's not all your fault.'

'Don't you bloody well dare!' said Cadfael sharply. 'It wouldn't do me any good. All it would do is drop you in it too.'

'You shouldn't have to carry the can on your own.'

'Look, don't be bloody stupid. Promise me you won't tell anyone how I got the pills.'

'Well, okay, I promise.'

'I mean anyone. Especially not Philomena or Woody. But not Bradders, Tarquin, Hypatia either. Nobody. Understand? Promise me.'

'Alright. Nobody. I won't tell a soul.'

We continued talking a while until I thought I had better close the door in case Woody returned. I left the door almost shut, but open a couple of inches so we could still converse if we wished.

Later Woody returned and demanded to know why the door was open. I explained I had let them out to go to the toilet and hadn't got around to shutting it again. Woody slammed the door shut and re-bolted it before I went back to my billet at Tarquin's.

The following morning Frankie was first out from the holding cell to appear before the community's disciplinary hearing. Philomena presided, Hypatia and Elsa beside her to form the panel of three judging the case.

'You are charged with attempted rape,' said Philomena, glaring. 'What do you have to say for yourself?'

'Yes, I did it,' Frankie confessed. 'I'm sorry. I don't know what came over me.'

'May I speak in mitigation?' I asked.

'What's the point?' said Elsa. 'He's guilty. He's confessed. What is there to say?'

'There are special circumstances,' I insisted.

'Attempted rape,' said Hypatia. 'Nothing can excuse that. Nothing.'

'Nevertheless, please hear me out.'

'Very well,' said Philomena irritably. 'Get on with it.'

'Brother Frankie is truly remorseful for what he attempted,' I pleaded. 'In mitigation, lacking experience and exposure to sexual intimacy, his reactions had been intensified by the novelty. His bad reaction could be ironed out with training in self-control. He deserves a second chance.'

Philomena impatiently waved me away before I could finish. 'There can be no excuse for Brother Frankie's conduct. It was toxic masculinity at its worst and must be excised from our midst. He must be cast out of the community forthwith.'

When it came to Cadfael's appearance, remembering my promise to him and the futility of my intervention on Frankie's behalf, I remained silent.

The judges reached their verdict faster than before, Cadfael was to be cast out for possession of chemicals detrimental for the health of Mother Earth for the purpose of boosting toxic masculinity.

Philomena, standing with ominous solemnity, facing the limestone cliff with the Abballon community gathered behind, held up her ceremonial blade, her sacred athame and addressed the cliff face.

'Hail Gaia, our beloved Earth Mother, open thine rocks to consume those to be cast out.'

A rumbling, grinding emitted from deep within the cliff. The ground vibrated. A slab of rock embedded into the cliff slowly parted to reveal a deep cave behind. The rock reached the extent of its travel and the noise ceased.

'Cast out those who have transgressed,' ordered Philomena.

Woody shoved Cadfael and Frankie forward towards the opening. Cadfael, still strong and proud, stood facing the opening defiantly. Frankie shrank back with fear. Woody grabbed Frankie by the arm and hurled him forward bodily.

Cadfael caught the cowering Frankie and steadied him.

'Come along, Brother Frankie, let's face this together, you and me. Show them what we are made of,' said Cadfael quietly.

Taking Frankie by the arm, Cadfael walked the two of them into the dark abyss. As they vanished, Philomena held up her sacred athame again.

'Beloved Earth Mother, take these transgressors within your body never to return.'

The rumbling started again, shaking the ground as the rock slid back, closing the opening, leaving the cliff face whole once more.

Tarquin stood back a little from the throng of onlookers, tears streaming down his face. I put my arms around his slightly built frame as he wept.

The Wild Side

'It's a job which needs to be done. Someone's got to do it,' I insisted.

'But why is it always us?' asked Bradders.

'Sure, we should do our part, but it should be shared around, man,' complained Huggs.

'Look, I'll be there too, doing my bit,' I said.

We were discussing digging latrines. As instructed by Philomena, I was now acting as one of Woody's deputies in his role as Moderator. Woody had made me responsible for the less desirable assignments and delegated the responsibility for recruiting people to carry them out, along with the resulting unpopularity.

As we talked Elsa arrived. The mingled aromas of farmyard animals wafted around as she sidled up to me and squeezed my bottom.

'Can't wait until later, you sexy beast,' she said with a salacious grin.

I forced a smile. I felt my loins involuntarily stir. I had the same love-hate feelings for Elsa as a drug addict for their habit, something filthy and degrading that I craved more than anything else in the world.

The next day, as I was by the stream cleansing myself after the day's labour on the latrines, alone as neither Bradders nor anybody else felt like talking to me, I perceived a little goat in the vicinity of Gaia's temple, presumably a stray from Elsa' herd. Not feeling gregarious, nor confident I would get a friendly reception from other folk, I lingered to observe the goat as it headed towards the steep rocky cliff.

The animal leapt onto the lower part of the cliff, located a gully or cleft in the rocks where it could get purchase, then in a series of scrambles and leaps ascended what at first glance appeared to be a sheer rock face before disappearing. Minutes later it re-emerged at the top, then vanished into shrubbery beyond.

Intrigued I made my over to the cliff. There was nobody else around, the other members of the community having already gathered in the great hall for the evening meal. Elsa would be wondering where I was, but would have to wait.

I made out the goat again, now grazing hungrily on pasture at the edge of the dense woodland on the Wild Side, separated from Abballon's land by the strip of bracken and scrub I knew from my experience was impassable, protected by a heat ray.

I found the area of cliff where the goat ascended. If the goat could do it, perhaps I could too. I ran my eyes up the rocky cliff. Set at a steep angle was a boundary of crumbly material between the layers of harder rock. I was inspired by the goat's success.

I hesitated for about ten seconds. What was there to remain for? I should seize the moment. Emulating the goat I reached up, grasping a rocky crevice. I had always been strong and athletic and by now, after weeks of hard daily labour I was in particularly good physical condition. I hauled myself up with ease, settling my feet onto ridges.

I was still only feet off the ground and the cliff towered above me, but it was a start. Seeing another handhold within reach, I grabbed it, pulled up my body weight, swinging my legs across to new footholds. Fortunately I had never been intimidated by heights. I got into a rhythm, scanning ahead to plot a succession of reachable handholds and footholds, stretching and hauling myself in planned stages, foot by foot, scaling up the slope. I did my best not to look down, focussing ahead. It was strenuous, but I enjoyed it. At last I was making a bid for freedom, one that might work.

Within a short span, perhaps ten minutes, although without any form of time keeping I couldn't say for sure, I had scaled over three quarters of the cliff's height. Although the end was in sight, looking up to assess my next moves, I realised further progress would be less simple than I had imagined.

At ground level I had already perceived a layer of rock smoother than the rest. Now I could see it wasn't rock at all, but a totally flat plane of smooth reflective glass about ten to twelve feet in height, cunningly disguised with a translucent surface printed in a camouflage pattern in the shapes and colours of the surrounding rock face. Above me stretched a vertical expanse of smooth slippery surface offering no grip or holds.

It was daunting to have come so far only to be faced with this insurmountable barrier. Were it not for the goat, I might have given up and retraced my route to the ground. From my vantage, with the wall of glass extending as far as I could see in both directions, there were no apparent routes over or around this obstacle. I began a traverse the base of the glass sheet.

This was not intrinsically more difficult than the vertical ascent, but, no longer buoyed by visible progress upwards, it felt tougher. Now tiring, I dug into my reserves, stretching to reach each handhold, fingers, tendons and muscles straining to hold my weight as I swung my body and legs to reach tiny ridges in the rock.

After what must have been another half an hour, I perceived around two hundred yards in front of me an end to the glass barrier and a resumption of the normal rock face.

Stretch after agonising stretch I pressed on to where, at last, I could resume my upward trajectory. With my last reserves I reached out over the top of the rock face, finding the sturdy gnarled stem of a well-established shrub, swung my leg over to get a foot on the top. In a final energy sapping heave I was atop the cliff.

Settling myself into a secure position on a clifftop rock I surveyed the surrounding scene as I gathered my breath. Laid out below, now slightly to one side after the long traverse, was the settlement of Abballon. From this aerial perspective the proportions and shapes differed subtly from my surface level mental map. Patches of planted vegetables dotted beside some hobbit homes with patterns on the roofs not visible at ground level. On the upper part of a windmill were small inset windows I hadn't noticed.

Beyond the village and its surroundings was Wild Side landscape invisible from the Abballon village, a valley with a gorge running through it, rocky outcrops, open stretches of heathland breaking up the masses of trees.

My heart raced from the elation of having escaped and the majesty of the view, but also from the realisation of the ever-present danger from savage beasts lurking in this prehistoric environment.

Recovered from my exertion I picked carefully through uneven overgrown terrain, alert for the slightest movement or white flash of fang or tusk, taking a wide berth around points from which fearsome sabre cats, wolves or bears might wait in ambush.

Without a plan, my mind raced to formulate a guiding principle or strategy. Ultimately, I had to find a way from this strange prehistoric world of Abballon to everyday twenty-first-century England, but first, I needed to understand the nature of this alien world. Could it be a time warp into prehistory? Or a parallel world on a different path? Whatever it was, Philomena flitted between the two routinely, so a conduit must exist. In the absence of clues, I could only explore in the hope of stumbling across something.

As I dropped down the gentle reverse slope away from the cliff, some distance out I saw a greyish fixture on the ground out of keeping with the wild surroundings, not so much its colour, but its straightness and regularity, fabricated rather than natural.

I was deterred from approaching the synthetic feature by the presence of wild beasts, not predators, but aurochs and mammoths. I resolved to return when the coast was clear.

If I was now in a prehistoric environment, what might this object be? Placed there by intelligent aliens, I speculated in a flight of fancy, to which the Abballon community attributed divine powers?

Skirting around in another direction I found a pond fed by a seepage of ground water from which I scooped up some to drink.

Emerging over the crest of a small hill I saw a rectangular impression in the ground that couldn't have been natural. With no sign of dangerous animals in the vicinity I approached cautiously.

It was the shape of a building, an old house built of brick. Kicking around in the dirt, I found remnants of electrical fittings that I noted were British, dating to the twentieth-century, killing the notion of being in the distant past. Could the presence of contemporary artefacts suggest a time warp into the far future?

By now, the sun had already gone down. Not relishing blundering about in the dark in this dangerous environment, I gathered bracken and fine twigs to form a makeshift bed, laying it in a spot providing a little shelter from the wind. Fortunately, there was no rain that night.

I woke cold, stiff and hungry as the first pre-dawn twilight emerged. There was nothing to eat, but I could at least get a drink of water from the pond. Refreshed and loosened up by having moved around, I made my way back to investigate the mysterious synthetic object I had seen the previous evening.

I was disappointed. Not only had the herds of aurochs and mammoths swelled but they had now been joined by an assortment of deer and wild goats.

There was a humming motorised noise. The object tipped itself upwards. The surrounding animals were getting excited, jostling. A fountain of greenish pellets spewed out, spreading out over a wide area, to about the extent of a football pitch.

After a couple of minutes, the fountain ceased and the motorised contraption closed back down. I observed from a safe distance while the animals tucked into their feast.

I was not the only one observing the scene. There was a commotion as a gigantic sabre cat dashed from where it had been lurking. The animals scattered, sprinting for cover. One unfortunate deer turned to avoid a set of claws, sufficient to receive only a glancing blow as the cat lashed out. The deer staggered, thrown off balance. The cat swung around for the kill, embedding its enormous fangs into its prey.

It was now the cat's turn to be hunted as a herd of mammoths formed up in confrontation. The cat grabbed the bloody carcase of the deceased deer, dragging it towards trees with several angry mammoths in hot pursuit.

Over the following minutes the prey animals returned, tentative and skittish, hunger overcoming their fear.

After what I guessed must have been an hour, the animals, having consumed most of the provided sustenance, dispersed in search of a second course on pasture elsewhere.

With the larger animals departed I felt bold enough to take on the few remaining deer, who edged away to let me through. The artefact was shut down now, flat and flush with the ground, its colour blended with the surroundings, but standing out as a modern metal construction coated with a special finish. A hinge construction permitted it to open to disgorge the animal feed. Embossed into the metal was a logo I recognised, Drembold Industries.

I picked up and sniffed some remaining food pellets, assaulting my nostrils with a stench of festering pond slime, evidently appetising to large herbivores, but not in the least appealing to serve as my breakfast however acute my hunger pangs.

Where to go from here? The Abballon village was evidently connected with and central to the enterprise so best to return and investigate its surroundings.

As I retraced my steps I breathed in a familiar aroma, manna, the nutritious bread-like material forming one of the mainstays of the Abballon community's diet. Like a bloodhound my nose tracked in the direction of the enticing scent.

With the smell as strong as a baker's shop around the corner, I noticed a discreet hatch built into the ground, like a manhole cover from which one might access a drain.

Uncertain how the hatch might be opened, I fumbled until I located a catch and lever allowing me to swing it open. Leading into the subterranean darkness there was an access ladder. I hesitated, wary. Realising I had to take my chances, I lowered myself.

There was no lighting below, but as my eyes became accustomed to the gloom the light from the open hatch above was sufficient to make out my surroundings. I was in a concrete lined tunnel encasing a trackway for a miniature underground railway. Pipes and cables ran along the sides. There was a splinter tunnel curving from the main one into a chamber from which the aroma of manna emanated.

I heard a trundling as a lightweight rail waggon emerged from the side tunnel. The smell of it told me it was laden with manna. Realising how hungry I was, I reached out and seized a couple of handfuls as the waggon passed. Thankful, I stuffed the sustenance into my mouth as the waggon continued on its way.

As I chewed I heard a rumbling along the main track, approaching me from the darkness. I glimpsed of another waggon as it loomed close. There was a hiss and thwonk consistent with a release of compressed air. I felt a thump and sharp prick on my chest as I was struck by a dart. My head spun as my grip slipped from the access ladder. A wave of blackness consumed me.

The chill from the damp moss and hard rock beneath made me shiver. I was back in Abballon. I knew it without opening my eyes. I wouldn't have been able to describe it to anyone, but the familiar scent in my nostrils was unmistakeable.

I could sense daylight through my closed eyelids. I blinked open my eyes. There were blurry figures around. I was laying on the same rock as I—and more recently Ivy and Frankie—had at their arrival, but this time the atmosphere was less welcoming.

As my eyes came into focus I made out Philomena flanked by Woody and Huggs. Anger blazed from Philomena's eyes. Woody's demeanour was of cynical aggression. Huggs's face lacked expression, an automaton who followed orders.

Philomena spoke. 'Brother Simon, you have transgressed Gaia's Law by straying into Wild Side. You will answer for this.'

With my senses still befuddled, I said nothing.

'Take him away. We'll deal with him tomorrow,' she ordered.

Woody and Huggs each took one of my arms and hauled me up, Woody roughly with a jerk, Huggs in a more supportive way as he aided me to my feet. Together they frogmarched me to the back of the great hall. Woody brusquely attached the metal shackles onto my wrists and ankles and shoved me into the small holding cell, then slammed the heavy door shut. The bolts grated as they slid across firmly securing the door shut, leaving me alone in the dark within the confined space.

Woody and Huggs exchanged brief words. One of them walked away. There were a few more steps and a scraping on the floor from what I assumed must have been a chair being dragged over. The bolts slid across and the door opened slightly.

'You alright in there, Brother Simon?' Huggs enquired.

'As alright as a condemned man can be, I suppose,' I replied.

'I'll leave the door open if you promise not to try anything on. You cool with that?'

'Yes, Huggsy, I'm cool with it. I won't do anything.'

'So, you got out then? How did you do it?'

'I climbed the cliff. Saw a goat doing it, so thought I could too.'

'Man, that's some climb. Good job. What did you find over there?'

'Well, there's the animals, of course. You need to watch out for those big cats. There're really scary.'

'Anything else?'

'I found where the manna comes from.'

'Really? Where from?'

'It was underground, in a tunnel.'

'Where does the tunnel go?'

'I don't really know. I'd only just got down there, found the manna, and the next thing I remember is being back here.'

'Wow. Quite an adventure. It's got you in trouble, though. I wouldn't want to chance it. Respect to you for giving it a try.'

'Thanks.'

We remained still a moment, until I broke the silence. 'How's things with you and Ivy?'

'Oh, cool. It's going good. I love her. She loves me too, pretty sure of it.'

'That's great. I'm really pleased for you both.'

Time passed. We chatted intermittently, but mostly sat quietly lost in our own thoughts. Eventually Huggs guessed Woody would be due back to relieve him, so he re-closed the heavy door.

Presently Huggs was gone and it was Woody outside the door. Woody looked in once to check on me and immediately slammed the door shut again without a word.

In the morning my meditation in the darkness was abruptly interrupted by the sliding the bolts and the heavy cell door swinging open. I blinked and screwed up my eyes as the light shone in. An unsympathetic Woody hauled me out roughly to face the disciplinary panel, presided as always by the imperious Philomena supported by Hypatia and Elsa.

It was established I had strayed into the Wild Side against Gaia's Law. No mitigating circumstances were offered, the panel quickly reached their verdict. I was to be cast out of the community without delay.

Woody and Huggs escorted me to face the same cliff face I had recently climbed. The whole Abballon community was assembled behind me. Philomena held up her sacred athame.

'Hail Gaia, our beloved Earth Mother, open thine rocks to consume he who is to be cast out.'

The same grinding noise as I had heard before reverberated from the cliff, even more ominous this time, as it was for me. The rock face parted revealing the deep dark passage, the way to oblivion.

'Cast out he who has transgressed.'

Woody came forward to execute her command, but I waved him away.

My legs trembled but I willed them to walk forward purposefully into the dark cave.

I took a few paces into the abyss, at which point the rumbling resumed. The rock face closed behind me and I was left standing in the most complete darkness imaginable.

There was a slight hissing and some movement in the air. I felt light headed and my legs crumpled. Not again, am I going wake up this time? was my last thought, as I lost consciousness.

The Outcasts

My first sensation as I came to was a smell of disinfectant overpowering a stale fug of unwashed people in a confined badly ventilated space. In the background was a distant reverberating hum of fans and other unidentifiable machinery. I lay on a thin sheet of foam matting giving off a rubbery vapour.

I opened my eyes finding myself within a cage formed of metal bars and mesh surfaced with a hard white plastic coating, presumably to facilitate hygiene and easy cleaning—as did the white plastic covering encasing my bed of foam matting.

My Abballon garb was gone and instead I was clad in a one-piece overall, which, like everything else here was white, sterile-looking and easily washable.

My own cage was set within one of two rows of similar cages facing one another on opposite sides of a large windowless echoing concrete chamber lined with a smooth white easy-clean render illuminated by harsh strip lighting.

A stainless steel squat toilet at the end of each cage formed an integral part of the cage floor, providing for sanitary performance of bodily functions but without privacy.

Stretched along the unoccupied central communal area between the rows of cages was a long table and benches. A small door in each cage would have provided access to the communal area, but when I checked mine was firmly locked, as presumably were the doors on the other cages.

I ran my eye along the other cages, roughly half were occupied. Most of the inmates were people I hadn't met, but I was pleased to recognise Cadfael in one on the opposite side of the chamber. I tried to catch his eye and waved, but his attention was elsewhere.

All at once there was a cacophonous clanking as the doors of the cages slid open simultaneously. Shortly after inmates slid themselves out of their cages into the central shared area. I did likewise.

I made straight across to greet Cadfael, whereupon we vigorously shook hands and grasped each other in bear-hug.

'Great to see you, Brother Cadfael.'

'Good to see you too, but sorry you've ended up in here with us.'

I sensed other eyes focussed on me. Frankie stood a few steps away, but beyond him my heart leapt as I saw Jenny at the far end of the room. I turned momentarily in Frankie's direction, greeted him briefly as I slapped him on his shoulder, before dashing for Jenny.

She was open-mouthed, momentarily stunned, then lit up in delight. Even in her uniform overall, she looked gorgeous. For moments we stood grasping each other tight.

'I thought I'd lost you,' I said eventually.

'You came for me. I never thought you would.'

'I was in Abballon, but you weren't there. It made it all feel pointless.'

'I'm sorry. Me and my big mouth. I upset Philomena.'

'Big mouth is right. You're the most opinionated woman I've met. But I love you for it.'

'How can you love me? We hardly know each other.

We went out a few times and since then we haven't seen each other for months.'

'I fell for you the first time we went out.'

Jenny paused. 'Well, you followed me all the way here. That says something.'

I looked back to where Cadfael and Frankie had taken a seat at the table.

'You must know Cadfael and Frankie. Let's join them,' I said, guiding Jenny in their direction.

There was plenty to talk about. The others were interested to hear of my escapade in the Wild Side. Jenny gazed at me in what I took to be admiration and adoration.

As we chatted a door opened to allow a group of four quadruped robots to trot into the room before clanging shut behind them. My companions took no notice of the incursion, but I broke off from conversation to observe the intruders. The robots had four legs and moved with a gait giving them the superficial air of a large dog, albeit one made of metal, wires and plastic. They emitted slight puffing noises like escaping compressed air as they moved. On their front they were fitted with two arms and mountings for sensory equipment such as cameras and scanners. On their sides I noticed the Drembold Industries logo.

Seeing I was preoccupied, Cadfael explained, 'Don't worry about them. They just come round to clean up the place and check on us. Don't mess with them, though.'

The robots went around the room methodically swabbing every surface, clearing out and wiping down each cage in turn. The cleaning completed the robots brought in trays and set them out on the table. It was manna, masses of it, and plastic bottles of water.

'Is that it? Is this all we get to feed us?' I enquired.

Cadfael nodded.

'What is this, some sort of a jail?' I asked.

'Well, kind of,' said Cadfael. 'But they take us out now and again and do stuff to us. Experiments and so on, as far as I can make out.'

'You mean we are test subjects in a laboratory?'

'I couldn't really say. We don't get told anything.'

As we ate and chatted on a variety of topics, I pondered how we might break out.

'Has anyone managed to get out of here?' I enquired.

'I heard some people have been taken out and not brought back,' Cadfael replied.

I pondered. 'But they didn't get out by themselves, though. And goodness knows what happened to them. I don't like the sound of it.'

'Exactly. It's not encouraging,' Cadfael agreed.

I looked around. 'There's the robots. We could take them out, perhaps. Or the doors…'

Cadfael vigorously shook his head and brought his fore finger to his lips. He looked around and cupped his hand to his ear.

'Oh, I see. I get it. We're being overheard,' I acknowledged.

The day passed. There were more conversations. I was introduced to other inmates. More manna and water arrived. The robots came in and cleared the food remains.

Eventually the robots came in one more time, but this time one spoke. 'Time for bed, return to your beds, please,' it said in a woman's voice.

The timbre took me by surprise. The robots' shape and

manner of movement suggested something fierce like an aggressive Doberman or German shepherd with a gruff bark, not the reassuring feminine voice I heard.

The inmates made their way back to their respective cages. How would we know which was ours, I wondered, before noticing each was labelled with an electronic display showing the occupant's name, mine reading 'Chewton, S'. As each person had entered his or her cage the door slid shut and locked itself with a solid clunk.

I lingered while the others complied. A robot advanced and stood close by. 'Time for bed, please,' repeated the robot in a patient feminine tone.

I stood where I was defiantly. A wire shot out from the robot and two sharp darts embedded in my arm. I doubled up in pain as my muscles went into an uncontrollable spasm from the robot's Taser. A pair of robots picked up my rigid body and slid me into my cage. One ripped out the wires leaving blood spots where the barbed darts had torn my flesh. Mercifully my spasms ceased. My cage door slammed shut and locked.

'Told you not to mess with them, didn't I?' called Cadfael, from across the room.

The lights went out. As I lay in the dark my body was still rigid, racked by agonising cramps and shaking after my encounter with the Taser. Over the following minutes the physical effects of my ordeal subsided, but I could not sleep. My confinement felt intolerable. The room's walls echoed with coughing and snoring. For hour on hour I lay awake, my body tense and mind in turmoil.

At some point I must have fallen asleep because I was rudely awakened by the horribly bright strip lighting illuminating the room with its dazzling clinical whiteness.

The routine was the same as it had been the previous day. The cage doors slid open and inmates emerged.

I greeted my companions and we struck conversations, but having less news to discuss, these were less animated than they had been. Having less to talk about with the others I took the opportunity for a more in depth private chat with Jenny, or at any rate as private as the circumstances allowed, bearing in mind, as indicated the day before by Cadfael, presumably someone or something was listening in to every word.

'You know I am besotted with you, don't you?' I confided.

'I don't know why. All I've done is bring trouble for you,' Jenny replied sadly.

'Yes, don't I know it! You've brought us both no end of grief.'

'So, what do you see in me then?'

'You've got passion, fervour and commitment to what you believe in. I love that.'

'But I've been foolish and impetuous, and it's got both of us into this desperate mess.'

'It may be so, but in so doing we are in the process of uncovering a fiendish conspiracy. It was your passion and idealism that led us here. I would never have dug out all this alone.'

'But nobody knows we're here. What good is it uncovering the darned conspiracy, if we can't tell anyone in the outside world?'

'I grant you, it's a problem.'

'I've just blundered into a terrible mess and dragged you with me and now there is no way out. I'm so sorry.'

'Don't be sorry. I made my own decisions. Anyway,

don't lose heart.'

'But how can I not lose heart, stuck here like this?'

'Something will turn up, I expect.'

'How can you say that?'

'Easily. I just did say it.'

'You're impossible,' Jenny exclaimed.

'What do you mean, I'm impossible? Being impossible is your department.'

'I suppose you're right. But you do still like me, despite being impossible and after what I've pulled you into?'

'More than like, I love you, actually,' I admitted, with a serious tone and looking into her eyes.

'Oh. I still can't think why.'

I put my arms around her and held her tight. We hugged and kissed passionately, oblivious to their surroundings and who might be watching.

Our canoodling was interrupted by the robot cleaning squad. We watched impatiently while the mechanical beasts bustled about. After the incident on the previous evening I gave them a wide berth. At the completion of the cleaning process one gathered the debris from the cleaning and took it to the far end of the room whereupon a small flat door slid open, allowing the robot to tip in the material. The opening swung shut again.

With things being quiet again I resumed our conversation. 'I know with us being stuck here like this, this will sound theoretical, but hypothetically if and when we ever get out, what should we do? About us, I mean.'

'Do? What do you mean?' Jenny queried.

'Well, about us. What is the future for us?'

'We don't seem to have much of a future, stuck here, do we?'

'I know, but just supposing we did manage to get out.'

'What about it?'

'Would we be an item? You know, would we be together?' I insisted.

'Well, we could be, I suppose. We could give it a try.'

'Hmm. Well, that's something I suppose. You don't sound hugely enthusiastic.'

Jenny reached out and held my hand. 'It's not that. You bounced me with it, that's all. I haven't had time to think about it.'

I smiled at her playfully. Jenny slapped me on the shoulder. 'What are you looking at me like that for?'

'I'm watching you while you think about it.'

'You're impossible.'

'Have you thought about it yet?'

'Oh, alright. I think we're stuck with each other now.'

This ended the day on a high note. Despite our difficult circumstances, I was relaxed and happy as I settled for the night and quickly fell into a peaceful sleep.

As I crawled out of my cage at the beginning of my third day of incarceration it felt as if I had already been in confinement for an age. I knew the routine, knew my surroundings and fellow inmates.

After we had chewed our way through our boringly familiar manna I settled to chat with Jenny, Cadfael and Frankie. We speculated about what might be going on in the outdoor world of Abballon.

'People much preferred you as Moderator compared with Woody,' I assured Cadfael.

'You're just saying that to make me happy.'

'No, not at all. Woody is a nasty piece of work,

unpleasant, vindictive and overbearing.'

'Did you get back with Philomena, after she cast me out?' Frankie enquired.

I cringed. Jenny looked at me with a disturbed expression. 'No,' I said, without elaborating.

Frankie might have been satisfied with my monosyllabic answer, but Jenny wasn't. 'What's this about you and Philomena?'

'Look, she took a fancy to me. I didn't have any choice, any more than Frankie did.'

Jenny looked me up and down. 'Oh yeah, so she forced you to shag her, as if she could, a great hulking brute like you,' she said sarcastically.

'Look, you were there, you know what it's like. You can't say no to Philomena. You defied her, and look what happened to you,' I protested.

Jenny narrowed her eyes. She was partially mollified, but I guessed she would be asking me tough questions later.

'You were better off with Elsa anyway,' said Frankie, naïvely indiscreet.

'Elsa, what's that about?' Jenny exclaimed, practically screaming.

'Look, I can explain,' I protested.

'You mean it's true. You've been shagging Elsa too. Is it true?' Jenny demanded.

'Well, yes, but I didn't want to do it. In Abballon you have to,' I insisted.

'Yes, it's true. I can vouch for that,' intervened Cadfael in support.

'True that he was shagging Elsa?' asked Jenny.

'Well, yes,' said Cadfael, 'but what I meant was, in

Abballon if you're a man you don't get the choice.'

'Oh come on! A big muscly bloke forced to have sex. Get out of here!' she exclaimed. 'And with Elsa, too. You don't even have taste. I should have realised what you were like when you brazenly chatted up that barmaid in Glastonbury, right in front of me.'

I sensed the hopeless position I was in. I could only shrug and stare at the floor. Thanks to Frankie, the atmosphere between Jenny and me was as cold as the South Pole.

That night as I lay in my cage, imprisoned indefinitely with no prospect of release and now apparently irretrievably estranged from Jenny, my mood submerged into a gloomy abyss.

Escape

I woke from my despondency determined to escape confinement at the earliest opportunity by any means. As Cadfael had warned, I could not share this intention. Taking Jenny with me wasn't an option. After Frankie's thoughtless indiscretions, she wouldn't have come anyway. I would have to go it alone.

After we were released from our cages I wandered over nonchalantly, as if taking a stroll, towards the main doors. Robust and I could only assume well-defended, I had noticed two successive sets of doors, which opened and closed in succession when the robots passed, always leaving one door secured. Even were I to slip out with the robots, I would be trapped, not to mention tasered to an inch of my life.

I resumed my outwardly carefree wander to the far end of the room where I had observed the robots disposing of detritus into a rubbish chute. I tested the door to the chute with a haphazard tapping of my heels, but it was solid as a rock. The chute and the doors evidently opened freely for the robots but not for inmates. The robots must be equipped with an electronic tag or device granting access. Should I have managed to get it to open it would have been just possible to squeeze myself through.

Instead of socialising with the others while the robots carried out their cleaning duties, I took a seat alone at the end of a bench nearest the chute, staring into space as if in deep thought.

When a robot approached the chute with the sweepings it had gathered, I was poised. As the chute door slid open I sprang like a gymnast using the robot as a vaulting horse to drop feet first into the opening. On the way through my shin scraped the metal frame, followed by a bang to my hip and a heavy thump against my chest that winded me. I had incurred torn flesh and bruises, but it hardly mattered given the stakes.

As I disappeared down the chute the robot shot out its fearsome wires. The metal barbs embedded in my neck. My whole body went into a rigid and agonising spasm as I continued my descent but it didn't last for long because the wires snagged, extracting the barbs, leaving bloody puncture wounds as if I had been attended by Count Dracula.

I flopped into a hopper among a mix of festering garbage. For seconds I remained still, recovering from the battering and tasering I endured, but knowing I could not safely remain for long, I scanned for a way out. I strained to reach up and pushed at a place where I could see chinks of light shining in from above. It was a lid I was able to swing up to open. I dragged myself over the lip of the rubbish hopper. Heaving down onto the floor I found myself within a subterranean chamber containing the paraphernalia for maintenance and domestic services.

I didn't waste time, making up a ramp offering itself as an escape route. Pressing a button mounted on the wall caused neighbouring double doors at the top to swing open providing access into a corridor lit by harsh strip lighting with the utilitarian and antiseptically clean appearance of a laboratory or office complex. Closed doors led off the corridor at intervals. The double doors closed behind.

I leaned against the double doors. They remained

firmly shut. There was a card scan lock on the doors I presumed must be the means for opening them from the corridor, but I had no such card. The other doors leading off the corridor also had cardkey access. All were shut. I was trapped there.

I paced along the corridor. One of the doors had been propped open. I ducked inside. It was a conference room. Projected on a large display screen mounted on one of the walls was a view of the room with the cages from which I had escaped minutes before. The screen showed a commotion. The robots were busy rounding up the other inmates and confining them to their cages. Presumably security arrangements for recapturing escapees would now be swinging into action.

The door being propped open suggested someone would soon return. I scanned the room for options for concealment or escape. There was some sort of a cupboard at the end of the room accessible through a door with louvres. The door was not secured and I peeped in. There was humming electronic machinery mounted in racks. Presumably the slatted door was designed to permit ventilation and prevent overheating of the computers and communications equipment contained within this annex.

I heard footsteps. I quickly closed the door behind me in the equipment cupboard. There was just sufficient visibility between the slats for me to see out into the main conference room.

A man pushed in a second large display screen mounted on a wheeled portable frame. He plugged it into a power socket. He sat at the table and typed away at a keyboard. Some graphs and statistics appeared on the newly arrived screen.

A woman stepped in through the door. My heart almost pounded out of my chest as I saw it was Philomena, awe inspiring as ever! What was she doing here?

The man at the keyboard greeted her. 'Please, do take a seat, Dr Shorbody will be with us shortly.'

Moments later a thickset man in his forties strode in purposefully. He looked familiar but for a moment I couldn't place him.

'Mr Drembold, please take a seat,' said the man, 'Dr Shorbody will join us in a moment.'

Of course, it was Alex Drembold, head of Drembold Industries. And Dr Marcus Shorbody was the eccentric scientist I had seen with the Marquess of Mendip on my first visit to Glastonbury and subsequently at his press conference at Britannica College about his genetic experiments.

Over the next minutes a few more people I did not recognise came in and arranged themselves around the conference table.

Eventually a pressured Dr Shorbody appeared in the doorway. He was preoccupied as he continued a conversation with another man who remained in the corridor.

'I trust full security measures are in place,' said Dr Shorbody.

'Yes, we have applied a full lockdown. He won't escape. The full robot team are on tracking duties,' said the other man.

'Good. Keep me informed.'

Dr Shorbody came into the room and the door closed behind him. Putting aside the crisis having just arisen he switched attention to his guests and colleagues arranged around the table.

'So sorry to keep you all waiting. There has been a security breach. One of our subjects has got out, but don't worry, he won't get far.'

'He won't get past our robot team,' chipped in Alex Drembold. 'Their tracking capabilities are second to none, if I say so myself.'

'We're counting on them,' said Dr Shorbody with a look of challenge.

Dr Shorbody passed along the table effusively greeting and shaking hands.

'Well let's get down to business,' said Dr Shorbody at last with an air of someone who has no time to waste. 'The latest developments for the Mythological Magick project.'

'What are the current timeframes for this?' asked Alex Drembold.

'As you know the next phase of the Mendip Themed Enterprises programme is the opening next year of the Pleistocene Panorama park. Most of this is now in place. The Pleistocene fauna, mammoths, wolves, sabre cats and so on, have been developed and are settled into the landscape and the prehistoric village of Aballon is populated. We only need to complete the arboreal rail circuit to convey our visitors through the scene while avoiding undue disturbance to the inhabitants.'

'I can understand how the prehistoric animals might become accustomed to an overhead rail circuit, but I can't see the human inhabitants accepting it so easily,' Alex Drembold observed.

'The humans don't get to see the rail system. It passes

behind a discreet viewing platform we built into the cliff above the settlement,' Dr Shorbody explained.

'In the event the Abballon inhabitants did see anything we have a theological explanation for it,' interjected Philomena. 'It would be a divine intervention by the goddess Gaia, a sort of Chariot of the Gods, if you like.'

'Mythological Magick is the next phase in the programme taking the visitors forward into the early classical era, the time of Homer, the Iliad, Greek Gods and the mythical beasts of the era. The Marquess is keen we are open for business with it two years from now,' continued Dr Shorbody.

'And from there it leads on to Knights of Camelot, I suppose,' said Alex Drembold.

'Exactly,' said Philomena. 'We are taking our visitors on a time travelling experience, starting from the Ice Age, through the classical era, then the pre-medieval mythical period and back to the present day, once they will have built a good appetite for the medieval banquets we offer, or for those with simpler tastes, fried chicken and hamburgers.'

'And it's Mythological Magick we are here to talk about today,' said Alex Drembold.

'Yes,' confirmed Dr Shorbody. 'In particular the development of the mythological beasts the Marquess requires for the attraction. The biology here is proving particularly challenging.'

'The team has already been successful with the beasts for the Pleistocene Panorama. Why is Mythological Magick proving so much more difficult?' asked Alex Drembold.

'For the Pleistocene Panorama we were re-creating animals that actually existed at the time. We didn't have to redesign the biology. We had to figure out the genetics by tracing back to common ancestors of animals we still have today. It had its difficulties, but it was way simpler than what we are trying now.'

'We could always use robotics. We at Drembold Industries provided the animatronic dragon for Knights of Camelot. We could do the same for Mythological Magick,' suggested Alex Drembold.

Dr Shorbody shook his head. 'The Marquess won't hear of it. The mythical beasts must be biological, flesh and blood. He is adamant.'

At this moment the door onto the corridor swung open and one of the Drembold Industries robots trotted into the room on its four legs.

'Excuse the interruption,' said the robot in meek feminine tones. 'We are searching for an intruder. We have reason to believe he may be in here.'

My heart almost stopped. I had been rumbled. I poised to make a desperate run for it, but truthfully I did not fancy my chances.

'Well, he isn't, as you can see,' said Dr Shorbody irritably.

The robot ran around the table checking each person in turn.

'He's not here. Get out of here,' shouted Dr Shorbody.

The robot hesitated, as if considering, but eventually turned and departed. Having been nervously holding my breath, I could breathe again. I sighed audibly. Realising what I had done, I froze, but fortunately there was no indication anyone had heard.

'In what respects was the development of the Pleistocene animals simpler than developing the Mythological creatures?' asked Alex Drembold, once the robot was gone.

'The Mythological creatures are chimeras, consisting of combinations of features from multiple animals together with some which have never existed in a real animal. We are having to devise completely novel biology to bridge the systems of distantly related creatures,' Dr Shorbody explained.

'Interesting. How?'

'Take the centaur. In this case we are doubling up on some of the features because we have the abdomen and thorax of both a horse and a human brought together into a single creature, so horse heart, lungs, gut, liver and so on as well the human equivalents. The nervous and endocrine systems need integrating, which is challenging.'

He typed onto the keyboard on the desk and a picture of an unusual dead animal came up on the screen.

'We have an animal model we have been using as a proof of concept,' he continued. 'This is a baboon torso mounted on the body of a donkey. This one you see on the screen is our tenth attempt, which remained alive three months. We are optimistic we'll iron out the remaining problems soon, paving the way for a human trial.'

'Do you have a human subject available for transformation into the centaur?' asked Alex Drembold.

'Yes,' said Dr Shorbody, as he typed. 'This one.'

A picture of Cadfael appeared on the screen.

After leaving the picture on the screen a few seconds, Dr Shorbody typed more and the picture changed. A monstrous ape appeared on the screen, but this was no ordinary ape. For scale the primate was shown next to one of the scientists in Dr Shorbody's team. I estimated it must be at least ten feet tall, the most monstrous yeti ever imagined. On top of its huge body was a grotesque face with a single gigantic staring eye in the centre of its forehead.

'A slightly simpler project has been the Cyclops. Here we see the animal model, a chimpanzee. There are two aspects to this. The formulation of the single eye and the increase in the animal's size.'

'And the human subject for this one?' enquired Alex Drembold.

Dr Shorbody brought up a picture of Frankie onto the display, before moving to a picture of a further monstrosity, a blend of a goat and orangutan with an exaggeratedly prominent phallus.

'Here we have the animal model for the satyr. Besides his combination of physical features defined to us by the mythology of ancient Greece, the essential requirement is his insatiable and indiscriminate sexual appetite. A key feature is the satyr must be triggered into sexual activity by proximate femininity unencumbered by higher mental inhibitions such as morality, loyalties and finer aesthetic considerations. Our selected human subject is this one.'

I was shocked to see my own picture appear. They'd have to catch me first.

Philomena intervened. 'We know from the time this individual spent with us in Abballon his sexual appetites take precedence over conditions that might inhibit others. Our animal husbandry specialist has mentioned to me in her personal experience his virility is reliably excellent at all times.'

Dr Shorbody moved on. A picture appeared of the bedraggled corpse of a peculiar specimen consisting of the torso and head of a rhesus monkey mounted onto the back half of a large fish resembling a salmon.

'The mermaid is proving the most challenging of our mythological creatures. Combining the metabolisms of a warm-blooded mammal with a cold-blooded marine creature has thrown up numerous problems. Nevertheless we think we have found a workable solution. By integrating the cold-blooded marine elements with the warm-blooded by means of an adapted placental interface in the mammalian uterus we have achieved a workable coexistence. Our human subject is this young woman.'

I gasped at Jenny's picture. I was now more determined than ever to make good my escape and mount a rescue.

There followed a general discussion on the technical intricacies of the programme after which the meeting broke up. Everybody left except the man who had come in at the start to set up the extra display screen. He packed the screen and tidied papers and other bits left lying around.

I realised it was now or never. I would never be able to evade capture as myself, but if I could assume this man's identity I stood a chance of getting away. I burst out of the equipment cupboard and in a single flowing dash launched myself at the man. I swung my fist at the man's jaw with the full power of my strong right arm. The impact was immense, the man's jaw broke with a sickening crack and the force took him off his feet. From the pain in my hand I figured my knuckle bones were probably broken too. The man fell back, smashing the back of his head against the table as he fell heavily onto the floor, unconscious at the least, possibly even dead.

I winced, shocked by what I had done. I hadn't really wanted to hurt the man and I didn't want him dead, but, needs must. I had to get away.

I quickly removed the lab coat from the man's body. I stepped into the corridor in his coat and badge. At one end was a lift. I used the man's card swipe to open it and stepped in. The floor numbers started from zero and went into the minuses. Evidently I was now on floor minus 3, three floors below ground level or some sort of base level. I pressed the zero button. As I had guessed it opened up into a reception area.

At the far end of the reception was a series of pods mounted on a light rail system. Without hesitation or inviting interest from peering around the place I jumped to the conclusion this was my best chance to make an exit. I walked briskly to the far pod, used my newly acquired swipe card to cause the pods doors to open and stepped in. Without pausing I perused the selection of options and pressed the button marked 'Camelot Grotto'. Seconds later the pod moved, gathering speed as it disappeared into a tunnel bored into the solid rock.

Within minutes the pod glided to a halt within another rocky cavern. I pressed the button provided to open the doors and stepped out. Fortunately there was nobody else, so I wouldn't be challenged. There was a door at the end of the room, which I used my borrowed card to open, stepping out into Grotto of the Knights of Camelot theme park where I could mingle with the excited holidaymakers. I had made it out.

Fanciful Work of Fiction

If Rebekah Nemmberg, the editor of *The Daily Trumpet*, was relieved to see me in one piece on the news floor of the paper's industrial style offices, she gave no indication.

'I assigned you for two weeks to investigate the strange happenings in Glastonbury. You disappeared for nearly three months, without getting in touch. Then you breeze back like everything is okay. It's not. Tell me a reason why I shouldn't fire you, here and now.'

'But I couldn't get in touch. I was stuck there, without means of communication.'

'It wasn't as if you were stranded in the Amazon or on the Moon. You were in England, not even 200 miles away.'

'But I may as well have been on the Moon. The bloody place is cut off completely from the outside world in a sort of prehistoric time warp.'

Rebekah brought up a document on her computer screen.

'Well, this brings us to this cock and bull story you've written about this whole affair, no doubt in a hopeless attempt to redeem yourself. It's the sort of fanciful stuff that might appeal to a publisher of pulp fiction, not a newspaper.'

'But it's the truth. I promise you. The truth can be stranger than fiction.'

'Really?' said Rebekah, eyes narrowed.

I wasn't convinced she believed me, but sensed she did not entirely disbelieve either.

'True or not, it doesn't make a difference. It's

unpublishable. There is no supporting evidence, and we would be stepping on the toes of powerful people who would sue our arses off. We've already been leaned on by some you wouldn't want to antagonise.'

'But we can't let this drop,' I pleaded. 'There are people in captivity who will have hideous experiments carried out on them, unless we can thwart this whole thing.'

Rebekah looked hard at me, weighing things up in her mind. 'Alright. You had better get your arse back to Glastonbury and dig up some proper evidence we can publish.'

'Thanks, I will.'

'No swanning off on your own for a three month holiday this time. I want a report from you daily, without fail. Got it?'

'Yes, will do.'

After leaving Rebekah's office I wandered over to see Tim Bennston, my ever-helpful and level-headed friend on the news desk.

'You know she was worried sick about you when you disappeared,' Tim confided. 'She's got a soft spot for you, if you ask me.'

'She gave no sign of it just now. Tore me off a strip and threatened to fire me.'

'When we couldn't get in touch with you, she had search parties hunting in all directions and your picture plastered all over the paper.'

'Really, let's have a look.'

Tim hummed cheerfully as he browsed back through the archive of old editions.

There was a front page headline entitled 'Glastonbury

Triangle' under which was an array of head shots of missing persons, including of me. The article below highlighted the large number of disappearances in the Glastonbury area, people who vanished without trace, among them a brave *Daily Trumpet* investigative reporter. The local police were lambasted for their feeble attempts to resolve the matter accompanied by insinuations of a cover-up by influential figures in the locality.

A later front page had the headline 'Enticed by Satan' accompanied by a picture of the lovely Ivy Langport adorned with pentangle jewellery and another of her worried parents, Elsie and Eddie, who were quoted saying their daughter, brought up by them as a good Catholic, had been enticed by a local coven of Devil worshipping witches. There was a photo of the outside of Megan's Magick Shoppe, which the article identified as the witches' lair. An accompanying piece highlighted the police failure to locate the many people who had disappeared accompanied by a large photo of me and smaller photos of other missing persons.

'And this one only went out yesterday,' said Tim, bringing up a two page feature that had occupied the middle of the paper entitled 'Demonic Menace in our midst'. It was a fleshed out version of the piece I drafted myself just before my departure for Abballon. A picture of Megan's Magick Shoppe was shown again, with blurred photos of the proprietors Nathan and Megan, together with other members of the Mendip Moon Coven. The article implied a host of sinister demons had been conjured up and now infested the premises.

'By the way, as you're going to be in Glastonbury,' said Tim, 'you may want to follow up on this.'

He handed me a garbled report about sightings of a strange wild beast reported to have strayed from a former Ministry of Defence facility in the Mendips. I recognised the name of the informant, Eddie Langport, Ivy's father.

'Yes, for sure. I'll chase it up.'

'I believe I have been reported as a missing person. I'd like to unreport myself.'

I was at the front desk of Glastonbury police station. The desk surface was mounted at a height requiring the supplicant to stand, forming the window between the lobby in the general public realm. The officer was behind this glass, situated within the inner police sanctum from which the general public were excluded unless under arrest.

'Right you are, sir,' replied the police woman in reassuring West Country tones. 'Can I have the name please and your date of birth.'

The police woman took down the details.

'I have information relating to other missing persons. I'd like to talk to someone.'

'Well, if you give me their names and dates of birth I'll take those down too.'

'It's not so simple. I really need to talk to someone in CID. Previously I was talking to Inspector Bellard and Sergeant Lunnton. Could you put me in touch with them?'

'I'm sorry but DI Bellard has moved on and Sergeant Lunnton has moved out of CID. Could I put you on to someone else in CID?'

I didn't like the sound of it. Involuntarily I stretched my lips, showing my teeth in a grimace. I could picture the disbelief and open incredulity I would face trying to explain my bizarre experiences to a stranger. I was in no hurry to have a policeman I didn't know write me off as a deranged lunatic.

'No, thanks, but I'll leave it for now. I might come back to you later.'

'You sure? If you've got information you really should let us have it.'

'I know you said Sergeant Lunnton had moved on, but would it still be okay to talk to him, informally. It's all a bit sensitive, you see.'

The police woman looked dubious.

'It wouldn't be his responsibility these days. Shouldn't really be involved in missing persons.'

'Well, it's not just missing persons. I want to talk to him personally.'

'Well, I don't know. I'm not supposed to pass stuff to officers from members of the public. You might be one of those stalkers. Got it in for him, or something.'

'I'm not a stalker and I haven't got it in for him.'

'But how do I know that? As a police officer you have to arrest people and sometimes they bear a grudge.'

'Could you just leave him a message to call me, if he wants? If he would rather not, he can ignore it.'

'Alright, I'll leave him a message.'

'Langport Farm, Mendip Estate' said the sign adorned with the Marquess of Mendip's family coat of arms.

I turned my modest rental car into the farm lane, following between a hedgerow and wire fence behind which cows grazed in a muddy field. At the end of the lane was a yard surrounded by a ramshackle assortment of farm buildings, an old barn, a utilitarian milking parlour fashioned out of concrete, now heavily stained with brown slurry and green slime, a newly constructed barn, steel framed and clad in corrugated cement board.

I bumped over the unevenly paved farmyard steering carefully around potholes. To one side was another small field in which alpacas grazed. I went on about another hundred yards to reach the farmhouse, a substantial but dilapidated building with a Georgian core, substantially altered in an ad hoc fashion over the intervening centuries. I parked in a convenient space a little way from the front of the house.

Despite it being the middle of the day in high summer, the curtains were drawn across the windows of what I assumed must have been one of the main reception rooms. Nosiness being part of the job description for a journalist, before making my presence known, I tiptoed to the window and peered through where one curtain left a slight gap.

Elsie and Eddie Langport, who I had last seen trying to drag their daughter Ivy from the Mendip Moon Coven's Esbat ceremony, were sat around a table together with a flamboyantly dressed middle-aged woman with wildly tousled hair and wilder flashing eyes, their fingertips touching on the table top.

'Is there anybody there?' demanded the flamboyant woman, the large wooden beads on here necklace bouncing on the cleavage of her heaving bosom.

I crept away and went to the front door, pulling on the old-fashioned bell pull. A bell jingled from within the house.

The homely farmer's wife Elsie Langport answered.

She blanched, reeling back.

'Hello Mrs Langport, you remember me, I expect, Simon Chewton. We met in Glastonbury and I'm a friend of Ivy's.'

Elsie nodded, her lips set tight.

'Is it alright if I come in?'

'Oh, yes, please do.'

Elsie led the way to the dimly lit dining room, where her husband and the exotic woman waited.

'This is Simon, he has come over to talk to us about Ivy,' said Elsie, still shaking.

'You have come over from the Other Side?' said the other woman.

'Yes, I suppose I have,' I said.

'What can you tell us about Ivy?' asked the woman.

'She is well, actually. She has found herself a fine young man, by the name of Huggs. They seem happy.'

'Oh, I see,' said Elsie. 'So, she's not bothered about Harry then?'

'You mean Harry Mallet. No, I think she has moved on as far as he is concerned.'

'So, she'd be telling him to go on and find someone else then,' chipped in Eddie Langport.

'Yes, I think it's what she'd want him to do,' I confirmed.

'Does she have anything to say to us?' Elsie enquired.

I stood and pondered. 'I'm not sure really. She didn't mention anything.'

'Is there anybody else who wants to talk to us today?' intoned the other woman as if addressing somebody in the ceiling.

Nobody else answered so I did. 'Not that I'm aware of.

I came over on my own.'

'Do you have any other message for us?' asked the other woman, holding up her hands in mid-air and letting them shake.

'Well, not exactly. Just to let you know Ivy is alright, I suppose.'

'But where did you all get to? What happened to you?' demanded Eddie.

'Well, it's a long story. It has been alright for some, like Ivy for instance. They're out in the light and fresh air. But there's those who have ended up in a different place. Locked up underground. It's not been good for them at all.'

Elsie smiled broadly. 'So Ivy's in heaven then! Thank you, sweet Jesus! The other folk, would it do any good if we prayed for them?'

'I was thinking more in terms of rescue,' I said.

'But you can't rescue people from Hell,' Elsie exclaimed.

It had been dawning on me since I arrived that my audience were under a major misapprehension. 'I think we are talking at cross-purposes. Nobody is in Heaven or Hell. They are all alive and kicking, for the time being. Ivy is fit and well, but it would be good to get her out of there. It's not a safe place.'

'You don't mean they're in Purgatory, do you?' said Elsie, with a puzzled look.

'No, it's not Purgatory either. It's right here in flesh and blood reality.'

'So, where is she then?' Eddie demanded.

'It's called Abballon. I'm not sure precisely where it is, but I believe it isn't very far from here.'

'Is it do with those witches, Devil worshippers and what not?' asked Eddie.

'Actually I think they are just cover for something more sinister.'

'You mean something to do with the Devil! Saints preserve us!' exclaimed Elsie.

'I am feeling bad vibrations in the aether. There is an evil presence,' intoned the psychic woman.

I was losing my patience. It was time to put a stop to this. I strode to the window and threw open the curtains to let the bright daylight shine in.

'There is no evil presence. Just me. I am flesh and blood, just like you.'

'But you were in the paper. Disappeared. Just like Ivy and the others,' said Eddie, indignant.

'Yes, disappeared. But I'm back. And if you give me a chance, I'll get Ivy back too.'

'Well, I'll be darned,' Eddie exclaimed.

'Thank the Lord,' said Elsie.

'Look, I could murder a cup of tea. Perhaps if you see me drink it, you'll believe I'm real. Then we can talk about it.'

Elsie bustled out to make the tea. I reached out my hand to greet the Langport's other visitor, the gaudily attired woman summoning up spirits.

'We haven't been introduced. I'm Simon.'

The woman shook my hand weakly. 'I'm Elona. I'm a psychic.'

She pulled out a lurid business card with a graphic portraying ghosts and ghouls in a deep purplish hue. 'Elona Silvana, Spiritual Medium,' it announced.

Elsie came swaying back in with a pot of tea and cups

on a tray. All eyes were on me as I took my first swig, confirming to all I was real.

'So, Ivy is alive then, definitely?' asked Eddie.

'Yes, definitely,' I confirmed.

'So how do we get her back?'

'Don't know yet. I'm working on it.'

'What can we do to help?'

'Can you put me in touch with Harry Mallet? I don't have his number or anything.'

Elsie rummaged around and scribbled on a piece of paper, which she handed over.

'One other thing. You said something to *The Daily Trumpet* about some kind of escaped animal. Could you tell me something about it?'

Elsie shuddered. 'Great brute of a thing, it was.'

'What sort of a brute?'

'A big cat of some sort, but with massive fangs, biggest you've ever seen,' said Eddie. 'It took one of our cows. Upset the whole herd. They were on edge for days afterwards. Our milk yields are way down.'

'And one of the alpacas,' added Elsie.

'That's true,' Eddie agreed. 'And they cost more than the cows.'

'So, what did you do?'

'Didn't know what to do. I called the police and this sergeant came round. He didn't know what to do either.'

'This sergeant, do you happen to have his name?'

'Lunnton,' Elsie chipped in. 'Sergeant Lunnton.'

'What then?'

'A bit later some men came round. Said they'd been sent over by the Marquess to take care of things. They shot the cat with a dart, then loaded it into a van and took off.

They needed a forklift, it were that big,' explained Eddie.

'What happened about the dead cow? Weren't you out of pocket?'

'No, not a bit. They gave me 10,000 quid in an envelope. Told me to keep quiet.'

'It was someone sent over by the Marquess. What's he up to, do you think?'

Eddie and Elsie looked at each other and shook their heads.

'I wouldn't say anything against his Lordship. Always been good to us, they have, the Mendip estate. We're fourth generation tenants here.'

Fortuitously it was only minutes after I left the Langports when I picked up a call from Sergeant Lunnton.

'Glad to hear you are back in circulation, alive and well,' he said.

'So am I, but we need to get the others out too.'

'Yes, I know. You're the only one who has reappeared, as far as I know.'

'Do you have any information at all about the other missing persons?'

'I don't really know. I've been reassigned to other duties, so it isn't my responsibility anymore.'

'Would you like to have a chat about it?' I offered.

'I can't talk to you about it officially, because it's outside my remit now.'

'How about unofficially, over a drink perhaps. I'm buying.'

'Alright, outside Glastonbury police station, at the end of my shift.'

I arrived outside the police station at the agreed time. I decided driving would not be a good idea after a few pints in the pub with Sergeant Lunnton, so I came on foot. The sergeant hadn't arrived.

After 15 or 20 minutes a police van pulled up. Sergeant Lunnton leaned out of the window. 'Sorry, held up a bit. Just got to deal with this lot, then I'll be with you.'

I heard clucking from the back of the van. A loud aggressive voice yelled from the back with a barely intelligible expletive ridden tirade in a thick West Country accent. Sergeant Lunnton drove the van around the corner of the brutalist concrete building, whereupon an electrically operated heavy duty steel gate opened to allow him into the enclosed police station compound.

It was a further half an hour before Sergeant Lunnton emerged, now in civilian clothes.

'Sorry about that,' he said. 'A case of chicken rustling. Caught the culprit red-handed. A handful, but we got him booked in. He can stew in the cells for the time being. Problem then was, what to do with the chickens. Farmer won't take them back because of the danger of fowl pox. There're stuck in the yard for now. Given them some water and chicken feed. Have to figure it out in the morning.'

Despite the kerfuffle he had just been dealing with Sergeant Lunnton was calm and unhurried as if such bother was just part of the daily routine.

'No worries,' I assured him. 'Let's go and get that drink.'

'Bloody need one, after that lot, I can tell you.'

He probably did, I reflected. Yet it did not show in his manner. His broad face was lit by a friendly smile, his voice languidly calm as he strolled with a steady purposeful gait. Despite being heavily built enough to appear threatening if he chose, Sergeant Lunnton gave off the vibrations of a cuddly teddy bear.

We adjourned to the Oak and Holly. I had proposed the Mendip Grenadier, but Sergeant Lunnton thought they would be suspicious of policemen, even ones dressed in mufti. A policeman was probably no more popular with some of the clientele at the Oak and Holly than at the Mendip Grenadier, I mused, but at the Mendip Grenadier there could have been a punch up, whereas at the Oak and Holly the purveyors of illegal substances would have just slipped out the back.

I brought us over two foaming pints of Meadow Dew ale.

'So what is your role these days, Sergeant?

'Call me Keith, please. I'm not on duty now. Agricultural Affairs squad. To do with livestock, mostly. You wouldn't believe some of the shenanigans what goes on in farming, you really wouldn't.'

'Funny you should say that; I heard your name mentioned just a couple of hours ago.'

'Nothing bad, I hope.'

'It was to do with some escaped big cat killing a cow and alpaca.'

'Oh, yeah, I remember that one. Very odd, that was.'

'How so?'

'Well, it was huge. Like nothing you've seen, with great big fangs. Don't know what it was. I certainly wasn't going to take it on. Well, I was going to go and call a zoo, or something, but I put in a call to the Marquess of Mendip's estate office first, since it was on their land. They just said, don't worry about it. Leave it to them. They'd deal with it. Well, I was dubious. Didn't see how they could handle it any better than I could. But I called back the farmer a couple of hours later and he told me it had all been taken care of. I even called back in person just to make sure there wasn't still some giant cat marauding around the place, but all was well.'

'Any idea where the cat came from?'

'Well, yes, I did wonder about it. Being huge it left bloody great footprints, so I took a look. I tracked it to the edge of the Ministry of Defence land bordering the Mendip estate. I couldn't go further though.'

'What's going on in there, I wonder?'

'Don't really know. But what about you, where have you been all this time?' Keith asked.

'Hm. Long story. Well, you will remember your boss DI Bellard had me fitted with a tracking device after I told you I was going off on the trail of the other missing persons.'

'Yes, I remember.'

'Well, I got through to where the other missing persons were, but it's completely cut off from the outside world. Phones, tracking devices, anything electronic, doesn't get through from there. And the big cat you dealt with, they have those in there too, as well as other weird beasts, mammoths, wolves, aurochs and all sorts. It's a new theme park the Marquess planned, I found out that much. The people in there are going to be part of the theme park, examples of prehistoric people for visitors to gawp at, as if they had gone back in time.'

'Well, I'll be damned.'

'Your colleague on reception at the police station asked

me if I wanted to tell someone from CID about it, but when I found out both you and DI Bellard had moved on, I bottled out. I couldn't imagine anyone believing such a bizarre story.'

'Yes, I see what you mean. They'd have had you down as a looney.'

'But you don't think I'm a looney, do you?'

'No. But then, for one thing, I already know you. And anyway, after my own experience with the monster cat, I'm more inclined to believe such things.'

'But how come you aren't in CID anymore? What happened?'

'Alright, but anything I say has to be off the record. You mustn't quote me. Okay?'

'Sure. I definitely won't mention your name in anything. Promise.'

'We always figured the Marquess and the Knights of Camelot theme park were involved, but it was tough to get the evidence. You were there when we did the first raid, but we didn't find anything and the Marquess and his friends in high places didn't take kindly to it. It made it hard to go back in to investigate further.'

'I can understand how he might block things. He has powerful connections.'

'After we lost trace of you we tried to get another search warrant. Initially our own bosses in the force wouldn't allow it. DI Bellard made a fuss and in the end we drew up a warrant, but then we couldn't get a JP to approve it. It seems our MP, Sir Nicholas Jardinair, had put a word in, so we couldn't get one.'

'That's interesting. I wonder how Sir Nicholas ties in with the Marquess's schemes.'

'After there was a lot of publicity about missing persons, with you having gone missing and then Ivy Langport. *The Daily Trumpet* made a big song and dance about it, complaining the police weren't doing anything. Police indifference and incompetence, they called it. We weren't at all happy. Anyway, afterwards we got our warrant.'

'Sorry about what *The Daily Trumpet* said. It wasn't me because I wasn't there. Must have been our editor. She can be a right cow when she puts her mind to it.'

'Well, here's the trouble. Before you disappeared we already knew the disappearances had something to do with the grotto in the Knights of Camelot theme park. It's underground so we couldn't track anything in there. So, what DI Bellard had arranged was to install a tracking device on the Royal Barge, which takes the people up into the cave. We kept it quiet though, didn't get any warrant or anything for it. We didn't want it to leak out it was there, you see, which it would have done if it had been official.'

'You managed to track me that far then?'

'Yes, right up to the end of the cave, which is where we lost you. But we did at least know this was the way through to wherever you folk were getting to.'

'Then what?'

'Well, we carried out our raid, searched behind the scenes in the cave, but we didn't get any further. But then, I guess someone on the Marquess's team wondered how we knew where to look. They had someone scan for bugs and found the tracker on the Royal Barge.'

'Oh dear. I suppose that's when smelly brown stuff hit the fan.'

'It certainly did. The Marquess got a court injunction against what his brief called further vexatious raids on Mendip estate properties and personnel. Effectively the police are now banned from investigating anything in connection with the Marquess and his properties. As for DI Bellard, well he isn't a DI any more. There was a disciplinary hearing and he was busted to sergeant and put back in uniform. He now works as a traffic officer in London. And me, well you know what happened to me, I'm now in the Agricultural Affairs squad looking after cows, chickens and big cats.'

Mindful of the shock I had caused at the Langports when I turned up unannounced I decided I had better first phone Jenny's parents, Delia and Henry Potterswell. Henry answered.

'It's me, Simon Chewton, I'm back in circulation.'

'Oh, my goodness, we were giving up hope. And Jenny, is she with you?'

'I'm sorry, she isn't. But I have seen her. She is okay, at least for the time being. We need to get her out of there, though.'

'Out of where exactly?'

'It's a long story. Is it alright if I come over?'

'Yes, of course.'

My finger was still on the glazed ceramic bell push as the imposing front door of the Potterswell's substantial Edwardian home swung open. It was Jenny's mother, Delia, who opened it. Jenny's father, Henry, was hovering just behind in the hall. He looked flushed, I'm guessing from having spent the time since my call anxiously pacing.

Delia as always was meticulous in her duties as hostess, using the rituals of social convention to contain her seething emotions. She was not one to let her standards drop regardless of the pressures of daily life. As always she was meticulously turned out, elegantly made up, wearing a sleek dress set off with tasteful pieces of understated jewellery. Only her haggard features, the boniness of her face and the sagging dry skin on her neck betrayed the stress and worry she had been under over recent months.

The worry had taken its toll on Henry too, but, like Delia, he would never have let it get the better of him. His face was redder. A man of action the pressure had wound him up like a spring, a caged tiger poised to break out and rip into anyone who got in his way.

As Delia took me through the entrance hall past the imposing clutter of a grand long case clock, ornate mirror and military memorabilia she gushed her relief and gratitude.

'So glad to hear you had got back after we had been so worried about you and the others who had vanished.'

'I'm glad too.'

'It was so good of you to come over right away. There must have been so many other things you needed to take care of.'

'Yes, there has been a lot.'

'So kind of you to take the time to talk to us about Jenny.'

Henry dutifully kept up the show of hospitality he knew was expected of him by his wife. He opened the military campaign chest serving as a drinks cabinet and I accepted a gin and tonic. Henry poured me a generous measure, a whisky and soda for himself and dry sherry for

Delia.

'Now, about Jenny, where is she and how do we get her back?' demanded Henry once hospitality had been attended to.

I sighed. 'I wish I had a simple answer, but I don't. I think I had better start from the beginning. I'll warn you now, this is going to be quite a tall tale you may find hard to believe. Nevertheless, it is all true, I assure you.'

Henry and Delia leaned forward. I began my yarn, from coming into the grotto in the Knights of Camelot theme park to meet Philomena right through to my eventual escape from Dr Shorbody's fiendish laboratory complex.

At every stage Henry was diving in with ideas for full scale military assaults, but I had to remind him we hadn't yet pinpointed the exact locations of either Abballon or the underground laboratories. Furthermore it was likely these were located on Ministry of Defence property, so we might be opposed by the full might of the British armed forces besides anything the Marquess had lined up.

'Well, there you have it, that's the full picture,' I announced, after a couple of hours and two refills of my gin and tonic.

'Well, that really was quite a yarn, I must say,' observed Henry. 'Has a ring of truth to it. I'm a good judge of character and a sound chap like you isn't going to make it up.'

'We have a few challenges. There is no chance of getting cooperation from the police. My editor has made it clear *The Daily Trumpet* won't publish anything more on this until I can get solid material to back it up. It is also clear the Marquess enjoys the support and protection of powerful establishment figures, such as our local MP, your neighbour, Sir Nicholas Jardinair.'

'I know some people from my army days,' said Henry.

'I just want to get Jenny out of there,' said Delia, her voice quivering as she struggled to hold back tears.

'Of course Jenny is the priority for us, but what we really need to be doing is busting this whole thing apart and rescuing all the poor sods trapped in there,' I said.

'Quite right. Clear out the whole rotten mess once and for all,' Henry agreed.

'Alright, look, I suggest you get your army contacts lined up, Colonel, and in the meantime I've got a couple more lines of enquiry of my own. Then we'll meet up again in a day or two.'

Gathering of Forces

I arranged to see Harry Mallet at the workaday ale house where we had first met, the Mendip Grenadier. Harry, gruff and impatient about social niceties, came straight to the point. 'What's this you've got to tell me about Ivy then?'

'She's out there with the other missing people who have been on the news, like I was.'

'Oh, yeah. I saw you in the paper. So, you were in the same place?'

'Yes, that's right.'

'Where's that then?'

'You know, I'm not sure, but I don't think it's far from here. My guess is it's on the Ministry of Defence place, Wookey Vale.'

'How come you're not sure?'

'We were kept confined. We couldn't see exactly where we were.'

'What? You mean locked up?'

'Well, sort of. Where we were, where Ivy is, is out in the open air, but there's some sort of heat ray thing keeping us so we can't stray from the village and farm. And beyond that there's wild animals. Dangerous stuff. Big cats, wolves, and so on.'

'Big cats? You mean like the one that killed a cow on Ivy's mum and dad's place. I saw it in today's *Daily Trumpet*.'

'Yes, exactly. I saw one kill a deer when I was there. One of them came after me too.'

'You're not having me on, are you?'

'I know it sounds strange, but it's true. Straight up.'

The two of us had been sitting side by side looking ahead and taking the occasional swig from our pints of Meadow Dew ale. At this point Harry swivelled to face me, concern appearing on his face.

'What about Ivy? Is she safe with all what's going on?'

'I'd say she's safe, at least for now. This is where the heat ray thing comes in. It keeps the people held in the village and farm they've got there, and it keeps the wild animals, big cats, wolves, mammoths and stuff out of the place as well. When I was there, I tried to get out, but I was beaten back by the heat ray. At the same time there was this huge cat thinking it would have a go at me. It rushed across at me, but then the heat ray back beat it back as well.'

'But you're here now, so how did you get out?'

'Well, first I got out into where the massive great wild animals are. I went up a cliff, where they hadn't put any heat ray or anything because I reckon they thought nobody could climb it.'

'What, you some sort of mountaineer then?'

'Nah. But I'm not scared of heights, particularly. It wasn't too difficult.'

'What happened then?'

'Well, I got caught, didn't I? They took me back to the village.'

'Then what?'

'I got what they call cast out. It's what they do, if you don't obey the rules.'

'Like not going out among the animals?'

'Yes, and a load of other stuff. There's loads not allowed.'

'Well, cast out. That's alright. You wanted to be out,

didn't you?'

'But that's not what it means. I ended up in this laboratory place. Underground, like a prison, except that they do experiments on you.'

'What sort of experiments?'

'Horrific. I saw what they were planning. I was going to be turned into a satyr.'

'What's a satyr when it's at home?'

'A sort of half goat, half human that does a lot of shagging.'

Harry turned to me aghast. 'You what?

'I know. It sounds unbelievable. It's the Marquess behind it. He wants to open another theme park with these mythical creatures in it. He's got a mad scientist setting it all up.'

'Mad scientist! Now you're pulling my leg. You're having a laugh.'

I turned to Harry and gave him a serious look. 'No, I'm not. I wish I were. This is serious. They really are doing this stuff. And I'm not barmy either, if that's what you're thinking. The Marquess and his mates have really got this set up.'

Harry looked me up and down through narrowed eyes, weighing me up. 'So how did you get out?'

'Down a rubbish chute, then through the laboratories. It's when I found out what they were planning. Then there was this little underground railway that gets you out at the back of the grotto at the Knights of Camelot.'

'So, now you're out, what now?'

'Got to go back and rescue them somehow.'

'Why would you do that?'

'My Jenny's there. In the laboratory. They're going to

turn her into a mermaid unless I can get her out.'

'Mermaid? Now you're really off your rocker.'

'Seriously. Half fish half human. Just like what they planned for me, half goat half human. And there's another bloke in there. He's going to be a centaur. In case you're wondering, half horse half human. We have to get them out.'

'Who's we?'

'You and me and whoever else we can get on board, if you're up for it.'

'Why me?'

'You want to get Ivy out, don't you?'

'Well, yes, she's alright from what you said. In the village, I mean.'

'For the time being. But they sent me and my Jenny and a load of other folk into the laboratories. It's only a matter of time before Ivy winds up there too.'

Harry had been taking a swig from his pint. He choked on it as he took in what I had just said. 'I see what you mean. I couldn't let that happen to her.'

I had hoped to be able to slip in without fuss to see my friend Nathan Oxbury in the Mendip Moon witches coven, but this proved impossible. From the end of the road I could already see a commotion taking place in Glastonbury High Street.

The gathering looked out of place in those surroundings, invaders from the world of conventional respectability uneasily intruding into the bohemian new age alternative lifestyle of witchcraft, mythology, shabby chic clothing, crystals and incense. The upholders of moral rectitude had congregated in front of Nathan's place,

Megan's Magick Shoppe, behind a catholic priest carrying out a ritual, holding forth with the vehemence of an Old Testament prophet.

'Strike terror, Lord, into the beast now laying waste your vineyard. Fill your servants with courage to fight manfully against the reprobate dragon,' intoned the priest in a loud commanding tone.

Another voice intervened.

'Ah, yes, what is it Henut? …Yes, it'll be Ala. She's a dragon who destroys crops.'

It was a woman's voice I recognised as Elona Silvana, the extravagantly theatrical spiritual medium I met at the Langports' place carrying out the séance. She was hovering in the front row of the crowd of onlookers, with her ever credulous clients, Elsie and Eddie Langport in proximity.

The priest turned and looked at her sternly, and then continued his haranguing of the evil spirits in his thick Irish brogue.

'I cast you out, unclean spirits, along with every Satanic power of the enemy, every spectre from hell, and all your fellow companions; in the name of our Lord Jesus Christ. Begone and stay far from this place of God. For it is He who commands you, He who flung you headlong from the heights of heaven into the depths of Hell. It is He who commands you, He who once stilled the sea and the wind and the storm. Hearken, therefore, and tremble in fear, Satan, you enemy of the faith, you foe of the human race, you begetter of death, you robber of life, you corrupter of justice, you root of all evil and vice; seducer of men, betrayer of the nations, instigator of envy, font of avarice, fomenter of discord, author of pain and sorrow.'

'Ah, Henut, yes… Surgat, he who can open of all locks, he is refusing to leave,' chipped in Elona, conveying a message from her supposed spiritual companion. The priest glared at her, before resuming his exhortation of the Satanic forces.

'Why, then, do you stand and resist, knowing as you must Christ the Lord brings your plans to nothing? Fear Him, who in Isaac was offered in sacrifice, in Joseph sold into bondage, slain as the paschal lamb, crucified as man, yet triumphed over the powers of Hell.'

The priest made three signs of the cross, glancing sideways at Elona to head off any further intervention.

'Begone, then, in the name of the Father, and of the Son, and of the Holy Spirit. Give place to the Holy Spirit by this sign of the holy cross of our Lord Jesus Christ, who lives and reigns with the Father and the Holy Spirit, God, forever and ever,' intoned the priest with finality.

'Amen,' called out those attending the proceedings. Among them was the earnestly devout Dr Theophilus Pottinger; dressed in an austere cassock, huge and hairy like a pious yeti, he knelt in prayer on the pavement. Also present was Ophelia Jardinair, the vociferous leader of the Moral Multitude accompanied by various of her followers including the Langports and their irritating companion Elona Silvana. Scattered around the periphery were a scattering of curious onlookers.

Eventually I eased my way through to the front of the throng where I managed to catch the eye of an enthralled Eddie Langport.

'What's going on?'

'An exorcism. Casting out the evil spirits from that place,' Eddie replied.

'Oh, I see. So now they're cast out, it'll be safe to go in then?'

'Oh, no, I wouldn't go in there,' he said, eyes flitting as he shook his head.

'Got to go in. Got to get Ivy out of where she is, and the others too.'

'You're braver than I am then, and no mistake,' replied wide-eyed Eddie gravely.

Members of the crowd gasped as I strode in through the front door of the shop. Some observers, who would have recognised me from my picture published in *The Daily Trumpet* as one of the missing persons, took me for a ghost.

I weaved through the racks and displays of crystal balls, tarot cards, pentangle emblems, athame daggers, chalices and cauldrons to find Nathan and his wife Megan crouching behind the shop counter from where they had been observing the spectacle.

'Simon, is it you?' exclaimed a nervous Nathan in surprise.

'Yes, Nathan mate, it's me.'

'So, you got back somehow. How did you do it?'

'It's a long story. But what's all this carry on about?' I indicated the commotion outside.

'It was the story in *The Daily Trumpet* the other day, the one that had a picture of the shop saying we're full up with devils and demons.'

His wife Megan spat on the floor. 'Filthy rag!' she exclaimed. She had an air of the fairground about her, showmanship done on the cheap, aged around 40 but trying to be in her 20s, decorated with tattoos, adorned with Wicca-inspired costume jewellery from the shop's stock, she had the care-worn look of someone who had struggled combined with the resilience of someone who had always fought through and survived.

'Oh, I see,' I said, embarrassed it was me who had unleashed this pantomime.

'That Moral Multitude woman has gone and organised a bloody exorcism,' Nathan explained.

'Hypocritical cow!' said Megan. She squared off towards me. 'Anyway, you've got a bloody cheek coming in here, after what your excuse for a paper published about us.'

'Nothing to do with me,' I said, lying through my teeth.

'A likely story.'

'Look, it's true. Don't you trust me?'

Megan looked at me with distaste. It was evident she had taken against me. 'No.'

'Why not?'

'You're too bloody smarmy and cocky to be trusted, with a typical masculine entitled attitude, that's why.'

'It couldn't have anything to do with me. The story went out before I ever got out of there.'

'Out of where exactly?'

'Place called Abballon, where all those missing people ended up.'

'So how come *you* managed to get away?' Megan asked.

'I grabbed my chance when I could, but I couldn't get anyone else out.'

'So, what's to stop the others coming out too?'

'They're confined. No communication with the outside world and the way out blocked.'

I turned to Nathan. 'By the way, the package you gave

me to give Cadfael. He got it and he was thankful.'

'Oh, that's good. How is he?'

'In a predicament, I'm afraid. The stuff you gave him didn't do him any good in the end.'

'Oh, what, you mean the stuff wasn't good for his health or something.'

'No, it's not that. It got him cast out of Abballon.'

'Oh, well that's alright. Sounds like it's good for him to be out from there.'

'Afraid not. When you get cast out you end up in a laboratory at the mercy of a fiendish scientist.'

'What sort of a laboratory?'

'The plan is to turn the folk there into mythical beasts for the Marquess's new theme park. Cadfael's lined up to be turned into a centaur.'

'What's a centaur?'

'Half horse, half human. There's a horse's body and legs and so on and where its head normally is, that bit's human, body, arms and head.'

'Far out,' said Nathan. Megan stared at me with deep scepticism.

'I was there too. They were going to make me into a satyr.'

'And what's a satyr?' demanded Megan, making her disbelief evident.

'Half goat, half human. Goaty back legs but stood upright, horns on the head,' I explained. I glanced down between my legs but decided not to mention that part.

'Yeah, right,' said Megan in a tone verging on ridicule.

'You think that's far out. My Jenny's in there too. Plan is to make her into a mermaid.'

Before we could continue we were distracted by

singing from outside. Dr Theophilus Pottinger was now leading the fervent congregation of Moral Multitude activists, his deep bass voice booming, in an uplifting hymn to the Lord.

'Look, you won't be getting any customers at the moment. Why don't we have a cup of tea and I'll tell you all about it,' I suggested.

Our growing rescue force met at the Potterswell's grand Edwardian home. I introduced my new recruits, bar room brawler Harry Mallet and bohemian hippy Nathan Oxbury.

'Megan not coming?' I enquired.

'No, she's sceptical. Doesn't believe it.'

'Can't say I blame her,' I confessed. 'It is all rather bizarre.'

'You're that bounder who was assaulting that young girl, aren't you,' bristled Henry Potterswell when Harry appeared. 'What the hell do you think you are doing here?'

'It's alright Colonel. He loves Ivy and wants to rescue her, just like I do for Jenny.'

Henry, visibly better now he had some action to prepare for, introduced an old army colleague, Captain Bill Sterning. Bill was a tough looking individual in his late 30s. He had an air of quiet confidence and authority combined with a steely determination few would have dared challenge. Although dressed in casual clothes, there was nothing casual about how he was presented. His trousers were perfectly fitted and pressed, his fleece top immaculately clean and tailored, his loafers polished. From the way he moved and held himself one could sense his hard muscular physique. I felt throughout Bill was quietly assessing the capabilities of Harry, Nathan and myself.

I kicked off the briefing. I explained we would not be getting assistance from the police, what had become of Sergeant Lunnton and former Inspector, now Sergeant Bellard, how I had made contact with Lunnton but not Bellard as yet. I noticed Harry was uncomfortable about the mentioning of policemen.

'Drembold is key to what's going on,' I continued.

'Who's Drembold?' asked Harry.

'Alex Drembold, boss of Drembold Industries.'

'What has he got to do with it?' demanded Henry.

'When I was over there, wherever I looked there were Drembold Industries logos, and I saw him there too. He is up to his neck in it.'

'What are we waiting for?' said Henry. 'Let's get him in for interrogation.'

'It would be a bit rash just to rush in,' I replied. I glanced at Bill and sensed a knowing look on his almost deadpan expression.

'Nearer to hand,' I continued. 'In fact literally next door, we have Sir Nicholas Jardinair. As Minister of State for Defence Establishments he must have knowledge of what the Marquess was up to; they are clearly carrying out their activities on land acquired from the MOD.'

'So, what are we going to do?' harumphed Henry.

'If I might suggest, Henry, with Harry and Nathan to help you, could you take care of surveillance of Sir Nicholas, which would leave Bill and I to pursue Drembold in London?'

I looked towards Bill, whose lip curled into the merest

hint of a smile as he nodded his head by barely a millimetre by way of agreement.

Reconnaissance and Infiltration

I made a call to my old friend Jim Mendolsen from Britannica College.

'Hello Jim, it's Simon.'

'Oh hello. Where are you? I thought you'd gone missing.'

'I had, but I'm back now.'

'So, what happened?'

'Too involved to clarify now. Come to my place for dinner and I'll explain everything.'

'Yes, I can't wait to hear.'

'There's a friend I'd like you to meet as well, when you come over.'

'Anyone I might know?'

'Shouldn't think so.'

'Love interest, perhaps?'

'You'll have to wait and see.'

I had only been back in my Earls Court flat briefly since my escape from the Dr Shorbody's laboratory complex. Not very clean from the outset it was now looking grubbier than ever with layers of dust on every surface and an air of musty neglect. There was also the matter of food. I had never been much of a cook at the best of times.

The capable Bill Sterning took command. He had me go out to obtain something decent requiring a minimum of preparation while in the meantime he would remain to spruce up the flat. I returned with in an Indian takeaway meal, the best desert I could find readymade in the supermarket and a couple of bottles of decent wine. The floors and furniture were now free of dust, rooms aired and the taps never gleamed so bright.

Jim, a shy and bashful person always anxious about meeting new people, was simultaneously nervous and buoyant as he stood on my threshold, evidently delighted at seeing me again after having thought I might be dead.

'Jim, this is Bill.'

Jim, guileless, hesitated with a look of astonishment before taking Bill's hand.

'What's the matter, Jim?'

'I was, sort of, expecting someone else.'

'I never said who. Bill is here to assist with a rescue plan for those I had to leave behind when I escaped.'

'Escape? From where?'

'Let's get ourselves a drink and I'll explain.'

Jim listened carefully as I related my experiences over dinner. Bizarre as the tale might have seemed, Jim showed no scepticism. For him it was the technical aspects he relied on for his assessment of a story's veracity, so as these came out he was quick to delve into the finer details. When these accorded with his detailed knowledge of the technologies involved, how they were employed by Drembold Industries and what he had heard about Dr Shorbody's bizarre ideas, any doubts were banished.

When I described how the police had been discredited by having illegally placed a tracking device in the Royal Barge of the Knights of Camelot grotto Jim blushed. I caught his eye and he hurriedly looked down, his untidy mop of blond hair flopping forward. He bent to scrabble on the floor for his heavy spectacles when they dropped off his nose. I waited for him to say something.

'Alright, it was me,' Jim confessed. 'Alex Drembold

called me in on the Marquess's behalf to scan for electronic eavesdropping devices. It was me who found it.'

'No need to blame yourself, Jim. The device shouldn't have been there and the Marquess was within his rights to check for bugs on his own property. You weren't to know the context.'

'Nice of you to see it that way,' said Jim.

After the dishes had been cleared I came to the point of why Jim had been invited.

'About those people trapped helplessly in the Marquess's scheme, we—Bill, myself and others—are proposing getting them out. You have great expertise that could help.'

Jim smiled and cast his eyes between us. 'I was wondering when you were going to ask me, otherwise why would you be telling me all this?'

'Well, what do you say?' I pressed.

Jim paused and tipped his head from side to side. 'Alright. The crazy stuff needs to be stopped. I'll help.'

'Fantastic. Any ideas about how we might go about it?'

Jim gritted his teeth and looked concerned. 'Look, I'm probably going to tell you some stuff I shouldn't. Classified information. I need you to assure me any secret things that come out will only be used for this rescue mission and nothing else.'

'You have my assurance, and especially that nothing secret will appear on the pages of *The Daily Trumpet*. You have my word.'

'And mine too,' said Bill.

'From your description I am pretty sure this Abballon place and the laboratory complex are within the Wookey Vale Military Facility. Originally it was for training soldiers in field craft and for military exercises, but with the cuts in the armed forces since the Cold War it isn't required for that any more.'

Bill nodded.

'However it does have another use, which you definitely need to keep quiet about.'

Jim looked meaningfully between Bill and I. We both nodded.

'It forms part of Britain's air defence and anti-missile capability, which is why over-flying of the area is prohibited and radio signals are blocked.'

'Right, it all fits.'

'But the secret stuff is underground in camouflaged silos. The MOD has no use for the surrounding landscape. They'd want to have something else going on there to further disguise its purpose.'

'You mean like the Marquess's new theme parks, Pleistocene Panorama and Mythological Magick,' I suggested.

'Exactly, they'd be ideal. Visitors to the parks would be carefully marshalled and controlled, so they wouldn't stray into any of the MOD installations,' said Jim.

'And the Wookey Vale facility borders onto the Mendip estate, so it can all be integrated with the existing Knights of Camelot setup.'

'Yes, it's handy for them,' agreed Jim.

'And the Marquess is best mates with Sir Nicholas Jardinair, who is Minister of State for Defence Establishments, so they could do a deal. As the local MP Sir Nicholas could also pull strings to hamper police from investigating missing persons.'

'Okay, but how are we going to get inside?' chipped in

Bill, anxious to restore focus.

'There are two aspects to this question,' Jim replied. 'I can help with the reconnaissance to figure out what's going on and where things are, but the actual getting ourselves in there in person, it's trickier because it'll be well defended.'

Bill and I rendezvoused with former Inspector, now Sergeant, Bellard in the car park of Ruislip Lido.

Although recognisable, with thinning gingery hair combed back, blue eyes that still had a sparkle, pale freckly face, compact wiry frame, Sergeant Bellard was a different man to the young upwardly mobile Detective Inspector with ambition to reach the police force's higher ranks. In the intervening months he had become middle aged, his ambition excised, now content to coast until he could draw his pension.

Sensing my embarrassment about referring to him by either of his former or now diminished rank when making introductions, Sergeant Bellard intervened. 'Please, call me Jeff. Glad you made it back from wherever it was you disappeared.'

'Glad to be back too. Sorry to hear about the difficulties you got into trying to track me down.'

'My own fault, I suppose. I was pushing my luck with the tracking device on the barge.'

We wandered around the lake a while until we found a bench on the edge of the woods set slightly away from the excited families on the beach and miniature railway.

'What are you doing these days?' I enquired.

'I'm Traffic Operations Supervisor for the Denham and North Harrow Metropolitan Police district.'

'What does it involve?'

'Mostly issuing speeding tickets, arresting drunk drivers and stopping people parking where they shouldn't when they drop off their kids at school.'

'Sounds fascinating.'

'There are more exciting jobs, but I'm making the best of it. Openings for former police officers with a dodgy reputation are limited. But what about you? I'm dying to know what happened.'

'You can see I managed to get out, but our concern now is for others still trapped in the Marquess's fiendish establishment, located as far as we can ascertain, within the Wookey Vale Defence Facility. We intend to get them out.'

'I wondered about that, but it didn't seem possible, him doing anything on MOD land.'

'We think he's done a deal to make use of the land with Sir Nicholas Jardinair, the Minister of State for Defence Establishments.'

'Makes sense. I am pretty sure it was Sir Nicholas who pulled the strings to get our investigation closed down and me out of the way,' said Jeff.

'After your experience I would understand if you didn't want to have anything more to do with any of this, but we were hoping you might throw a bit more light on things for us.'

'Just so long as everything I say is strictly off the record. I've still got my pension to think about.'

'Is there anything we should know to help us in what we are doing?'

'We did find out the name of the company that excavated the tunnels and installed the infrastructure behind the grotto in the Knights of Camelot theme park. We were just about to pay them a visit when the plug was pulled on our investigations.'

'Who were they?'

'Mendip Constructions plc, based in Glastonbury.'

I have a mind like blotting paper for absorbing seemingly pointless information and for once this paid off. 'That's where Harry Mallet works. I'm sure of it.'

After Bill and I returned from London, with the rescue squad assembled among the comfortable accumulated military themed clutter in the Potterswells' sitting room, Henry, pumped up with anticipation, launched the proceedings with a detailed account of the surveillance operations on prime target Sir Nicholas Jardinair.

Sir Nicholas had spent the week in London where during the working day he had been in his office at the Ministry of Defence. On one occasion he had lunch at the Café Royal with Alex Drembold. One evening he had visited a basement flat in Earls Court where he been entertained by a woman in a black leather catsuit, identified as Miss KattyKins. On the Friday evening he was back in Glastonbury addressing the annual dinner of the Young Farmers Association. On the Saturday morning he was at the Conservative Party committee rooms in Glastonbury talking over the issues presented by a succession of local residents. In the afternoon he had accompanied his lady wife Ophelia to open the Lower Saunterton village fete, the proceeds of which went to the Church Restoration fund. On the Sunday morning Sir Nicholas and Ophelia had attended a celebration of Matins at Lower Saunterton church, whose roof was to be renovated by the previous day's fete. Henry's wife Delia had ascertained Sir Nicholas had shareholdings in both Drembold Industries and Mendip Leisure Parks, the operator of the Knights of Camelot theme park.

I congratulated Henry on his thorough investigation into Sir Nicholas, without mentioning I was grateful he had been successfully diverted from blowing our cover by launching raids on the Marquess's property, or worse, interfering with installations at the Wookey Vale Military facility.

Harry Mallet, who had access to his employer's, Mendip Constructions, computer systems had downloaded plans of the extensive underground excavation for the Knights of Camelot grotto extension project. When overlaid against the detailed maps of the area Bill Sterning had brought along, it was clear the tunnelling operations extended far beyond the Marquess's estate and deep into the confines of the Wookey Vale Military facility. After scrutiny I could correlate my recollection of the laboratory complex against matching features on the Mendip Constructions plans. Bill Sterning laid out satellite photographs, correlated with the plans. On these the village of Abballon could be identified as well as the cliff overlooking it.

We discussed the question of how we might overcome or circumvent the formidable defences of the Wookey Vale facility. Jim Mendolsen explained the constraints.

Over-flying had been prohibited so any flying object would be assumed by the military to be hostile and shot down out of hand. Furthermore radio control was impossible because of the deployment of automated radio frequency signal cancellation technology provided by

Drembold Industries. He knew it worked because he had developed it himself. However, he could offer a solution. The weakness in the defences was that it allowed bird life to pass freely.

He opened the large case he had brought in to reveal what could only be described as a robotic seagull. Jim explained it gave out neither a heat nor radar signature, appeared to be a bird to any human observer and flew itself autonomously so that it neither received nor transmitted any radio signal. With this we could carry out preliminary surveillance.

Nathan Oxbury had been a keen caver for years. He pointed on the map to a pothole he knew in the vicinity of Wookey Hole caves. It was not open to the public, nor did it feature on any map. He thought it was unlikely it would be guarded and probable it would connect with caves existing close to the laboratory complex.

We resolved that Jim would utilise his bird-like drone to carry out a detailed aerial survey while Nathan and I surveyed access via the Wookey pothole network. In the meantime Bill and Henry would source explosives, weapons and combat personnel.

Rescue Operation

To begin with, the break-in to the Marquess's secret installation went smoothly.

Over the previous hour Nathan Oxbury had led the way crawling and hauling ourselves through crevices within the damp cold labyrinth of twisting passages and chambers within the hard limestone rock, the light from our head torches reaching feebly into the eerie darkness, each of us struggling to suppress exhaustion and claustrophobia.

At last we had reached our launch point for the mission, a wall of concrete forming the lining of one of the underground railway tunnels, as marked out on the plans obtained by Harry Mallet from his employers.

A specialist member of Bill's squad of military veterans placed a shaped charge of explosive against the concrete. The detonation reverberated and shook each person as if we had been inside an oil drum while it was hit with a sledgehammer. Chunks of rock fell off the insides of the pothole but mercifully inflicted no more injury than slight bruising. Dust blew around, filling nostrils and choking throats. When it settled, light could be seen shining through a ragged man-sized hole piercing the concrete.

Bill's team of six former members of the British special forces led the way through the tunnel into the laboratory complex's reception area, with the remainder of us following close. Retired colonel Henry Potterswell, nominally in command, made a lot of noise in an enthusiastic tally-ho fashion, but the combat forces took their lead from former captain Bill Sterning. Tagging along were myself, gangly potholer Nathan Oxbury, tough Harry Mallet and Jim Mendolsen with his expert knowledge of the complex's security systems. Swooping and flitting around the group was Jim's robotic seagull.

Electronic access control presented no barrier as Bill's explosives specialist blew out the main door into the laboratories with a shaped charge.

The concussion from the explosion was still reverberating with dust and smoke hanging in the air when the loud repeated klaxon sound of the complex's alarm sounded. Our advantage of surprise was gone.

From one end of the complex's main corridor the military team systematically blew open each door with a shaped charge, threw in a stun grenade and followed up quickly to check and clear each of the rooms. In each case the robotic seagull followed behind to record a video of the room's contents.

Once several rooms were cleared, above the sounds of explosive demolition and the incessant blaring of the klaxon we heard a clatter of scampering steps on the floor from the far end of the corridor. Approaching fast were a squad of four-legged guard robots.

'Careful, they're dangerous,' I said, speaking from bitter experience.

The robots were quickly cut down by a hail of gunfire from the Heckler and Koch MP5 automatic close quarter battle submachine guns carried by Bill's assault team. The robots fired tasers and anaesthetic darts in retaliation but they were well beyond effective range. One by one they toppled, crippled by the bullets smashing up their delicate electronic and mechanical components, waving legs helplessly in the air like crippled insects.

Until this point the cleared rooms had been empty, but shortly after the assault team resumed room clearance, we encountered one of the occupied rooms, a large laboratory with a plethora of specialist equipment in the centre of which was an operating table surrounded by people in white scrubs and surgical masks.

The surgical team scattered as the rescue forces burst in. One I recognised as the dangerous fanatic himself, Dr Shorbody. I lacked time to identify more of the white coated individuals or their intentions. Laid out naked and unconscious was Jenny Potterswell. Besides assorted fiendish apparatus surrounding the table were screens depicting the anatomical details of a mysterious human fish hybrid, the mermaid the Marquess required for his new Mythological Magick theme park.

Without hesitation I swept Jenny up in my arms. There was sheet of green cloth lying around nearby, which I grabbed and wrapped around her to protect her dignity. I heaved her onto my shoulders in a fireman's lift.

Jenny's father, Colonel Henry Potterswell almost exploded in apoplectic fury. His face bright red, veins throbbing and eyes popping he gave his command.

'Open fire. Take them out. No prisoners.'

The assault troops looked at Henry and then over towards Bill, who shook his head slightly, held his palm out and indicated down with his fingers. He faced Henry.

'No sir. We need to let justice take its course. We are not here to kill anybody except in self-defence. Those are the rules of engagement,' he said, quietly but firmly.

Henry's rage ebbed. He seemed relieved to see Jenny safely in my arms.

'Very well. But I do need to do this.'

He advanced briskly towards the cowering group of white clad figures. In an explosion of ferocity he slammed his fist into Dr Shorbody's face with every ounce of his strength. Dr Shorbody reeled from the force, landing flat on his back with blood streaming from his nose and mouth. Dr Shorbody's clinical collaborators backed away unnerved by the ferocity of Henry's attack and the robotic seagull swooping over as it captured the action on video.

Bill commanded the clinicians to remain, informing them that should anyone set foot in the corridor, they would be shot without warning.

He gathered the rescue team to proceed to our next objective, the chamber within which the unfortunate human specimens for Dr Shorbury's experiments were held.

Explosive charges made short work of the inner and outer doors of the prison chamber. The robots that might have opposed us had already been dispatched during the earlier confrontation in the laboratory complex corridor.

We were not greeted by the detainees as we burst in because they were locked in their cages, presumably having been confined by the robots when the alarm went off. As the dust and smoke from the explosions cleared Bill Sterning assessed the situation, before giving his instructions to those confined.

'Get yourselves right to the back of your cages please. Put your mattresses in front of you and turn to face the back. We are going to blow open the cage doors.'

Bill's explosives expert came towards Bill and shook his head. He opened his bergen and let Bill look inside. Bill clenched his fist and hit the air with it. He gestured to Henry and I.

I was still carrying Jenny's inert form across my shoulders. I laid her out flat on the top of the table running down the middle of the chamber.

'Sorry, but we don't have enough explosives to blow all the doors,' Bill explained.

I indicated to Jim to join us.

'We can't use explosives on the cage doors. We don't have enough. We need to find another way to get them open,' I explained as Jim arrived.

'Well, the doors and locks are operated electrically,' Jim observed. 'We could try to figure out how it's wired.'

'Can you get onto it?'

'Will do,' said Jim. He wandered around looking for wires and other clues for how the doors operated, before wandering out of the room through the blown-open doors.

The others, especially Henry, observed Jim while feeling a mounting impatience. All the while the alarm klaxon blared, reinforcing the urgency. Jim's robotic seagull swooped and circled like an annoying insect.

'We need to get a move on,' Bill observed. 'There will be forces gathering to oppose us. We don't have much time.'

'If anyone can figure this out, Jim can,' I said reassuringly.

Jim was no longer to be seen. Presumably he was doing something.

'I've had enough,' Henry exclaimed. 'We need to take action.'

He strode rapidly out of the room through the open doors. I followed a short distance ready to intervene, fearing Henry might cause further delay by interfering with Jim's efforts. There was a trolley laden with cleaning materials standing in the corridor. Henry grabbed a mop mounted on a metal pole and hurried back into the room. He sprang up to one of the cages and frenziedly smashed the pole against the door lock.

I was distracted from further supervision of Jim and Henry when I noticed Jenny raising her head and propping herself on one elbow. I ran over and sat next to her on the bench next to the table.

'Jenny, are you alright?'

'Yes, I think so. What's going on?'

'We're getting you all out of here.'

'Who is we?'

'Me, your dad and some of our mates.'

'You've got a lot of mates.'

'Enough, I hope. We're not out yet and we may face opposition.'

'Last I remember one of the robots fired a dart at me. I don't remember anything afterwards,' Jenny recalled.

'We got to you just before Dr Shorbody and his accomplices were going to do some fearful atrocities on you. Then we came in here to get the others out.'

'What atrocities were they going to do?'

'I'll tell you later. In the meantime I'll get your dad. Don't go anywhere.'

I sprang over to Henry who was still doggedly smashing into the cage lock, which refused to give.

'Colonel, Jenny's come to. She'd like to talk to you.'

Henry dropped his metal pole and followed me to the table. He wrapped his daughter in a bear hug.

'Thank God. We thought we'd lost you.'

I left Jenny with her father and went out quickly to see

how Jim was progressing. Noseying in the corridor outside I found Jim buried in a wiring closet.

'How's it going, Jim?'

'Not bad. I think I may have got it. This seems to be the power circuit for the doors.' He bridged across one wire with another. From the main chamber we heard a click and a whirring, followed by a loud cheer.

We ran back to see the cage doors slid open and the inmates emerging from their confinement. All except one. The door Henry had been smashing with his metal pole was now jammed shut, leaving the unfortunate Frankie beleaguered inside.

Bill indicated to Henry and I to join him.

'We'll have to leave this guy. We can't afford to waste any more time,' he advised.

Henry nodded.

'Bugger that. We are not leaving anyone behind, and certainly not Frankie,' I insisted.

I picked up the metal pole from where Henry had dropped it and rammed it forcefully against the lock over and over in a frenzy of pent up anger. On about the fourth or fifth strike my efforts bore fruit and the door released, but, bent out shape, it only opened a crack. Further kicking forced it open a little more, not even half open, but perhaps just sufficient for Frankie to squeeze through. Thanks to Frankie's slight build, after some squirming and wriggling he emerged.

The now much larger group scurried back through the laboratory complex corridors, across the reception area and into one of the railway tunnels. The map Harry had obtained indicated this would take us through in the direction of the village of Abballon. Jenny was now fully conscious and capable of making her own way, but I kept close in case she might need assistance.

We had not progressed more than a few hundred yards along the dimly lit roughly formed concrete tube when we felt the rails vibrating and heard the trundling noise of an approaching waggon, which I recognised as the same as the one that had subdued me with a dart during my escapade in the Wild Side.

'Careful, it'll be armed,' I shouted.

Bill's assault team opened up on the waggon with their Heckler and Koch MP5 submachine guns, riddling its components and sending it out of control, which far from coming to a halt, caused it to surge forward gathering speed along the track, which was sloped slightly down in our direction. Pressed tightly against the tunnel walls, we felt the rushing air on our faces as the waggon rattled past with barely an inch to spare.

The waggon now past us, continued to pick up speed, rocking from side to side, tipping up off the rails and scraping against the tunnel walls as it followed a curve in the track around a bend out of sight towards the reception area. A moment later we heard a loud crash and explosion as it came to grief.

Having verified there were no injuries other than slight bumps and scratches from the passing leviathan, Henry urged his troops to press along the tunnel.

After minutes we emerged into a large open area lit by an enormous picture window stretching along into the distance, sufficient to allow hundreds of theme park visitors to step out of their rail transport onto a viewing platform from which they could look over a vista.

I heaved myself up off the track onto the platform,

turned and helped Jenny up to join me and together we approached the expanse of plate glass. We were situated near the top of the cliff face forming Abballon's border, from which we could see the settlement stretched out below. We could see little ant like figures tending the fields and labouring on Woody's construction projects.

'It's been a while since you were there, hasn't it?' I observed.

'First time I've seen it from this angle,' said Jenny.

'Not my first time,' I admitted, remembering the view I had seen from the cliff top while making my temporary escape into the Wild Side.

I called Henry and Bill over to take a look.

'There is our next objective, getting those folk out. Then we're done and we can get out of here.'

'Wow, it's quite a setup,' said Bill.

'No time for sightseeing. We need to keep moving,' chided Henry.

'Yes, sir,' Bill agreed.

We led the group onwards towards the end of the platform where Harry's purloined plans indicated there was a route to ground level. There was a large lift with people starting to gather.

'No, we could be trapped in there. This way,' said Bill, directing people towards a door marked 'Emergency Exit'.

The door led onto a narrow spiral staircase winding into what appeared to be a bottomless shaft. Bill's military assault team led the way with Henry and I just behind, the remainder trailing in the rear. Jim's robotic seagull zigzagged, flying awkwardly in the confined space, keeping pace with the leading members of the group. The metal staircase vibrated and rocked from the thumping of dozens of footsteps, the clatter echoing off the walls of rock and concrete.

After a monotonous winding more times than we could count we reached a hollowed out cavern at the bottom. I went forward with Bill and Henry to survey the scene. I could make out the reverse side of the screen standing behind the altar at the rear of Gaia's temple where it butted out from the base of the cliff.

I eased forward to check it out. As I approached the screen I felt a familiar heat on my face. I stepped back quickly.

'What's the matter?' Henry demanded. He strode forward purposefully, then a moment later reeled back in shock falling backwards onto the floor. At this point the figure representing Gaia rose up.

'Go back. How dare you enter this sacred place!' said the figure accusingly, before it gradually faded.

'It's the heat ray system. It's not letting us through,' I explained.

By this time Jim had joined us.

'Jim, we need you to do your magic again.'

Jim looked around critically, considering the physics involved for how microwaves might be directed and where they could emanate from. He just managed to pick out a faint electric fan. A little more searching revealed heavy duty power cables embedded within the concrete.

'This will be the power supply. If we can take this out it should be disabled.'

Although our stock of explosive charges had been depleted there was enough remaining for this job. The explosive expert rigged the charges, the rest of us stood back and behind whatever cover we could find and the charges went off. Bright sparks and crackling came from the fractured high tension cables.

Bill advanced cautiously. He smiled broadly as he passed from behind the altar screen and waved for the rest of the group to follow.

I led the team quickly to the Abballon community's great timber hall. Those present, my friends and comrades from the community quickly assembled to meet us, Tarquin, Bradders, Hypatia, Elsa, Ivy, Huggs and the rest. They were simultaneously confused and delighted to see their old friends, Cadfael, Jenny, Frankie, myself and many more.

Interrupting the excited greetings and chatter I jumped up onto the table and clattered some crockery to get the crowd's attention.

'We are here to get you out from this place, to rescue you,' I announced.

There was a murmuring and shaking of heads from the Abballon residents.

'We don't need rescuing. We are happy where we are,' Hypatia declared. There was a general nodding from her fellow Abballonians.

I tried to reason with them.

'Look, this whole setup is part of a fiendish experiment. You are being exploited. They have terrible things planned for you.'

I could tell from the sullen and resistant reaction I was not cutting through.

'There is a massive laboratory in there where they plan to turn people into mythical monsters. It's what they do to the people who get cast out.'

My audience was now looking at me as if I was insane, one of those weird lunatics with conspiracy theories about alien abduction.

Before I could enlarge on my tall tale about a fiendish plot by a mad scientist, Abballon's inhabitants' attention was drawn by a commotion among them. There was jostling and raised voices between Harry Mallet and Huggs.

'She's coming back with me,' Harry asserted aggressively.

'No, I'm not,' insisted Ivy.

'You heard her. She wants to stay here,' said Huggs.

Harry raised his fists and lunged at Huggs, who ducked parrying the blows.

'Cool it, man. There's no need for this,' said Huggs stepping back.

'Come on, fight like a man,' shouted Harry.

Eventually, after trying to avoid the fight, Huggs leant forward and shoved Harry backwards. Harry regained his balance and rushed forward again with his fists flailing.

The fight was curtailed by an amplified voice booming in from outside projected over a loudspeaker.

'Give yourselves up. We have you surrounded.'

Bill, Henry and the assault team dashed out of the hall to investigate, followed by Jim and I. The assault team hunkered down with guns ready in a formation to provide all round defence.

While the conversations took place inside, the robotic seagull had been ambling in the air outside the hall. Jim aimed a laser pointer at it. The seagull broke off from circling and took off rapidly in a straight line away from the area.

There was a brief burst of heavy machine gun fire. Half a dozen rounds thudded into the ground nearby.

'I repeat, give yourselves up. You are surrounded by superior forces,' said the voice on the loudspeaker.

'Back to the temple,' shouted Bill urgently.

Keeping low and skirting whatever cover we could find the assault team moved back.

Another burst of machine gun fire clattered out, this time from our front directly in the direction of the temple itself. Again the bullets slapped into the ground with squelches as they embedded themselves into the wet soil.

'Come on, move! Let's go!' shouted Henry loudly as he continued to run forward.

The answer was another burst of machine gun fire whizzed by, now very close to Henry. One of the rounds made a whining as it ricocheted dangerously off a rock.

Bill leapt forward and grabbed Henry by the arm.

'If they had wanted to take us out they could have done so easily. The situation is hopeless, sir,' Bill stated.

Henry looked around and considered. 'I suppose you are right,' he agreed, reluctantly.

Bill led the group to the open area where the Abballon inhabitants carried out their ceremonies. Bill and his men tossed their weapons to one side and waited with hands raised.

Quickly we were surrounded by tough looking troops.

'Royal Marines,' Bill observed. 'Best not mess with them.'

Negotiation

I stared at the blank walls of my cell. Besides the artificial strip light set into the ceiling behind a reinforced frosted glass panel a little daylight shone through some clouded glass bricks built high into one wall. My bed was a narrow foam mattress covered in easy clean vinyl laid onto a built in platform. Being incarcerated was becoming a habit, I reflected.

Since being rounded up by the marines the only conversation I had was with the impassive Military Police corporal taking details of my identity, cataloguing the meagre effects I was carrying and ascertaining whether I suffered from any medical conditions.

A voice shouted out in the corridor.

'Chewton.'

A booted heel stamped down on the hard concrete floor.

'Sir!'

Cromp, cromp, cromp went the boots as they approached my cell. The door swung open. There were two military policemen. One advanced into the cell, while the other remained outside.

'Chewton, come with us,' ordered the corporal who had come into the cell.

The two soldiers marched me briskly along the echoing corridor, escorting me into an interview room. An officer sat behind a small table, in front of which was an empty chair, stackable and made of moulded plastic attached to a metal frame.

'Take a seat,' ordered the officer.

I sat in the empty chair. The two military policemen marched briskly behind, placing themselves on either side, stamping their heels as they took up a military at ease position.

'Well, Mr Chewton, what is your role in this affair?' demanded the officer.

'What affair?'

'An armed incursion onto a Ministry of Defence site threatening national security.'

'It had nothing to do with national security. We were rescuing people held against their will, subjected to horrendous scientific procedures. What has it got to do with the MOD?'

'Your group was armed and on MOD property.'

'We weren't intending anything against the armed forces.'

'What is your role in this?'

'I managed to escape and I was trying to release the others being detained.'

'So, you organised the whole thing.'

'I've got nothing more to say until I get a solicitor.'

'As an armed combatant you don't get those civilian niceties.'

'I've still got nothing to say.'

The officer sat and thought, then indicated to the two military policemen.

'Take him back. We'll talk again later when he is feeling more forthcoming.'

Cromp, cromp, cromp went the boots as I was escorted back to my bleak cell.

I was left to stare at the wall for what must have been

another hour before further stamping feet preceded the arrival of a tray thrust through a slot in the cell door. It was a meal divided between compartments moulded into the plastic tray. In one there was some beans, watery potatoes and a gristly over-grilled burger. In another was peach slices that must have come from a tin. I ate it using the provided plastic fork and spoon.

After a couple more solitary hours cromping of boots announced the return of the military policemen. We marched out further, out of the guardhouse where the cells were located and into another basic single storey building, where I was shown into an office to be greeted by a smooth looking man in a well-cut civilian suit.

'Mr Chewton, please take a seat,' said the man in a friendly fashion, indicating an office chair.

'Could you wait outside, please,' said the man, phrased as a request but there was no doubt it was a command. The soldiers marched smartly out of the room leaving the two of us.

The man was around 40, slightly thinning hair, well-spoken and well-groomed. At first glance his outfit was plain and unobtrusive, but on closer inspection his suit was of the highest quality and expertly tailored. The way he held himself suggested he was tough and athletic.

'I am Julian Smith.' I did not believe him.

'I understand from the others you are the one I need to be talking to about this whole unfortunate business,' said Mr Smith. On the surface he was polite, friendly and soft spoken, yet I sensed beneath the urbane exterior he could be ruthless.

'Which others might that be?'

'Oh, we have had some very interesting conversations with members of your group.'

'Look, I won't be saying anything until I see a solicitor.'

'Mr Chewton, please, or should I say Simon, you can call me Julian. You have taken arms against your own country. In those circumstances all this civilian stuff about rights and so on just doesn't apply. We are totally within our rights to just shoot you out of hand. You were armed on MOD property after all.'

'I'm still not saying anything.'

'Well, let's get a cup of coffee and take it from there. How do you take it?'

'White, two sugars please.'

Julian poured the coffee for both of us into cups with saucers.

'Now Simon, what I want is to figure out a solution to all this suitable for everybody and avoiding anybody needing to be hurt. But for that I need you to help me.'

'How is it I could help?'

'You obviously knew something about what is going on within the Wookey Vale facility. Where did you get that information?'

'I learned about it by being held there.'

'You obviously knew more than you could have found out that way. You couldn't have organised all this on your own. Who put you up to it? Who are you working for?'

'Nobody. Everybody involved are people I know personally.'

'What? You have a fully trained squad of heavily armed former soldiers among your circle of personal friends. That just isn't credible, is it Simon?'

'I have nothing further to say.'

'You will need to discuss this sooner or later, Simon. This isn't going to end well for you if you don't.'

As I sipped my coffee I was thinking. 'I am prepared to negotiate, but not with you.'

'Oh, Simon. I'm shocked. What's wrong with me? What have I done to upset you?'

'Nothing wrong with you, Julian. You have been charming. But I want to talk to someone who can make decisions.'

'Simon, I do have a certain amount of discretion you know. Why don't we explore things a bit before you make a hasty decision.'

'I want to talk to Sir Nicholas Jardinair.'

Julian looked at me askance and shook his head sadly. 'What, to the minister? You couldn't seriously think he would handle this personally, could you?'

'I think he would. Just tell him I know what happened at Bramston Gardens, Earls Court. He'll want to talk to me then.'

Henry's dogged pursuit on the wild goose chase I had dreamed up to divert him from anything rash and impulsive could be paying dividends.

Julian pursed his lips. 'Alright then. I'll pass on the message, but I fear it is only wasting time. I feel sure we will be talking again.'

I waited in my cell while more time passed, marked only by the arrival of another unappetizing meal.

Cromping boots announced the return of military police guards. On this occasion I was escorted some distance, out into the open where I could stretch my legs and enjoy breaths of fresh air in the outdoors. We passed a parade ground with a soundtrack of clumping marching feet, stamping of heavy boots and crisp words of command, eventually reaching the facility's officers mess, proceeding into a comfortable lounge area with easy chairs and sofas. I couldn't help smiling in triumph as, at the far end of the room in a discreet corner, Sir Nicholas Jardinair rose from his seat to greet me. Julian Smith, or whoever he really was, with him.

'Mr Chewton, nice to meet you again,' said Sir Nicholas, although I suspected he didn't think it was nice at all.

'The pleasure is all mine,' I said, and did mean it.

'Mr Chewton, what would you like to drink?' Julian enquired, friendly yet projecting toughness.

In another setting I would have ordered a foaming pint of Meadow Dew ale, but I realised this was probably not the thing to have in the officer's mess.

'Thank you, a gin and tonic would be very nice.'

The mess steward, hovering, left to attend to it. My military escort, neither acknowledged nor offered any refreshment, stood smartly at ease a few paces away, discouraging members of the mess who might otherwise have joined the conversation.

'I understand you are on friendly terms with Jenny Potterswell, one of my neighbours?' asked Sir Nicholas.

'Yes, we know each other.'

'Quite well, I gather.'

'She is why I came to be in Wookey Vale.'

'I suppose she is also why Colonel Potterswell joined forces with you on this wild escapade of yours.'

'As her father you can understand why he would want to rescue her.'

'Quite so.'

The mess steward returned with a tray of drinks.

'You mentioned an address in Earls Court that was supposed to mean something to me,' observed Sir Nicholas, once the mess steward was out of earshot.

'Yes, Sir Nicholas. I have a feeling the friendship you have with Miss KattyKins would not be pleasing to your lady wife.'

'I see. What do you think you know about that?'

'Enough to make a good story in *The Daily Trumpet*. It could play quite well.'

'What have my private friendships got to do with anything?'

'You would be amazed who else Miss KattyKins is friends with, in the Russian embassy, for example. I can see parallels with the Profumo scandal. National security put at risk by defence minister's private life, along those lines.'

'But you are here, Simon. How do you suppose such a story would be published, if you were to, well, you know, disappear? It wouldn't surprise anyone if you were to vanish, after what has happened already when you joined a crazy Satanic cult.'

'The story is ready, written up and stored in a safe place. If I don't get out to intercept it within the next day or two it will end up with my editor, who you can be sure will publish it.'

Julian and Sir Nicholas looked at me intently, assessing. I looked back confidently.

Sir Nicholas spoke first. 'It's no good Mr Chewton. There is no doubt such a story would be embarrassing for me personally and I would probably lose my job, but I could not compromise national security for it. For one thing Julian here knows about it, so the matter is out of my hands.'

'Sir Nicholas is right. In this situation national security comes first. In that context Sir Nicholas is expendable, as we all are, even if he is my boss. We would take it to the prime minister if necessary. Your blackmail won't work,' said Julian conveying a hard certitude.

'There is another story that will be published if I am not released in time to intercept it. You might not be so blasé about that one,' I responded.

'And this story is?' challenged Julian.

'The story about the fate of a large number of missing persons, how police investigation into their disappearance was sabotaged and the laboratory complex where gruesome experiments were to take place. How about that?'

'But how is such a story going to see the light of day? You are here and here is where the story will remain,' observed Julian.

'No, it won't. The story is already waiting on the outside. It will go out if I don't intercept it.'

Sir Nicholas looked concerned, but Julian shook his head.

'You're bluffing. There is no way you could have got the story out. All radio traffic is suppressed. All over-flying prohibited and any attempts result in the aircraft being shot down. Heat ray shields would have caught anybody who slipped away from your group.'

Sir Nicholas looked relieved.

'You are mistaken,' I said confidently. 'The story is out there, I promise you. You can verify that with Jim

Mendolsen, who presumably you are holding somewhere around here. Ask him about a seagull he had flying about the place. You don't shoot down birds flying around over here, do you?'

Julian frowned slightly, betraying for the first time the merest hint of vulnerability.

'Alright, supposing your friend did manage to smuggle something out on this seagull. What would the seagull do with it, unless you or Mr Mendolsen pick it up later?' countered Julian.

'Check with Delia Potterswell. She will confirm she picked up the bird and its cargo and sent it to me, for my personal attention at *The Daily Trumpet*. If I don't reappear soon the editor will open the contents and deal with them accordingly.'

Julian and Sir Nicholas looked at each other. Sir Nicholas inclined his head slightly.

'Do you have any other matters you want to mention?' Julian asked brusquely.

'No, I think you have the full picture,' I said.

'Very well, it's time for you to return to your quarters.'

Julian gestured to the military policemen to come forward and escort me away.

It was early the following day after a night's sleep on the thin mattress and a disgusting breakfast of baked beans and a shrivelled burnt sausage I was marched out again.

I really didn't know what to expect. Perhaps they didn't believe me and had decided to keep me quiet, permanently. I had visions of being shot at dawn.

I was relieved when we took the same route as on the previous day and even more relieved when I found myself back in the officers mess.

This time I was greeted by another player in the affair, Alex Drembold, the founder and chief executive of Drembold Industries, a solidly built middle aged man with an air of someone who, despite being a civilian, was in charge of the officer's mess if not the military base.

'Hello again Simon,' said Alex cheerfully. He appeared to be genuinely pleased to see me, which was a little surprising considering we had not parted on the best terms.

'Oh, hello. This is unexpected.'

'It's a bit early for a drink, but I'm told they'll do you an excellent bacon sandwich here. Fancy that?'

'Not half.'

'And a pot of coffee to go with it?'

'That'll be nice.'

The steward went away to attend to it.

'Bloody good job, that raid of yours,' said Alex.

This hard-nosed business man was suddenly my best friend. I didn't know what to make of it.

'Really? Isn't it rather inconvenient for you?'

'Well, yes. But it's an opportunity too.'

'How so?'

'I think you are a pragmatic sort of fellow. Let's figure it out between us, shall we?'

Enmeshed within the Enterprise

The library of Mendip House, the renowned Palladian style country house, was just as I remembered when I first visited in the days I was on the staff of *The Daily Trumpet*.

Barstairs, the impeccably turned out butler, was the same, hovering in the background. The dust of ages hung in the air. The same classic leather-bound volumes adorned the shelves. There was a timelessness about the place. Wars, revolutions, plagues come and go, business ventures rise and fall, throughout which the dynasties of the English aristocracy persist.

I recognised one book. I glanced towards Barstairs and caught his eye as I reached for the volume. Barstairs nodded and smiled benignly. When I placed it on the table it fell open at a familiar page with an illustration portraying a satyr, the well-endowed hybrid of man and a goat. It could have been me, I mused, had I not thwarted Dr Shorbody's fiendish scheme.

The door leading to the Marquess's study opened. A big man, heavy and hairy like a bear, in priestly garb, was talking earnestly as he emerged, followed by the Marquess. I recognised the man as Dr Theophilus Pottinger, the chaplain from Royal Pentonville College.

The Marquess nodded to me in acknowledgement as he passed, but Dr Pottinger was too intent on his pronouncements to notice my presence. The reproduction of Glastonbury Abbey in the full glory of its heyday would inspire the younger generation to return to the fold of the church, declared Dr Pottinger. The exhibitions he had planned for the Cradle of Christianity park would engage with people, encouraging them to consider important theological questions, such as the meaning of the Holy Trinity.

Dr Pottinger was still holding forth as they reached the far end of the room.

'The parting of the waters would be another one we could consider, incorporated into one of the rides, along with pursuing Egyptian chariots.'

'Certainly worthy of consideration.'

'People will be getting hungry as they go round, which is where we can bring into play the parable of the feeding of the five thousand with loaves and fishes.'

'Intriguing. How would that work?'

'A figure representing Jesus would preach his sermon to the visitors, while simultaneously bringing forth a fish burger with optional chips, feeding both body and spirit simultaneously.'

'We'll pass the suggestion to the catering team. Certainly food for thought, along with the many other excellent concepts you have laid out.'

Barstairs, holding the door open, leaned in a few inches to encourage Dr Pottinger to proceed through it.

The Marquess had an affinity for obsessive eccentrics, I mused, first a mad scientist and now a religious obsessive.

With Dr Pottinger finally on his way the Marquess followed by Barstairs walked with deliberation back towards the Marquess's study. The Marquess continued as Barstairs came level to where I stood.

'His lordship will see you now,' he announced, indicating the way.

The Marquess paused to greet me as we entered the

study. If the Marquess felt any distaste or irritation towards me for having disturbed his plans he gave no sign, showing only immaculate politeness, civility and good manners while maintaining an air of effortless superiority.

'Mr Chewton, so glad to see you again. I understand I should congratulate you on your recent nuptials. You married Jenny, Colonel Potterswell's daughter, I understand.'

'Yes, your lordship. As it happens we're staying with my in-laws while I'm here.'

There was something in the Marquess's manner that conveyed within seconds of meeting him that he would be in command in any encounter. No need for anything to be said, no need for it to be stated. He was adorned in his timeless uniform of the English upper class, in an expertly tailored Saville Row tweed outfit. This time I was more formally dressed than had been my custom, in a well-tailored business suit, which gave me an air of authority, Jenny told me.

The Marquess cast his eyes to the far end of the comfortable and spacious room on the corner of the building, giving it a bright double aspect. Around the place were scattered models featuring attractions planned for the Marquess's theme parks. Drawings and sculptures of mythical beasts, centaurs, griffins, mermaids as so on were still prominently scattered.

As we walked to the sofa and easy chairs positioned near the window, the Marquess's muse, the dangerously seductive Philomena stood to greet us. On this occasion she was adorned in an outfit I supposed represented a Greek goddess, perhaps Artemis.

'Simon, so nice to see you again,' said Philomena. As

usual, I sensed something predatory in how looked at me. Lovely as she undoubtedly was, on this occasion I would be resisting her charms, I resolved, though I could appreciate why the Marquess kept her around.

'Well, Mr Chewton, perhaps you could describe what Drembold Industries are proposing to populate the Mythological Magick park.'

I pulled my laptop computer out of my bag. As I fumbled to set it up, plug in my security dongle, enter my password, click my mouse on the correct presentation and so on, filling time while the computer hummed and whirred, I delivered my standard company spiel on autopilot.

'As you will know Drembold Industries are world leaders in robotics. Our humanoid robots are so convincing they can mingle in a crowd and blend in completely. They are deployed by several law enforcement organisations so as to avoid putting their human resources in harm's way.'

The expressions on the faces of my audience betrayed impatience.

The Marquess intervened. 'Yes, yes, we have seen Drembold's robots in action. What about the beasts for the Mythological Magick park? Have you had any thoughts on the Minotaur?'

This question put me on the back foot. 'To be honest we have struggled a bit with the Minotaur. We know it is supposed to be a hybrid of a bull and human, was hidden away in a labyrinth and was in the habit of devouring young men and maidens, but there isn't much out there on its physical appearance. Our people are working on it, though.'

'Well, what exactly have you got for us?' demanded Philomena.

My momentary embarrassment was alleviated when an image appeared on the laptop's screen.

'This one you can see now is our centaur,' I explained. I clicked the mouse and the centaur broke into a computer generated gallop. 'As you can see, its movements are entirely convincing. As far as anyone seeing it is concerned, they will believe they are witnessing a living, breathing creature.'

'I resisted a robotic solution because I never thought you would be able to achieve sufficient realism, but I must say, seeing it now, I am impressed,' said the Marquess.

I clicked the mouse again and a mermaid appeared.

'The mermaid was a little tricky, because of the need to combine human and fish style movements into something elegant. For this we consulted a choreographer from the English National Ballet.'

I clicked my mouse and the mermaid launched into sinuous swimming movements.

'She looks rather nice,' said Philomena. 'I'm sure the visitors will enjoy it.'

I clicked my mouse again, blushing as a satyr appeared on the screen. I could hardly forget it was so nearly my own fate to embody this creature and even the damned robot resembled me, as if I was looking at a distorted version of myself in the mirror. Seeing the damned thing's oversized private parts fully exposed made me feel naked. I crossed my legs involuntarily.

'It could almost be you,' Philomena observed, adding to my embarrassment. 'Is it functional in every respect? I mean in terms of activities that might frighten the horses.'

She had her eyes on the creature's crutch.

Nervously I clicked my mouse, then instantly regretted having done so. On the screen the satyr ran through an ancient Greek landscape of mountain rocks and olive trees, coming across a pool fed by a glittering waterfall. Bathing in the pool were three naked nymphs. In a moment the satyr was in the pool in flagrante delicto with a nymph.

'We had better save this one for the adults only tour,' the Marquess observed.

I was saved from further embarrassment by Barstairs entering the room.

'It is Mr Sterning, your lordship, to see you on an urgent matter.'

Bill Sterning entered. He and his companion, who I recognised as one of the assault team from the rescue operation, were dressed in park ranger uniforms. Bill and I nodded in acknowledgement.

On the laptop screen the satyr moved on to a second nymph, who for some reason had failed to run away while he had been violating her companion. I hurriedly clicked the mouse and the screen moved on to a display of the giant Cyclops.

'Mr Sterning, what is the matter?' the Marquess enquired.

'Demonstrators have broken into the Theme Hub complex, my lord,' Bill replied.

'Oh dear. Who are they and what do they want?'

'They claim to represent BUFUIG, my lord.'

'Who are they, exactly?'

'The British UFO Investigation Group, my lord. They are claiming the theme parks are a front for a secret government conspiracy to hide the presence of alien creatures in what was formerly the Wookey Vale Military Facility.'

'Have they done damage?'

'We have them contained, but we've had to close tours of Pleistocene Panorama until we can get them cleared out.'

'What have they got against Pleistocene Panorama?'

'They claim the big cat that escaped from the Wild Side recently is actually an escaped alien.'

I pondered what BUFUIG would make of the robotic centaurs, satyrs, mermaids and the minotaur the Marquess wanted for his Mythological Magick theme park. It was not a subject I was going to explore on this occasion. The Marquess turned to me.

'Mr Chewton, I am very sorry, but we'll need to cut this short. I am impressed though. Send me through the draft contract and we'll take it from there.'

Having parked my new company Lexus, I took a stroll through Glastonbury town centre. I had imagined it would have been a quiet stroll among the purveyors' exotic whole foods, carved wooden faeries, glittering coloured minerals and botanical remedies, but for some reason whenever I happened to be there it was never quiet in Glastonbury.

There was a loud confrontation outside Megan's Magick Shoppe between members of the Mendip Moon Coven led by the corpulent Hetty and local farmer Eddie Langport accompanied by street fighter Harry Mallet. I gathered the coven had purloined the Langport's herd of alpacas on the grounds their animal rights had been infringed. The alpacas had been liberated and were now wandering freely on the sacred hill of Glastonbury Tor. I wondered how long they would remain unscathed before sabre cats or wolves from the Marquess's Pleistocene Panorama park got out on the loose.

Voices were raised, shrill screeching from the coven, gruff and agricultural on the part of Eddie and Harry. A one-sided punch up between infuriated brute Harry Mallet and intimidated beanpole Nathan Oxbury was just starting to develop when Sergeant Keith Lunnton of the Agricultural Affairs squad appeared to break things up.

Once order was restored I stepped into the meeting place for the cosmopolitan alternative lifestyle, the Oak and Holly where I was delighted to see my old friends, sturdy weather-beaten Cadfael, brash hearty Bradders and nerdy sensitive Tarquin who had called in for a pint at the end of one of their stints in Abballon. As I had negotiated, the members of the community were now salaried staff who could come and go freely using the railway access to the Knights of Camelot Grotto. Over a pint of Meadow Dew ale I caught up on the latest news.

'I saw Philomena today,' I said.

'How was she?' said Bradders. 'Not seen her for ages.'

'She was done out as a Greek goddess, not sure which one.'

'Bet she looked good,' said Bradders.

'Yes, she always does,' I concurred. 'Bit intimidating too.'

'What, still fancies you, does she?'

'Yes, I have an idea she does.'

'You lucky devil,' said Bradders.

'I'm a married man these days. She can look elsewhere.'

'It's been so long I've almost forgotten about her,' said Tarquin.

'So, you don't get to see her in Abballon at all these days?'

'No, she went off to do something with that new Mythological Magick thing.'

I snorted into my beer as I imagined what Philomena might move on to when she finished with Mythological Magick.

'Share the joke,' demanded Bradders.

'I suddenly imagined Philomena as the Virgin Mary.'

'What brought that to mind?'

'New theme park idea they were talking about, Cradle of Christianity.'

'Jezebel or Delilah more like,' said Tarquin.

'So, who is in charge, now she's gone?'

'Hypatia took over as Ethereal Guide,' said Cadfael.

'What about Woody? He had just been made Moderator when I was cast out.'

'I'm back as Moderator,' said Cadfael.

'Woody's quieter than he was,' said Bradders. 'Shagged out, literally. Does his building work during the day and Elsa keeps him busy all night.'

'Who does Hypatia keep busy?'

Cadfael blushed and Bradders sniggered.

'That'd be me,' Cadfael confessed.

I steered my Lexus into the Potterswell's driveway between the avenue of shrubbery, once distinct specimens since merged into a tumble of dark foliage, gliding in smoothly alongside Henry's classic Jaguar.

Jenny was there to meet me, now conventionally and

minimally made up, dressed in casual but elegant slacks and a dark blouse with a pattern of spots, barely recognisable as the goth witch figure she had been when we first met.

Like most men, although I noticed her change of style, it didn't particularly concern me how she presented herself. For me she was and always had been the vision of loveliness who had got me where I was today, albeit taking me over some rocky and dangerous ground in the process. I wrapped her in my arms and kissed her softly on the lips.

'Good day, was it?' Jenny enquired.

'Yes, I'd say so. The Marquess liked what we're offering. Got cut short though. A bunch of demonstrators have broken into the theme parks and he was dragged away to deal with it.'

Jenny winced slightly. 'Oh dear. Was it Hetty and her coven?' She looked embarrassed, mindful of her past association with the witchcraft mob.

'No, not them. They were busy in Glastonbury High Street fending off the Langports who were cross about them pinching their alpacas.'

'Who then?'

'BUFUIG, the UFO people. They are claiming the Marquess is hiding aliens from another planet in his theme parks.'

'There're barmy, those people.'

'Some, your mum and dad for instance, would say witchcraft aficionados are equally as barmy.'

'Hm. We'll have to keep working to educate my mum and dad and their friends, I suppose.'

'Personally I don't hold out much hope of changing their outlook.'

'Anything else? I can tell you stopped off for a beer somewhere.'

'Saw some of our old mates in Glastonbury. Cadfael, Bradders and Tarquin. They're all in good spirits.'

'So how many beers was it then?'

'Just the one, honest.'

I wasn't going to get away with so much, now I was a married man, I mused. It was true I had only had just the one, but in the absence of a wife and needing to drive it could easily have been several.

I hadn't been counting on settling down to married bliss after the dramatic rescue, bearing in mind the rocky patches our relationship had been through and Jenny's attachment to far out ideas. It hadn't even been a major consideration for the rescue operation. The priority had been to get her and the others out of danger. What happened after would have to take care of itself.

After the Military Police had been persuaded to release us all, I had wasted no time getting our relationship resolved, one way or the other, and telling her a few home truths.

'I hope this is going to be the last time I'll have to rescue you from your own stupidity.'

'But you did such a great job,' said Jenny. 'You're the world's best rescuer.'

'I don't intend to make a habit of it.'

'So, do you mean another time you wouldn't bother?'

'I don't intend there to be another time.'

'How are you going to prevent it?'

'It's up to you of course, but I think the best plan is for us to get married so I can keep a close eye on you.'

'You mean that, us getting married?'

'Yes, but be warned, if we do get married, I'm not going to let you swan off with a lot of crazies whenever you feel like it.'

'I'll have to think about it.'

'Alright, but don't think too long. One other thing. It wasn't just me, your mum and dad dote on you and you put them through the wringer, not to mention your dad putting himself in danger on your behalf. You need to make peace with them and return some of the love they have for you.'

'You sound like my dad.'

'Is that good or bad?'

'I'm not sure.'

Looking at her, I could tell she thought it was good, but didn't want to say so.

I anticipated her coming back with heated rhetoric about toxic male arrogance but to my amazement she was melting like butter in the sun, liking the way I asserted myself. In no time all was harmonious with her parents and wedding plans were underway.

The Potterswells' neighbours, the Sir Nicholas and Ophelia Jardinair, joined us for dinner that evening.

The Potterswells were in fine form as hosts. Delia was looking better every time I saw her these days. For the first time in years she could relax, free of the worry that had escalated since Jenny had entered her teens, now I had taken her troublesome daughter off her hands. The relief showed in her features and her more tranquil demeanour. Henry was still Henry, impetuous and forthright, yet somehow more mellow. In her rebellious phase heaven knows how Jenny might have presented herself for dinner, but this time she had taken the trouble to wear the simple but stylish dress her mother might have chosen for her.

I congratulated Sir Nicholas on his new cabinet role as Foreign Secretary. Sir Nicholas reciprocated regarding my new position at Drembold Industries. He did not say so, but I sensed Sir Nicholas felt much more comfortable having me around since I had moved on from *The Daily Trumpet*.

Ophelia observed she had seen some stray alpacas wandering around near the Tor. Had anyone else seen them? I strongly suspected she knew all about the alpacas and how they had arrived there, but was testing the water to see how Jenny would react.

'Just in case you were thinking I had something to do with it, well, on this occasion it had nothing to do with me,' Jenny replied, picking up Ophelia's insinuation.

'I suppose you have lost touch with the witchcraft side of things, now you're married?' said Ophelia.

'Actually no, I haven't,' said Jenny.

'Oh, but didn't you get married in church?'

'Yes, because it was what mum and dad wanted. We had a handfasting as well, out on Berkery Hill.'

'But is that compatible, marriage in church and something, well, pagan?' said Ophelia, not entirely hiding her distaste.

I cringed and pursed my lips; sensing fireworks.

'I keep an open mind about beliefs,' said Jenny, diplomatically, restraint being something she had been learning under my tutelage.

'You're back at college, aren't you dear?' chipped in Delia Potterswell, in a bid to head off trouble.

'Yes, I'm doing an MA in Pagan Belief Systems at Royal Pentonville College. I am thinking I might go on to do a PhD.'

'Oh, Royal Pentonville. I have a very good friend there. You may know him. Dr Theophilus Pottinger,' said Ophelia.

'Yes, I know him,' said Jenny, with gritted teeth.

'Lovely gentleman. Very active with us in the Moral Multitude. I expect you must have some lovely discussions,' said Ophelia.

'Yes, we discuss things from time to time,' said Jenny.

I snorted, vainly trying to disguise my burst of laughter as a cough. Jenny had described the slanging matches between her and Dr Pottinger in graphic detail.

The following day Jenny and I set off early for our marital home, the opulent property we could now afford on my substantial salary from Drembold Industries, a prestigious four bedroom detached property in Weybridge situated in a neighbourhood of neatly mown lawns, gin and tonics, luxury cars and golf courses.

The place was still in flux, only partially furnished and decorated. I was confident between us we would eventually get it into good shape, but apart from the time constraints with my new job and Jenny's college work, we didn't feel quite ready to make the transition from youth culture into middle class gentility.

First on the agenda after our arrival was a video conference call with my boss, Alex Drembold.

It had been Alex's idea for me to work for him in Drembold Industries. The move required me to sign the Official Secrets Act in respect to the specialist technologies the company was involved in. By bringing me into the fold, the move had reassured the Ministry of Defence about my future conduct. Likewise concerns about Bill Sterning and his team had been neutralised by bringing them onto the Marquess's staff.

I updated Alex on the robotic creatures for the Mythological Magick theme park.

'Is he reconciled to them being robotic rather than flesh and blood?' Alex enquired.

'I would say, yes. He was impressed by the visual impressions I showed him and I didn't get objections.'

'Well, his options are limited, now Marcus Shorbody is out of the way,' observed Alex. 'It was him who had convinced the Marquess they had to be living and breathing creatures.'

'Where is Dr Shorbody these days?' I enquired.

'Last I heard of him he had disappeared into Porton Down, doing something weird and wonderful for the MOD. I always thought his ideas were harebrained.'

'Not just harebrained. Bloody immoral. Barbaric.'

'I can understand how you feel, given what he was planning for you and your Jenny.'

'You were in there with him. I don't know how you could do that.'

'You can't mix morality with business. Can't say I'm sorry you managed to kill it off, though. It's a great opportunity for us.'

'It's a bit more personal for me than just a business opportunity.'

'I get that. By the way, talking of business opportunities, once we close the deal on Mythological Magick, we should open discussions with the Marquess about doing something with Marcus Shorbody's laboratory complex. I was thinking of something along the lines of Frankenstein's Fortress, with lightning flashes and creatures coming to life, that sort of thing. What do you think?'

I clinked my glass of wine against Jenny's.

'Here's to us,' I said.

'Yes, to us.'

'I'm surprised you're here with me, to tell the truth. You were always so idealistic.'

'But I am idealistic,' Jenny insisted.

'Our life now, that's not idealistic. I've sold out on all sorts of principles to get here.'

'How so?'

'Nobody has been held to account for the diabolical things being cooked up. The Marquess, Alex Drembold, Dr Shorbody, Philomena, they're all just carrying on as if nothing happened. And I've been bought off with a nice job.'

'But you did get everyone freed, the folk in Abballon are proper paid staff who can come and go as they like. That was quite an achievement.'

'Well, okay, it was probably the best that could be negotiated, and in negotiations compromises have to be made. Idealism fades, like beauty, crumbling in the face of the hard rocks of reality.'

Milton Keynes UK
Ingram Content Group UK Ltd.
UKHW010238190624
444371UK00004B/115

9 781788 648912